From inside the house there was an animal-sounding howl, and then a gruff shout: 'It's locked!' I wrenched the gate open and ran out into the lane, Mum staggering after me. Pure terror sang through my veins; I could hardly breathe. When I looked over my shoulder I saw Mum clutching her knife in one hand, the other pressed against her bump, her hair hanging in sweat-soaked strings around her face.

'Keep going,' she gasped. 'Don't worry about me.'

I heard that howl again, echoing up into the trees, and crashes as the Fearless tried to break down the front door. I tried to run faster, but my legs felt weak; I wasn't sure I could keep going. Acid burned up into my throat, nearly choking me.

Behind me, Mum moaned and fell to her knees on the track.

I ran back to her. Another shout – 'There's something in front of the door!' – and more crashes drifted towards us. 'Mum, get up!' I said, frantically tugging on her arm. She shook her head. She'd dropped her knife. 'You go, Cass. Get to Sol's.'

'No, I'm not leaving you!'

I heard the sound of glass breaking. It sounded as if the Fearless had given up trying to get out of the front door and were smashing their way out through a window instead. I pleaded with Mum to get up. Then I heard another sound at the top of the lane.

A car.

It was coming towards us, fast.

Also by Emma Pass:

# ACID

# THE
# FEARLESS

## EMMA PASS

CORGI BOOKS

THE FEARLESS
A CORGI BOOK 978 0 552 56615 5

First published in Great Britain by Corgi Books,
an imprint of Random House Children's Publishers UK
A Random House Group Company

This edition published 2014

1 3 5 7 9 10 8 6 4 2

The Random House Group Limited supports the Forest Stewardship Council
(FSC®), the leading international forest certification organization. Our books
carrying the FSC label are printed on FSC®-certified paper. FSC is the only forest
certification scheme endorsed by the leading environmental organizations,
including Greenpeace. Our paper procurement policy can be found at
www.randomhouse.co.uk/environment.

MIX
Paper from
responsible sources
FSC® C016897

Set in Bembo

Corgi Books are published by Random House Children's Publishers UK,
61–63 Uxbridge Road, London W5 5SA

www.**randomhousechildrens**.co.uk
www.**totallyrandombooks**.co.uk
www.**randomhouse**.co.uk

Addresses for companies within The Random House Group Limited can be
found at: www.randomhouse.co.uk/offices.htm

THE RANDOM HOUSE GROUP Limited Reg. No. 954009

A CIP catalogue record for this book is available from the British Library.

Printed and bound in Great Britain by
CPI Bookmarque, Croydon, CR0 4TD

For my support crew: Duncan, G-Dog and The Hound.
We miss you, big guy, and we'll never forget you.

# INVASION

INVASION!

**Neurophyxil - exciting results**
**Sent:** Monday 15th September 2014 10:21
**From:** "Dr Edward Banford" <EG.Banford@Pharmadexon.co.uk>
**To:** "Professor Simon Brightman" <SA.Brightman@Pharmadexon.co.uk>;
"Professor David Brett" <DB.Brett@Pharmadexon.co.uk>

Hello Simon and David,

I hope this finds you and your families in good health. I have been at Camp
Meridian for two weeks and am reasonably comfortable – well, as comfortable
as it's possible to be when one is in an army tent in the middle of the desert. It's
quite strange to think that I left England cloaked in cloud and rain! But I am not
emailing you to grumble, my friends – far from it. The results for the new drug are
simply astonishing – like nothing I have ever seen.

As you are both aware, Neurophyxil has now been administered to 95% of troops
on active service worldwide. Just two soldiers here have suffered the more serious
side effect associated with the drug – an increase in aggression – that disappeared
once they ceased taking it.

The drug appears to start working around five days after beginning treatment.
Although soldiers still suffer stress reactions to trigger events, their stress levels
recede far more quickly than those who have not taken the drug. There has been
a noticeable decrease in nightmares, emotional outbursts and depression.

And, as studies earlier this year have already shown, levels of post-traumatic stress
disorder and other emotional disturbances among soldiers no longer in active
service have gone down by almost 85%. But you already know all this, of course
– do forgive me for rambling on! The reason I'm emailing you is because of the
other effects the drug seems to be having – effects that were not previously
noted. Approximately half of all the soldiers taking Neurophyxil have reported
increased energy and motivation, as well as enhanced strength in combat
situations. Not only that, but levels of anxiety when entering combat situations
have fallen. It would appear that Neurophyxil not only has an effect on stress
levels after trigger events but also helps control fear itself.

If Neurophyxil can dampen down the fear mechanism, then just think what the
possibilities for this drug could be! On my return I will, of course, file a proper
report. Exciting times, my friends!

And now I must go as I've just been informed that 'grub's up'. (And I can tell you,
excitement or no, army rations are one thing I won't miss once I'm back on home
soil!)

Very best wishes,

Edward

white powder. **NEUROPHYXIL**
...ely 5mm in diameter. Each ta...
...5%
...olene yellow (E104), sunset...
...de, and other inactive ingredie...

**NEUROP...**
(neuro...

Neuro...
appears...
contains...
Inactives...
yellow (E110...

**...S AND USAGE**

Neurotryptine hydrochloride is a partial dopamine agonist in the fourth generation... atypical antipsychotics, which have additional antidepressant properties. It has been... found to promote enhanced augmentation of brain-derived neurotrophic factor in the... infralimbic prefrontal cortex. It has been shewn to be particularly effective in... preventing post-traumatic stress disorder in users who are regularly exposed to... trigger events.

**CONTRAINDICATIONS**

**NEUROPHYXIL®** is contra-indicated in patients under the age of 18, and in anyone... who has known or suspected hypersensitivity to any of the ingredients.

**WARNINGS**

No studies have been carried out of **NEUROPHYXIL®** in pregnant women. It should... not be administered to anyone who is, or suspects they may be, pregnant.

**PRECAUTIONS**

Only take **NEUROPHYXIL®** if it has been specifically prescribed for you. Not to be... administered to patients under the age of 18.

**POSSIBLE SIDE EFFECTS**

The most common adverse reaction to **NEUROPHYXIL®** is nausea and indigestion. Symptoms usually pass within 7-14 days. Some patients have reported dizziness... and vomiting

In a small number of patients (1%), **NEUROPHYXIL®** has caused increased... aggression, which passes within 7 - 21 days of administration being stopped. The... reasons for this are, at the time of printing this leaflet, unknown. **Tell your doctor**... **immediately if you develop the above symptom.** Remember that your doctor h... prescribed this medication because he or she has judged that the benefit to you i... greater than the risk of side effects. Most people taking this medication do not ha... serious side effects.

**DOSAGE AND ADMINISTRATION**

**NEUROPHYXIL®** should be taken orally, twice...

**HOW S...**

...**UROPHYXIL®** is supplied in blister... ...ainers of 28 tablets.

...each of chil...dren

NE...

Keep out of the re...

# Allied Forces Defending Civilians On Continent Forced To Retreat As NATO Say Effects Of 'Fearless' Drug Are 'Totally Devastating'

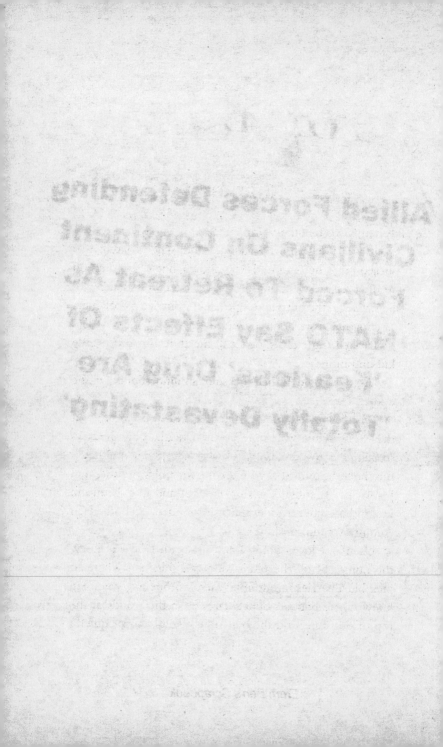

# Chapter 1

When I was ten, the world ended.

It was the summer holidays. Dad, who worked as a surgeon at a hospital in the next town, had a few days off so, after tea, we went out for a walk. 'Dad, wait!' I called as he strode up the hill. He stopped, and I hurried to catch up.

'Sorry, Cassie-boo,' he said.

I rolled my eyes. 'Don't call me that. I'm not a little kid any more.'

'As if I could forget,' he said, smiling slightly as he added, 'Cass.'

We climbed to the top together and stood looking at the view while we caught our breath, our shadows stretching across the dry, silvery grass. Blythefield Hill was the highest point in the landscape for miles around, and below us, I could see our village and the beautiful Hampshire countryside that surrounded it, bathed in August evening sunshine.

Usually, I loved going for walks with Dad. He knew the names of all the plants and animals, and where to pick blackberries in autumn where no one else went. He knew where badgers built their setts in the woods at the top of our lane, and the best time of night to sit quietly and wait for them to come out. Mum normally came with us, but now she was eight months pregnant, her feet were swollen all the time, she still felt sick most days, and the doctors said she had to stay at home and rest.

But that evening, it wasn't wildlife or my baby brother I was thinking about while Dad and I stood on top of the hill. Instead, my thoughts kept returning to the newspaper I'd found last night while I was sorting out the recycling.

Mum and Dad had been in the front room, Mum watching TV and Dad checking emails. We kept the re-cycling box in a kitchen cupboard to stop our cat, Kali, from getting into it, and when I pulled it out I saw the newspaper wedged behind it. Assuming it had fallen out of the box, I picked it up. Dad used to buy a paper every day on his way back from work, but lately, he'd stopped – or so I'd thought. This one was dated from a week ago. THOUSANDS OF CITIZENS FORCED TO FLEE AS FEARLESS INVADE FRANCE, the headline shouted.

I sat down and began to read, my gaze skimming over words like *carnage* and *rising death toll* and *unstoppable* and *pain*. A sick, cold feeling started in the pit of my stomach and coiled up into my chest. As I turned the page and saw the pictures – piles of bodies, ruined buildings – my hands were trembling. The worst was one of a skinny, ragged-looking man in an army uniform with horrible wounds on his face and head, his clothes soaked in blood. He was grinning at the camera, his expression crazed and twisted, his eyes a weird silvery colour, and even though it was only a photo, you could see they were filled with hate and madness. Underneath was a stark caption: *The face of the Fearless.*

I heard footsteps coming towards the kitchen. Leaping up, I shoved the paper into the recycling box and turned to face the door, my heart hammering. 'Are you all right?' Mum said as she came in to get a glass of water. 'You look a bit pale.'

'I'm fine,' I said quickly. I knew that whoever had stuffed that paper behind the box – Dad, I reckoned – hadn't wanted me to see it. I tried to smile at Mum, although it was the last thing in the world I felt like doing, and took the recycling outside.

That night, I had a terrible dream about a man with silver eyes. I shouted myself awake, bringing Dad running into my room. But when he asked me what was wrong I said I'd had a nightmare about a monster. I was scared that if he knew I'd read the newspaper, he'd be angry.

Now, though, standing on the top of the hill with Dad, I couldn't keep my worries to myself any longer. I'd carried them around inside me all day, and they were getting bigger and bigger.

'Ready to head back?' Dad asked.

'Dad,' I said. 'What's happening in France?'

His face immediately grew serious. 'Where did you find out about that?'

I told him about the newspaper.

He sat down on the soft, springy grass, and patted the ground beside him. 'There have been wars going on in the Middle East for a long time,' he said, putting his arm around my shoulders. 'Our army has been fighting over there, and when our soldiers come home, a lot of them suffer terrible problems because of all the horrible things they've seen there. It's known as Post-Traumatic Stress Disorder – PTSD. Our government paid for some scientists to invent a drug that would stop this happening. At first, the drug was very successful. Not only did it dramatically reduce the number of soldiers suffering from PTSD, but it meant they could fight better while they were out there.'

He hesitated for a moment, then went on. 'But then it was discovered that the drug had a devastating side effect. The soldiers who'd taken it – and by now, there were thousands of them – stopped feeling fear altogether. They started doing terrible things. At the same time – no one's sure how – the enemy got hold of the formula for the drug and made an even more concentrated version of it, so the side effects kicked in immediately. And then . . .' He swallowed, shifting position slightly and plucking at the dried grass, tearing a clump up and twisting it between his fingers. 'And then they started forcing it on anybody and everybody. Even . . . even people who aren't soldiers.'

My stomach lurched. 'Are those . . . the Fearless?' I said, remembering again the man with the silver eyes who'd stalked me in my dreams.

Dad nodded.

'But why couldn't our army stop them?' My heart was beating faster and faster.

'They're trying,' Dad said. I noticed he wouldn't quite meet my gaze.

**10**

'So how come the Fearless are in France?' France was close – we'd been to the Dordogne on holiday last year. 'Will they come here?'

'No,' Dad said firmly. 'We'll be all right. There aren't going to be any Fearless here. The government and the army are making sure of that.' He gave me a quick hug. 'Please don't worry about it, sweetheart, OK?'

By now, the sun was dipping towards the horizon, streaking the sky with gold and pink. 'Dad,' I said as we stood up.

'Yes?'

'Can Sol come over after my riding lesson tomorrow?'

'I don't see why not. Come on. We should head back. Mum'll be wondering where we are.'

'Race you down the hill,' I said. The path we'd just climbed was wide and flat, perfect for sprinting.

'OK,' Dad dropped into an exaggerated crouch, like an athlete about to run a race. I assumed the same position, giggling.

Then, behind us, I heard a blasting roar, so sudden and deafening that Dad and I both jumped and ducked. As the sound streaked overhead I saw, already way off in the distance in front of us, the black arrowhead silhouette of a fighter jet flying south. Another went over, then another, and another. Then a dull, low thudding filled the air. Following the jets was a line of huge helicopters with two rotors; I counted five, seven, ten. The sound made the air vibrate around us.

Dad's mobile rang. He put it to his ear. 'Clare, are you

OK?' he said. He listened for a moment, and all the colour drained out of his face. He ended the call. 'We need to get home, *now*,' he said.

'Dad, what's—' I started to say. He grabbed my hand. We pelted down the hill, going so fast that my feet tangled and I almost fell over. By the time we got to the road and the *Welcome to Blythefield* sign, my chest was burning, but another formation of fighter jets streaking overhead kept me moving. The streets were empty, and eerily quiet.

When we reached our house, which was tucked away up the lane at the edge of the village, Mum was waiting for us at the front door. She was clutching her bump, her hair standing out around her head in a tangle of flame-coloured curls, and for one horrible moment, seeing her pale face and tear-filled eyes, I thought the baby was coming early.

'What's happened?' Dad asked frantically. 'I couldn't hear you properly over the helicopters.'

Mum hustled us inside, locking the door behind us. All the curtains were drawn and the blinds were down, even though it was still quite light outside. Kali appeared from the kitchen and began winding around my ankles, miaowing; I picked her up, burying my face in her sleek, coal-coloured fur.

'I'd turned it on to watch the news,' Mum explained, pointing at the TV, 'and the screen went blank. Then that came on.'

Dad and I both looked at the same time. On the screen, there was a message, white writing on a black background.

'Oh, God,' Dad said.

If you are seeing this message on your television or computer screen, it means the Invasion has taken place and all broadcasting and internet services have ceased.

## TAKE ACTION NOW – DO NOT WAIT.

• Find a place of safety for you and your family. Do not stay anywhere you could be easily cornered or trapped. Plan your escape routes and practise using them.

• Arm yourself. Although guns and ammunition are in short supply, many other items can be used as weapons, such as garden and DIY tools, knives, lengths of wood or heavy kitchen implements. Use any force you feel is necessary to protect yourself.

• Make sure you have the facilities to collect and boil rainwater for drinking, cooking and washing. Good hygiene is essential for the prevention of disease, particularly among the young, elderly and those with existing health problems.

• Make sure you are aware of basic first aid techniques. With medical facilities now severely limited, it could save your or a loved one's life.

• Do not venture out of your safe place unless you have to, or draw attention to yourself by making unnecessary noise, using lights if not needed, etc.

# Chapter 2

I stared at it. I understood what it was saying, yet I couldn't make sense of it. I kept thinking about what Dad had told me up on the hill: *There aren't going to be any Fearless here. The government and the army are making sure of that.* 'What's happening?' I asked, my voice thin and high with fright.

'I don't know.' Dad grabbed the remote and flipped through the channels. They were all showing the same message. He turned the TV off and grabbed the laptop off the coffee table. I watched him try to connect to the internet. The same message flashed up on the screen.

'What the hell?' he murmured.

'What about the radio?' Mum said.

Dad fetched them. We had two – a brand new digital one and an ordinary one. When he turned the digital one on, there was nothing but a low hum. The ordinary one crackled and hissed; he switched it from FM to AM, twisting the dial. I heard a burst of sound – a voice. It startled Kali, who wriggled out of my arms and darted out of the room.

'What was that?' Mum said.

Dad turned the dial again, more slowly this time. Out

of the hiss of the static, the voice emerged. It was a man, talking very fast, his voice high and panicked. '. . . here,' he was saying. 'They reached the coast an hour ago and it's carnage. I don't know if anyone can hear me, but I'm in Dover, at . . .' Another burst of static obscured his words. '. . . and I'm using this . . .' More static.

'How's he doing that if the radio stations have stopped broadcasting?' Mum said.

Dad shook his head. 'Maybe he's got some sort of police radio.'

The man's voice rose out of the static one last time. '. . . to send this message to warn you. The Fearless are here! There are thousands of them! And they . . .' Then the static grew to a buzz, and no matter which way Dad turned the dial, he couldn't find the man again. He switched the radio off.

I didn't cry easily, but I felt a tear leak from the corner of my eye and trickle down my cheek. 'What's *happening*?' I said.

'Sweetheart, I don't know.' Dad's face was grim. He took his mobile out of his pocket, dialled someone's number, then cut the call. 'That's gone now too.'

'What about the landline?' Mum went into the kitchen, and came back a few moments later holding the handset. She shook her head. She was breathing fast, clutching her bump.

The doorbell went.

'Wait here,' Dad said with a nervous glance at the blank TV screen. He went into the hall. I heard the chain

**15**

on the front door rattle, then voices – familiar voices.

'Sol!' I cried, running into the hall as Dad let Sol and his parents into the house.

Dad showed them into the living room. Mr Brightman limped across to one of the armchairs and sat down with a grunt, sticking his left leg out. Two years ago, he'd been in a terrible car accident. He was rushed to Dad's hospital, and it was Dad who'd operated on him and saved his life.

Mrs Brightman perched in the other chair, her mouth pinched into a thin line. As always, her blonde hair was sleek and gleaming, her clothes, a cream blouse and white trousers, immaculate.

'Do you have any idea what's going on?' Mum asked Mr Brightman.

Mr and Mrs Brightman exchanged glances. 'Perhaps we should send the kids upstairs for a bit,' Mr Brightman said. 'There's something we need to talk to you and Pete about, Clare.'

Mum turned to us. 'Why don't you and Sol go up to your room, Cass?' she said in a too-bright voice. 'I'll bring you up some biscuits and juice as soon as we've finished.'

I glanced at Sol. I felt as if I was on the verge of tears again. I couldn't stop thinking about the fighter jets and the helicopters. I knew that they were connected to that message on the TV, and the man on the radio. *The Fearless are here!*

'Kids, upstairs, please,' Dad said, going over to the door and opening it for us.

'But Dad—' I wanted to know what was going on. I *needed* to know.

'No arguing, Cassandra,' Dad said in his best I-mean-it voice. He watched us go up the stairs. As we reached my bedroom, I heard him go back in the living room and close the door.

'Did you see those planes and helicopters go over earlier?' I asked Sol as he sat down on my bed. Kali padded in and jumped up beside him, but he ignored her, and nodded solemnly.

It was getting dark now. I switched on the light and went to the window, where I stood for a moment, looking out at the shadowy garden before whisking the curtains closed. The room looked exactly the same as it had when I woke up this morning: the walls the same shade of pale duck-egg blue, the desk in the corner comfortably cluttered with books and pens and the beginnings of a patchwork cushion me and Mum were making. Hound, the worn brown-and-white toy dog I'd had since I was a baby, was still sitting on the end of my bed, one ear sticking up and one flopping down as always. But nothing looked familiar. I didn't feel as if I belonged any more.

'We should go down and listen,' Sol said.

'What?'

He wrinkled up his nose, like he always did when he was worried, his freckles disappearing into the creases. 'I heard Mum and Dad say something last night about moving away.'

**17**

I gasped. 'You can't move!' I said. Sol and I had only known each other a few years, but as our teacher Mrs Pamett said, we were joined at the hip. I'd never had a best friend before Sol came along. He shouldn't even have gone to my school – Mrs Brightman wanted to send him to a posh boarding school, but Sol failed the entrance exam. Mrs Brightman was really disappointed. Once, a couple of our other friends and I went round without being invited first and as we left I heard her arguing with Mr Brightman, saying stuff like *those dreadful village children* and *should never have moved here in the first place.*

'It was the father of one of those "dreadful village children" who saved my life,' I heard Mr Brightman snap back at her, and with a shock, I realized he was talking about Dad. Which meant Mrs Brightman had been talking about me.

'I don't want to move either,' Sol said.

'OK, let's go back down.' I was as desperate to know what was going on as he was. We crept downstairs, and I pressed my ear against the living-room door.

'Everywhere's been overrun,' Mr Brightman was saying. 'Europe, Asia, America, Canada. And now here.'

'But are you sure?' I heard Mum say. Her voice sounded high and panicky.

'You've been watching the news, haven't you? And you saw that message on the TV and the internet.'

Dad murmured something I couldn't quite make out.

'What does he mean?' whispered Sol, who had an ear

pressed to the door as well. I realized I hadn't told him about the newspaper in the recycling yet.

'. . . why we came over,' Mr Brightman was saying. 'I recently invested in some property – a small, man-made island off the coast between Portsmouth and the Isle of Wight. The previous owners were developing it as a holiday resort, but they were based in Dubai, and when the trouble started overseas their backers pulled out and they went bankrupt. It's nowhere near finished yet, but I'm setting it up as a safe place for people to ride out the Invasion. A select few people.' He cleared his throat. 'Pete, I've never forgotten what you did for me after my accident. I wouldn't be here today if it wasn't for you. And your medical skills would be invaluable. That's why I've reserved a place for you and your family on Hope Island.'

Inside the room, there was silence. It didn't occur to me to wonder how Mr Brightman had managed to be so well prepared for the Invasion when it had taken the rest of the country by surprise. Not then, anyway. All I could think was, *does this mean we'll be moving?* And how had Mr Brightman been able to buy an island? I didn't know a lot about what he did, only that it was something scientific that he never talked about, not even to Sol. And I knew it made him enough money for the Brightmans to live in the huge house at the top of the lane, which had its own swimming pool and tennis court. But a *whole island*?

'What about the baby?' Mum said.

'Like I said, the facilities are basic at the moment, but there's medical equipment. We'll make sure you're OK.'

This time it was Mum's reply that was too quiet to hear.

'Of course, you'll only be able to bring the bare minimum with you,' Mr Brightman went on. 'A few changes of clothes and other essentials. No pets, I'm afraid.'

*Kali.*

I grabbed the handle and flung the door open. 'If Kali can't go, I don't want to either!' I said as the adults stared at me. 'We can't leave her!'

'Cass—' Dad began.

Mrs Brightman cut across him. '*Solomon!*' she snapped, crossing the room in two steps and grabbing Sol's arm. 'Were you eavesdropping? *What have I told you about that?*'

Her eyes looked like bits of black flint. She gave Sol a hard shake, her fingers digging into the top of his arm. He tried to twist away. 'Ow, Mum. You're hurting me!'

'I don't know what's got into you recently, Solomon,' Mrs Brightman said. 'I've told you it's rude to listen in to grown-ups' private conversations. I've told you—'

'Diane, leave him,' Mr Brightman said, but she seemed not to hear him.

'Apologize at *once*,' she hissed at Sol.

'I – I'm sorry.' Sol's eyes swam with tears, and I took a step back, just in case she decided to start on me next. Last time I'd gone to Sol's, she'd yelled at me for dropping a glass. That's why I usually asked Sol over here.

'*Diane*,' Mr Brightman said, a little more forcefully, and she seemed to come to her senses. She let go of Sol, who blinked and rubbed his arm. 'I'm sorry,' he said again in a small voice.

'I'll deal with you when we get home,' Mrs Brightman said.

Dad cleared his throat. 'So, when are you leaving?'

'As soon as possible,' Mr Brightman said.

'Dad!' I said. 'Do we have to go?'

The adults all looked at each other. 'We're still trying to decide, sweetie,' Mum said. 'Nothing's definite yet.' I noticed she hadn't really answered my question.

'We'd better get back.' Mr Brightman stood awkwardly. 'We need to pack up some things. We'll be back in half an hour – if you want to come with us, be ready. And until then, stay indoors.'

Dad showed the Brightmans out.

'Mum, Dad, what's going on?' I demanded as soon as he came back. '*Please* tell me.'

Mum patted the sofa. I perched beside her, and Dad sat down in the armchair where Mr Brightman had been a few minutes before. Both of them looked pale.

'That message on the television,' Mum said, moving her hands in small circles across her bump. 'It's there because, in the countries where there are wars happening, people have been given a – a sort of medicine to make them fight better—'

'She knows,' Dad said in a gruff voice. 'She found last week's newspaper when she was sorting out the recycling.'

Mum looked sharply at him, and I realized that my parents must have known about the Fearless for a long time – and that they'd kept that knowledge from me.

'What's happened to the army and the police?' I said. 'What's happened to the *government*?'

Dad swallowed. 'I'm not sure.'

I looked from Dad to Mum and back again. The dread I felt when I read the newspaper yesterday was back, stronger than ever. 'Have the Fearless killed them?'

'I'm not sure,' Dad repeated. 'But we're going to go with the Brightmans, just in case. If the Fearless do come to Blythefield, it'll be too dangerous for us to stay.'

'I don't want to go!' I cried. 'Not if I can't take Kali!'

Dad pressed his lips together. 'Cass, we don't have any choice.'

'But Dad—'

'Sweetie, don't argue, please,' Mum said. 'Come back upstairs. We need to pack.'

We went up and quickly, silently, stuffed some of my clothes into a bag. In Mum and Dad's bedroom next door, I could hear Dad opening drawers, banging them shut again, and a thud as something fell over. My skin was prickling all over and I couldn't catch my breath properly; I felt as if everything was happening too fast. Only Kali, rolling around on my bed, purring, seemed oblivious to the tension in the air. I paused for a moment to rub the soft fur on her neck, an ache growing in my throat. I couldn't leave her. I couldn't. I'd had her since she was a kitten.

Mum folded me into an awkward hug. 'Who's going to look after her, Mum?' I said into her shoulder, my eyes hot. 'Who'll feed her?'

'She'll be OK,' Mum comforted. 'She catches things all the time. Sometimes she eats so many mice she doesn't want her food, remember?'

I nodded, sniffling.

Then Mum groaned and arched her back, pulling away from me.

'Mum?' I asked, at the same time as Dad, walking past my door with a suitcase in his hand said, 'Clare?'

She shook her head. 'It's nothing. Practice contractions.'

'Already?' Dad said, putting the suitcase down.

'I'm *fine*, Pete.'

Dad frowned. 'If you're sure.' He didn't sound convinced. 'I'm going to go down and check all the doors and windows.'

'Let's put Kali out now,' Mum said, holding out her arms. I passed Kali over, feeling like my heart was being ripped out of my chest. As Mum carried her over to the door, she started wriggling. She twisted out of Mum's arms, and thundered down the stairs. 'Pete!' Mum called. 'Can you let the cat out?'

Dad's voice drifted up to us. 'Done it!'

A few minutes later, he came back upstairs. 'Everything's locked, and I'll turn off the gas, water and electricity just before we leave,' he said. He was holding my granddad's old walking stick. It was stout and gnarled, with a brass handle, and he was clutching it so tightly his knuckles were white. 'The Brightmans should be back soon.'

I grabbed Hound off the bed and stuffed him in a side pocket of my bag. Then I carried it downstairs and put it with Mum and Dad's suitcase by the front door. Back in the living room, Mum sat down and pressed her hands against her bump, taking deep breaths. Dad fiddled with the radio again, but there was nothing but white noise, and when he turned on the TV and the laptop, there was just that sinister message. I tried to read a book, but I couldn't concentrate, so I picked up my DS. Only I couldn't concentrate on that either. I kept thinking about Kali. What if I never saw her again?

The back door rattled, making us all jump.

'Who's that?' Mum said. 'Not the Brightmans yet, surely?'

'I'll go and check,' Dad said. 'Stay here.'

'Be careful!' Mum called after him as he went out, carrying the stick. I heard the back door open. A few moments later, he came back. 'No one there. It must have been the wind.' He glanced at his watch. 'I'll get the car out and bring it round to the front so I can start loading the bags into it. Then we'll be ready to go as soon as the Brightmans arrive.'

The garage was separate from the house, standing at the back of the garden at the end of a short gravel drive. I crept to the living-room window and pushed the curtain aside a couple of inches, watching Dad walk across the lawn. It was completely dark now and the security light had come on, casting a long shadow in front of him.

Halfway to the garage, he stopped, patting his pockets. A few seconds later, the outside light, which was on a timer, went out. All I could see was my own reflection in the glass. I felt an irrational burst of terror. Had he forgotten the keys? Suddenly, the light flashed on again; Dad was shaking his head, the car keys dangling from one finger as he marched towards the garage.

And then, through the hedge at the back of the garden, ten feet or so away from him, I saw something move.

# Chapter 3

A split second later, the light went out again.

When it came back on, I saw a woman standing in front of a gap in the hedge where a cow had got through in the spring. It had raced around the garden, churning up the grass with its hooves, and Dad had had to call the farmer to come and get it; he hadn't got round to patching up the hole yet.

The woman was a bit younger than Mum, tall and slender, wearing a grubby-looking army uniform with a pouch belted around her waist. Her dark hair was in a ponytail that had come half-undone, and there was blood all down the side of her face, soaking into the collar of her jacket. In the harsh glow from the outside light, it looked black. She took a few steps towards Dad, who hadn't seen her yet – he was unlocking the garage door, and she was just out of his line of sight – then stopped, looking round her in a dazed sort of way.

'Come away from there,' Mum said in a sharp voice.

'There's someone out there,' I whispered. I let the curtain drop and darted across the room to turn out the light. Then I returned to the window. Mum came to stand beside me.

'Who is that?' I said. I didn't recognize the woman. I'd never seen her before.

Mum didn't answer me.

'*Mum*. She's hurt – maybe we should go out and—'

'No!' Mum said loudly, and I saw the woman's head twitch as if she'd heard her, although she couldn't have because she was too far from the house.

'No,' Mum said, lowering her voice again. 'We mustn't go out there.' She took in a sudden, hissing breath, pressing her hands into the small of her back.

Dad finally looked round and saw the woman. He opened his mouth, saying something to her. She lunged at him and, before he could even move out of the way, never mind defend himself, she punched him in the face. Even though he was twice her size, he staggered back and collapsed on the gravel in a heap, his eyes rolling up, blood bursting from his nostrils like someone had just turned on a tap. Mum and I both screamed at the same time and the woman's head jerked towards the house again.

Mum pulled me away from the window, crushing me to her and clapping a hand across my mouth before I could scream again. '*Keep quiet*,' she whispered fiercely. Her breath was coming in ragged little gasps. My heart was banging and my legs had gone weak. Against my back, I felt the baby kick savagely, as if he too sensed something terrible had just happened.

Mum took her hand away from my mouth.

'Mum, what's happening?' I said in a shaky whisper. 'Is Dad—'

I couldn't say it. I couldn't say *dead*.

From outside, I heard a piercing whistle.

'Don't move,' Mum whispered back. With her back against the wall, she inched towards the window, peering around the edge of the curtain. I crept to her side, ignoring her hissed 'Cass, I told you not to move!'

Dad was lying on his back, blood still oozing from his nose. The woman put two fingers to her lips and whistled again, then folded her arms, looking round impatiently as if she was waiting for someone. Her movements were sure and strong. I realized she must have just been pretending to be dazed – or else the attack had energized her in some way.

The woman looked at the house. Mum made a sort of squeaking noise and drew back, but I stayed where I was, peeping around the curtain.

There was something wrong with the woman's eyes. They were silvery and dull, and her pupils were enormous.

Suddenly, I remembered the photograph of the man in that newspaper article.

Dad began to move.

It was like he was only half-awake. His feet twitched and his hands pawed at the air. But he was alive. *Alive.* As his eyelids flickered open, I started to cry, half from fear, half from relief. 'Mum, he's waking up! We have to help him!' I whispered through my sobs. But all she did was stand there, her back to the wall, gasping.

Dad raised an arm and let it drop. His eyes were still

half-closed. I remembered a few years ago when Sol and I were bouncing on the top of his bunk bed. Sol jumped up, hit his head on the ceiling, then fell off the bed and hit his head on the floor. Afterwards he was really sleepy and kept being sick, and said he couldn't see properly. He had to go to hospital, and stayed off school for two days. When he came back, he told me proudly that he'd hit his head so hard it had shaken his brain against the inside of his skull and given him concussion. *It's really dangerous*, he told me. *I could have DIED.*

What if that was what had happened to Dad?

'Mum,' I moaned, tears spilling down my cheeks. '*Do something.*'

But her eyes were closed. She didn't even seem to hear me.

The woman looked over her shoulder. A few moments later, two men pushed their way through the hole in the hedge. One was quite young, also dressed in an army uniform that was crusted with mud. The other was older than Dad, wearing an ordinary jumper and jeans. They were filthy too. Both men had the same weird silver eyes as the woman.

The older man bent over Dad, put two fingers under his jaw and tilted his head back. Dad struggled feebly, trying to push him away. The younger man straddled him, kneeling on his arms and legs to pin them down. The woman unzipped the pouch around her waist, taking something out – a syringe with a long needle that glinted cruelly in the glow from the outside light. It was full of liquid that looked like watery blood.

Grabbing Dad's hair with her free hand, she pulled his head roughly to one side and brought the needle down hard, stabbing it into the back of Dad's neck.

Dad jack-knifed, hard enough to throw the man sitting on him off and send the empty syringe flying out of the woman's hand, his eyes springing open and his mouth opening in a soundless howl. Then he collapsed again.

I squeezed my eyes shut, telling myself that the last few minutes had just been a bad dream, and that when I looked through the window again, I'd see Dad walking towards the back door with the stick in his hand.

He'd smile and give us a thumbs-up to say *everything's OK*.

He'd come inside and we'd load up the car and wait for Mr and Mrs Brightman and Sol to arrive.

And we'd all be safe.

'Oh God,' I heard Mum say behind me in a high, trembling voice. 'Oh God, oh God, oh God.' When I opened my eyes again I saw the older man lifting Dad over his shoulders.

The woman looked towards the window and pointed.

Mum grabbed my hand and dragged me into the kitchen, where she pulled out the two biggest knives from the block by the cooker.

'*Mum!*' I wailed as she led me out into the hall. We were going towards the front door. Going *outside*. I tried to pull away from her, but she was still holding my hand too tightly. It wasn't until we got to the door that she let me go.

'We're going to try to get to the Brightmans' house, OK?' she said. Her voice was croaky and thick with tears.

'I don't want to go out there,' I said, shaking my head.

'We have to. They know we're here. That woman heard us scream.' She tried to hand me the smaller of the two knives, and when I shook my head again, pushed it at me more insistently. 'I don't want you to use it unless you absolutely have to. I'll try to protect you. But if anything happens to me, don't stay with me. Run.'

I started crying again, so hard I couldn't speak. The knife was heavy, and the thought of having to use it, even on that woman or one of those men, turned my stomach.

'Cass, snap out of it!' Mum's voice was suddenly hard and angry. She pulled me round to face her. 'You have to—' She drew in her breath sharply, letting go of me to press her hands to the small of her back and closing her eyes. 'Oh, *God*, not *now*,' she groaned through clenched teeth. Fresh terror zigzagged through me, the shock strong enough to stop my tears.

'Mum? What's wrong?' I said. 'Is the baby coming?'

Mum let out a slow breath and straightened up. 'No. It just . . . kicked me a bit too hard, that's all.' She slid her key into the front door lock. 'We have to be quiet, OK? Very quiet, and very quick.'

As she pulled the door open a few inches to look out, my palms were so slippery with sweat I was scared I'd drop my knife.

'When I say run, we run,' she whispered. 'Don't stop until we get to Sol's house.'

I heard the back door rattle, and a bang as if someone had kicked it hard. Then another, and a splintering sound. I looked over my shoulder to see the Fearless woman clambering through the hole she'd kicked in the door, her lips pulled back in a snarl.

'*Quick!*' Mum hissed. We slipped out of the front door and Mum locked it. Then we dragged the recycling bin and the rubbish bin, both of which were almost full, in front of it. '*Go!*' Mum said in my ear.

I got to the gate first, fumbling with the latch. From inside the house there was an animal-sounding howl, and then a gruff shout: '*It's locked!*' I wrenched the gate open and ran out into the lane, Mum staggering after me. Pure terror sang through my veins; I could hardly breathe. When I looked over my shoulder I saw Mum clutching her knife in one hand, the other pressed against her bump, her hair hanging in sweat-soaked strings around her face.

'Keep going,' she gasped. 'Don't worry about me.'

I heard that howl again, echoing up into the trees, and crashes as the Fearless tried to break down the front door. I tried to run faster, but my legs felt weak; I wasn't sure I could keep going. Acid burned up into my throat, nearly choking me.

Behind me, Mum moaned and fell to her knees on the track.

I ran back to her. Another shout – '*There's something in*

*front of the door!'* – and more crashes drifted towards us. 'Mum, get up!' I said, frantically tugging on her arm. She shook her head. She'd dropped her knife. 'You go, Cass. Run. Get to Sol's.'

'No, I'm not leaving you!'

I heard the sound of glass breaking. It sounded as if the Fearless had given up trying to get out of the front door and were smashing their way out through a window instead. I pleaded with Mum to get up. Then I heard another sound from the top of the lane.

A car.

It was coming towards us, fast.

Headlights burst out of the darkness, so bright they blinded me, and the shriek of the engine filled my ears. There was no time to get out of the way. I flung a hand across my eyes, screaming, hearing Mum screaming too, time seeming to slow as I waited for the car to slam into us, and wondering how much it would hurt.

# Chapter 4

The vehicle jerked to a halt just inches away from us, the engine stalling. I heard a door open. Then a voice. 'Clare? Cass?'

Mr Brightman.

He helped me to my feet, then Mum. 'Where's Pete?' he asked her and, when she didn't answer him, 'Clare? *Where is he?*'

'He's – he—' I started to say, but the words stuck in my throat.

'They were soldiers!' Mum said. '*British soldiers!*'

Mr Brightman stared at us, his face pale in the light from the Range Rover's headlamps.

Down the lane, I heard the Fearless woman call, '*Come on! I heard them!*' and one of the men make a roaring sound.

Mr Brightman ran back to the Range Rover, yanking open the back door. 'Get in, quick.'

I scrambled in next to Sol, who was sitting bolt upright. In the front, Mrs Brightman was gazing out through the windscreen. She didn't look round as Mum clambered in too and sat with her arms across her bump, bent over.

'Mum,' I said as Mr Brightman slammed the door and got back into the front. '*Mum*. Are you OK?'

Then I heard a ratcheting sound from the front of the Range Rover. Mr Brightman was holding a gun with a long double barrel.

'Everyone strapped in?' he said as he opened the window next to him a few inches. 'This could be a bumpy ride.'

I quickly fastened my seatbelt, and helped Mum with hers.

'I've locked the doors,' Mr Brightman said. 'Everyone hold on, OK?'

He twisted the keys in the ignition, revved the engine, and we jolted forwards. Even with my seatbelt on, I had to cling to the edge of the seat. The Range Rover bounced down the potholed lane, Mr Brightman steering with one hand and pointing the gun out of the window with the other.

Suddenly, a shape jumped in front us, silhouetted in the headlights. The Fearless woman. There was a thump and the Range Rover skidded sideways. Sol, his mum and I screamed. Mr Brightman swore and yanked on the steering wheel, never slowing. He fired the gun out of the window once, twice. '*Simon, slow down!*' Mrs Brightman shrieked at him.

'Slow down?' he yelled. 'Are you crazy, woman?'

He fired again, and at last, we reached the road. Mr Brightman put the gun down on the floor between the seats. I sat back, trembling.

To start with, the road was empty, but not for long. As we drove, we started to see more vehicles — cars, vans, even buses and lorries — heading in the opposite direction.

'Simon, don't you think we should be going north too?' Mrs Brightman asked as Sol and I twisted round to see if anyone was following us, and saw nothing but the dark, empty road behind us. 'If the Fearless have come up from the coast—'

'Diane, *look* at them,' Mr Brightman said, indicating the slowly-moving lines of traffic on the other side of the road, the vehicles' headlights shining brightly into the Range Rover. 'They're going nowhere, and the Fearless'll pick them off like flies. Hope is ready. All we have to do is get there.'

I gazed out of the window at the vehicles on the other side of the road, trying to process the knowledge that I'd never see Dad again; that the life I'd always known had come to a sudden, brutal end. There was still part of my brain that kept insisting all of this was a dream, and that soon, I'd wake up back in my own bed, and nothing would have changed.

The inside of the Range Rover filled with dazzling light. I saw a pair of headlights on our side of the road, coming straight towards us. Mr Brightman swore and hauled on the wheel. The other car swerved too, just in time to avoid ploughing into us, and bumped off the road into the ditch. 'Idiot,' Mr Brightman snarled.

'Cass,' Sol whispered. It was the first time he'd spoken

since Mr Brightman rescued me and Mum. 'What did they look like? The Fearless, I mean?'

I swallowed. 'Like – like ordinary people,' I whispered back. *Except for the eyes*, I reminded myself. *Don't forget the eyes.*

A shiver wrenched down my spine.

Mr Brightman had been right about the traffic on the other side of the road. By the time we reached the motorway it had stopped moving altogether. People were sounding their horns, but there was nowhere they could go. We kept having to swerve to avoid people driving up our side, and at one point, we passed a van that had crashed into the central reservation, its front caved in, another car all the way up the steeply sloping verge opposite with its windows smashed and its tyres shredded. We were the only people who seemed to be going south.

Then I started to see them: shadows and shapes, trying doors and thumping their fists against windows. We were going so fast it was hard to see them properly, and I wondered if I was imagining them.

Right until one of them leaped over the central barrier and out in front of the Range Rover, and Mr Brightman tried to swerve and didn't manage it. A body flipped up onto the bonnet and a face thumped against the windscreen: a snarling, bloody face with silvery eyes. I screamed. Somehow, Mr Brightman kept going, swinging the Range Rover from side to side until the Fearless let go and slid off the bonnet, leaving a spider-web of cracks on the windscreen where he'd hit it with his head. One of the headlights was out too. As we sped forwards I saw his body tumbling towards the steep bank at the side of the motorway, and then he was gone.

Beside me, Mum let out a cry, arching her back, her eyes screwed shut. 'Mum!' I shouted. 'What's wrong?'

'The baby,' she groaned through clenched teeth. 'It's coming.'

Mr Brightman glanced back over his seat. 'What did she say?'

'She says she's having the baby!' I said. Mrs Brightman twisted her head to look round over the seat, her eyes wide. '*What?*'

Mr Brightman swore again. 'Clare, we're half an hour away if the road stays clear. Just hang on, OK? *Hang on.* I'm going as fast as I can.'

Mum hung her head, grinding her teeth together, lost in her own little world of pain.

I reached for Sol's hand and we clung to each other, our fingers locked tight.

Not long after that, we turned off the motorway, leaving the lines of traffic behind. But even though the narrow lanes we were racing along were almost empty, and the few cars we did pass were heading towards the motorway despite Mr Brightman's frantic gestures for them to turn round, in my head, I was still there. I kept thinking about the Fearless making their way along the rows of cars; finding doors that were unlocked or smashing windows; reaching in to—

*No, no, no, don't think about that,* I told myself.

Mum hadn't said a word since she told us the baby was coming. What if she gave birth right here in the Range Rover? I had no idea how to help someone have a baby. I don't think *any* of us did – Dad was the doctor and he . . .

*Don't think about that either.*

And the baby was coming early . . . one of my friends' brothers was born three months early last year. They got him to hospital, but there was something wrong with his lungs, and he—

*STOP, OK?* I ordered myself.

We drove through a village where lights blazed from windows, doors stood open and, in one driveway, a car burned so fiercely I could feel the heat of the flames through the window as we passed. And nearby . . .

'Don't look, kids,' Mr Brightman said in a shaky voice, but it was too late. I'd already seen the man and the woman lying unconscious on the ground, the orange glow from the flames flickering across their faces. A figure crouched over them, binding their wrists with rope. Nearby, another small group of people sat on the ground, also tied up, their faces slack with despair.

I closed my eyes, so far beyond being scared now that I didn't even know what I felt any more. *A bad dream, a bad dream, a bad dream,* I chanted over and over inside my head, as if saying it enough times would make it come true.

Once we were out of the village, Mr Brightman slowed the Range Rover down. 'Diane,' he said. 'I need you to hold the gun while I look out for the turning.'

He tried to hand it to her, but she batted it away. 'Get that thing away from me!'

'Diane—'

'I don't want it! I don't want *any* of this!'

'Well, I hate to tell you this, but you don't have a choice!' Mr Brightman bellowed at her, and for some reason hearing Sol's parents yelling at each other made my terror sharp and real again in a way nothing else had been able to. Tears welled up in my eyes and spilled down my cheeks.

'Mum, Dad, *stop it*!' Sol cried, bursting into tears as well.

'Don't you *dare* shout at me, Solomon!' Mrs Brightman snapped.

Mum screamed, her head thrown back, tendons standing out in her neck.

'Hold on, Clare!' Mr Brightman shouted. 'Ten more minutes!'

He thrust the gun at Mrs Brightman again, hunching forwards over the steering wheel and trying to see where he was going in the light from the remaining headlamp. A bright full moon had risen overhead, but trees covered the road, and the moonlight only broke through in a few places.

Then he exclaimed, 'There!' and yanked hard on the wheel. Through my tears, I saw a sign that said *Dockyard ½ mile. Permit holders only. Trespassers will be prosecuted* flash past.

A high chain-link fence flanked the road we were on now. Mr Brightman stamped on the accelerator and we surged forward, the engine howling. Mum cried out again. 'Nearly there!' Mr Brightman said.

Ahead, I saw lights. Mr Brightman put the brakes on so suddenly I was thrown forward and my seatbelt locked, biting into my neck. 'This is it,' he said, grabbing the gun back from Mrs Brightman. 'All of you stay here. I'm going to find someone who can help us with your mum, Cass. When I get out, lock the doors behind me. Don't unlock them till I come back.'

When he'd gone, Mrs Brightman jabbed a button on the dashboard, and I heard the locks clunk. The only other sound was Mum's rapid breathing. Peering through the windscreen, I saw other cars in front of us, parked all over the place, and beyond them, huge buildings and gigantic cranes silhouetted in the moonlight.

Mr Brightman returned a few minutes later with another man carrying a powerful torch, a rifle strapped to his back. He tapped on the window, making us all jump. Mrs Brightman unlocked the doors again. 'This is Ian Denning,' Mr Brightman said, indicating the man with the rifle. He was about Dad's age, and had a light-coloured moustache and sandy hair. 'We're going to get your mum to a boat, Cass. You and Sol stick with us, OK? Diane, I need you to get the bags out of the back.'

'I can't carry all those! They're too heavy!' Mrs Brightman said, sounding outraged.

'So just take the essentials!' Mr Brightman said. 'For God's *sake*, Diane!'

Mrs Brightman muttered something and pushed her door open. As she stamped round to the back of the Range Rover I saw she was wearing a pencil skirt and little heels.

It took her for ever to pick which bags to take, and watching her, I realized Mum and I had left everything at the house. All we had with us were the clothes we were wearing.

'Diane, hurry up, for crying out loud.' Mr Brightman marched to the back of the Range Rover and started pulling bags out himself. 'These'll do. Sol can carry his rucksack.' Ignoring Mrs Brightman's protests, he slammed the boot shut and hefted one of the bags onto his own back.

'Ready?' he asked me and Sol as he put an arm around Mum. We nodded. 'OK, Clare, we need you to walk as fast as you can. Kids, stay close. You too, Diane.'

Mrs Brightman scowled at him. Her hair was coming out of its clip and hanging in her face.

We followed Mr Brightman and Ian Denning, who were helping Mum walk, through the haphazardly parked cars towards another set of gates, where people were standing in a messy, jostling queue. Some people were crying. Others had stunned expressions on their faces, as if they couldn't believe this was happening. A girl my age with long hair even curlier than mine was lying on the ground screaming, despite her mother's pleas to calm down.

At the gate a man and a woman with rifles were trying to break up two men who were squaring up to each other with furious expressions on their faces. 'Come on, then,' one of them kept saying. 'Come on!'

'Coming through!' Ian Denning shouted as we got nearer. 'Let us past, please!'

'What's so special about them, then?' one of the men called. He was fat and balding and dishevelled-looking. 'Slip you a few tenners, did they?'

'That's it,' the female guard said as we hurried past them. 'One more word out of you and you're not coming in.'

Her threat didn't stop the mutters that started rising around us. 'Yeah!' someone else shouted. 'Why can't they wait in the queue like everyone else?'

Ian Denning turned and pointed his gun at them. 'This man is the reason you're all here in the first place,' he said, indicating Mr Brightman. 'Now shut up, or none of you'll be getting in.'

The queue went quiet, save for the girl still sobbing and screaming on the ground, but I could feel their anger, radiating towards us. I was glad when we got through the gates.

Mum gave another one of those terrible groans, her legs buckling under her. Mr Brightman swore. 'We need to be quicker than this, Ian,' he said.

By now they were almost carrying Mum between them, Mr Brightman limping heavily but moving so fast that the rest of us could hardly keep up. As we hurried after them through a dark maze of warehouses and machinery, I saw the silhouette of an enormous ship rising up over one of the warehouse roofs. At last, we reached a long wooden pier that jutted out to sea. We were surrounded by ships. Balanced on their keels in dry concrete channels, they looked truly gigantic.

And in front of us, across the water, was the dark shape of an island, the moonlight making a glittering path on the waves between here and there.

Hope.

'This way,' Ian Denning said, leading us onto the pier, where the smell of salt and seaweed was so strong it stung my nostrils. At the end a ladder led down to the water. I peered over the edge and saw a little wooden boat bobbing on the waves, with two men sitting inside. When they saw us, they began climbing up the ladder. Sol and I retreated behind Mrs Brightman, our eyes on their guns.

Just then, Mum screamed, and back in the direction of the dock gates, I thought I heard someone else scream, too. But the sound didn't come again. Maybe it was just an echo.

Mr Brightman crouched next to Mum and explained she'd have to climb down the ladder. Mum shook her head. 'You have to, Clare,' Mr Brightman told her. 'You can't have the baby here.'

He and Ian Denning got Mum to her feet and guided her over to the ladder. Somehow, she made it down to the boat. 'Diane, Sol, Cass, come on,' Mr Brightman called hoarsely, beckoning us over. Then, behind us, we heard a

**44**

yell. I whirled to see a man running along the pier. At first I thought it was the man from the queue, the one who said we'd bribed Ian Denning to let us through the gates. Then I realized he was younger, with longer hair, matted and filthy.

And that his eyes were as silver as the moon.

Ian Denning wrenched his gun from his back and fired it at the man. The sound of the shot was deafening, but he missed and the man kept coming. Sol and I both screamed and ran for the ladder. Mrs Brightman ran too, but she wasn't quick enough, and the Fearless grabbed her and started to pull her back along the pier. As she shrieked and struggled, Mr Brightman fired his own gun – just as the Fearless turned back towards us, his face frozen in a manic grin and Mrs Brightman held like a shield in front of him.

The bullet slammed into her stomach, and her shriek turned to a screech.

She and the Fearless crumpled to the ground together. 'Diane!' Mr Brightman yelled hoarsely. '*Diane!*'

As he ran towards her the Fearless got to his feet again, blood pouring from a hole in his abdomen, his face twisted in a grimace. Ian Denning tried to shoot again, but his gun jammed. Mr Brightman just stood there, staring at his wife, who wasn't moving.

'Dad!' Sol yelled. Even with the horrific wound in his stomach, the Fearless moved frighteningly fast. '*Dad!*'

Mr Brightman ran for the ladder and we all scrambled down it. Mum was already curled up in the bottom of the boat. The Fearless reached the ladder too; as he started to climb down, one of the men fired his own gun at him and hit him in the shoulder. His body jerked and he toppled into the water with a splash.

The two men started to row frantically, pulling away from the Fearless who, incredibly, was still alive, hissing garbled curses and trying to swim after us. At last, he went under the water and didn't come back up. Then Mum made a noise that was half-groan, half-howl. 'It's coming! It's coming!' she gasped, sitting up.

One of the men thrust his oar at Ian Denning, and he and Mr Brightman scrambled to help her. I'd always thought having a baby would take ages, but within ten minutes, it was over. My brother was born while Hope Island was still rising up out of the water in front of us and the docks and the mainland were still falling away behind.

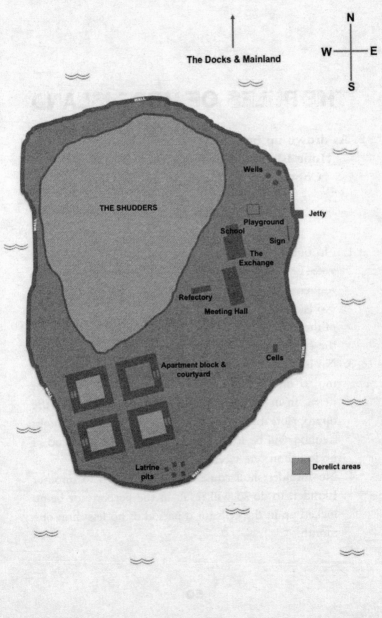

# HOPE ISLAND

The Docks & Mainland

N
W — E
S

Wells

THE SHUDDERS

Jetty

Playground
School
Sign
The Exchange

Refectory

Meeting Hall

Cells

Apartment block & courtyard

Latrine pits

Derelict areas

# THE RULES OF HOPE ISLAND

**As drawn up by S. Brightman, Island Mayor, the Hope Island Governing Committee and the Captain of the Patrol in the first year of occupation** (Invasion Year Zero).
**Amended** I.Y.3; I.Y.5

1. No outsider is permitted to land on Hope ~~without a vote first being cast by the IGC and the island's residents~~. Any trespassers will be shot by the Patrol.
2. No Islander will have children without the permission of the HIGC. This is essential to conserve resources for the community.
3. No Islander will take food or any other items belonging to another Islander, or take food or any other items from the Exchange without presenting the appropriate number of tokens. Any Islander caught stealing will be locked up in the cells for a period of no less than one week.
4. No Islander shall cause deliberate injury to another Islander. To do so will result in the perpetrator being locked up in the cells for a period of no less than one month.

5. No Islander shall deliberately cause the death of another Islander. To do so will result in the perpetrator being outcast.
6. All Islanders aged 17 and over are expected to contribute to the community on Hope Island by working in the roles chosen for them by the HIGC.
7. All Islanders aged between 5 and 17 years must attend school from Monday to Friday.
8. No decisions are to be made that affect the island community without consulting the HIGC.
9. Any Islander who leaves the island without permission may be denied re-entry.
10. Any Islander who is taken by a Fearless and does not return of their own accord, unAltered, will be considered lost.

# Chapter 5

*Seven years later*

## CASS

When I look at myself in the piece of mirror fixed to the wall above my sleeping mat, even my restless night can't dull my excitement. My shirt and trousers, although patched and faded, are clean, and the worn leather of my boots gleams in the light from the oil lamp. My armband is blue, embroidered with the words *Hope Junior Patrol*. If my assessment goes well, today will be the last time I wear it.

On the mat beside mine, Jori stirs and sits up. '*Please can I come and watch you do target practice?*' he says as he kicks his blankets back, the same question he's asked a hundred times a day since he found out I was graduating from the Junior Patrol. His breath forms clouds in the chilly air.

'*No*, Jor.' I twist my mousy curls back into a knot, wishing, not for the first time, that I'd inherited Mum's flaming red hair like my brother did.

Jori pushes his lip out. 'But I want to!'

'*No*. It's too dangerous.' I help him tug his favourite bright green T-shirt down over his head. 'But you can join the Junior Patrol when you're twelve, and then you'll get to learn to shoot a gun yourself, eventually.'

Jori rolls his eyes. 'But that's *ages*. I'll be *old*.'

'Are you trying to say I'm old?' I lunge at him and he shrieks, trying to dodge away, but I grab him and start tickling him while he squirms in my arms and giggles.

Then the Meeting Hall bell starts to ring, signalling breakfast. Jori wriggles free, still giggling breathlessly, and I chase him out of the apartment to the rickety communal stairs. If these apartments had been finished, we'd've had lifts, but whoever owned the island before Sol's dad only got as far as putting in the shafts. Hope's maintenance crew have boarded them over so no one falls down them.

Outside, the slowly lightening sky is iron grey, an icy wind gusting off the sea, and I can hear the waves crashing against the shore. Sadness tugs inside me. Despite the cold, winter used to be my favourite time of year before we came to the island. Mum and Dad's too. Now, it just means me and Jori wearing every item of clothing we own in bed to keep warm because I can only spare enough fuel to light the stove for a few hours in the evening.

'There's Sol!' Jori says, breaking into my thoughts. I look up and see a tall, broad-shouldered figure walking across the courtyard. My face heats up, and all thoughts about Mum and Dad are driven from my head. Damn.

'Sol! *Sol!*' Jori shouts. Sol turns, and my heart sinks a little.

'*Jori,*' I hiss.

'What?' Jori says. I sigh inwardly. I can hardly tell my seven-year-old brother that last night, after we'd been to our final Junior Patrol meeting, Sol asked me to go for a walk down to the jetty, and despite the sinking, *here-we-go-again* feeling in my stomach, I'd agreed. Or that, when we got there, pink-faced in the light from his lantern, he stammered, 'Cass, I was wondering if . . . that is, if me and you might—' He cleared his throat, his Adam's apple bobbing, then gazed at me with a helpless expression while I wondered what on earth to say.

The thing is, I *like* Sol. But the thought of us being a couple – of Captain Denning marrying us at the Meeting Hall, of having his kids and us getting old together – makes me feel restless and trapped.

It's ridiculous, I know. Even if I make it through my assessment, I'll never leave Hope. The barterers have to come to us, bringing their boats over to a specially re-inforced area by the jetty where we trade goods, scavenged from the abandoned towns and cities and empty houses or swapped with other barterers. This place is going to be my home for ever, so why *not* settle down with Sol? With no one from outside allowed onto the island – a consensus reached once we hit one hundred residents to try and conserve resources – who else is there? Sol and I should be like a pair of boots so battered and old they've moulded themselves to the shape of your toes and heels. We should fit perfectly.

And yet, for some reason, we don't.

'I'm sorry,' I told him gently as the waves slapped against the jetty behind us, the boats creaking and rocking. I was uncomfortably aware that I was repeating the exact same words I'd said to him last time he told me he wanted us to get together. 'I just don't feel ready yet.'

I could see in his face that he was thinking, *why not?* A lot of the other Islanders our age were pairing up. 'I'm sorry,' I repeated. I didn't want to stick the knife in any further.

Sol's face hardened. 'Forget it,' he said. 'I'll walk you back to your apartment.'

And I couldn't argue because he was the only one with a lantern, and on a cloudy night the island's too dark to find your way around without one.

Jori skips across to him, grinning. With a stiff smile on my face, I follow.

'Hey.' I look up, searching Sol's face for any sign of bitterness or resentment. A few years ago, he started shooting up, going from a scrawny kid whose nose was level with my shoulder to a six-footer who could easily pass for twenty. His eyes are a clear, pale blue, he still has a light dusting of freckles sprinkled across the bridge of his nose and in summer his hair, eyebrows and eyelashes are bleached almost white by the sun. No wonder Marissa thinks I'm crazy for not being interested in him.

'Hey,' he replies. His tone is as neutral as his expression.

As we start walking again, I decide the best approach is to act as if last night never happened. 'You all ready for today?' I say. 'I'm so nervous.'

'Why? You've been practising, haven't you?'

'Yes, but . . .' I trail off. So he is still annoyed. I sigh inwardly.

We climb the steps that lead out of the courtyard and are greeted by the view of the rest of the island. The remains of Hope's half-built 'town' begin a few hundred yards from the Meeting Hall and the Exchange, and have been nicknamed the Shudders because of the way, every so often – usually after a bad storm or a long winter – yet another building shudders itself into a pile of rubble and dust, with a rumble you can feel in your bones if you're close enough, and which is why a fence with hand-painted signs warning of the danger has been put up by the maintenance crew to keep people out. Beyond the Shudders is the sea wall, the Patrollers on duty at their posts, and then the sea, as grey and churned-looking as the sky. When we first got here, everyone had to camp out in the bare, unfinished apartments until there was enough manpower and resources to fix everything up. It was better than the alternative, though. From a young age, kids on Hope are taught about the dangers of the Mainland – how it's still crawling with Fearless, waiting to pounce on anyone stupid enough to set foot there. How the barterers manage to survive, I have no idea.

'Come on, Cass.' Sol's voice breaks into my thoughts. 'We don't want to miss breakfast.'

All meals on Hope are eaten communally in the Refectory, a long building between the Meeting Hall and the Shudders. When we get there, Jori hurries off to find Sam, his best friend, while I join the other Junior Patrollers – Rob Cole, Marissa Yuen, Andrej Zadac and Shelley Hopkins – at a table in the corner. They're all wearing armbands too. Everyone except Sol and Rob looks nervous. As Rob bumps fists with Sol, Marissa rolls her eyes. I hide a smile. Marissa is the girl who was lying on the ground screaming the night we arrived at the Docks. Strange to think that she's now my closest friend on the island after Sol. She's half-Chinese, with a delicate figure and long eyelashes I'd kill for, her thick, wavy hair tied back in a plait.

After a silent breakfast – hard bread and coffee, which isn't really coffee at all, but some bitter, vaguely coffee-tasting substance the barterers make from dried, ground-up dandelion roots and God knows what else – the six of us head over to the Meeting Hall, lining up at the bottom of the steps.

'Good luck, Cass!' Jori yells as he passes us on his way to school, a building at the back of the Exchange.

'Get to class!' I call back, but I'm smiling. Jori grins and scuttles after Sam.

At last, Patroller Yuen – Marissa's mother – opens the Meeting Hall door. As we troop inside I feel another shiver of excitement, mingled with nerves. What if I fall over, or forget something, or say something stupid?

'Good luck,' Marissa whispers, squeezing my arm.

'You too,' I whisper back.

We follow Patroller Yuen into the Meeting Hall's main room where Captain Denning and the other Patrollers are sitting behind a long table. The Meeting Hall was going to be grand; you can see the remains of ornate plaster cornices on the ceiling, and the richly patterned paper still shows beneath the many layers of whitewash slapped on the walls.

The Patrollers' gazes bore into us as we line up and salute. *Am I really ready for this?* I wonder. But I want to stand watch on the sea wall. I want to trade with the barterers. If I can't do that, what else is there? I can't see myself teaching at the school – I'd do anything for Jori, but a whole class of kids would wear me out in about five minutes flat. I have zero skill with a needle or a hammer or a saw. Numbers tie my brains in knots, so handling goods at the Exchange isn't an option. I suppose I could work in the Infirmary, but I don't like the thought of being cooped up all day. So the Patrol it is – as long as today goes OK.

Anyway, I'm curious about the barterers. I've never met any, but I've heard about how tough they are. Almost everything we have on Hope – clothes, shoes, herbs to make medicines or tobacco, tinned food, paper, crockery – comes from them. I want to hear first-hand what life is like on the mainland now and their stories about the Fearless they encounter as they scavenge for goods in the abandoned towns and cities. I want to know how they manage to survive without the protection of a

**58**

community like ours. Although their life must be frightening and dangerous, it sounds exciting, and excitement's not something we get much of on Hope.

'Good morning,' Captain Denning says. His gaze flicks over to me and away again, hard and flat. It was him who found Mum that morning five years ago, sprawled across the rocks beneath the sea wall with seaweed in her hair, looking like some sort of ghastly, blue-lipped mermaid. People tried to tell me it was an accident, but I'd already found her note. *I'm sorry. Please look after your brother. Love, Mum. Xx*

She'd never really recovered from the horrors of the Invasion, or from losing Dad so brutally. Almost from the start, it was me who gave Jori his bottles and changed his nappies, who rocked him to sleep and read him stories and took him over to the Infirmary when he had a fever or a rash, while Mum sank deeper and deeper into the grips of the depression that would eventually make her walk into the sea with her pockets full of rubble and stones.

Captain Denning will never forgive Mum for putting the Islanders through that, and because I'm here and she isn't, he's transferred his hatred to me. I'm lucky, really, that I've been allowed to join the Junior Patrol at all.

*This is not the time to start thinking about Mum*, I tell myself as an old, familiar sadness swells in my chest. *You need to focus.*

Captain Denning smoothes his moustache with the tip of one finger. 'I'm sure I don't need to remind any of you how important today is. You have been training with the Junior Patrol for five years now. This is your final chance to show us the skills and knowledge you've gained, and prove you have what it takes to graduate into the Patrol. You will be assessed on not only your physical combat skills, but also your knowledge of the Fearless, of survival, and of self-defence. Are you all ready?'

We nod, almost in unison.

'Excellent,' he says. 'Then we'll begin.'

# Chapter 6

## SOL

We're put into pairs – Cass with Andrej, Marissa with Rob, and me with Shelley. The Patrol always puts girls and guys together because if we ever have to defend ourselves against Fearless, we won't have any choice about who we end up fighting. I try to catch Cass's eye as she crosses the room. She doesn't notice.

*Forget it*, I tell myself, taking a few deep breaths through my nose. *Focus.*

With the eyes of Captain Denning on us, I settle in to the moves I've been practising for so long, I don't even have to think about them any more. I pretend to gouge Shelley's eyes out, and make as if I'm going to cut off the blood supply to her brain by placing my thumbs against the pressure points in her neck. Then I twist her head sideways just to the point where, if I went any further, her neck would snap like a stick of driftwood.

When Captain Denning calls, 'Time!' and I step away from her, I see a spark of fear in her eyes. It's strangely satisfying.

Next, it's hand-to-hand combat, using blunted

61

wooden sticks instead of knives. I force Shelley to the floor within seconds, the end of my stick digging into the soft spot beneath her jaw. Then we have to demonstrate our fitness, doing press-ups and sit-ups, jogging on the spot. I'm the only one who's not out of breath when we finish.

*Lightweights.*

Except for Cass, of course. I don't mean her. I try to catch her eye again, but she's still not looking at me.

I clench my fists, take another deep breath and try to forget the surge of humiliation I felt as she stuttered, *I'm sorry. I just don't feel ready yet.*

'OK,' Captain Denning says. 'Now we'll test your firearms skills.'

Behind the Meeting Hall, Patroller Cary is waiting with the guns – mechanical, pump-action Brownings with the barrels sawn off, the stocks cut down to a pistol grip to make them lighter. The Patrol has Lee Enfield rifles, too, but bullets are in short supply these days. The Brownings use cartridges and shot, which are easy to make ourselves.

We line up. I make sure I'm next to Cass. Every time I look at her I get this ache in my chest. What am I doing wrong? Does she think my feelings for her are just some stupid crush? We've been through so much together. We have a connection.

I *love* her, dammit.

And she doesn't see it. At all.

I squeeze my eyes shut. Open them again.

Patroller Cary hands Cass a gun.

We have one shot each. I watch Cass turn to face the target, a painted board nailed to a post. She lifts the gun, extends her arms, pulls the trigger. The shot smacks into the target, dead centre.

The others get close to the bullseye but never quite hit it. Finally, it's my turn. Despite the cold, my hands are steady as I aim at the target. The gun kicks against my shoulder, the shot spraying the centre of the target.

I glance at Cass, wondering if she saw. But she's talking to Marissa.

'OK, everyone, back inside, please,' Captain Denning says as I hand the gun back. 'We're moving on to the theory part of your assessment now.'

'Cassandra,' Captain Denning says when we're lined up in front of the table again. 'Please give a brief rundown of the events that led to the Invasion and the defeat of our armed forces by the Fearless.'

I watch her take a deep breath. 'The Fearless drug was first used at an army base called Camp Meridian in the Middle East,' she says. 'It was meant to stop soldiers from suffering from Post-Traumatic Stress Disorder, and it was so successful that the government secretly approved it for immediate use for all our troops worldwide, even though no long-term tests had been carried out. Um . . .' She clears her throat. *Stop acting so nervous,* I think. *They'll mark you down.* 'Then it was discovered that the drug had a dreadful side effect – it stopped people who took it feeling any fear at all, or love, or empathy. They started

**63**

doing awful things like killing and torturing people just for the sake of it.'

I resist the urge to shake my head. Does she realize how emotional she sounds? Why does she always let her feelings get the better of her?

'By the time people realized what was happening,' Cass continues, 'the enemy had got hold of the formula – no one knows how – and strengthened it so the side effects started straight away. They also changed it from tablets to an injection so that they could force it on people more easily.'

I smile wryly to myself, wondering what everyone in this room would say if they knew that *I* know how the enemy got hold of the serum formula. My father's little secret is the reason everyone who lives on Hope was invited here at the last minute, just like Cass and her parents were. The adults are (or were) all friends and acquaintances of my parents – people Dad knew would be useful additions to the community here – and the last thing he wanted was for them to realize he'd known what was coming before the government made their announcement. That would have been way too risky.

'After that,' Cass goes on, 'our Fearless and the enemy Fearless started banding together to create a huge army that invaded countries all over the world. They used whatever force they could – bombs and missiles – to terrify people into submission, until there were so many of them that civil defence forces couldn't cope. Eventually they didn't even have to use those sorts of weapons any more. By the time they invaded the UK, there were basically no unaltered soldiers left to fight them, and ordinary people stood no chance. Society collapsed almost immediately.' Her voice wavers a little, and I know she's thinking about that night we fled Blythefield. 'It was hopeless.'

From outside, there's a faint rumbling sound – another part of the Shudders giving way. I feel it vibrating up through the floor. Everyone turns to the windows.

'Thank you, Cassandra,' Captain Denning says. He looks at me, barely bothering to conceal the contempt in his gaze. He's been like this ever since the last mayoral election, as if my dad winning was somehow my fault. 'Solomon, please explain to us the changes that take place in someone who's received a full dose the Fearless serum, and why it makes them so hard for an ordinary person to defeat.'

I almost roll my eyes. Really? That's all he's going to ask me? Then I remember that until I graduate, I have to keep pretending I respect the guy, even if I hate his guts.

'The Fearless serum causes permanent changes to the amygdala, a part of the brain, which plays a key role in processing emotions, in particular the fear reflex,' I say. 'It also permanently raises stress hormones and adrenaline levels. As Cass said, they lose the ability to feel any fear, love or empathy whatsoever, and become highly aggressive.' I glance at her, but she's looking at her feet.

'After they Alter, they're left with intense cravings that can only be controlled with continued use of the serum.

There are also marked physical changes, which as yet have not been explained. When someone is fully Altered – and with the strengthened serum, this takes just one dose, with people Altering in a matter of days – their irises turn cloudy and their pupils become permanently dilated, making the Fearless's eyes highly sensitive to light and giving them excellent night vision. The serum also heightens their sense of hearing and smell. Their vocal chords lengthen, their voices becoming deeper and hoarser. They are slower to react to injury, even if they're mortally wounded, although they can still die. They also become faster and stronger. This makes them hard to defeat unless you're armed, which most ordinary people during the Invasion weren't. They heal very fast, too, and—'

I'm interrupted by the sound of someone running down the corridor outside the hall. The doors fly open and Olly Fleet, a Patroller who graduated last year, bursts in, his face glistening with sweat.

'What is the meaning of this?' Captain Denning snaps.

It takes Patroller Fleet a few moments to get his breath back. He bends over slightly, his hands on his knees.

'Well?'

Patroller Fleet looks up at him. 'We have a breach!' he gasps.

Just in time, I manage to stop a smile spreading across my lips.

*Finally*, something's happening around here.

# Chapter 7

## CASS

Captain Denning jumps up, his chair screeching against the floor. 'What?'

'We have a breach,' Patroller Fleet gasps again. A chill creeps up the back of my neck.

'A Fearless?' Captain Denning comes round the table, drawing his gun.

'No, just a guy, but we don't know how he got here – there are no boats anywhere.'

Patroller Cary grabs the clipboard he's been writing our marks on, and the Patrollers hurry from the room.

As soon as they've gone, Rob goes round the table and flops down in one of the chairs. 'Goddammit. Why can't this be over already?'

A silence falls, broken only by the sound of him stabbing one of the Patrollers' pencils repeatedly into the table. *Tock . . . tock . . . tock.*

'Do you think it is a Fearless?' Shelley says, sounding anxious. In all the years I've lived on Hope, we've only ever had one breach. It was in the middle of the night, a few months after we got here. My memories of it are jumbled: lights flashing, shouts and gunfire, and Jori, who was just a tiny baby then, screaming and screaming until I went to pick him up. Mum lay on her bed throughout the whole thing, her face turned to the wall, and I thought she was asleep until, in the moonlight coming through the window, I saw her eyes were open.

I never found out the full details of what happened that night, or how the Fearless managed to get on to the island, but after that, the Patrol doubled their numbers and traded for more guns.

Outside, we hear shouts.

Rob chucks the pencil down. 'Screw this. I wanna know what's going on.'

He stomps over to the door. 'Anyone else coming?' he says over his shoulder.

Sol shrugs. 'Yeah, why not?'

'I'm staying here,' Shelley says. 'Captain Denning'll go ballistic if he sees us.'

Andrej nods in agreement, hanging back. Marissa looks round at me, eyebrows raised.

We follow Sol and Rob to the door.

A crowd has gathered outside the Meeting Hall. No kids, I'm relieved to see – the Patrol must have told the teachers to keep them indoors – but plenty of adults. In the middle of them all, Captain Denning and Patroller Cary are struggling with someone.

The someone doing the shouting.

Sol, Marissa, Rob and I go closer. I see, with a shock, that it's a boy about our own age, dressed in faded combats, a patched blue hoodie that looks damp at the cuffs, and battered black boots. He has thick black hair with a long fringe falling over his face like a curtain, and an eyepatch over his right eye.

'Let me go!' he yells, still struggling. 'I'm not here to steal anything, I swear!'

He has a Scottish accent, a broader version of James Craig's, our head Maintenance Engineer.

'Shut up,' Captain Denning says. The boy bucks and twists, and despite the fact that Captain Denning is almost twice his size, nearly gets free. Patroller Yuen steps forward and points her gun at the boy, who goes still, his face twisted in a scowl and his eyes – or rather his eye, because only his left is visible – glinting with anger.

Captain Denning turns to Patroller Fleet. 'Where did you find him?'

'In the Shudders. We heard shouts. A wall had collapsed, and he was trapped.'

I remember the noise we heard a short while ago, and for the first time, I notice that the boy isn't putting his full weight on his right leg.

'Why are you here?' Captain Denning asks him.

'It's my – my friend's bairn,' he says. 'She's sick – she needs medicine. I heard from one of the barterers that you have a doctor here – I thought they might be able to help.'

'So you sneak on to the island and hide out in the Shudders. Why not send a message with this barterer if you were so desperate, eh?'

'He wouldn't do it. He said no one here would agree to it.'

'He was right,' Captain Denning says, and I'm reminded of the time, four years ago, when a small group of Invasion survivors turned up at the docks from who-knows-where and tried to bargain their way onto the island, the first new people to come here in as long as I could remember. Mayor Brightman ordered them to be put in the cells immediately, and there were meetings long into the night about them. Then all Islanders over the age of seventeen had to vote. Only one person wanted to let them on; the rest decided against it, and the group was taken back to the mainland without us even finding out who they were.

'We have limited resources here,' Captain Denning says. 'We don't just go handing them out to strangers, *especially* not strangers who sneak on to the island and try to—' He frowns. 'How *did* you get here, anyway?'

The boy doesn't answer him.

'How. Did. You. Get. On. To. The. Island?' Captain Denning's jaw is clenched.

'I swam across from the mainland and climbed over the wall,' the boy says, quite matter-of-factly, as if this is something anyone could do.

'When?'

'Last night.'

'Impossible. The sea wall is guarded twenty-four hours a day. If anyone came over it, we'd know.'

'There wasn't anyone watching the bit *I* came over,' the boy says.

'And where was that?'

'Back there.' He points over his shoulder. 'There's a load of boats moored at the bottom.'

'Patroller Fleet, I believe you were on duty at the jetty last night, weren't you?' Captain Denning says loudly, looking round at Olly.

The crowd falls silent. Even the sound of the sea seems to fade. I see Olly swallow, and colour steals into his face. 'I – I had to go back to my apartment for something,' he says, after a long moment of silence.

'*WHAT?*' Captain Denning roars, so loudly I almost jump out of my boots. 'You did *WHAT?*'

The colour drains out of Olly's face, leaving him ghost-pale. 'Clara's been ill again,' he says. 'And Ella's exhausted. I wanted to check they were OK.'

I feel a pang of sympathy for him. His daughter, Clara, was born four weeks ago. It was a difficult birth, leaving Ella weakened and sickly. On top of his Patrol duties, Olly's having to take care of both of them.

'I – I'm sorry,' he stammers.

'I don't want to hear it,' Captain Denning says. 'Take off your armband, give me your gun, and go and wait for me in my office.'

Olly does as he's told, slinking away with everyone scowling at the back of his head. Rule number one of being in the Patrol: *never leave your post without permission*.

'Please,' the boy says when Olly has gone. 'Let

me go. I'll find someone else to help my friend's kid.'

'You're going nowhere,' Captain Denning says. 'Why are you wearing that eyepatch?'

'Lost my eye. It was gouged out by a Fearless.' He says out to rhyme with *boot*.

Captain Denning looks at him for a moment longer. Then he says, 'Right, you're coming with me.'

'No!' The boy leaps forward, startling Captain Denning, who steps back and loses his balance, sitting down hard on the ground. The crowd scatters in alarm.

'Oh, no you don't,' Sol snarls, and he and Rob grab the boy as he tries to shove past them. Sol twists his arm up behind his back and forces him to the ground.

'Sol, Rob, take him to the cells,' Captain Denning says, getting to his feet and brushing grit off the back of his trousers. He's unhurt, but his face is pink. 'I'll deal with him later.'

'Give me your gun,' Sol says to Patroller Yuen, who glances at Captain Denning. He nods, and she hands Sol the gun. Sol drags the boy to his feet and presses it into his back.

'Don't hurt him!' The words are out of my mouth before I've even had time to think. Rob and Sol look round at me, Sol's expression puzzled, Rob's sardonic.

'Who asked *you*?' Rob sneers, and I feel my face heat up. What did I say that for?

'What's going on?' Everyone turns. Simon Brightman is limping towards us, leaning heavily on a cane. The crowd parts to let him through, and Captain Denning's shoulders stiffen. Before the Invasion, he and Mr Brightman were friends – they'd gone to university together, Sol's told me – but not any more. Sol's dad has held the position of Hope's Mayor ever since he came here. Two years ago, at the first Mayoral election, Captain Denning stood against him, and didn't even get a quarter of the vote.

Patroller Cary explains about the boy, and Olly Fleet not being at his post when he should have been. Mr Brightman's face is grave. 'Where is Patroller Fleet?' he asks Captain Denning.

'In my office,' Captain Denning says.

'We'll go and talk to him. And we'd better send a team into the Shudders to make sure there's no one else there.'

Captain Denning nods. Then he spots Marissa and me. 'What are you two doing out here? I thought I told you to wait at the Meeting Hall.'

He doesn't say anything to Sol or Rob. Most of the Patrol treat Sol as an equal because he's the Mayor's son, and Rob benefits by association.

'C'mon,' Marissa mutters, and we turn to go back to the Meeting Hall.

I can't resist one last look over my shoulder, though, and as Rob and Sol start leading the boy away I realize he's looking back at me. Our gazes connect for a second and I see despair. *Help me*, he mouths.

*How?* I mouth back.

Then I see Captain Denning glaring at me again.

I look away, and keep walking.

# Chapter 8

## MYO

I don't know why I did it. Maybe it's 'cos she said, *Don't hurt him.* Or because she's the only one who looks back at me when everyone else is walking away.

'What were you staring at?' the tall lad with the blond hair says.

'Nothing,' I mutter.

'You were staring at her.' He's holding the top of my arm so tight it's cutting off the blood supply.

'I wasn't looking at anything,' I say, thinking of my bag, back in those ruins. I wish I'd not left my knife in there.

'Get moving,' snaps the other lad, the one with a face like a bulldog. They march me across the island. It looks just like everywhere else in this God-forsaken, Fearless-blasted country: run down buildings, weeds growing everywhere. I think about fighting the two lads off, then remember Lochie waiting for me back at the docks. If I want to make it back to him in one piece, I can't get into any fights.

We reach a concrete building that has four stalls with

gates across the fronts. Blondie unlocks one and gives me a shove. 'Get in there.'

'What happens now?' I say as I half step, half-fall into the cell.

'They'll have a meeting. Decide what they're going to do with you.'

'And what about after that?'

Blondie smiles. 'Dunno. Perhaps they'll tie you up and throw you in the sea.' His smile widens. 'If you're lucky, they might shoot you first.'

*Shit.* Does he mean that? Maybe panic's what makes me open my big mouth again instead of keeping it shut like I know I should. 'You think your girlfriend'll be happy about that?'

'You what?'

'You heard.'

He lets go of me, and for a moment I think he's just gonna storm out of the cell and lock the gate.

You'd think I'd know better, right?

'She's not my girlfriend,' he hisses, and his tone tells me everything I need to know about how he feels about that girl.

'Here,' he tells Bulldog-face, handing him the gun. He lunges at me and I twist, expecting a punch. Instead, he tries to grab my eyepatch. *Shit, no.* I give him a push, sending him flying back into Bulldog-face, who staggers and almost drops the gun.

I see the surprise in Blondie's eyes. He's thinking, *I'm twice his size. He shouldn't be able to do that.*

'What the hell *are* you?' he snarls, and launches himself at me again. This time, I'm ready. I throw my arm out, blocking his blow, and then we're grappling, shoving each other across the cell.

'Are you going to answer me, or what?' Blondie tries to slam me against the wall and I jerk my body round just in time. I drive him back a few steps and swing my fist into his jaw, rocking his head back with a satisfying crunch.

Meanwhile, Bulldog-face is staring at us like he can't quite believe what he's seeing, his mouth hanging open, the gun forgotten.

*Your pal here might be twice my size, but looks can be deceiving*, I want to tell him, and I would, if I had any breath in my lungs to do it with.

Blondie tries to head-butt me. I bring my knee up, aiming for his balls. Then Bulldog-face, who's been staring at us, open-mouthed, runs into the cell and slams the butt of the gun against my head. My legs tangle; I go down, seeing stars, and they start raining blows down on me, kicking me in the stomach and the ribs, and all I can do is curl into a ball to protect myself.

'Should I shoot him?' Bulldog-face says when they've finished and I'm lying there, trying to remember how to breathe.

'No.' Blondie's panting, like he's just run a race. 'We'll tell Captain Denning he attacked us. He can deal with him.'

'D'you think he's—' says Bulldog-face, and my heart,

which is already pounding, starts to beat even faster.

'I don't know what he is,' Blondie says. 'Come on.'

He spits in my face.

After the cell gate clangs shut behind them, I roll over, groaning. When I lift my arm to wipe my cheek, my side hurts something awful. Feels like Blondie and his pal have busted a rib or two. *You idiot*, I curse myself.

But what was I supposed to do? Let him tear off the eyepatch?

I sink back against the floor, thinking of Lochie, alone over at the docks. Of Ben and Gina, back at the bunker, wondering where I am right now, and probably still furious with me for leaving in the first place. And of Mara. I can't believe I managed to keep up with her all the way to this island, and then lost her in those ruins. With those guards or whoever they are searching the place, she and the Fearless she was with will be long gone.

I was so close to getting my sister back – there is no sick baby; I just told the soldier guy that 'cos it was the first thing that came into my head – and now it looks like I followed her all the way down here for nothing.

What am I gonna do?

# Chapter 9

## CASS

Marissa and I return to the Meeting Hall, where Shelley and Andrej demand to know what happened. When Marissa explains, they stare at us with shocked expressions.

'Patroller Fleet *left his post*?' Andrej says. 'Is he crazy? Anyone could have got onto the island – there could be a Fearless hiding out in the Shudders, waiting for a chance to—'

'Ugh, don't.' Shelley makes a face, wrapping her arms around her middle. She only joined the Junior Patrol because her parents pressured her into it. 'There *can't* be anyone else here. The Patrol will search the Shudders, right?'

'D'you think that boy was Fearless?' Andrej asks me.

I shake my head. 'No. His eyes were brown. His eye, I mean. I saw it.'

'What're you talking about that freak for?' Rob says loudly behind us as he comes in with Sol. We all gasp. Sol's clothes are scuffed and dirty and his knuckles are grazed; a huge bruise is blossoming on his jaw.

'What *happened*?' Shelley says.

'He attacked me,' Sol says. He touches his jaw gingerly, and winces.

Then we hear Captain Denning's voice in the corridor outside. We quickly form a row in front of the table again as he and the other Patrollers come back in. Rob hands Patroller Yuen her gun, and I listen in disbelief as Sol explains how the boy had a knife up his sleeve and tried to stab him with it, and how it was only Sol's years of training that meant he was able to disarm him without getting cut.

'Where is this knife?' Captain Denning asks, frowning.

'I got rid of it, sir,' Sol says.

*Hang on*, I think. *You and Rob had a gun. Why didn't you just point that at him?*

It doesn't add up. Even if the boy has some sort of death wish, a knife is no match for a gun, especially not a Browning, and *especially* not at close range.

No one else seems to notice the hole in Sol's story, though. They're gazing at him in awe.

'Are you able to continue with your assessment?' Captain Denning asks.

Sol nods.

'Very well. Patroller Cary, if the boy is violent, I want someone to stand guard at the cells. We can't spare any of the Patrol proper, but one of the older members of the Junior Patrol would do. Go to the school and tell Adam Hopkins he's excused from his lessons. Make sure he has a gun.'

I see anxiety flicker across Shelley's face as Patroller Cary heads for the door. Adam is her younger brother, and has eighteen months left in the Junior Patrol.

Patroller Cary salutes and leaves.

'We will now conclude your assessment,' Captain Denning says. 'Marissa Yuen, you are stranded on the mainland with only a bottle of water, some rope and a striking flint. Please take me through the steps you would take to ensure your survival.'

As Marissa tells him, I zone out, thinking about the boy again, and the way he mouthed *help me* as he was led away. I don't know why, but when he said he was here to try and get medicine for his friend's kid, I believed him. Bringing Jori up practically single-handed has given me a sixth sense for lies – which is why Sol's story about the knife has me wondering – and anyway, why go to all that effort, swimming from the mainland (a superhuman feat in itself, especially at this time of year, when the sea is close to freezing), and try to break into a community you knew was going to be hostile, if you weren't truly desperate?

I wonder where he's from. Has he come all the way from Scotland? I've heard tales of a few other communities like ours on the mainland – second-hand, from people on the island who've been told about them by the barterers – but we've never come into contact with them. For all I know the stories could be just that – stories. Perhaps it's just him, battling for survival, alone.

I realize Marissa has finished speaking and force

80

myself to pay attention. Andrej's up next, then Shelley, then Rob. The Patrollers listen as they answer Captain Denning's questions, their faces impassive, making pencil notes which will be erased later so the paper – a rare and precious resource these days – can be re-used.

Captain Denning sits back. 'We will discuss your responses this afternoon, and the names of those of you who have been successful will be announced before the Patrol Graduation Ceremony tomorrow morning.'

Everyone groans, although we all knew we wouldn't find out straight away. The Patrol likes to drag this part out as long as possible.

The Meeting Hall bell rings, signalling lunchtime, and Captain Denning dismisses us.

'Are you OK?' I ask Sol as we go down the Meeting Hall steps.

'Oh, so you care now?' he says.

I feel a little flash of anger, mixed with guilt. 'Of course I do. You should get that bruise looked at – it's nasty.'

'I'll be fine. He came off worse.'

'You beat him up?'

'What was I supposed to do?' Sol sounds angry again. 'The guy had a *knife*. Anyway, he was trespassing.'

I don't answer this time. The way he's looking at me unnerves me. 'Forget it,' I say, and catch up with Marissa. When Sol's in this sort of mood, there's no speaking to him. Sometimes he reminds me so much of his mum, it scares me.

As soon as we get to the Refectory, we're mobbed by a crowd of kids from the school, Jori among them, wanting to know about the boy. In a tiny place like Hope, news travels and grows as fast as a flame up a lamp-wick. Soon, the boy's not just a boy but a Fearless, and Sol is the one who single-handedly defended the rest of the Islanders from him with his quick thinking and bravery. 'I helped bring him down as well!' Rob keeps saying, but no one's really listening to him.

When I've collected my lunch – more hard bread and a thin, salty broth made from the last of the previous year's supplies of dried fish and kelp – I find a quieter spot at the edge of the Refectory where I can eat in peace. My thoughts keep returning to the boy. Maybe it's because he's the first outsider I've seen since I came here, but he fascinates me.

I look around. All the Islanders are here except for the Patrollers on watch duty and Sol's dad, who keeps himself to himself, eating meals in his office at the Meeting Hall. Almost everyone is still gathered round Rob and Sol. 'You know, I'm sure I'm missing some buttons and thread,' mutters Sheena Drake, Hope's seamstress, her voice as sharp as her pointed chin and blade-like cheekbones. 'He could have been hiding out in the Shudders for weeks – if that building hadn't collapsed we'd never have known!'

As the conversation swells to an indignant crescendo, I gulp down the rest of my broth and drop my last piece of bread into my pocket. Because it's assessment day, I don't have any duties this afternoon – a rare few hours of freedom. I slip out of the Refectory and head over to the cells, trying to make it look as if I'm actually just returning to the apartments – which, if anyone challenges me, is exactly what I'll do.

Adam is standing outside the cells with a gun tucked into his belt. He's only wearing a thin jacket, and has his arms wrapped around himself, shivering. When he sees me, he looks relieved. 'Cass! Are you busy?'

'Why?' I say.

'Can you watch the cells for a few minutes while I go back to my apartment and get my coat?'

'Sure,' I say, suddenly grateful it's so cold.

'Thanks!' He hands me the gun, and runs off in the direction of the apartments.

The boy is in one of the middle cells, hunched over with his back against the wall and his knees drawn up. The gate is fastened with a rusty padlock. 'Hey,' I hiss, tucking the gun into my belt.

The boy jumps, sucking in his breath sharply as he looks up at me, as if something's hurting him. With a jolt, I see his face is bloody, one side of his mouth swollen. What did Sol and Rob *do*?

I take the piece of bread from my pocket and hold it through the bars. 'This is for you. Sorry there isn't more.'

The boy gazes at me for a moment. Then he looks away again. He doesn't take the bread.

'Please,' I say. 'You need to eat. I don't have any water on me right now, but I can bring you some.'

'Who sent you?' His voice sounds muffled because of his injured mouth.

'No one,' I say. 'I came by myself.'

'Why?' He looks up at me again, his gaze filled with something that looks a lot like anger.

'I . . . wanted to check you were OK,' I say, only realizing as I speak the words that this is, in fact, the truth. 'Are you?'

The boy's hard gaze softens a little. 'I've felt better,' he says. His accent is almost exotic after hearing the same voices around me for so many years.

I indicate his face. 'Does it hurt? I've got some salve back at my—'

He shakes his head. 'I'll survive. Thanks, though.' The undamaged side of his mouth lifts in a smile. I smile back uncertainly, trying to imagine him launching himself at Sol with a knife. 'I'm Cass, by the way,' I say. 'Cass Hollencroft.'

'Myo McRae. D'you know what they're gonna do to me?'

I shake my head.

'Your pal thinks I'm Fearless, you know.' Myo winces again as he tries to shift his position.

'Are you?' I say.

He snorts. 'What do you think?'

'Considering you didn't leap at the bars and bite my hand off when I tried to give you that bread, and that you can speak normally and you don't have, um, silver eyes, I'm pretty certain you're not.'

I hear the Meeting Hall bell start to ring, signalling the end of lunch. 'I have to go,' I say. 'If anyone sees me talking to you, I'll be in big trouble. But take the bread, OK? I'll try to bring you some water later.'

The boy nods. Then, just as I'm turning to go he says, 'Cass?'

I turn back.

'Can you do me a favour?'

I glance round to check if Adam's coming back. There's no sign of him. 'What? If you want me to talk to the Patrol about letting you go, I'm sorry, but—'

Myo shakes his head. 'I know you can't do that. It's just . . . I had a bag with me. There are some clothes in it. Could you get it for me? I need my jacket – it's freezing.'

I frown. Although the Shudders is technically off-limits, as kids, Sol and I and the others used to sneak in all the time. We'd scavenge for bits of wire or other stuff we could barter at the Exchange, or pretend to be Fearless, hunting each other down through the ruins. And if the Patrol discovered one of our ways in and blocked it off, we'd just find another.

But that was before I joined the Junior Patrol. Before Mum drowned herself, and Jori became my responsibility.

Myo looks pleadingly at me. 'I'm so cold.'

I still don't answer. Going into the Shudders would be crazy, but I can't give him my coat — someone would recognize it. And I can't exactly ask Sol if I can borrow something of his.

'Where were you?' I ask hesitantly.

'It looked like a cinema. I left the bag under an old board on the stage when I went out to see if anyone was around. That was when the building next to it collapsed and I got stuck.'

I know the old cinema well; it used to be one of our favourite haunts. 'OK, I'll try. But I mean *try*. I'm not promising anything.'

'Thank you.'

As I turn away from the cell, I wonder what I've just got myself into.

# Chapter 10

## CASS

I'm just in time. Adam's coming back, bundled up in a coat, and out of breath. 'Sorry! I sneaked into the Refectory to grab some food.' He holds up a piece of bread and grins.

I shake my head. 'I hope Captain Denning didn't see you.'

'Nah.' He bites into the bread.

I hand him the gun and hurry back to the apartments, where I tidy up, not because it's messy but to keep warm. Jori is back at school, so I have only my clamouring thoughts for company as I try to figure out how on earth I'm going to get into the Shudders to retrieve Myo's bag. If it was summer, I could wait until early morning, but this time of year, the sun doesn't rise until after the Meeting Hall bell rings to wake everyone up. If I leave it until then, there'll be too many people around, and he'll probably freeze overnight. But I have the same problem in the evening; it's dark before the evening meal, and if I don't turn up for that, someone might notice. I'll have to go in a few hours, after everyone's gone back to their apartments for the night.

*You do realize what a stupid idea this is, don't you?* I tell myself as I sweep non-existent dust across the bedroom floor. *If anyone – ANYONE – realizes what you're up to, you'll get kicked out of the Patrol and put in the cells yourself. Maybe even kicked off the island. And going into the Shudders at night? Really?*

A couple of hours later, Jori comes back, and I help him with his homework – making a simple fishing net out of bits of nylon rope scavenged from the high-tide line on Hope's beach. Did we have homework when I was seven? I can't remember; my life before the Invasion feels like a distant dream. Sometimes, I feel sorry for Jori, knowing he'll never get to be a kid in the way I did, living a truly care-free life.

'Are you OK?' Marissa says as she and I leave the Refectory after the evening meal, where all the talk has been about Myo again (although I'm the only one who knows he's called that, of course). The Patrol's search of the Shudders revealed nothing – they didn't even find Myo's bag, so it must be well hidden – and the news he was alone has been greeted with a mixture of relief and bewilderment. 'You seem pretty preoccupied.'

'I was just thinking about today,' I say, adding hastily, 'about the assessment, I mean.'

Sol passes us. He glances at me, but doesn't say anything. You can almost feel the awkwardness between us. 'Did you guys fall out or something?' Marissa asks, watching him walk off with Rob.

I shake my head. I really don't feel like trying to explain right now, or have her ask me for the millionth time *why* I don't want to get together with Sol when we'd be perfect for each other.

Jori runs up to us. 'Cass! Can I go to Sam's? Pleeeease?'

'Yeah, go on,' I say. 'I've got to go to the Exchange, anyway. Be back by eight, OK?'

He runs off, grinning. Marissa and I collect our ration tokens from our apartments and head over to the Exchange. It's where all Hope's supplies are stored – everything we make, find, or trade with the barterers. Every year, each Islander over the age of fifteen receives four flat, round tokens carved from driftwood and threaded onto a piece of rope or leather. One's for food, one's for fuel, one's for clothing and shoes and one's for everything else. Every time you go to the Exchange, the tokens have notches cut in them in exchange for whatever it is you need. Everyone has a maximum number of notches per year, and the more valuable a good is, the more notches you get, so you have to be careful to make the tokens last.

As we go inside, it occurs to me that I don't have enough lamp fuel for my expedition into the Shudders. Over the years, I've become an expert at calculating how much Jori and I need, and I wasn't going to get any more until next week, but I can't look for Myo's bag without a lamp. The Patroller at the storeroom door raises an eyebrow when I ask for a bottle of fuel – after food and shoes, it's the most precious commodity on the island – but notches my token without comment.

Back at my apartment, I fill our spare lantern with oil, change the light blue jumper I'm wearing for a black one, and dig my summer shoes, a pair of faded black canvas plimsolls, out of the cupboard in the bedroom. It's too cold for them, but I'll be much lighter on my feet. I stuff my flint and steel and a couple of the strips of dried seaweed we use as firelighters into my trouser pockets, and put the shoes by the door.

Jori comes back from Sam's just before eight. I get him wrapped up in extra layers of clothing, and then we get under his covers and he snuggles down in my arms as I tell him a story about what my life was like before the Invasion. He never tires of hearing about Mum and Dad, or our old house, or the village, or what my school was like. It used to be painful telling him these things, but I've spoken about them so often now that they feel like dreams, or things that happened to someone else.

Gradually, he relaxes in my arms, his breathing becoming deep and steady. I extricate myself carefully. Then I stand beside his sleeping mat and gaze at him for a moment. With his skin permanently dry from the weather and the salty air, and his penetrating gaze, my brother often seems older than he really is. But when he's asleep, the furrow between his eyebrows smoothes out, and he's just an ordinary, innocent seven-year-old. I sigh. Part of me wishes he could stay this way for ever.

Then I remember Myo. I feel a burst of nerves. Am I *really* going to do this?

*Half an hour*, I tell myself. *If it takes any longer than that, I'll come back.*

I put my coat, hat and scarf on, trying not to make any noise, and step into my plimsolls.

'Cass? Where are you going?' a sleepy voice says behind me.

I jump and look round. Jori's eyes are open. Crap.

'Um, nowhere,' I say.

'Why have you got your bag?'

'I borrowed something from Sol and I need to take it back. Go to sleep, OK? I'll only be a few minutes.'

Feeling guilty and flustered, I grab the spare lantern, turning away so he doesn't see me tucking it under my coat, and hurry out of the apartment before he can ask what I borrowed from Sol. Outside, frost glitters, the moonlight making everything look like the old black-and-white films they used to show on TV before the Invasion, the ones Dad liked so much. I dart between pools of shadow to the courtyard steps, cursing the moon for being so bright.

The fence around the Shudders is too high to climb; I'll have to do what I used to do when I was a kid – look for a way under or through. I feel my way along it until I find some loops of wire that have been used to fix two pieces of the fence together. Blowing on my frozen hands to warm them, I untwist them, pulling the mesh apart to make a Cass-sized hole. As I squeeze through, the wire catches at my jacket and hair.

Once I'm on the other side, I pull the hole closed and stand there for a moment, listening to the thunder of the sea and the wind moaning through the ruins. Now I'm here, I'm glad of the moonlight. Without it I could easily smack my head on a beam or fall down a foundation hole.

As I duck through a doorway, the Shudders fence rattles in the place where I came through. I freeze, listening for the crunch of footsteps across the rubble-strewn ground; the bark of a Patroller's voice as they shout, *Who's there?*

Nothing happens. It must have been the wind. I let out a slow, shaky breath, trying to see where I am. I haven't been here in years, and everything looks so different in this eerie, silver light. At last, I spot something I recognize: a dented metal sign advertising a restaurant, lying at an angle against a pile of rubble. I'm on the street that runs through the middle of the 'town'; under my feet are paving stones, almost buried by the sand that's blown here in winter storms, and all around, leafless saplings have taken root and struggled up through the rubble, many more of them than I remember. Shivering, I thread my way through piles of brick and stone, carefully making my way down to the cinema, which is at the bottom of the street.

Behind me, I hear a skittering sound, like a stone being kicked. I look round, but I can't see anything. Perhaps it was just a piece of brick falling from a building.

Then, as I start walking again, I hear the sound for a second time. This time, it's more distinct.

Footsteps, light and quick.

# Chapter 11

## CASS

'Who's there?' I hiss. I'm certain it's not the Patrol. They'd march up, grab my arm, demand to know what I was doing here.

No answer. The hairs on the back of my neck prickle. What if it's a Fearless?

*Don't be stupid*, I tell myself. *The Patrol searched the Shudders top to bottom after they found Myo, remember? There's no one else here.*

So why do I feel as if I'm being watched?

I crouch, feeling around for a lump of brick.

'Whoever's there,' I say as I straighten up, 'Stop messing about or I'm going to chuck this brick at your head. And I'm a great shot.'

I grip the brick harder, feeling its sharp edges dig into my palm and fingers. I'm almost certain that someone's playing a joke on me. Maybe Rob. It's exactly the sort of thing he'd do.

The footsteps start again, coming towards me, then stop.

'I mean it,' I snarl.

'Cass, it's me,' a small voice says.

*Jori?*

'Where are you?' I say.

My brother emerges from behind a pile of concrete blocks just a few feet away. He's still bundled up in all the clothes I put him to bed in, and my spare scarf is wound around his neck.

'For God's *sake*, Jor.' I hold out my hand to help him over the rubble. 'I told you to go to sleep!'

'I couldn't.'

'Did you follow me?'

He nods. 'I saw you go through the fence.'

Goddammit, he must have been right behind me when I left the apartment. And there's no time to send him back. If he gets caught . . . 'I s'pose you'll have to come with me, then. But you'll have to be careful.'

'Come where?'

'The cinema. I've got to look for something.'

A smile flickers across his lips.

I frown. 'I guess that means you can tell me the best way in there?' I say, and he gets such a guilty look on his face that any other time, I'd laugh.

'You won't tell anyone, will you?' he says.

Still frowning, I shake my head. 'No. But you shouldn't come here, Jor. It's dangerous.'

I know my words will probably have no effect, though. Nothing stopped *me*. 'Come on,' I tell him, lighting the lantern. 'Before we freeze to death.'

The cinema looks almost exactly the same as it did

when I last came here, a few days before my twelfth birthday, and two weeks before Mum walked into the sea. The lobby and the steps leading up to the auditorium are coated in a thick layer of dust and seagull crap, bundles of cable hanging from the ceiling from when the building work was abandoned. Shafts of moonlight coming through holes in the ceiling illuminate speckles of mould on the walls, and here and there more of those spindly trees have taken root in the carpet.

'You can still get in there,' Jori says, pointing at the auditorium steps. At the top are two doors with round windows, half hanging off their hinges. As I squeeze through them after my brother, I get a shiver of déjà vu. How many times did I do this when I was younger, with Sol or one of the others?

Once we're on the other side, I put a hand on Jori's arm to stop him and hold out the lantern. 'Are the steps still safe?'

'Not the ones at the side,' he says. 'The ones in the middle are OK, though.'

We descend them carefully, the boards creaking and cracking under our feet. At the back of the stage, there's a vast screen. I remember how I used to wonder what would happen if we still had electricity and could've switched the projection equipment on. Would we see films from seven years ago – films of life as it used to be? Even now, the thought makes me shiver.

Jori hauls himself up onto the stage and goes pelting across it. 'Come back here!' I say as I jump up after him.

There used to be steps here too, but most of the treads have rotted away.

He giggles.

'I mean it,' I say. 'Stay where I can see you.' Then, to my right, I hear a scuffling sound. 'Jori! What did I just tell you?'

'I'm not doing anything,' my brother's voice says at my left elbow, making me jump.

'But I just heard you—' I hold the lantern up, but all I can see is the screen. 'Never mind.' Maybe it was a rat. There are plenty on the island, despite the maintenance crew's efforts to get rid of them. *Maybe I should make sure,* I think. I shine the lantern into the corners, trying to ignore the chill creeping up my spine. To my relief, there's nothing there.

I find Myo's bag underneath a board at the back of the stage, just like he said. It's a large, battered-looking leather satchel. I can't resist peeping inside. He has all sorts of stuff in there: a knife – *hang on*, I think. *Didn't Sol say Myo attacked him with his knife and that he got rid of it?* – a rolled-up jacket, some binoculars, the first battery operated torch I've seen in years, some foil pouches with *MRE* and *Meal, Ready to Eat* on the front, and ... chocolate bars? I take one out and frown at it. It *is* a chocolate bar – a Cadbury's Bournville, in a crackly red plastic wrapper. Where did he get it? I've never known the barterers to trade stuff like this. Not the ones who come down this way, anyhow.

'What's that?' Jori says, and I realize he's never seen

chocolate before. We had it on the island when we first came here, but he was too little to eat it, and after six months or so, it was all gone.

'Chocolate. Want to try some?' I say. After we've come in here to get his bag back on this freezing cold night, running the risk of being caught by the Patrol, I reckon Myo can spare us one chocolate bar.

'You mean like that stuff you used to buy with your allowance?' he says. I've told him about the food we used to eat before the Invasion many times.

I nod, and tear open the wrapper. The chocolate has a white bloom on the surface, and the texture's weird – kind of brittle and powdery – but I still get a wave of nostalgia as I nibble on it. When Jori tries it, though, he makes a face and spits it out. 'This is *horrible*. It tastes like dust.'

He's right. This stuff is definitely past its best. Regretfully, I chuck the half-eaten chocolate away and pick up Myo's bag, slinging it across my chest.

'Come on,' I tell Jori. But he isn't beside me any longer.

'I heard something,' he whispers, his voice carrying through the darkness to where I'm standing.

'So did I. A rat or something. Nothing to worry about.'

'No. It sounds like *breathing*.'

We both go quiet. All I can hear is the thud of my heartbeat in my ears, and the ever-present sound of the sea outside.

'There's nothing there,' I say. 'You probably heard—'

Then I stop. I *can* hear breathing, steady and rasping and slow.

I turn, holding up the lantern. 'Who's there?' I say sharply, wondering if Myo had someone with him after all. But wouldn't the Patrol have found them? Wouldn't whoever was with Myo have come to *help* him?

I hear a creak as something – or some*one* – moves. 'It's coming from over here,' my brother whispers.

'Stay with me.' I reach into Myo's satchel for the knife.

Jori screams.

Something barges past me, jolting the lantern and making it go out.

'*Cass! Help! HELP!*' Jori yells.

'Where are you?' I cry, whirling around.

Jori's screams cut off abruptly.

I give up trying to find the knife and grab the torch instead, shining it in the direction Jori's screams were coming from. There are two people at the back of the stage: a man with filthy bandages wrapped around his head and covering one arm, and a girl in a thin blue dress, her long, black hair hanging into her face. The man is holding Jori, one hand clamped across his mouth to silence him. In his other is a gun, which he's pressing against my brother's temple. Despite this, Jori's struggling to get free, his eyes wide and terrified. The man grins at me, showing rotted, blackened teeth. A terrible smell comes off him in waves.

That's when I see both he and the girl have silver-coloured eyes with enormous pupils.

'This one'll do,' he says in a growling voice that brings memories of that terrible night seven years ago flooding back.

Before I can move, cry out, do anything, he leaps off the edge of the stage into the shadows, the girl flitting after them like a ghost.

'JORI!' I scream as they crash through the auditorium and up the steps. I run after them; my feet meet empty air as I plummet off the edge of the stage, and I land in a crumpled, winded heap, the torch flying from my hand and going dark as it skitters away across the floor.

I haul myself to my feet again, taking in a groaning, sobbing breath. *The Patrol*, I think as I stagger up the steps and through the moonlit lobby. *The Patrol will stop them*. I keep shouting my brother's name as I run back up the street to the fence. As I frantically tug the mesh apart, I hear a cry, then a muffled-sounding *crack* over by the sea wall. My heart leaps. The Patrol must have caught the Fearless and shot them as they tried to get off the island. I push through the fence and start running again, my legs going weak with relief.

It isn't until I get closer that I realize other people are shouting too. I see a cluster of lanterns; a small crowd of Patrollers gathered around a huddled shape lying at the base of the wall; other people running from the direction of the Meeting Hall and the Exchange. I reach the huddled shape at the same time as Rob and Sol, praying that it's the Fearless man, that someone has Jori, and he's safe.

But it isn't the Fearless man. It isn't the girl, either. It's Patroller Cary, his eyes open but sightless, his mouth frozen in an 'O' of surprise, a small, bloody hole in the centre of his forehead.

There's no sign of the Fearless or Jori anywhere.

# Chapter 12

## CASS

I clap my hands across my mouth. Someone's making a low keening sound which, when people start looking round, I realize is coming from me.

'What the hell's going on?' Captain Denning pushes his way to the front of the little crowd gathered round Patroller Cary, and swears.

'It – it happened so fast,' Patroller Yuen says. 'We heard screams from the Shudders, then someone running – Mike shouted, and there was a shot. By the time we got here . . .'

She indicates the body on the ground, her face drained of colour.

Captain Denning opens his mouth, then closes it again.

'Who fired their gun?' he says at last.

The Patrollers around him shake their heads.

'It was a Fearless,' I say. My voice is hoarse from screaming. 'He was in the Shudders. There were two of them – a man and a girl. The man had a gun, and he's taken Jori.'

Captain Denning stares at me. '*What?*'

Shaking, I tell him a version of what happened, leaving out the bit about going to look for Myo's bag.

'But what were you *doing* there? And whose bag is that?'

I pull the bag round behind my back. 'Does that even matter? There was a Fearless! *He took my brother!*' In my head, I can see the Fearless swimming back to the mainland through the black, icy water, and Jori, terrified, choking, frozen . . . 'Please! You have to go after them. You have to get Jori back!'

Captain Denning doesn't answer me. The people around us are muttering to one another, their expressions frightened and shocked.

'It was that boy,' Sheena Drake says suddenly. 'I bet he had the Fearless with him. They all helped each other get over here.'

My mind whirls. Is that what happened? Did Myo bring the Fearless with him?

*No, that's insane*, I tell myself. *How could he? And why would he? After all, he's not Fearless himself.*

'Forget about Myo!' I cry, knowing that with every minute – every *second* – that passes, my brother is getting further away. 'He's got nothing to do with them!' But no one's listening, except Sol, who turns and frowns at me.

'Who's Myo?' he says.

I grab his arm. 'Sol, the Fearless took Jori! The Patrol have to go after them!'

Sol seems to be about to reply when Captain Denning

says, 'Patroller Greene, Patroller Zadac, take Patroller Cary to the Infirmary. Patroller Yuen, escort everyone back to the apartments, find every Patroller who isn't here yet and make sure we have sufficient people on watch. Then we need to search the rest of the island and make sure there aren't any other Fearless here. I'll go and warn the Mayor. And I will deal with you later, young lady,' he adds, glaring at me.

'Wait!' I say. 'What about Jori?'

'Sorry, there's nothing I can do.' Captain Denning turns away.

'*NO!*' I scream. I start to run after him but Sol catches hold of me, pulling me back. 'Cass, stop it!'

'Let *go* of me!' I try to wriggle out of his grip, but he tightens his fingers around my arm until my fingers start to tingle. I stare at him. 'Sol, don't you get it? *The Fearless took Jori!* If we don't get him back, he'll be Altered!'

'And what do you want the Patrol to do? Take a boat out in the middle of the night, go over to the docks and put themselves in even more danger? Cass, you know the rule.'

*The rule.* Just one of many drawn up by Sol's dad and the Patrol after everyone first came to Hope. The rule that says anyone taken by a Fearless who doesn't return of their own accord, unAltered, will be considered lost, because the safety of the Islanders is paramount and the limited resources of the Patrol are considered too precious to be used for anything other than defending the island.

Which means no one's going after my brother. He's as good as dead – or Altered – already.

I want to collapse against Sol and wail. But that isn't going to get Jori back. *Nothing's* going to get Jori back, unless I go after him myself. But how can I do that? How will I get off the island?

The people around me start to disperse as Patroller Yuen ushers them back towards the apartment blocks.

'Captain Denning wants all the Junior Patrol who are about to graduate to take part in the search,' Rob tells Sol. 'Apart from Cass, obviously.'

'OK.' Sol lets go of my arm. 'Cass, you need to go inside.'

I shake my head. I can't move. Can't even speak. Grief is building inside me like a storm, vast and dark and roaring.

'*Cass.* Go back to your apartment. It's not safe out here.'

'Please, Sol,' I whisper. 'Help me get him back.' For a second, I think about telling him that if he helps me, I'll go out with him.

His face hardens. 'Go *inside*, Cass.'

I watch him and Rob walk off.

My brother is gone.

The only family I have left, and he's gone.

Even now, part of my mind refuses to accept this. *Any moment now*, I tell myself, *he's going to come running over, grinning all over his face at the joke he's played on everyone.*

But he doesn't.

My eyes burn, but no tears spill over. Instead of returning to the apartment, I head to the Meeting Hall. Mr Brightman will help me. He has to. My dad was a close friend of his. He helped deliver Jori in the boat on our way over here.

On the way, I bump into Marissa, who's got a gun and a lantern, her expression grim. 'Cass, where are you going?' she says gently. Someone must have told her about Jori. 'You should get back to your apartment – as soon as the search has finished I'll come and find you.'

I grab her arm. 'Mar, you have to help me get him back!'

'What? No, we *can't*.' She glances round nervously. 'We'd have to steal a boat. And take a gun. And even if we do make it back, once the Patrol realize what we've done they'll kick us off Hope for ever. I'm really sorry, Cass.'

From across the island, I hear a long whistle – the signal from the Patrol that the search is about to start. 'Just hang in there, OK?' Marissa says, her voice cracking on the last word.

I stumble away from her. When I get to the Meeting Hall, Captain Denning is just leaving. I wait in the shadows until he's gone, then run up the steps. Mr Brightman – I can't think of him as *Mayor* Brightman, no matter how hard I try – spends most of his time in his office; even now I can see a line of flickering light under the door. I knock. 'Come in,' he calls.

When he sees me, he looks surprised. 'Cass. You should be at home. It's not safe.'

'You have to help me get Jori back!' I say. '*Please!* He's my *brother*, we can't let the Fearless take him!'

I know I sound almost hysterical, but I don't care.

Sol's dad shakes his head. 'I'm sorry, Cass. I can't spare my men to go on a wild goose chase over to the mainland. You know that. I'm truly sorry about Jori. But those are the rules.'

I stare at him for a moment. Then I turn and run out of his office.

Outside, I walk blindly, not knowing where I'm going and not caring. I don't realize I'm near the cells until I hear someone hiss, 'Cass.'

I stop. The moon shines on Myo, standing at the front of his cell. 'Oh, God, I thought you weren't coming,' he says, and I remember his bag, which is still slung across my shoulder.

No one's guarding him; Captain Denning must have decided that getting the Patrol to search the island was more important. I go over and shove the bag through the bars. He snatches it from me and pulls out the padded jacket, shivering and hissing in pain as he pulls it on.

'Hey, what just happened?' he says as I start to walk off. 'I heard a gunshot, and someone screaming . . .'

I turn back. 'There were two Fearless in the Shudders. They killed one of the Patrol and took my little brother.'

Myo's eyes widen. '*What?*'

'Were they with you?'

'No! No way!'

'You sure?'

Myo shakes his head. 'I swear, I had no idea.'

'They must have followed you here, then.' I swallow hard against the ache in my throat. 'The man shot Patroller Cary so he could escape with Jori.'

'The man?'

'There was a man, and a girl.'

'Why didn't anyone go after them?'

'It's a law we have here. If anyone's taken or Altered, they're lost. There aren't enough of us, or enough weapons, to go after people.'

'That's crazy,' Myo says.

If it had been anyone but Jori who'd been taken, I'd tell him he was wrong. I'd have argued that the survival of the Islanders was more important than the life of a single person, repeating the words we've had drilled into us for as long as we can remember.

But it's my brother who's gone.

My brother who the Patrol are refusing to help.

I close my eyes, leaning my forehead against the cold metal bars of the cell gate.

'What're you gonna do?' Myo says softly.

'Go after him,' I say. 'I have to. Even if he's dead, I want to get him back.'

'Take me with you.'

I open my eyes. 'Eh?'

'I need to get out of here and back to the mainland. If *you* were thinking those Fearless were with me, the rest of your lot are gonna string me up. If we go now we might be able to catch up with the Fearless and get your brother back. I know where they're taking him.'

My stomach lurches. 'What do you mean?'

'I've heard about this place from the barterers, where they say the Fearless are bringing people to *alter* them,' he says. 'They reckon the Fearless are trying to get their numbers up again.'

I hold my breath, aghast, and hardly daring to believe that the answer to my predicament might be right here, in front of me, with this boy I don't even know.

'Can you get us off this island?' Myo says.

'I don't know.' My mind is whirling as I try to work out how I can get us to the jetty and onto a boat, unseen. 'I – I can try. But I'll need to get some stuff – water and food—'

'How long will it take you?'

'Ten minutes.'

'Go. I'll get this lock open.'

I don't need telling twice. I turn, and run back in the direction of the apartments.

# Chapter 13

## MYO

I work frantically at the lock with my knife. My ribs are killing me and I'm terrified Cass won't make it back, or someone — one of those guards — will turn up first. Why did I promise her I'd help her find her brother? I must be crazy. Either we'll catch up with Mara, which will be a disaster, or I'll have to take her all the way back to the bunker to get weapons and supplies. It's not gonna work.

But I have to get off this island. Next time someone tries to take my eyepatch off, I might not be able to stop them. Once we're on the mainland, and we're on Mara's trail, I'll have to find a way of ditching Cass. I feel like a total bastard just thinking about it, but what choice do I have?

When she comes back, she's wearing a pack and a pair of sturdy boots instead of the pumps she had on before. I give her a thumbs-up and start to push the gate open, but she holds up her hand. She takes a bottle of lamp oil out of her pack and tips a bit onto the gate hinges so it opens without making a sound.

'Good thinking,' I whisper as I limp out and snap the

lock closed again. I have my satchel across my chest, even though it makes my ribs hurts like hell. 'How are we gonna do this?'

She tells me her plan for getting off the island. 'Are you OK?' she adds as I take a couple more steps, hissing in pain.

'Don't worry about me,' I say. 'I've had worse. We're heading for the jetty, right?' I don't want her to know that I'm wondering how on earth I'll make it that far.

She nods. 'Follow me. And be *quiet*.'

We creep along, keeping to the shadows. When we're almost at the sea wall, Cass drops into a crouch. I crouch too, breathing fast. The pain's making me feel sick. My ribs are broken for sure.

'That's where they put ladders over to get down to the boats moored on the other side,' Cass whispers in my ear, pointing, and I see one of those guards standing on top of the wall with a lantern by her feet. We watch her for a moment. Cass eases the pack off her shoulders and gives it to me.

It's heavy. 'What's in here?' I ask.

'Food, water and clothes. I've got a knife tucked in my boot, too.'

I feel relieved. At least she'll be able to look after herself.

She runs across to the wall.

'Patroller Yuen!' I hear her gasp. 'That boy has escaped from the cells!'

'What?' she says. 'Cass? Is that you?'

'I was in my apartment! He came in, threatened me with a knife and made me give him all my food! I managed to get away but I think he's still in the building somewhere!'

The soldier swears, grabs her lantern and gives a shrill whistle. 'Cass, you need to go and find Captain Denning,' she says. 'I think he's on the south wall.'

'Come *on*,' Cass hisses as soon as the soldier's run off.

I throw her the pack, clenching my teeth as fresh pain stabs through my side.

'Keep low so the rest of the Patrol don't see our silhouettes or shadows,' she whispers as we clamber up onto the wall. Ten feet below us are a group of wooden rowing boats with oars in the bottom, and next to me is a rolled-up rope ladder secured to a pair of metal hooks. Cass gives it a shove and it unrolls. '*Go!*' she hisses. I climb down as fast as I can and drop into the nearest boat, biting back a cry of pain. A few moments later she lands beside me. 'Untie the boat,' she says, grabbing the oars. I lean over, untie the mooring rope and push the boat off against the wall before collapsing back with a groan.

Cass picks up the oars. 'Wait!' I hiss, sitting up again. 'Let me row to start with. If they see you, they'll know you helped me.'

'They'll know anyway. I left a note,' she hisses back.

'You what?'

She gazes at me for a moment. I lean forward and snatch the oars from her hands.

The pain is awful; it takes everything I've got to pull

the oars through the water and steer away from the jetty. Soon, the shouts start. I see lanterns above the wall. There's a shot, and a bullet whizzes past my ear, another grazing the boat's prow. '*Shit!*' Cass says, ducking her head. I pull harder at the oars and manage to put on one last burst of speed.

A few minutes later, we're out of range. I collapse back against the side of the boat, groaning.

'Did they get you?' Cass asks, sounding panicked.

I shake my head. 'No. It's my ribs. Some bruises from when your pal decided he was gonna try and kill me.'

'What?' She leans over and before I can stop her, she's pulled up my jacket, hoodie and shirt. In the moonlight, the bruises on my ribs look black. Cass gasps. 'Did Sol and Rob do that?'

'Aye.' I tug my clothes back down.

'They said you had a knife, but I saw it in your bag.'

I snort with laughter. 'I didn't have anything.'

Cass goes quiet, grabs the oars and starts rowing. I wonder how she feels about Blondie. He said she wasn't his girlfriend. Has she turned him down or something? He sounded pretty bitter.

Jesus, why do I care? I need to think about what I'm gonna do next. I need to think about getting Mara back. The longer she's with those bastards, the more danger she's in of ending up like them – half-dead and rotting from the inside out.

My sister has already been through hell. I can't let it happen again.

# Chapter 14

## CASS

When we're almost at the mainland, I stop rowing, gasping for breath. The docks look black against the star-scattered sky. Dread squeezes inside me like a cold hand. What if the place is crawling with Fearless?

Then I think of my brother, of the Fearless man clapping his hand over his mouth so he couldn't even cry out before he was dragged away. I row the rest of the way to the mainland with my teeth clenched together, while Myo rests against the side of the boat with his eyes – or rather his eye – closed. When I remember the bruises on his ribs, I feel slightly sick. *God*, why did Sol *do* that?

It isn't hard to find somewhere to moor the boat. Wooden piers still jut out into the water all along the shore, although most are rotted and collapsing now, their pilings slimed with seaweed and crusted with barnacles. I find one with a ladder that still looks safe, and tie the boat up alongside it. I've got the knife I told Myo about – the biggest and sharpest of my kitchen knives – in my boot with a piece of oilcloth wrapped around the blade. Checking it's secure, I shoulder my pack and climb the ladder, my fingers clamped around the spray-slick rungs. Then I help Myo up. He falls to his knees, breathing hard again and clutching his side. But when I step towards him, he waves me away.

Trying not to listen to his ragged breathing, I turn and look at the docks again. Everything is washed in moon-light, just like it was the first time I was here seven years ago. *That was the last time I was on the mainland*, I think with a chill, as memories of that night come flooding back. Those ships are still in their dry docks, rust blooming on their sides like sores, and beyond them is the jumble of warehouses and buildings we ran through with Mum.

Myo limps towards me, grimacing. 'I'm sorry, I need to rest for a bit. I can't carry on like this.'

'Oh. OK,' I say, although inside, I'm screaming, *What about Jori? If we don't go now, we'll never get to him in time.* I chew my lower lip. I'll never find my brother on my own. I wouldn't even know where to start. Like it or not, I'm relying on Myo, and if he needs to rest, then I have to let him.

'I've got the rest of my stuff in one of those buildings,' he says.

I look at the warehouses, which are half-lost in inky shadow. 'Is it . . . safe?'

'Aye.'

I wish I could feel so sure. *Perhaps he lives here*, I think. Is his friend here too? I wonder what's so wrong with their baby that Myo was prepared to risk everything to get onto Hope and try and find someone to help her.

As he limps past me, I reach down and take the knife out of my boot, my stomach tightening with nerves as I unwind the oilcloth from around the blade. At the end of the pier is a towering stack of shipping containers – cargo for a ship that never arrived, or was never able to leave – and nearby, weeds tangle through the arm of a toppled crane, which lies along the ground like the skeleton of some gigantic, prehistoric animal.

I follow Myo across to the containers. He holds up a hand, peering at the entrance to a large warehouse. 'Do you want a lamp?' I whisper. He shakes his head. I grip my knife tighter.

Myo gives a low whistle. '*Don't!*' I hiss.

He looks round at me, a half-smile playing on his face. 'Why? Who d'you think's gonna hear me?'

Inside the warehouse, something moves. A wave of terror crashes over me. Myo's tricked me into getting him off Hope and lured me over here by promising to help me. Inside the warehouse, the Fearless who took Jori are waiting, and now they're coming to get me too.

Every muscle and nerve ending in my body is on fire with adrenaline, my mind screaming at me to run. I take a step back. Then another. Myo glances at me again, but this time he's frowning. 'What's wrong?'

Out of the shadows pads the biggest dog I've ever seen.

The top of his head reaches Myo's elbow, his wiry, dark grey fur hanging in shaggy fringes over his eyes and along his muzzle, legs and tail.

'His name's Lochie,' Myo says as the dog nuzzles him, his tail sweeping from side to side. 'He's a Wolfhound.' He rubs Lochie's ears. 'You waited,' he murmurs. 'Good lad.'

When he lets him go, Lochie comes over to me. I freeze, hardly daring to breathe. I didn't even know you could get dogs this big.

Myo smiles. 'He won't hurt you. Hold out your hand.'

Nervously, I do as he says. Lochie sniffs my fingers. It takes all my willpower not to snatch them away as he swipes at them with a huge, wet tongue. Myo makes a strange sound, and I realize he's trying to stifle a laugh.

'What?' I say.

'Your face.'

'I've never had a dog, only a cat,' I say, and feel an unexpected twist of sadness. It's the first time I've thought about Kali in years. 'Anyway, when I heard him coming, I thought—' I stop, feeling my face heat up.

'What?'

'Nothing.'

'No, what?'

'That those Fearless were in there, and you were calling them to come and get me.'

Myo's amused expression vanishes. 'Why would you think that?' he says sharply. 'Let's get one thing clear right now. I'm not a Fearless, and I'm not in league with them either.'

He sounds angry, and that makes me start to feel angry, too. I look him straight in the eye. 'I don't know you. I don't know anything about you. And two Fearless

**116**

just took my brother, so excuse me for being completely paranoid right now.'

We glare at each other for a moment. He looks away first.

'Aye, well,' he mutters. 'Are we gonna get some rest, or what?'

I follow him and Lochie into the warehouse, taking my lamp out of my pack. But it isn't as dark inside as I was expecting – moonlight leaks through gaps where parts of the roof have fallen away, painting stripes of light on the cracked, stained concrete floor. Old wooden pallets and bits of machinery are strewn everywhere, and a profusion of skinny, leafless trees, just like the ones in the Shudders, have sprung up among them.

'Over here,' Myo says, making for a stack of metal crates in one corner. Between the crates and the wall there's a sleeping bag, a dish of water, frozen solid, and a fire barrel with a metal rod balanced across the top. In the corner is a pack, twice the size of mine.

I take off my pack. 'Can we light a fire?' I say. My clothes are damp from sea spray, and I'm cold all the way to my bones. Myo nods, pulling his satchel off over his head with a grunt of pain. He takes out a bottle of water, knocks the ice out of the dish and refills it, while I go to find wood. In less than ten minutes, I have a fire going in the barrel, moon-silvered smoke spiralling up towards a hole in the roof above us, the flames casting a shuddering orange glow onto the crates and the walls.

'Nice job,' Myo says.

I step back from the barrel, brushing off my hands. 'What d'you think I do all day on Hope, sew dresses and sweep floors?'

He holds up his hands. 'Did I say that?'

I narrow my eyes at him. Grimacing, he sits down. Lochie lies down beside him with a grunt. His paws are almost the same size as my hands. Myo reaches out and rubs the dog's ear.

'You want to eat?' he says.

I'm about to tell him I'm not hungry, then remember what we were told, time and time again, in the Junior Patrol. *If you find yourself in a survival situation, your priorities must be shelter, water and food. Without shelter, your body will weaken. And without fuel, it'll give out on you altogether.*

'Yeah, OK,' I say. I take bread, dried fish and kelp strips out of my pack. They look even less appetizing than usual, although Lochie shows a great interest in the fish strips, raising his head and sniffing the air loudly as I unwrap them.

Gritting his teeth again, Myo turns and pulls one of those foil pouches I saw in his satchel out of his pack. 'Want one? There's ravioli, chicken stew, chilli or spaghetti bolognese. I wouldn't recommend the bolognese, but Lochie likes it.'

Frowning, I take a pouch. It's a year or so out of date, but that doesn't worry me. The barterers occasionally trade canned food, and everyone on the island knows that unless the tins are split or bulging, they're safe. I assume these are the same.

The pouch is full of packets. I stare in wonder at the labels: *Chicken Stew, Strawberry Dairy Shake, Mango Peach Sauce, Sugar Free Raspberry Beverage*. There's even a pack of crackers, a spoon and a wet wipe.

'Where did you get these?' I ask as he shows me how to prepare the stew by sliding it into a pouch marked *Heater*, tipping a small amount of water into the top and propping it up against the wall while the chemicals inside react and heat the food.

'Ben found a load of them at the bunker when we—' He stops and clears his throat.

There's a few seconds' silence.

'Who's Ben?' I say. 'And what bunker?'

He starts eating, pretending he hasn't heard me.

'*Myo.*'

At last, he looks up at me.

'Do you have a community too?' I say.

He nods.

'Where?'

'Up north. Staffordshire.'

'And you live in a bunker?'

He nods again, and starts eating his chilli. A pouch of bolognese for Lochie is cooling nearby.

'How many of you are there?' I say as I take a cautious spoonful of the chicken stew. To my surprise, it tastes OK – a little salty, but it's definitely edible.

Myo tries to shrug, and winces, sucking in his breath. 'Twenty of us, including me.'

'Twenty? Wow.' *So the barterers' stories about other survivor communities are true.* 'Is Ben your leader?'

'I guess so. He found the place.' Myo turns stiffly to empty Lochie's water dish and tip the bolognese into it. Lochie gobbles it down in just a few mouthfuls. 'Sorry, boy,' Myo says when the dog whines at him for more. Lochie lies back down with a grunt.

I can tell from his body language that he doesn't want to tell me anything else about the bunker, so I say, 'You said you thought you knew where those Fearless might be taking Jori.'

He nods. 'Sheffield.'

My stomach sinks. 'But that's going to take . . .'

'The Fearless are on foot too. And they're only human, same as us.'

'They are not,' I snap.

'Not what?'

'The Fearless are not human. They're monsters.'

'Aye,' Myo murmurs.

'And what if they've given Jori the serum already? He could have Altered by the time we get there!'

'He won't have.'

'How do you know?'

'The serum they use these days isn't as effective. It takes at least a couple of weeks and multiple injections to Alter someone.'

I stare at him. 'What? How do you know that?'

He shakes his head. 'Everybody knows that.'

I think back to what we were told about the serum in

**120**

our lessons at Hope's school. Did nobody realize things had changed? Why didn't the barterers say anything?

My head is full of questions – I want to ask Myo about his friend's baby, and if he still intends to try and find medicine for them – but he's turned away, busying himself rinsing out and refilling Lochie's dish with water. It's clear that this conversation's over, too.

A silence settles over the little space, broken only by the sound of Lochie sighing occasionally, and the crackle of the flames in the barrel. Every now and then a piece of wood shifts, and sparks drift up into the air along with the smoke, winking out as they float towards the warehouse roof.

'We should get some kip,' Myo says at last.

'Shouldn't one of us keep watch?'

Myo jerks a thumb at Lochie. 'We've got the best security guard on the planet right here. You'll listen out for any trouble, won't you, boy?'

I notice that whenever Myo talks to him, Lochie's shaggy eyebrows twitch up and down, as if he understands every word.

'Here.' Myo holds out a blanket.

'I've got one.'

'Yeah, but you can't lie on the floor. You'll freeze. Take it.'

He thrusts it at me. I spread it out, and dig my own out of my bag to wrap round myself. Myo gets slowly into the sleeping bag, his teeth clenched together, his face pale.

'Are you sure they didn't break something?' I ask him.

'I don't know. I hope not.' He lets out a slow, shuddering breath.

I lie down too. I'm not expecting to sleep, but when I close my eyes, exhaustion rolls over me in a great wave. Before long my thoughts start to fragment, sliding over each other like pieces of broken glass, and I'm sucked down into a deep, dreamless dark.

# Chapter 15

## SOL

'What happened?'

'Where is he?'

'Did you catch him?'

As I join the rest of the Patrol in the Refectory, everyone crowds round us. *Get away from me*, I want to tell them. I'm scanning the room for Cass, but I can't see her.

After she raised the alarm, everyone was evacuated from the apartments to the Refectory. The Patrollers who weren't guarding them or on watch duty were sent on another search, and Captain Denning came to find me, Rob, Shelley, Marissa and Andrej and told us to join them. That was how we found out we'd graduated.

And then, just as we were about to start, we discovered the boy had stolen a boat. The Patrollers on the wall had shot at him, but he was already too far away.

He'd escaped.

I clench my hands into fists. I want to punch something. A table. The wall. I can *see* that freak laughing at us. Laughing at *me*. How the hell did he get out of the cells?

And how the *hell* did he manage to steal a boat?

I touch the bruise on my jaw and wince. One thing's for sure. If I ever see him again *anywhere*, I'll kill him. No one makes a fool out of me. No one.

'Everybody! Your attention, *please*!' Captain Denning climbs onto a bench at the front of the Refectory, banging the butt of his rifle against the wood.

Everyone falls silent except for Olly and Ella's brat, who's doing that horrible, high-pitched screeching thing babies do.

'It appears the boy has escaped from the island,' Captain Denning says. 'We believe he managed to steal a boat.' A gasp goes up from around the hall. '*Please*. I don't want anyone to panic. The Patrol are going to conduct another thorough search of the island, and . . .'

I tune him out and squint over everyone's heads again. Where *is* she?

'Where you going, man?' Rob murmurs as I start to edge away.

'To look for Cass. Cover for me, OK?'

As I slide through the Refectory door, I try to remember the last time I saw her. It was before the first search, when I told her to go inside. Perhaps she stayed in her apartment – the evacuation of everyone back to the apartments was chaotic, and I'm pretty sure no one thought to do a roll call. They were too busy freaking out about the boy, and the Patrol were too busy getting ready to start looking for him.

I take the stairs up to Cass's place two at a time and go in without knocking.

The apartment's cold, dark, quiet.

'Cass?' I say, turning the thumbwheel on my lantern to make it brighter.

As I go to the bedroom, my heart's beating fast. What if she's done something stupid?

*No, she wouldn't*, I tell myself.

I swing the lantern round. The room's empty, but something's not right. Normally, Cass's apartment is tidy. Now, her stuff is scattered all over the floor, like someone came in and ransacked everything.

I look round again, taking in details. The blanket is missing off her bed. Her boots are gone, and so is the pack she keeps on a hook by the door. The clothes on the shelves near the sleeping mats are jumbled up; all the warm clothes – the jumpers and thermals – have been taken. And back in the other room, the cupboard where she keeps all her food and supplies is wide open. Loads of stuff is missing – food, lamp oil, her water bottle, purification tablets.

*Oh, shit, she hasn't.*

She *can't* have done.

Then I remember the way she looked at me, the way she begged: *Please, Sol, help me get him back.*

And I see the scrap of paper on top of the cupboard, weighted down by a tin of peas.

I snatch it up.

*Whoever finds this, I'm sorry*, the note says in Cass's

slanting scrawl. *Jori is my family. He's all I have. I can't abandon him. C.*

'You *idiot*,' I breathe.

*Maybe you* should *have helped her,* a little voice in my head says as I read the note again, trying to take it in. *How?* I ask it. *By taking her off the island? By risking both of us getting kicked off Hope for ever?*

Dammit, I should have stayed with her. I should have kept an eye on her. I should have—

*What if she went with the boy?* the little voice says suddenly.

About to rush out of the door, I stop dead. What? No. That's *absurd*.

*What if she helped him escape?*

No. No way. Not Cass.

And then I hear her call *Don't hurt him!* after Rob and me as we led him away to the cells. See the imploring look on her face.

And hear *him*, the freak, sneering *You think your girl-friend'll be happy about that?*

*Maybe he forced her to go with him,* I tell myself.

*What? But gave her time to pack a bag with food and clothes?* the voice says.

The suspicion inside me blooms into a dark, terrible certainty.

When Dad and the Patrol find out about this, she'll never be able to return to Hope, even if she does find Jori.

I stare at the wall with unseeing eyes. The thought

**126**

that I might never see Cass again is far worse than knowing she's run away with the freak.

I crumple the note in my fist, stuff it in my pocket, and run back into the bedroom, where I pull the clothes all the way off the shelves, kick over furniture, yank the blankets off Jori's sleeping mat and throw them in the corner. After that, I ransack the other room as well.

Then I run out of the apartment, back to the Refectory, where I yell, 'She's gone! He's kidnapped her!'

'Who's gone?' Rob says. 'What are you on about, man?'

'Cass, you idiot,' I growl. 'The freak's made her go with him.'

I shove past him to find Captain Denning and tell him the terrible news.

# Chapter 16

## CASS

I don't know what wakes me, but suddenly my eyes jerk open, and the jumbled nightmare I've been having about the Fearless man snatching Jori blows away like smoke.

The moon has set, and the fire in the barrel has almost burned down. Shivering, I sit up and rub my arms, which ache from rowing the night before. It's so dark I can hardly see anything. I light my lantern.

Myo's gone.

Panic rises inside me. I scramble to my feet. His pack and sleeping bag have gone too. So has Lochie's water dish.

*He's abandoned me*, I think, my heart thudding. A wave of nausea rolls over me. I have no map, no compass. How will I ever find my way to Sheffield on my own?

Then I hear Lochie whine.

I turn, holding out the lantern. He's standing behind me. '*Lochie!*' I hear Myo hiss nearby. '*Come on!*'

But Lochie doesn't move, just whines again, his gentle gaze fixed on me.

A few moments later, Myo appears, wearing his pack,

the sleeping bag rolled up and pushed through the top.

'Shit,' he says. He must have seen my light.

My panic turns to fury.

I pull my knife out of my boot and, yanking off the oilcloth, push Myo backwards against the crates with the blade against his neck. Lochie gives a single bark, but stays where he is.

'You bastard,' I spit at Myo. 'You promised you'd help me.'

His eye goes wide. 'I – I was just—'

'Just what? Planning on leaving without me? I risked *everything* getting you off Hope. I can probably never go back.' I press the knife blade harder against his throat.

He doesn't try to struggle or push me away, just stands there, his hands curled into fists by his sides, his chest rising and falling rapidly.

'Well?' I say.

'OK. OK. I'm sorry. I was—'

'Save it. I'm not interested in your excuses.' I lower the knife, half expecting him to turn and run, but he stays where he is. I wrap the blade in the oilcloth again and shove the knife back in my boot.

'At least your dog can be trusted,' I say as I turn to gather up my things, not bothering to hide the anger in my voice. Lochie whines again. Tentatively, I reach out and rub him under the chin. His fur is a lot softer than it looks. He leans his head on my hand.

Myo takes off his pack again and sits down, holding his ribs. There's a livid mark on his neck where I held

**129**

the knife against it, but I haven't broken the skin.

I get the fire going again, and we have a silent breakfast of fish strips and coffee.

'So, how long is it going to take to get to Sheffield if we don't catch the Fearless up first?' I say when we've finished, my tone chilly as I emphasize the word *we*.

Myo heaves himself to his feet. 'If we don't catch them up, we'll need to go back to the bunker. We can't go to Sheffield without guns. They don't call it the Torturehouse for nothing.'

*The Torturehouse*. A shiver crawls up my spine. 'Is that this place you talked about? The place where you think the Fearless are going?'

'Aye.'

'So how long will it take to get to the bunker?'

'About eight or nine days.'

'What?' Desperation builds inside me as I think about how far behind my brother and the Fearless we could already be. Myo said it takes a couple of weeks for someone to Alter now – but what if he's wrong? And there are so many other things that could happen to Jori before then. I don't stand a chance of getting him back.

'Keep your hair on,' Myo says. 'I know someone who might be able to help – a barterer. He has horses, and if he's around, and heading that way, he might take us with him.'

*If* he's around. *Might* take us. 'And what if he's not around?'

'Then we'll think of something else, OK?' he snaps.

I'm about to snap back, then notice how every breath he takes in seems to hurt him still, and how pale he is, his face glistening with sweat.

'Are you sure you're up to this?' I say.

Myo gives me a hard look. 'If we're going to get to Danny and April's by nightfall, we need to get a move on.'

Danny must be the barterer he was just talking about. I put the fire out. As we leave the warehouse, Myo limping again, I briefly consider offering to help him carry his stuff. Then I remember he tried to abandon me. Screw him.

Outside, the sky is the colour of dull steel; frost crunches under my boots. Soon, we reach the road that leads out of the dockyard. The cars left by the people who were trying to get onto the island that night seven years ago are still there. As we weave our way through them, Lochie trotting ahead with his nose to the ground, I try not to look at anything too closely, but my gaze is drawn as if by a magnet to the doors hanging open; a doll lying on a back seat that stares out at me with sightless eyes; a single child's trainer, weathered and rotted; the decayed remains of a suitcase resting on the verge.

We reach Mr Brightman's Range Rover, which is leaning sideways, its tyres flat, its windows smashed. More cars are parked behind it, stretching up the road as far as I can see. I stare at them as memories of that night return with full force – the crazy, terrifying drive down the motorway; the Fearless who tried to leap into our path;

that house where the car was burning and two Fearless were crouched over that couple; Mrs Brightman getting shot; Mum's cries as my brother was born.

I'd hidden my face and put my hands over my ears to block out Mum's screams while it was actually happening, too traumatized by everything else that had happened to watch. But then I'd heard a different sound: a thin, sharp wail. Someone nudged me, and I looked up to see Mr Brightman holding out my brother, wrapped in his jacket. I remember trembling as I took him and placed him in my lap, awed at how tiny and perfect he was. His face was red and scrunched up, his fists opening and closing as if protesting at being born too soon, and into such terror and chaos. I held him close to my chest and rocked him until his wails subsided, and when I looked down at him again he was gazing up at me.

At that moment, I knew I'd do anything I could to protect him. I put out a finger and he hung onto it, his grip surprisingly strong. 'Hello,' I whispered. 'I'm your big sister. I'm Cass.' And when we reached the island, and we were being registered, I was the one who named him. *Jori*.

'What's wrong?' Myo says, jolting me back to the present.

'That was the car we came in,' I say. 'Me, my mum, Sol and his parents.'

'What about your brother?'

'He was born as we were on our way to the island.'

'So he's just a bairn?'

'Yeah.' The words catch in my throat as I think of how frightened Jori must be right now.

*That's if he's still alive*, a nasty little voice in my head says. I tell it to shut up.

We reach the main road. The hedges are wildly overgrown and the trees lean at an angle down towards the tarmac, their bare branches forming a tunnel over our heads. The rest of that morning, Myo and I travel more or less in silence. I'm still angry about earlier, and he must sense it because he keeps his distance, walking a little way ahead with Lochie between us. All I can think about is Jori. Are the Fearless giving him anything to eat? Is my brother warm enough? Is he alive? I have no way of knowing whether each step I take is bringing me closer to him or taking me further away. Myo could be taking me anywhere. But until I come up with a better plan, I have to stick with him.

Near to what we both estimate is midday, we stop to eat again, sitting on our packs by the side of the road. Lochie disappears into the woods behind us, barking. I hear twigs snapping as he plunges through the trees.

'Bring us back a rabbit, eh, boy?' Myo calls after him.

I take a swig of water and am about to pass the bottle to Myo when he jumps to his feet.

'What's wrong?' I say, my heart beating faster.

He holds up a hand. 'Shh.'

I listen, but I don't hear anything. Myo picks up his pack. 'We need to get off the road.'

'Why? What's—'

'Into the trees, now.' Myo's tone is urgent. I snatch up my pack and follow him into the wood. He's almost running, his bruised ribs seemingly forgotten. A little way back from the road is a wide ditch, choked with dead leaves, twigs and ancient rubbish. 'In there,' Myo whispers, dropping his pack into it and jumping down after it. He digs in his satchel, pulling out his knife.

'What about Lochie?' I whisper back as we crouch side by side, looking towards the road, which is half visible through the trees. The food I just ate has turned sour in my stomach, and my heart's pounding so hard it feels like it's going to burst right out of my chest.

'He's got enough sense to keep away, I hope.'

'From what? The Fearless?'

'No, this is worse than the Fearless.' He's breathing fast, his jaw clenched. He's *scared*.

I stare through the trees, wondering what on earth is coming along that road. And then I hear it – a sound I haven't heard for so long that at first, I can't place it: a low, throbbing hum that gradually gets louder.

Engines.

# Chapter 17

## MYO

'That's a car!' Cass says, turning to stare at me with wide eyes. 'Who would have a car these—'

'Be *quiet*.' I stare at the road, my knife clenched in my fist, the pain from my busted rib forgotten. 'If they find us, we're screwed.'

*If they find ME, we're screwed.*

She shuts up. Thank God. I pray Lochie stays away. If the Magpies find him, Christ knows what they'll do.

They come into view, heading in the direction we've come from. It's the same jeep I saw five days ago, open topped with a camouflage pattern painted on the sides. The same people are in it too, four men and a couple of women. I was near what used to be Oxford. They'd stopped to cook a meal, which I should have been able to smell from miles off, but it was a breezy day and the wind wasn't blowing in the right direction. Me and Lochie came round a corner and almost walked straight into them. Just like before, they're bundled up in heavy black coats and black caps, with trank guns across their laps. The only difference is this time, they don't have two

Fearless chained up in the back of the jeep. As they pass the spot where Cass and I are hiding, the guy beside the driver turns his head. It feels like he's staring straight at us.

I hold my breath. Until a month ago, none of us had ever seen the Magpies. We'd only heard about them from the barterers. Then Ben almost got caught by another group of them when he was out on a salvage run with Cy. They were in the remains of one of the villages on the moors, searching one of the houses and not being awful quiet about it, because they thought there wasn't anyone around to hear them. And because of all the noise they were making, they didn't hear the jeep pull up outside. There were four of them, and Ben and Cy had to hide up in the attic while the Magpies pulled the house apart, looking for them. By sheer chance, one of the ceilings came down before they could get up into the roof, and they gave up and left. Ben and Cy were both pretty shaken up, though, and it freaked everyone else out too.

After that, Ben found out from one of the barterers exactly who they were and what they were doing. He gathered everyone in the Communications Hall and told us. 'We have to be incredibly careful,' he said. 'If they find out about us, it'll be the end of everything. From now on, no one leaves the bunker in groups of less than three, and if you do go anywhere, you take a gun.'

It was like the first couple of years after the Invasion when the country was crawling with Fearless all over again.

Like everyone else, I promised I'd take care, but all I could think about was Mara. It was almost two weeks since she'd escaped, after I took her outside for some air, and somehow, she'd managed to get away from me. I guess I was lucky she'd run instead of attacking me, but that was the only good thing about it. We searched for her across the moors, but she was nowhere, and then the weather started to get really cold, and Ben decided we needed to postpone our search until it improved again. All I could think was, *What if the Magpies catch her?* The thought of having to wait to go looking for her again made me feel sick with worry.

It was a few days later, after another barterer brought the news she'd been seen with a Fearless man, heading south, that I decided whether Ben liked it or not, I was gonna go after her straight away, and started squirreling away food and supplies to take with me. Who knows how she managed to hook up with him, but I wasn't gonna let her go back to them. Not after I'd fought so hard to keep her away.

'What were they—' Cass starts to say when the first jeep's gone past. I hold up a hand. I can hear a second jeep now. It's going even slower than the first. The guy with the scar on his cheek, the one who was barking orders when I nearly bumped into them last week, is driving.

Something rustles behind us, making us jump. It's Lochie, a small, furry body dangling from his jaws. 'Stay,' I hiss, holding up a hand. Lochie stops, ears

**137**

pricked, putting his head on one side and then the other.

We wait until the sound of the engines has died away. Then I climb out of the ditch and walk to the edge of the trees, looking in both directions up and down the road. I wish I could take off my eye patch; only being able to see out of one eye makes everything more difficult. But I daren't.

'It's OK,' I say as Cass joins me. 'They've gone.'

She hands me my pack. 'Who were they?'

'No one we want to run into, ever.'

'Why?'

'They're rounding up Fearless,' I say.

She frowns. 'But that means they're on our side, doesn't it?'

'They're on no one's side but their own,' I say flatly. I turn to Lochie. 'What you got there, lad?'

It's a rabbit, which I tie to one of the loops on my pack by its feet. But Cass won't be so easily distracted.

'Wait,' she says as I start walking again. 'If they're rounding up the Fearless, surely that's a *good* thing? Maybe they could help us find the ones who took Jori.'

'Cass, they're not good people, OK?' I whirl around to face her, the pain from my ribs forgotten again for a moment. 'They're not interested in helping people. Especially not people like you and me. If you've got any sense you'll keep out of their way.'

She looks shocked at my outburst, but she doesn't ask any more questions, and I'm relieved, because I'm not sure I could answer her if she did. The Magpies seem to

**138**

be some sort of army, and Danny, who had a run-in with them himself not long ago, told me a lot of them come from overseas. Presumably they've been rounding Fearless up there too. He says that they're taking the ones they catch to a camp somewhere in the countryside near London – or rather, what used to be London, before the fires. But he doesn't know what they're doing with them down there. No one does.

I turn back round and start walking again, cursing myself for not getting away this morning when I had the chance, and cursing myself even more for feeling guilty that I tried.

*Guilt is good*, I remind myself. I'm terrified a day will come when I don't feel guilt any more, and I become as cold-hearted and inhuman as they are. But, dammit, it makes it so hard because the longer I let Cass tag along with me, the more danger I'm putting myself in. There's no *way* she can come back to the bunker. Somehow, we have to catch up with Mara and the other Fearless before then, and somehow, I have to get Cass's brother away from them without Mara coming to any harm – or Cass finding out that Mara's my sister.

I start to walk faster, even though it hurts my ribs. 'Come on,' I say gruffly over my shoulder. 'We've got a few hours of walking ahead of us yet.'

*And I don't want to be out here in the dark with the Magpies roaming around*, I add inside my head.

# Chapter 18

## CASS

We don't see the Magpies again after that, but a couple
of times we skirt around the edges of villages and towns.
The houses, some cloaked in ivy or creepers that have
grown unchecked, have smashed windows, crumbling
walls and sagging roofs, destroyed by the weather or the
Fearless – perhaps both. No one comes out to meet us.
I'm starting to feel as if, while I've been living on Hope,
the rest of the world has upped and vanished. Where is
everyone? Where are the Fearless?

I've got a blister on my left heel. Eventually it bursts,
making me grit my teeth every time I put my foot down.
I struggle on, reminding myself that I'm doing this for
Jori, but by late afternoon it's so sore that Myo notices me
limping. To my surprise, he makes me sit down on the
verge and take off my boot. 'Jesus,' he says when he sees
the blister. 'Why didn't you say something?'

'It's fine,' I say, although the sight of the raw pink flesh
on the back of my heel makes me feel queasy. I reach for
my pack, where I've got some basic first aid stuff – a
bandage and some seaweed salve – stashed in a side

pocket, but Myo has already pulled an old pencil case out of his satchel.

'If that gets infected, you're in trouble,' he says, taking out bandages, tape and a tube of antiseptic cream, blue with a white cross on it, like the stuff we used to have in the bathroom cabinet at home. I'm in for another surprise when, instead of thrusting the stuff at me and telling me to sort myself out, he gently cleans and dresses the blister, then helps me inch my boot back on.

'Better?' he says when I stand up again.

I test it, grimacing in anticipation, but it's not nearly as painful as before.

'Thank you,' I say.

'You're welcome.'

'What about you?' I say. 'How are your ribs?' He hasn't mentioned them all day.

'Sore,' he says. He gathers up his stuff, turning away from me again, shutting me out. Clicking his finger at Lochie, who's investigating something in a ditch, he starts walking again.

As I limp after him (both of us are hobbling now, an irony which doesn't escape me) I get a sudden, fierce ache in my throat. I don't often think about my old life – I don't let myself, because it's easier that way – but all of a sudden I have a terrible longing for things to go back to the way they used to be. Hot baths, frothing with bubbles. My soft bed in my cosy bedroom, and my bookshelves stuffed with books. Going swimming with Sol. Watching cartoons after school with Kali purring on my lap. Mum.

Dad. And instead, here I am in a cold, empty landscape with a strange boy who will barely speak to me – who tried to abandon me. My old house is probably nothing but weathered ruins now, like the ones we've passed. There's no running water, no central heating, no TV, no anything. And Mum and Dad and Kali are gone for ever.

I just hope I'm not too late to save Jori.

At last, with dusk turning the air blue around us, we round a bend and Myo points through the trees that line the road. 'There.'

I'm so tired I don't see the barbed wire strung between the tree trunks until I almost collide with it. 'Watch it!' Myo says sharply.

'How do we get through?' The strands of wire are too near to the ground to crawl under, too close together to squeeze through, and too high to climb.

'Like this.' Myo walks along the line of trees, grabbing the trunks of the smaller ones and shaking them. He reaches one that's just a little bit taller than he is, grips the trunk in both hands and pulls. The tree comes clean out of the ground and I realize it's not a tree at all – at least, not a living one. It's been turned into a fencepost: the roots have been cut away to make a sharpened point, and the branches have been left on to disguise it.

Myo pulls the post to one side. As we squeeze through, I get a prickling feeling across the backs of my hand and my neck, as if we're being watched. I turn, but no one's there. I yawn. I can't remember the last time I felt this exhausted.

Through the trees is a clearing with a tiny, ramshackle house in the centre made out of a patchwork of metal and wood. Its windows are boarded and smoke curls out of the chimney. To one side is a paddock and an outbuilding; I hear a whinny and realize it must be a stable. A lot of the barterers keep horses as they have to travel long distances.

We climb up onto the dilapidated porch, Lochie's claws scrabbling on the wood, and Myo knocks on the door. I tuck my hands into my armpits, shivering.

A few moments later the hatch in the door scrapes back. A piece of wire mesh has been fastened across the hole. Whoever this barterer is, it's clear he's taking no chances. 'Who is it?' a voice says, male and gruff.

'It's Myo and Lochie, and a friend,' Myo says.

'Myo!' the voice says. 'We were expecting you yesterday. Thought summat had happened. Wait there a minute, mate.'

The man shuts the hatch, and opens the door. He's in his thirties, with a neat beard and short brownish hair. 'Come in, quick,' he says. 'It's bloody freezing out there.'

We hurry into the house, and the man, who's carrying a lantern, frowns out at the trees for a moment before he locks the door behind us.

The first thing I notice is how warm it is. Blissfully, deliciously warm. We're in a narrow hall with all sorts of stuff stacked in neat piles – bicycle wheels, bits of furniture, pieces of wood, an old oil drum, a sweeping brush, a guitar with no strings, and who knows what else. And I can smell food cooking. My stomach growls.

'Danny, this is Cass,' Myo says without looking at me. 'Cass, Danny.'

Danny steps forward and holds out a hand for me to shake, grinning again. He's wearing patched trousers and a jumper that's coming unravelled at the cuffs. 'Nice to meet ya.' I shake his hand, and he turns his attention to Lochie. 'Hey, boy, you been keeping Myo outta trouble, then?' he says, scrubbing the dog's ears so roughly I'm surprised Lochie doesn't yelp or try to get free. Instead, he presses his face against Danny's legs.

'Daft dog.' Danny steps round Lochie and wraps Myo in a hug, thumping him on the back. Myo flinches, but he doesn't say anything. 'So what happened?' Danny says, releasing him. 'Me and April was gettin' worried. And you look like you've gone ten rounds with a Fearless.'

'Not a Fearless. I'll explain in a minute,' Myo says.

'So,' Danny says as he leads us down the hall. 'Did you find out where—'

Myo glances sideways at me. 'No. I'll talk to you about it later.'

Danny frowns. So do I. What's *that* about?

A woman appears in a doorway at the top of the hall. This must be April. She's tall and slender, with long curly hair, and for a second, she reminds me so strongly of Mum it takes my breath away. Then she steps forward and I see her hair is dark, not red. She wears combats and a jumper like Danny, and in her arms is a blanket-wrapped bundle, from which a tiny fist emerges, the

**144**

fingers opening and closing on thin air. 'Dan? Who is it?' she says squinting in the light of the lantern. I stare at her in surprise. I've never imagined the barterers living in houses and having families. I always assumed that they lived on the hop, moving from place to place to evade the Fearless.

The baby gives a cry. 'Shh, shh,' the woman soothes, jogging her up and down. When she sees Myo, a smile spreads across her face. 'Oh, thank goodness,' she says. 'We were worried.'

This time, Danny makes the introductions. The baby is called Tessie. April gives Myo an awkward, one-armed hug, and then, to my surprise, hugs me too. I look down at Tessie, who's gazing at me like I landed from another planet, her eyes round. I put out a finger and she grabs onto it. A lump rises in my throat. 'Hello, you,' I whisper. This must be the baby Myo was trying to find medicine for. 'Is she better now?' I ask April.

April frowns. 'Better?'

'She wasn't feeling well when I was here last time, was she?' Myo says.

'Well, she had colic, but—' I see April meet Myo's gaze over my shoulder, and her frown smooths out. She gives me a quick smile. 'Oh, yes, she's much better now. She had a fever, but it broke last night. Thank you.'

She and Danny take us into a little living room. It's as packed with junk as the hall: tin cans, bits of rope, pieces of cardboard, and even, I see in a corner, a stack of books. Although I'm starving and exhausted and frozen, I have an overwhelming urge to look through them. I've read the books on Hope so many times I could recite them in my sleep.

*This must be all the stuff he trades,* I think as Danny clears a space on a sagging couch. Although everything is shabby, it feels like a real home. There's even a grand-father clock in the corner, ticking ponderously, the pendulum swinging from side to side. The hands point to four forty-five.

'Sit,' Danny says. 'You must both be knackered. April, is there enough grub for all of us?'

'There can be,' she says with another of those smiles. 'Give me half an hour.'

'Here.' Myo unties the rabbit from his pack and hands it to her.

Thanking him, she passes Tessie to Danny and disappears through another door. The whole house smells comfortingly of cooking and woodsmoke. I take off my boots, sink onto the couch and close my eyes. I can't remember the last time I sat on something this soft.

'So what you been up to?' Danny asks Myo as Tessie gurgles on his lap, talking to herself in secret baby language. I keep my eyes closed. I'm so tired that if it wasn't for the hunger gnawing at my middle, I'd fall asleep in seconds.

I listen as Myo tells Danny what happened, Danny getting more and more indignant. 'They did *what*?' he says when Myo tells him about Sol beating him up. When Myo reaches the part of the story about the

**146**

Fearless man and girl following him onto the island, and Jori being taken and everyone refusing to help me get him back, Myo's voice cracks, making me open my eyes for a moment. I glance at him, but he's looking away from me.

'Are they *crazy*?' Danny says. 'They'd let a Fearless get away with one of their own? That's never right.'

I prise my eyelids open again. 'It's the rule. We don't have enough resources or weapons to go after people if they're taken, even kids . . .' I trail off, not trusting myself to say any more.

'They're a right funny lot down there,' Danny says, shaking his head. 'No offence, like, but—'

I shake my head too. 'It's OK.'

'If I'd known that was where you were going, I'd've told you not to bother,' Danny says to Myo. 'Who told you about it?'

'Shane,' Myo says. I'm guessing he means another barterer.

'Yeah, well, do us a favour and take whatever Shane says with a pinch of salt next time. He's a nice lad, but he's never been down that way. He don't know what they're like.'

'What are we like?' I say. I'm curious to hear an outsider's view of the island. 'Why do people think we're funny?'

'Just . . . suspicious, like. Won't help anyone. It's as if everyone who don't live there is Fearless. I mean, I know we all got to be careful, but you'd think the people in charge want that place to stay cut off from the rest of the world for ever.'

I remember how everyone is told as soon as they're old enough to understand the dangers that the mainland is crawling with Fearless, waiting to Alter us if we're ever stupid enough to set foot over there. And I remember how, two winters ago, the barterers stopped coming for months, and everyone assumed that their luck had run out and they'd finally all been picked off by the Fearless. Food supplies almost ran out, but Sol's dad and Captain Denning wouldn't let anyone go over to the mainland – they said there was nothing we could do but wait it out. Then, in spring, the barterers suddenly appeared again. We never found out what had happened, although there was plenty of speculation about it.

And yet . . .

Apart from Danny and April, the only people Myo and I have seen all day are the Magpies.

'Where *is* everyone?' I ask Danny. 'I thought there'd be Fearless everywhere, or that we'd come across another community, but there's no one.'

Danny frowns. 'There used to be more communities,' he says. 'Small groups, mostly in the towns and cities. But a bad flu went round the winter before last, and then the measles. It wiped a lot of 'em out – apart from Myo's lot, there's only a few groups left now, one in Wales and a couple up north that I know of. 'Course, if we still had hospitals and the like, it would have been a different story, but . . .' He shrugs. 'We both got the flu pretty bad ourselves, but we were lucky and avoided the measles. I guess your lot must have been all right too, what with being isolated on that island.'

I stare at him. So that's why no one came that winter. Epidemics like that have always been Hope Island's biggest fear. Like Danny said, our isolation from the mainland must have kept the illnesses away. But how could something on that scale have happened and we didn't know?

*Perhaps Sol's dad and the Patrol did know, and kept the barterers away,* a little voice in my head says. *And they wouldn't let anyone go to the mainland because they were scared they might bring the illnesses back.*

But if that's so, why didn't they tell us what was going on? Why did they let us nearly starve, thinking the barterers were gone for ever?

'What about the Fearless?' I say. 'Did the flu and the measles get them too?'

Danny shakes his head. 'Nah. Illness don't seem to affect 'em like that. It's the serum that's doin' for 'em.'

'Myo said it's not as strong as when the Invasion first happened – that it takes longer to Alter people now.'

'Yeah. There's no one with the facilities to make the real thing any more – all the scientists who made the drug originally are dead or Altered or gone – so the Fearless brew up something themselves. It'll Alter anyone they give it to who's not had it before, but after that it wrecks 'em proper quick. 'Cos the cravings are so bad, they have to keep takin' it – drives 'em mad otherwise – but

**149**

eventually it rots 'em from the inside out. It ain't pretty.'

'What do they make it out of?' My voice is shaking as I remember the filthy bandages around the Fearless man's arms and head, his blackened teeth and the terrible stench coming off him.

'Who knows. But if you can get your brother back before he Alters, he might be OK.'

'Do you think that's why they took him?' I say. 'Because the drug's making them ill, and they want to make new Fearless? Because otherwise they'd've killed him straight away, right?'

'I reckon,' Danny says. 'I've heard about other people getting taken recently – young 'uns like your brother, mostly. Most of 'em – the Fearless, that is – stick together these days. My guess is the two who took your brother will be taking him to one of their hideouts somewhere to start giving him the drug.'

'But why kids?'

'Couldn't tell ya. Might be because they're younger – stronger.'

I feel sick. 'But why don't they just have kids, then?'

'This new stuff made 'em infertile, or so they say. And most of the original Fearless have been takin' it too, so . . .' Danny shrugs.

I stare at the tabletop. 'But *why*? Why keep trying to make new Fearless?'

'People think it's another effect of the serum,' says April, who's come to check on Tessie. 'That it gives them this compulsion to make others like them, even though the drug is a death sentence. Of course, no one's actually *studied* them – how could they? But that's our best guess.'

As she goes back into the kitchen, I carry on staring at the table, trying – and failing – to process all this information.

'We think the two who got him are taking him to Sheffield,' Myo cuts in.

'To the Torturehouse?'

'Aye.'

Danny's frown deepens. 'And if you don't get this kid back before, you're going up there?'

Myo gives me another one of those sideways glances, like he did out in the hall. 'Maybe.'

Danny raises his eyebrows, but doesn't say anything.

Shortly after that, April comes back through to tell us the food's ready. In the kitchen, a pot is bubbling merrily on top of an iron wood-stove. At first, I don't think I'm going to be able to eat anything – my stomach is in knots after my conversation with Danny – but the smells coming from the pot are so delicious that I start getting hunger pangs again. Danny places Tessie in a cradle near the stove, and then we sit down at a table in the corner while April fills bowls with a thick stew that contains beans, lentils and shreds of meat from Myo's rabbit. Lochie gets some too, pushing his bowl around with his nose as he tries to hoover up every last molecule.

'Did you see if that . . . person was still lurking around in the woods when you answered the door?' April asks Danny as we scrape our own bowls clean.

Danny shakes his head.

'What person?' Myo asks.

'There was someone hanging around on the road earlier,' Danny says. 'No idea who. You didn't see anyone, did you?'

Myo shakes his head too. 'We saw Magpies earlier, but that's all.'

Danny makes a face. 'Those crazy bastards. I hope you didn't let them see you.'

'No fear,' Myo says.

'Are you two going to stop here for the night?' April says. 'It's bitter out there.'

'If that's OK,' Myo says.

'Of course.'

'I need to ask another favour, too,' Myo says, glancing at me. 'You said you might be taking the horses up north in a couple of days . . .'

Revived by the food and warmth, I'm more alert now, so I see the look that passes between Danny and April. My heart sinks.

'I've decided not to go,' Danny says at last. 'The weather's supposed to be getting worse up there – they say snow's coming. If I didn't have Tessie to think about, of course I'd take you, but I can't risk getting stuck. April needs me here.' He turns to look at me, his expression filled with regret. 'I'm sorry, love.'

'It's fine,' I say dully. 'I understand.' My heart sinks even further as I contemplate the days of walking Myo and I have in store. The Fearless don't need as much rest or sleep as we do. They're probably way ahead of us already. There's no way I'll get to my brother in time.

A gloomy silence falls. Seeing Myo stifle a yawn, April says, 'Would you two like to get some sleep?'

I nod. So does Myo. He looks exhausted.

April takes us back through to the living room, where she clears the rest of the stuff off the couch. 'One of you'll have to sleep on the floor. We've got plenty of blankets, though.'

Before she leaves, she hangs a lantern on a hook near the door. I make Myo take the couch, even though I'm still annoyed with him about this morning, and spread my blankets out near the piles of books. After applying some more antiseptic cream to my heel, I lie down, listening to the rhythmic clunk-tick of the clock and thinking about Jori. Where will he be sleeping tonight?

Lochie pads across to me and flops down against my back with a grunt. I tense. Myo laughs. 'If he's squashing you, give him a shove. He won't mind.'

Give Lochie a shove? Is he *crazy*? I stare up at the ceiling, my body rigid. Lochie give an enormous sigh and relaxes against me.

Eventually, I relax too. It's quite nice having him there; he's like a big, hairy hot water bottle. I close my eyes and drift off to sleep.

Myo and I are walking again. It's just past dawn, the air still, everything silver with frost. We don't speak. Lochie lopes silently alongside us. There's an atmosphere of tension, of waiting, hanging around us like smoke.

I hear a buzzing sound.

Engines.

*Magpies.*

Fear bursts through me as I remember what Myo said yesterday. *They're not interested in helping people. Especially not people like you and me.* 'We have to get off the road,' I tell him in a low, urgent voice, but he keeps walking, head down, like he hasn't even heard me. Lochie doesn't respond either. 'Myo!'

The engines grow louder. I scream Myo's name, trying to get him to look at me, and when he won't, I try to run. But all of a sudden, I can't move. I look down and see that the ice on the road has crept over my boots, freezing me to the tarmac. As I struggle to get free, it spreads, running up my legs in a crazed spider-web pattern. I can feel the cold biting into my flesh through the fabric of my trousers, and as the sound of the jeeps gets closer, I realize that this is something the Magpies have engineered, that they've done this so they can catch me. *But I'm not Fearless!* I scream. I look at Myo, but he and Lochie aren't there; they've run off into the woods and left me. The ice has got to my waist. I'm so cold. Soon it will reach my throat, and then my mouth, and then it'll creep down into my throat and lungs, and I'll die . . .

Suddenly, Lochie bursts out of the trees behind me, giving a deep bark.

I sit up, gasping for breath.

Lochie's no longer lying beside me. I must have been

asleep for a while because, although the lantern's still burning, I've kicked the blankets off myself and the house has gone cold.

I look over at the couch. Myo's sitting up, frowning at the door, where Lochie's got his nose to the crack at the bottom. Suddenly, Lochie barks again – the sound I heard in my dream.

'Why is he barking?' I whisper.

'Dunno. He must have heard something.'

We both fall silent, listening, but all I can hear is the thud of my pulse in my ears.

'Lochie,' Myo hisses. 'Come here.'

He starts to growl.

Myo stands up. 'What is it? Who's there?'

My heart thudding, I reach for my boots and my knife, which I left inside them. Myo grabs his knife too, and goes over to the door, opening it a little.

I grab the lantern off the hook. Then I hear something – metal scratching against metal, a tiny, secretive sound. It's coming from down the hall.

'Is that Danny?' I whisper. Feet thud on the floor above our heads; first one pair, then another, quicker and lighter. Lochie's still growling, a deep rumbling in his chest. I hear Danny coming down the stairs. 'Myo?' he calls. 'Is everything OK? I heard the dog—'

There's a bang, and a flash of light. A gunshot.

Then a shout from Danny as the door's flung open and whoever's out there bursts inside.

# Chapter 19

## MYO

Lochie goes crazy, baying and trying to lunge past me. I wrap my arms around his neck, wincing as pain shoots through my side. Danny shouts something.

'Where is it?' I hear a rough, flat voice say in between Lochie's barks.

'Where's what?' Danny says.

'The baby. I know you have one. I heard it crying.'

It's a Fearless. Maybe even the Fearless who took Cass's brother and who's with Mara, the one we've been trying to track down. Danny said there was someone hanging around on the road earlier. *Christ.*

Cass must be thinking the same thing, 'cos she whispers, 'Myo, what if—'

'Shh!' I say as Danny tells the Fearless, 'Get out of my house.' My mind's racing. Has Danny got a gun? If this is the Fearless who was with Mara, I need to get to him, find out what he's done with her – and Cass's wee brother.

'Stay here,' I tell Cass. 'Hang onto Lochie.'

She puts her arms around his neck. Gripping my knife,

I open the door just wide enough to get through. Lochie barks again and yanks out of Cass's arms and through the door. '*Lochie!*' I yell, running after him. The Fearless man lashes out with the butt of his gun, catching Lochie hard on the side of the head. He yelps and drops to the floor like a sack of rocks.

'The baby,' the Fearless says in that droning voice as Cass comes rushing up behind me. Danny isn't holding anything except a lantern, and no way is my knife gonna stand up to a bullet. *Shit*.

'We don't have a baby here,' Danny says.

Upstairs, Tessie begins to wail.

I look at Cass. Her face is white and strained. 'That's him,' she murmurs. 'That's the one who took Jori.'

*So where the hell is Mara?* I think. Lochie's still lying on the floor near the door, not moving. I'm desperate to go to him, but the Fearless is pointing the gun at all of us. Mebbe I could try throwing my knife and knocking it out of his hand. But it's hard to judge distances properly when I can only see out of one eye. If I missed and hit Lochie I'd never forgive myself.

The Fearless fixes his dull gaze on Danny. 'The baby. Now.'

Tessie's still crying. 'April!' Danny yells over his shoulder. 'Don't come down here!'

The Fearless is still staring at Danny. I glance at Cass again, and nod towards the Fearless. Her eyes widen. *He has a gun,* she mouths. *He's not looking at us*, I mouth back.

She presses her lips together. Then, very slowly,

she puts the lantern down on the floor, out of the way.

'Give me the baby, and I'll let you live,' the Fearless drones at Danny. The stench coming off him is awful and his skin looks grey, tinged with green. The thought of Mara ending up like this living zombie makes me sick to my stomach.

I give Cass a nod.

We charge at the Fearless, slamming into him and sending him staggering backwards, the gun dropping out of his hand and clattering to the floor. He's way stronger than me, even with the Fearless drug rotting him from the inside out.

'No . . . you . . . don't.' I force his arm back against the wall. He roars, trying to bite my cheek and blasting me with his hot, stinking breath.

'Jesus, you need to clean your teeth,' I tell him. I don't know how much longer we can hold him. 'Danny,' I say over my shoulder. 'Get April and Tessie out of here. Go.'

Then someone runs through the door, bending to snatch up the gun and sprinting up the stairs. The figure is moving so fast all I get is a glimpse of blue fabric and long black hair.

Danny gives a shout and chases after them. 'No!' I yell. The Fearless yanks his arm free. He punches Cass and she crashes to the floor beside Lochie, her knife spinning out of her hand. I head-butt him as hard as I can. As I stumble back, rubbing my forehead, the Fearless slumps face-first to the floor.

Lochie whines; he's beginning to come round. I check

on him first – no blood, thank Christ – then reach down to help Cass to her feet.

'Where's Jori? Is he here?' she says in a groggy voice. Upstairs, I hear Danny shout, then two bangs – the gun being fired.

I leave Cass leaning against the wall and run up to the bedroom. Danny's standing by the bed, still holding his lamp, his free hand pressed to his side. He's breathing hard, and his face is grey. I can't see April or Tessie anywhere.

Mara is standing in the middle of the room, holding the gun.

'Mara!' I say. She turns her head, fixing her silver eyes on me.

'Mara, it's me. Put the gun down.'

She doesn't give any sign that she recognizes me. She turns away again. Her hair is tangled and greasy. Where it parts at the back of her neck, I can see a raw red puncture mark.

'Oh, Jesus, Mara,' I moan.

Danny's eyes go wide. 'I thought you said you hadn't found her.'

'I hadn't.' Glancing behind me, I lower my voice, aware that Cass could come up the stairs any minute. 'She's one of the Fearless who took Cass's brother. We were tracking them.'

Danny's still staring at me. I can tell he doesn't believe me. Under his fingers, a dark stain is starting to seep through his shirt.

'*Mara*,' I hiss as she steps towards the bed. She must be taking the drug again, 'cos her serum sickness is gone. She'd get so bad, nothing could touch it; even the sedatives Gina found in the bunker's infirmary didn't help. All we could do was lock her in her room and ignore her screams. Now, her movements are strong and steady again.

*How am I gonna get her out of here with Cass around?* I think.

Then I hear a faint cry, coming from the other side of the bed.

Mara smiles.

'*No!*' Danny drops the lamp. It shatters and goes out, and for a moment, I can't see anything.

Mara screeches. I tug off my eyepatch and everything turns to grainy black and white. Danny's half across the bed, struggling. He's got a handful of Mara's hair, holding her head back, and in his other hand – God knows where it came from – is a knife with a long, curved blade.

'No, leave her!' I yell, leaping towards them, just as Mara gives another screech and lashes out, smacking Danny in the face and making him fall back across the bed. The knife flies from his hand. Mara bends down and gathers something up in her arms, jumping across the bed with it in two leaps. I try to grab her, and she slams into me hard enough to send me staggering back against the wall, knocking all the air out of my lungs and sending a bolt of pain through my ribs.

As I slide to the floor, groaning and clutching my side, she runs out of the room and she's gone.

# Chapter 20

## CASS

I knew as soon as Myo and I tried to pin the Fearless against the wall that the self-defence training I'd had in the Junior Patrol was useless. Those moves would work on an ordinary person, sure – maybe one of the Magpies, if what Myo said about them was true – but not a Fearless. His strength was terrifying. He looked half-dead, yet power thrummed through his skinny body like an electric current. How Myo managed to hold on to him for so long, never mind knock him out, I have no idea. Thinking about how close I came to being Fearless food makes black spots swim in front of my vision, as if I've been punched in the head all over again.

He starts to come round just after Myo runs up the stairs after the second Fearless, and I'm still so groggy from being knocked out myself that it's instinct rather than reason that makes me snatch up my knife and slam the blade into the back of his neck at the top of his spine. He takes for ever to die, just like the Fearless who tried to swim after us the night of the Invasion. I must have cut through his spinal cord, because he can't move his arms or legs any more, but he snarls a stream of gibberish at me, his blackened teeth gnashing together as blood wells up around the blade, which has gone in all the way to the hilt. As I back away from him, sick and shaking, my head pounding, Lochie scrabbles to his feet and hurries back into the front room, ears down, back hunched, tail tucked between his legs.

At last, the Fearless lets out a bubbling sigh and goes still.

Someone comes thundering down the stairs – the Fearless girl. She's got Tessie tucked under one arm like a doll. Before I can do anything, she rushes past me and out of the door.

'*Hey!*' I scream. If the girl's here, Jori must be nearby – he could be just outside the house. I dash out onto the porch, frantically calling my brother's name again, although it's too dark to see anything. But there's no answer. And no sign of the girl.

A few moments later Myo comes running out onto the porch too, clutching his ribs. In the light spilling out of the house I can see his face is flushed, his hair hanging messily across. When he reaches me he stops, his arms falling to his sides.

'*Shit.*' He slumps onto the porch steps, burying his face in his hands. His eyepatch is threaded between his fingers.

I stare out into the darkness. My mind is screaming at me to carry on chasing the girl, but I know it's already too late. Moving that fast, she'll be long gone.

I close my eyes and see myself slamming the knife into

the back of the Fearless's neck again, feel the blade grating against bone and gristle. A wave of nausea rolls over me and the pain in my head becomes a white-hot needle between my eyes. I lean over the porch railing, retching.

By the time we get back inside and I've closed the front door behind me, Myo's put his eyepatch back on.

'Where's Lochie?' he says.

'He went back in the front room. Where's Danny?'

'Upstairs. I think he's been shot.'

'We have to see if he's OK.' I pick up the lantern and we run up to the bedroom.

Danny's doubled over on the bed, his face a mask of pain. As I crouch down beside him, he moves his hand, and I see the palm is slick with blood.

I look round at Myo. 'Where's April?'

He turns towards me, and when I see his expression, I understand.

I go round the bed. April's lying on the floor by the wall, her eyes open, her throat a ragged, bloody mess of tendons and gristle. The girl must have shot her, too. More bile rises in my throat.

'We need bandages,' I say, turning away from April with a huge effort and forcing myself to sound calm and practical. 'And boiling water.' I'm this close to losing it completely; my hands are shaking; I feel hot and cold all over.

Myo nods. He's shaking too.

I go back over to Danny. 'Can you stand up?' I ask

him. I know it's dangerous to move him but we need to get him out of this room, away from his murdered wife.

Between us, we pull Danny to his feet and walk him over to the door, Myo holding the lamp. 'Shit,' Danny whispers. '*Shit*.'

'You'll be OK,' Myo says. Danny tries to look round for April, but I gently steer him out onto the landing so he doesn't see her.

'Are they all right?' he says, panic rising in his voice as we help him to the top of the stairs.

'They're fine. We'll see to them in a minute,' I say. 'Can you make it downstairs?'

Somehow, we get him down to the front room, where Lochie is standing in a corner, back hunched, quivering all over. Myo lets go of Danny and crouches beside him, murmuring, 'Are you OK? Did he hurt you?'

'Help me get Danny onto the couch.' I'm amazed at how steady my voice sounds. 'Then we'll sort Lochie out too.'

'Where are April and Tessie?' Danny keeps asking after we've eased him onto the couch. 'Where are they?' He has a glazed, distant expression, his skin a funny bluish colour. Myo helps me pull up his shirt and jumper. There's so much blood I can't see the wound underneath properly.

'Can you light the stove?' I ask Myo. 'We need some warm water.' I grab a cushion and press it against the wound, trying to stop the bleeding.

With another agonized glance at Lochie, Myo goes into the kitchen.

'Cold,' Danny says suddenly. 'I'm c–cold.' He's shivering harder now, his teeth clattering together.

'I know,' I say. 'Myo's getting the stove going.'

'Where are Tessie and April?' He stares at me with terror in his eyes. 'I need to see them – I need to know if they're all right.'

He tries to get up, sending the cushion tumbling to the floor. With an effort, I push him back down onto the sofa. 'You have to stay still,' I tell him. I pick up the cushion and hold it back in place. Danny mutters, his face twisting.

Myo comes back through. 'Water's heating up. How is he?'

'Delirious.'

'He's lost too much blood.'

'Can't we stop it?'

'I don't know.' He scrubs a hand through his hair until it's standing on end. 'Maybe we should forget about cleaning it and tie that cushion on with something.'

Even though the window is boarded, a pair of faded curtains hangs across them. I rip one down, and Myo cuts a wide strip off it so I can bind the cushion against Danny's side. As we finish, I hear a whistling sound coming from the kitchen. 'That's the kettle,' Myo says.

As he goes into the kitchen to take it off the stove, Lochie comes over. He doesn't seem as unsteady on his feet now, but his tail is still tucked between his legs.

Glancing at Danny, who's gone quiet, I gingerly feel the dog's head for cuts. Although he has a lump above his eye, the skin isn't broken.

'I think you'll be OK,' I murmur, rubbing his neck like I've seen Myo do. I'm both startled and pleased when he puts his head down and leans against me with a groan. By the time Myo comes back in the room, he's stopped trembling.

'How bad is it?' Myo says.

'He's fine,' I say. 'Aren't you, boy?'

Lochie stretches up and swipes his tongue across the end of my nose.

The ghost of a smile flickers across Myo's lips as I wipe my face with my sleeve. 'That's it, you're proper pals now,' he says. Lochie goes to him for another neck rub, then flops down on the blankets I was sleeping on and puts his head between his paws.

Danny's eyes are still closed, his chin resting on his chest. 'Danny,' Myo says softly. There's no response. I press two fingers against the barterer's neck. He has a pulse, but it's rapid and faint. His breathing's rapid too, and wheezy-sounding.

It takes him three hours to die. His breathing gets shallower, his pulse weaker, and he starts to make an awful rattling sound in his throat. It goes on and on. Myo and I sit either side of him, waiting until the rattling stops, and the only sound in the room is the hollow ticking of the grandfather clock.

'*Shit.*' Myo turns and punches the couch arm.

Lochie whines. I look at the clock and see it's almost five a.m.

'I need some air,' Myo says in a hoarse voice, standing up and rubbing his hand across his face. He walks out of the room before I can say anything.

I gaze at Danny. Twelve hours ago, he was inviting us into his home, introducing us to his wife and showing off his baby daughter. We were sitting at his kitchen table, eating stew.

And now all three of them are gone.

I get up too, grab the lantern, and go after Myo.

He's outside on the porch, his back to the house. His shoulders are shaking. When he looks round at me, I see his face is wet with tears.

I set the lamp down and touch his arm, and for a moment – just a moment – I feel something pass between us, a jolt of electricity that makes my skin tingle.

Then he steps back. The spell breaks.

'I have to do something for them,' he says, swiping at his face with the backs of his hands. 'I can't leave them here. They were my friends.' His voice is cracked, full of pain.

'Can we bury them?' My heart is thudding; I feel flustered and weirdly guilty.

'The ground's too hard. We'd never manage it.'

Then, from the stable at the side of the house, I hear the horses nickering. I'd forgotten all about them. I look at Myo, and he looks back at me.

'Right, this is what we're going to do.' His voice is still

raw. 'We'll take the horses. We'll get to the bunker quicker if we ride. We'll take some supplies, too – we'll need them if there's snow coming. But before that, we'll get that bastard Fearless out of the house. And—'

He swallows, looks away from me for a moment. I wait for him to compose himself.

'And then we'll torch the place,' he says at last. 'I can't just leave them there to . . . you know.'

As I pick up the lantern, Lochie pads out onto the porch and sticks his nose into Myo's hand, then mine, as if sensing we need comforting. I stroke his neck again. I don't feel scared of him any more, despite his size. It seems strange to think that I ever was.

We gather supplies first, replenishing our packs with whatever food we can find in the kitchen, and more first aid stuff from a kit under the sink. The Fearless is still lying face-down on the floor near the front door, the knife handle sticking out of the back of his neck. Before we take him outside, I reach down, pull it out and wipe the blade on my trouser leg. The horror of the last few hours has numbed me. No point in wasting a good knife on a monster like that.

The body is heavier than it looks; rigor mortis has started to set in, making getting it down the porch steps a slow, awkward business. We drop it on the ground near the fence. Then we go to the stable, taking a lantern each and a set of keys I found hanging up in the kitchen. 'Do you know how to ride?' I ask Myo as I undo the door.

'Aye,' he says. 'Danny showed me one summer. How about you?'

I nod. 'I had lessons before the Invasion.'

The stable smells of hay and dung and horse, a familiar smell which give me a rush of longing for my old life. Near the door, there are racks full of tools and tack, and at the far end are two stalls with horses tethered inside. One is brown with a white blaze on its face, and the other is black with white patches all over, their coats shaggy and long to protect them against the cold. As we walk across, the piebald snorts and stamps its feet, its ears back, its eyes wide.

'Shh.' Myo slips in beside it, laying a hand against its face. 'They're spooked,' he says. 'They must've heard the noise earlier.'

When the piebald has quietened down, he takes his hand away. 'This is Apollo, and the bay is called Flicka. We'll need food for them – can you see what's in those bins in the corner?'

There's a row of them, metal with numbers painted on the sides. I prise off the lids and see they contain grain. Myo and I find some hessian sacks and fill them with as much as we think Apollo, the biggest, can comfortably carry, packing them into a set of saddlebags. 'There's an abandoned farm on our route – I used it for shelter on my way down,' Myo says as we grab some full hay nets. 'It has a barn that's still got hay in it. It's years old but I reckon it'll be better than nothing if they've got through all this lot by then.'

I put bridles and rugs on both horses, saddle them and load them up with our supplies, and we lead them outside, tethering them to the fence around the paddock.

Myo and I look at the house.

'We should move April downstairs,' he says. 'Danny would want to be with her.'

It's an unpleasant task; April's body is also stiffening, pooling blood turning the backs of her arms and legs purple. We wrap her in a blanket, propping her up on the couch beside Danny.

Myo takes a box of matches from his pocket. 'I won't be long.'

I carry our packs outside. After a while, smoke begins to drift out of the front door. Just as I'm starting to wonder where Myo's got to, if I should go back in, he walks out onto the porch, his eyes streaming, his face grim. He's carrying the Fearless's gun.

'Didn't think this should go to waste,' he says, putting the strap over his head and coughing. Inside the house, I can hear the fire spitting as it takes hold. With all the stuff in there, it won't be long before the whole place is alight.

'We'd better get out of here.' Myo untethers the horses and I give him a leg up onto Apollo before mounting Flicka. As soon as I'm in the saddle, my body remembers what to do; it feels quite natural to pick up the reins and squeeze my legs against the horse's side to get her moving. The gap in the fence is already open – it looks like the two Fearless got in that way too – and we ease through it and out onto the road, Lochie leading the way.

It's still dark, but we have our lanterns, and their light is strong enough for us to be able to make out where we're going. Frost has formed again, and the horses' hooves ring against the icy surface of the road. 'Better go steady,' I say. 'We don't want them to slip. Can we cut across country a bit once it gets light?'

Myo nods. Before we ride away, I take one last look over my shoulder. Through the web of tree branches behind us, I can see the orange glow of the flames consuming the house, sparks flying up into the air, and hear the wood popping and cracking. Sadness and anger squeeze inside my chest, forming a tight band around my ribs. *I hate the Fearless*, I think. *HATE them.*

Where's Jori right now? The thought of how close he must have been when the Fearless man and the girl broke into the house makes me feel sick with despair. That girl is taking him and Tessie to the Torturehouse *right now*. We *have* to catch up with her.

And when I find her, I'm going to take that gun hanging around Myo's neck, and I'm going to shoot her right between the eyes.

# Chapter 21

## SOL

In the morning, when I open my eyes, everything's OK for a moment.

Then I remember.

*She's gone.*

*I might never see her again.*

I sit up and grind my fists into my eyes. Yesterday was horrible – hours spent on watch on the sea wall with no one to talk to, nothing to do except stare at the sea and think about Cass. It took me hours to fall asleep last night, too, and when I did, I dreamed about *him*. He and Cass were sitting together in someone's house, a fire burning in a grate nearby. They were talking, laughing. Cass was smiling at him in a way she's never smiled at me.

She preferred *him* to me.

I get up, pace across the room. It's still dark – about half an hour to go until first bell, by my reckoning – but Dad's sleeping mat is empty. Either he's in his office already, or he spent the night there. He does that a lot. The island is more important to him than his son, I guess.

I don't know why I even bother getting angry about it any more.

*Cass. Cass. Cass.* I'm still the only one who knows what's really happened to her. Everyone else, including Captain Denning and my father, thinks she's been kidnapped. I did a pretty good job of spreading that story round yesterday, acting all grief-stricken about it, and because everyone was weeping and wailing over Patroller Cary, who is going to be buried at sea later today, they were quite happy to weep and wail over Cass and Jori, too.

Inside, though, I was furious – with her for going off with him, and *him* for ever coming here in the first place. I wonder where they are now, and what on earth he said to make her believe he'd help her. *Oh, Cass,* I think for what must be the hundredth time. *I never thought you could be* that *gullible.* Her note is hidden in a book on the shelf by my bed. I can't get rid of it; it's the last connection I have to her. A memorial's been planned for her, Jori and Patroller Cary next week, and my father's asked me to do a reading because Cass and I were friends for so long (*stop talking about her in the goddamn past tense!* I wanted to scream in his face when he suggested it). God knows what I'll say.

As I get dressed, the Meeting Hall bell begins to clang. I grab my armband and head down to the Refectory to have breakfast before I go on duty. Another day of staring out to sea. *Great.*

To make matters worse, it's raining. Standing at my

post above the jetty, I glare across the water, hunched up under an oilskin, my gun cradled in my arms. With Cass gone, this feels like a waste of time. All I want to do is take a boat and go after her, shoot that freak in the head.

Only, of course, I can't. I'm stuck on this stupid island, without Cass, for ever.

And there's absolutely nothing I can do about it.

Down the wall, Patroller Yuen whistles, pointing out to sea. Squinting, I see a shape emerging from the curtains of rain obscuring the view of the docks.

A boat.

An incredulous grin spreads across my face. It's her. She's back. *She's back.* I want to whoop, punch the air.

But as the boat gets closer, my grin fades. It's much too large to be one of ours. There are three people inside, not two, and it has an engine. Where did they get the fuel?

As they get closer, I see one of the people inside is a man, one is a woman, and the third is wrapped from head to toe in a blanket, their face covered up. The man and woman are wearing uniforms – black coats and trousers and caps.

Not Cass. And they're not barterers, either.

I thumb the safety back on my gun.

'*Ahoy there! Turn around!*' Patroller Yuen shouts through cupped hands, her voice echoing across the water. '*You are not welcome here!*'

'*Go and fetch Simon Brightman!*' the man, a guy about

my father's age with a jagged scar down one cheek, shouts back. '*Tell him David Brett wants to speak to him!*'

'*I said, turn around!*' Patroller Yuen aims her gun at the boat, although it's out of range. I point mine that way too, my heart beating faster at the mention of my father's name. How does this David Brett know him? How does he know he's here? And why is the third person on board wrapped in a blanket? Are they ill? I grip my gun harder, my finger resting on the trigger.

'*This is your final warning!*' Patroller Yuen shouts. '*Turn back, or we'll shoot!*'

'*Fetch Simon Brightman, or we'll shoot!*' David Brett cuts the engine, and the woman lifts something out of the bottom of the boat, hefting it onto her shoulder. I only know what it is because when I was younger, before the Invasion, I was obsessed with the military, and a cousin bought me a huge book full of different weapons and machines which I'd spend hours poring over, dreaming of the day when I'd be old enough to join the army.

It's a surface-to-air missile.

Or, to be exact, a FIM-92 Stinger — a personal portable infrared homing surface-to-air missile.

My mouth goes dry. I run along the wall, yelling, 'Don't shoot at them! *Don't shoot!*'

'Listen to the boy!' David Brett calls as I reach Patroller Yuen, a smile curving his lips. I scowl. Who does he think he's calling a *boy*?

'Is that what I think it is?' Patroller Yuen mutters out of the corner of her mouth, slowly lowering her gun.

'Yes,' I say. 'And if they fire it, they'll annihilate half the island.'

She turns and looks at me. 'Go and get your father.'

'What? No – he won't—'

Patroller Yuen's expression grows cold. 'Patroller Brightman, I am giving you a direct order. Do as I ask, *now*.'

I glare at her for a moment, then remember that for the first three months I'm in the Patrol, I'm on probation. And I can't afford to mess up. Not unless I want to get redeployed to Maintenance, or, worse still, stuck in the school helping look after all the bratty little kids.

'Yes, Patroller.' With an effort, I resist the urge to inject sarcasm into my tone, and jump down off the wall. Who the hell do those people on that boat think they are, coming here and threatening us like this? How do they know my father? And where on earth did they get a Stinger from? Are they ex-army?

As always, the door to my father's office is closed. I barge in without knocking.

'Sol!' he says, jumping. 'Why didn't you—'

'Because there's a crazy guy with a missile launcher sitting in a boat out in the channel, asking to speak to you.'

'What?' My father reaches for his stick. 'Sol, if this is your idea of a joke . . .'

'He's asking for you *personally*. He says his name's David Brett.'

I'm expecting my father to say he's never heard of him. Instead, his eyes widen. 'What?'

'So you know him?'

'I – yes.'

'You'd better hurry up before he decides to fire a rocket at the Meeting Hall or the apartments, then,' I say, turning on my heel and walking out.

I return to the sea wall, where Patroller Yuen is waiting. 'He's on his way,' I tell her.

Patroller Yuen relays the message to David Brett, who nods and folds his arms. The woman behind him keeps the Stinger trained on the island. When my father arrives, Patroller Yuen helps him up onto the wall. He squints out at the boat.

'Ahoy, Brightman!' David Brett calls, waving.

I hear my father swear under his breath. He doesn't wave back.

'What do you want?' he calls.

'To talk to you!'

'Why?'

'We have a proposition to make to you!'

'Who's that in the blanket?'

'Don't worry, he isn't sick,' David Brett says. 'I think you might be interested to meet him, though.'

My father's frown deepens. 'Let them onto the island,' he tells Patroller Yuen. 'Bring them to my office. And tell someone at the Refectory to bring us coffee. Cake, too, if we have any.'

'What?' Patroller Yuen says.

**177**

'Do it.' My father climbs awkwardly down off the wall again and limps back in the direction of the Meeting Hall.

Patroller Yuen stares after him for a moment. Then she calls to David Brett, 'Bring your boat in!'

David Brett grins. Gunning the boat's engine, he brings it alongside the jetty and ties it up, and he and the other occupants disembark, the woman carrying the Stinger. That's when I notice the second man has a chain snaking out from under his blanket. Brett has the other end wrapped tightly round one hand. He tugs on it as he marches up the jetty, and the man stumbles. His gait is awkward and shambling.

'Patroller Brightman, show these people the way to the Meeting Hall, and go to the Refectory,' Patroller Yuen tells me. Brett looks up at me, his eyes narrowed. 'You Brightman's son?'

I narrow my eyes too. Brett smiles. 'Thought so. You look just like him.'

'Patroller!' Patroller Yuen snaps.

Curling my hands into fists, I nod, bristling inside at being used as an errand boy. If my father wants to give these people coffee and cake, why can't he go and ask for it his damn self?

As I lead them across the island, I notice the stench. It's coming off the man wrapped in the blanket, thick and rotten. I have to swallow to keep from gagging. What *is* that? They said he wasn't sick, but he smells like death.

Instead of heading to the Refectory, I stay with them,

clutching my gun. Inside my father's office, the smell is overpowering. My father coughs and covers his mouth and nose with his hand.

'What's wrong with him?' I demand before anyone else can speak. 'Why is he covered up like that? He *stinks*.'

'Oh, that.' Brett shrugs. 'Yes, he does, I'm afraid. He hasn't been looking after himself. But he's getting the care he needs now.'

'*Who* is, David?' my father says as I wonder again how on earth he knows this man and what Brett wants with him.

Brett looks at the woman, who hefts the Stinger into a more comfortable position on her shoulder and raises her eyebrows briefly.

Gripping the chain tightly, Brett pulls the blanket off the second man.

My father and I gasp simultaneously. He's pale, hollow-cheeked, his thinning hair lying lank against his scalp. Around his neck is a metal cuff with a bandage underneath it, yellowish fluid leaking from beneath the gauze and soaking into the collar of his threadbare shirt.

But it's his eyes that have caught my attention. They're silver, with enormous pupils.

He's a Fearless.

My father scrabbles under his desk, pulling out a pistol, and I jerk my shotgun up, finger ready on the trigger.

Brett laughs and puts a hand on the barrel of my gun, pushing it back down. 'Calm down, both of you. This one wouldn't hurt a fly.'

I look again at the Fearless and see its expression is dull and vacant. It's just standing there with its arms hanging by its sides and its mouth slightly open, like someone got inside its head and turned off all the lights.

Slowly, my father lowers his gun too. 'How—'

'I'll explain once we get that coffee,' Brett says, glancing at me, but I stay where I am.

'Why have you brought him here?' my father demands.

Brett gives another one of those smiles. 'You helped create them, Simon. Now's your chance to help us make things right.'

# Chapter 22

## CASS

After we leave Danny and April's, Myo estimates we have nearly two hundred more miles to travel. The first day passes like a strange dream: we don't see anyone, and we don't talk much, either. I'm not angry with Myo any more – how can I be after he stopped the Fearless from killing me? – but he's wrapped up in his thoughts, and I'm wrapped up in mine. That night, we shelter in the remains of a collapsed house, Apollo and Flicka tethered close by outside while Myo and I take turns to sleep and keep watch.

The next morning, the landscape starts to look familiar, but it's not until I see the hill in front of us that I realize why.

My heart and stomach jolt, as if I'm walking down a flight of stairs and I've missed the last one.

Myo, who's leading, looks over his shoulder at me. 'The road goes straight through the middle of the village here. But it should be safe. There wasn't anyone here when I came through before.'

I nod, not trusting myself to speak. Five minutes later I see the sign, leaning to one side and rusted, but still readable: *Welcome to Blythefield*.

In my head, Blythefield is the same as when Mum, Sol, his parents and I left: a row of pretty cottages along the road, the shop and the post office opposite the little green with the duck pond in the middle, the primary school, church and village hall clustered near the lane which led up to my family's and the Brightmans' houses.

But now the road is cracked and potholed and weedy, and the cottages are empty and ruined – windows smashed, doors hanging off, gardens overgrown, roofs sagging from years of bad weather and no maintenance, a tree felled by a storm lying across the wreckage of what was once a beautiful barn conversion belonging to a friend of Mum and Dad's. Cars, some burned out and crumpled, are parked haphazardly across the road. The post office is a shell, the whole front of the building reduced to soot-stained rubble, and there's a van in the pond, which is sludgy and coated with a thin rime of ice.

Everything looks cold and grey and dead.

As we get closer to the turning for my lane, I grip my reins so hard my knuckles turn white. The trees are bigger, their bare branches denser and leaning closer to the ground, but otherwise, it looks exactly as I remember it.

I gently squeeze Flicka's reins, nudging my leg against her side to make her turn, and steer her up the lane.

'Hey, where are you going?' Myo says. 'Cass!'

I ignore him, pressing my legs against Flicka's sides again to make her go faster. We reach my house just as Myo catches up with me.

Or rather, what used to be my house.

'What the hell are you doing?' Myo says. 'This isn't the right way.'

'This was where I used to live,' I snap. I get down off Flicka and tether her to a tree.

The front door is open. I take a deep breath, then step through. A sour odour of damp and rot slaps me in the face.

The hall looks like a tornado has ripped through it. The wallpaper is hanging down in shreds, the plaster is bulging and crumbling where water has seeped into the walls and the carpet squelches under my boots. The antique plant stand Mum bought at a car boot sale and lovingly restored is on its side at the bottom of the stairs, its porcelain top in pieces, and the photos and pictures we had on the walls lie face-down on the floor. I pick one up, but the photo inside is a pulpy, rotted mass, sticking to the inside of the glass.

I head upstairs. In what used to be my bedroom, part of the ceiling has given way, the window is broken and obscene graffiti has been daubed across the walls. Most of the furniture has gone, but my bed is still there, collapsed in the middle, as if someone's jumped onto it with great force.

Then I see the tattered remains of a small, stuffed toy dog sitting in the middle of the floor. Hound. I remember that evening we left, Mum helping me to pack my bag and me stuffing him into the side pocket. Now, his plush brown and white fur is black, mouldy stuffing leaking from a hole in his side. It looks like someone found him with the stuff we left downstairs and brought him back up here. *Why?*

'The Fearless must have come back and wrecked everything after they realized Mum and I had escaped,' I murmur.

'Aye, and there'll have been people passing through on salvage missions, too, taking whatever they thought was useful and trashing whatever they didn't. Everywhere's the same,' Myo says behind me.

I jump. I didn't even realize he was there. 'Never mind. I don't know what else I expected, really,' I say, my voice cracking on the last word. I gaze round me, looking for something I could take away with me – something that might remind me of the life I once had. But everything is ruined. This could be any post-Invasion house anywhere in the country. Anywhere in the *world*, for all I know.

That's when it really, truly hits me that my old life is over. The past seven years haven't been a pause while we wait for things to go back to normal. I'll never live in this house again. I'll never see my parents again. And unless we catch up the Fearless girl, I'll never see my brother again either.

'Let's go.' I turn and march back out of the house, and we ride away without looking back.

*How could the government have let this happen?* I think. *Why didn't they try harder to fight the Fearless? Why didn't everyone try harder to fight the Fearless?* It's as if, as soon as the Invasion hit, people just . . . gave up.

'What do you miss?' I ask Myo, desperate to distract myself from the dark thoughts swirling around inside my head. 'From before the Invasion, I mean?'

For a moment, I don't think he's going to answer me, but then he says, 'Sometimes I'd give anything for a Burger King or a McDonald's, you know? One of those burgers that had cheese and bacon in it.'

'Mmm. And don't forget a huge side order of fries drowning in ketchup . . .'

'And Coke with loads of ice . . .'

I laugh – the first time I've laughed since I left Hope. 'Maybe not today. I'd rather have hot chocolate.'

He smiles too. 'OK, hot chocolate, then. But I'd definitely have one of those ice cream things with bits of chocolate and biscuit mashed up in them to go with it. What were they called?'

'I can't remember. They were nice, though.'

Myo sighs. 'I don't miss a lot of things from before, but I miss the food.'

It's the most light-hearted conversation we've had, and for a moment, it seems as if it might break the ice between us, but afterwards, Myo seems to withdraw again, and we spend another day riding more or less in silence. The further north we go, the colder it gets, meaning we have to make several detours to find streams big enough not to have frozen over. We take turns carrying the gun, looking out for the Fearless girl or Magpies, but the whole time, we see just one person, a lone figure on horseback like us, riding along a ridge at the top of a hill. 'A barterer, probably,' Myo says, squinting through his binoculars from where we've stopped to hide in a stand of trees. 'I don't recognize him, though.'

Two days later it starts to snow. Soon there's an inch of it on the ground, then two, then three. The horses slow to a plod, balls of compacted snow forming in their hooves and on the shaggy fur on their legs, which we have to stop to remove. We finally solve the problem when Lochie catches a pigeon; we stop to cook it for our lunch, sheltering in a ruined barn, and use the leftover fat to grease Apollo and Flicka's hooves.

The effect created by the curtains of falling snow is utterly disorientating. If it wasn't for Myo's compass, we'd be turning in circles by now. 'How much further have we got to go?' I ask Myo, who's hunched in his jacket, the collar turned up and the hood of his jumper pulled down over his face.

'We should reach the bunker tomorrow evening as long as this doesn't slow us down too much,' he says.

*Great.*

It snows steadily all day, finally stopping just as we reach the old farm Myo discovered on his trip down to Hope. By now, it's starting to get dark, and our clothes are wet through.

'We should sort the horses out first,' Myo says, his teeth chattering. 'They need to eat.'

I need to eat too, and I'm desperate to get warm, but he's right; Apollo and Flicka have already finished all the hay we brought with us, and are going through the grain much faster than either of us had anticipated. We dismount and lead them through the farmyard, Lochie at our heels. As Myo said, there's a barn still piled with hay, and when we've dug our way through the snow and mouldy bales on the outside, some of the stuff in the middle is still OK, although it's dusty and smells of mice. We rub handfuls of snow over it to clean it a little, then tether the horses inside another outbuilding, leaving them the hay to pick at, and go to look at the house.

The only obvious damage is from the weather – rotted door and window frames, and tiles missing from the roof. We kick the front door open and Lochie pushes past us, as desperate to be out of the snow as we are. When he doesn't bark or growl, we follow him, Myo carrying a lantern and his knife, me holding the gun.

Inside, the house looks a little like Danny and April's, but there's less junk and more grime and cobwebs. The air is chilly and dank, and the stairs are blocked by a fall of wood and plaster.

'I slept in one of the barns on my way down south,' Myo says, his tone apologetic.

The front room, however, still has signs that this used to be someone's home: a dog bed by the mouldering sofa with dust-coated toys and blankets piled in it; a kids' rug with letters of the alphabet on it, its once bright colours dull with grime; a table in one corner, chairs arranged haphazardly around it and a doll and felt tip pens scattered across the top. On the wall above it is a huge canvas, speckled with mildew. When I go closer, I see it's a studio portrait of the family who must once have lived here – three little kids, a woman kneeling behind them and a man with dreadlocks standing beside her with his hand on her shoulder. They look happy and healthy, like they don't have a care in the world.

Where are they now? Were they killed or Altered? Are they roaming the country, looking for people to turn into new Fearless like the man and the girl who took Jori? A shiver twists up my spine.

At the other end of the room, we discover a fireplace, the grate half-buried by another pile of plaster. 'Do you think the chimney's still OK?' I ask Myo as we clear the rubble away.

'I reckon we should risk it, don't you?' His face is pinched with exhaustion and the cold, and I know I don't look much better.

In one of the outbuildings, we discover a dresser and some old chairs, which we smash up into kindling with an axe I find in a shed.

'I could do with a wash,' Myo says when the fire's built and lit and we've moved as close to it as we can, Lochie nosing in between us. The chimney must be OK, because the smoke spirals cleanly up it and away. I look down at myself and realize how disgusting I feel. Since leaving Danny and April's, all our energy has been focused on riding, eating, sleeping and keeping watch for the Fearless and the Magpies. As I thaw out, I'm starting to give off a strong smell of sweat and horse. My fingernails are black with grime and my hair, which I've kept tied up for days, is a mass of greasy tangles. I make a face. 'Me too.'

We unearth some large saucepans from a cupboard in the kitchen, fill them with snow and place them in the fire. 'You go first,' I tell Myo when the snow's melted, averting my gaze.

I hear water splashing. 'Crap,' he says. 'Can you pass me the soap out of the side pocket of my pack?'

Studiously avoiding looking at him, I find it for him. I'm expecting it to be the sort of soap we have on the island – yellowish, greasy stuff made by the barterers from ash and animal fat – but it's a bottle with a plain label, stamped with the words LEVER 2000. It must be from the bunker.

I reach behind me to pass it to him, but he's not where I thought he was and I have to turn round. He has his back to me, his right arm held out, and he's wearing absolutely nothing. The first thing I notice, with a jolt, is that his bruises are almost gone. How did he heal so fast? The second thing I see is the masses of thin, silvery scars criss-crossing his forearm, and a tattoo just above his right hipbone: a tiny silhouette of a swallow, delicately inked in black with *Mara* spelled out above it in inter-twined letters. I remember that flash of *something* that went between us on Danny's porch, and heat floods my entire body.

'Ta,' he says as I turn away again, my heart beating harder than ever. How did he get those scars? And what does that tattoo mean? Who's Mara? A girlfriend, I suppose.

'OK, your turn.' I take a deep breath and look round.

He's wrapped a couple of the blankets around himself. He sits down in front of the fire next to Lochie with his back to me, and, feeling horribly self-conscious, I strip and wash as fast as I can, using the Lever 2000 soap. It has no scent, just a clean, soapy smell, but the sensation of the lather on my skin is blissful. I take a pan of water to the sink in the kitchen to rinse my hair. When I'm done, I rinse my underwear, wrap myself in the remaining blankets and try to comb the worst of the knots out of my hair with my fingers. 'We need to dry our clothes,' I say. Even though I'm right by the fire, and the blankets are thick, I can still feel the cold nipping at my skin.

Myo points at the dining table. 'What about those chairs? We could put them near the fire and drape our things over them.'

We drag the chairs across. Sour-smelling steam rises off our clothes as they begin to dry. I wish we could wash everything, not just our underwear.

When we've eaten, Myo stares into the fire. I watch him surreptitiously, looking at him properly for the first time. He has a slightly upturned nose, a wide, serious mouth and a thick fringe of black lashes around his right eye. The light from the flames casts shadows under his jaw and in the hollows of his cheekbones. I remember how he looked when I passed him the bottle of soap, and look away, my heart beating faster. *Don't even GO there*, I tell myself sternly.

When our clothes are dry we pull them back on, laying the blankets out in front of the fire. 'I'll go and check on the horses,' Myo says. 'Then I'll do the first watch if you like.'

I nod, stretching out beside Lochie. I'm warmer than I've been for days, and I can feel exhaustion sinking into my bones like cement. Myo takes the gun and goes out of the room, and I close my eyes.

# Chapter 23

## MYO

Outside, it's started snowing again. As I trudge across to the barn, I flip my eyepatch up so I can see better in the dark and think about Cass handing me that bottle of soap, wondering how much she saw. I know she looked, 'cos she couldn't quite meet my eye afterwards. The scars on my left arm are much worse than on the right, purple and angry-looking even after all this time. I haven't cut for years now, but at one time it was the only way I could cope with what had happened.

The horses are at the far end of the barn, munching on the last of the hay. I check them over, wondering what Ben will say when I turn up at the bunker with a stranger. We've had no outsiders there for years. Stuck up on the moors in the middle of nowhere, it's easy to pretend the outside world doesn't exist, and that's how we like it.

But Cass and I are in this together now. I'd never've been able to stop that Fearless guy at Danny's by myself. I have no idea how we'll get Mara and her brother back without her finding out Mara's Fearless, but there must be a way. There has to be. And when I'm not so knackered, maybe I'll be able to figure it out.

When I get back, Cass is already asleep, her hair fanned out around her head. I sit down on one of the chairs, the gun across my lap. The old house creaks and groans around me. Riding will be slow tomorrow, but I still think we can make it back by nightfall.

I look over at Cass again, remembering that moment on the porch when she touched my arm. It makes me go hot and cold all over. What was that?

My eyes keep wanting to close, but every time my head sags forward I snap awake again. It's been the same every night since Danny and April died. Two of my friends, dead, at the hand of my own twin. And she could have been dead too if I hadn't stopped Danny from cutting her throat. I feel guilty because I couldn't stop it from happening, guilty because I couldn't save Danny, guilty for being relieved that Mara got away, guilty that she has Tessie and probably Cass's brother, too. Guilty, guilty, guilty.

Maybe it's crazy, trying to help her, but she's all the family I've ever had. Our ma and da were junkies and we got taken away from them when we were two, after the police found us on our own in their shitty flat where we'd been left for two days with no food or water. We were passed around a few foster families, then put in a home. All we had to rely on was each other. Even after she was Altered, I couldn't abandon her. Thank God Ben and the others agreed to take her in.

*But I should've got there sooner . . . I should've stopped them from getting shot . . . I should've stopped Mara taking Tessie . . .*

Cass gives a cry, making me jump. She's having a bad dream, her face twisted, her arms twitching, her eyes rolling behind their lids. Lochie lifts his head, looking at her with his ears up. I put the gun down on the floor and kneel beside her. 'Cass,' I say softly. 'Wake up.' When she doesn't respond, I say it louder. With a gasp, she sits up, clutching at me like she's drowning and pressing her face against my chest. I can feel her heart pounding through her back, and smell soap and the smoke from the fire in her hair. I get waves of that hot and cold feeling again and scramble back, embarrassed and confused, my own heart pounding almost as hard as hers was. 'Are – are you OK?' I stutter. 'What were you dreaming about?'

She gathers her blanket around her. 'We were out on the road – me, you and Lochie – and the Magpies came, but I was frozen to the road and couldn't move. The ice was all over me. They'd done it to trap me because they thought I was Fearless. And then you disappeared . . .'

She's shivering, even though the room's still warm. 'It's just a dream,' I say.

'I know, but I had the exact same one at Danny and April's, just before the Fearless got into the house.'

'That doesn't mean it's gonna happen again.'

She looks at me like she doesn't know whether to believe me or not. I can feel where she was pressed against me, like she's imprinted on my skin.

'Do you want me to go and check outside?' I say,

wondering if Cass's dream means Mara is out there somewhere again.

'Yes.'

I start to get up. 'No. Stay here,' she says.

I cross my legs, settling myself a little more comfortably, my skin still tingling all over for no good reason I can think of. The firelight makes a halo around her hair. I catch myself staring at her for a second too long, and have to make myself look away.

'I hate them,' she says suddenly.

Startled, I look round at her again. 'Who?'

'The Fearless. Who do you think?'

I nod, trying to ignore the coldness rising in the pit of my stomach.

And trying to push away the image of Mara that jumps into my head.

'They're evil,' Cass says. 'I wish there was a way to get rid of every last one of them.'

The tingling on my skin has disappeared. Instead, I feel like a gap has opened up between us, a hundred miles wide.

I get to my feet. 'I think I will check outside. Better safe than sorry.'

I pick up the gun and walk out of the room without looking back.

# Chapter 24

## CASS

I have no idea what I said to Myo to make him walk off like that, but the next morning, he's gone from not speaking much to barely speaking at all. When I remember his arms around me after I woke up from that nightmare, and then how he jerked away from me, I feel a thud of disappointment in my stomach, followed by a wave of embarrassment.

*Maybe* that's *it*, I think as we pack up and damp down the fire, ready to leave. *Maybe he's embarrassed too. Maybe he's worried you'll read something into it.*

*But why would he like you like that?* I tell myself as we head out to the barn. It's still dark, but the clouds have gone, stars shimmering overhead. *Why would YOU like him like that? You hardly even know each other.*

And then I wonder why I'm even thinking about this. I swing myself up onto Flicka, my face warming up.

'Want the gun?' Myo says as he climbs onto Apollo. Apollo's ears twitch back at the sound of his voice, first one, then the other. It's like the up-down movement of Lochie's eyebrows; the horses are always listening, even when you're not speaking directly to them.

'You carry it.' I'm not quite able to look at him. 'My hands are too cold.'

He grunts something that sounds like, 'OK,' and leans forward to adjust Apollo's bridle, not looking at me either. We ride out of the barn with Lochie loping alongside.

As we head further north, the sun rises on a transformed world. Everything is white and glittering, the snow stretching away either side of us as far as we can see. It's so dazzling we have to wrap our scarves around our faces, leaving a gap just big enough for our eyes. If Myo's calculations are correct, it's our last day of travelling, and now we're almost there, the reality of what I'm doing is sinking in. I've left my home and will probably never be allowed back. I've travelled hundreds of miles with a boy who's still practically a stranger, and who blows hot and cold on me for seemingly no reason. I'm about to enter a community that could be even more hostile to outsiders than Hope. And, if nothing terrible happens to me there, I'm going willingly into a Fearless lair. I want to ask Myo what the people at the bunker are going to do when I turn up there, but I can't be bothered when I know all I'll get is shrugs and grunts.

*It will all be worth it if I can get Jori back*, I tell myself, and as Myo and I ride on through the snow, it becomes a mantra, keeping all other thoughts and anxieties at bay. As long as I have that tiny thread of hope inside me that my brother's still alive, that I'll reach him in time, I can face anything and anyone. And I pray we can get Tessie back, too.

That afternoon, it clouds over and starts to snow again.

'We need to head over the moors now,' Myo says as flakes of snow spiral down from the sky, the first words he's spoken to me since we set off the farm. He's pointing to a rocky ridge that looks like the backbone of a dinosaur. 'The bunker's on the other side of that hill.'

It's hard going once we leave the road. The snow limits visibility, and hides rocks and gullies on the ground. Only Lochie seems to navigate the slopes without trouble, bounding ahead of us. We try to follow him as closely as possible, but my heart is in my mouth the whole time.

Then, just as we're nearing the summit, Apollo catches his hoof, stumbles, and with a terrible, screaming whinny, crashes down onto his side. Myo manages to jump clear just in time, the soft snow breaking his fall.

He swears and leaps to his feet. Flicka snorts and stamps, her eyes rolling, the whites showing all the way round the edge. 'Shit,' Myo says as he tries to calm Apollo, who's struggling to get up.

Looking round, I see an old fencepost sticking up out of the snow. I manoeuvre Flicka close enough to it to dismount and tie her up. 'Where's he hurt?' I say, running across to Myo.

'He's done something to his front right foot.' Myo's voice is sharp with panic. He starts pulling the packs and saddlebags off Apollo. 'We need to get him up if we can.'

I help him unstrap the rest of our gear. 'Give me some of those ropes,' Myo says. 'We'll try and roll him over so he can push up on his good side.'

I hand them to him, and he ties one around Apollo's back leg and one around his chest. Gently, we pull on the ropes, bringing Apollo over onto his chest, and he scrabbles to his feet. He stands with his sides heaving, holding his front right hoof up off the ground.

'Is it broken?' I ask as Myo, making soothing noises, feels Apollo's leg.

'I don't know.' The panic in his voice has subsided, but only a little. 'If we can get him to the bunker, we can get Ben to take a look at it. He was training to be a vet before the Invasion.'

'How far is it now?'

'Less than a mile.'

'Let's load the gear onto Flicka so Apollo isn't carrying any extra weight,' I say. 'If it's less than a mile, we can walk, and lead them.'

Our journey up to the ridge is slow and painstaking. At last, we reach the top, and make our way equally slowly down the other side, Apollo hopping on three legs.

'There,' Myo says.

Through the curtains of snow, I see two upright slabs of rock. The gap between them is big enough to lead the horses straight through. The path turns a corner and then, under an overhang of rock, I see a little stable with a corrugated iron roof, icicles bristling along the edge.

'It's for the barterers,' Myo says as we lead the horses into the stalls. I know he's thinking of Danny. The sadness in his voice is so raw that for a crazy second I want to hug him.

But I don't. I turn away from him and busy myself unloading our gear from Flicka. Once she and Apollo are in the stalls, Myo clicks his fingers at Lochie and we carry on along the path, carrying our packs in our arms. It's like a cave down here, claustrophobic and chilly. Our boots slip and slide on the frozen ground.

We reach a heavily reinforced metal door set into the hillside with no visible handle on the outside. Lochie barks. Shushing him, Myo taps the handle of his knife against the door, a series of knocks that remind me of the Morse code Sol and I learned years ago at school and used to send secret messages to each other. The sound echoes hollowly around us.

Several minutes pass. Then a little porthole opens at the top. Lochie whines, his tail starting to wave slowly from side to side.

'Who's there?' a male voice calls through the porthole.

Myo stands on tiptoe and waves. 'Hey, Cy. It's me.'

'Myo! Shit, hang on, mate.' The porthole slams shut, and with a rusty squeal, the door opens.

On the other side is a guy with a gun. He has metal studs through his ears, nose and bottom lip, his shaved scalp is tattooed with a spider-web pattern and his eyes, which are watering slightly – from the cold, perhaps – are a startling shade of blue. He steps through the door and wraps Myo in a hug, pounding him on the back.

Then Cy catches sight of me. His gaze becomes colder, harder. 'Who's this?'

'Cass,' Myo says.

I lift a hand in greeting. 'Hi,' I say. My voice is too high, and I clench my other hand into a fist, cursing myself for sounding so nervous.

'You're gonna have to wait here for a moment,' Cy tells Myo, rubbing his eyes and blinking to clear them.

Myo nods. 'No worries.'

'What's going on?' I say as Cy goes back inside, slamming the door behind him.

Myo shakes his head. 'Nothing.'

At last, Cy returns. 'OK, you can come in,' he says, glancing at me. He holds the door open and Myo and I duck under his arm, Lochie shoving past us. I just have time to see that we're in a tunnel lined with mould-speckled tiles, thick cables running along the walls near the ceiling and lights, dark and dead, hanging down at intervals, before Cy slams the door shut again.

The darkness presses against me like a blanket. Just as I'm starting to wonder if the next thing I'll feel is the muzzle of Cy's gun against my head, I hear a click and the tunnel is flooded with light. Cy's got a torch, a boxy-looking thing with a little winding handle sticking out of the side.

'Did you find Ma—' he begins to ask Myo as we start walking.

Myo cuts him short with a shake of his head. 'No. I'll talk to you later.'

I remember him saying almost the exact same thing at Danny's. I frown at the backs of their heads.

We make our way along a downwards-sloping corridor. The deeper underground we go, the higher the temperature rises until it's almost comfortable. Then I see a door propped half-open with a cracked plastic crate. On the other side, lights – real lights – shine weakly; I wonder how on earth they power them. I can hear voices, too. A sign above the door says *COMMUNICATIONS HALL. AUTHORIZED PERSONNEL ONLY.*

The hall is high-ceilinged, more signs fixed to the walls saying things like *NO SMOKING* and *IN EVENT OF SIREN SOUNDING PLEASE DON THE PROTECTIVE SUITS STOWED UNDER YOUR DESKS AND AWAIT FURTHER INSTRUCTION*, and in the middle of the room is a square of desks with flat-screen computers on them and chairs in front of each monitor. Everything is coated in dust.

The far end of the room looks more homely. Someone's painted a mural on one of the walls – trees and flowers and animals. There are tables, rickety book-shelves stacked with books and magazines and a battered acoustic guitar leaning up against them, and some couches and armchairs covered with brightly coloured blankets and sheets.

And standing round the couches is a group of people, about twenty of them, all staring at me.

As we walk across, I'm struck by something: the oldest person here looks as if they're in their thirties, and there are no kids. Maybe they're somewhere else in the bunker?

Cy is standing between a skinny woman with her hair in little plaits, and an Asian girl with short, curly hair. Next to her is a tall guy with green eyes the colour of sea glass.

'Before you ask, I didn't find her,' Myo tells him.

The man raises an eyebrow. 'Who's this?' he says, as I wonder for the third time who Myo hasn't found, and what he's not telling me.

'My name's Cass,' I say.

The man acts like he hasn't heard me. 'Myo?'

'I got into some pretty bad trouble,' Myo says. 'Cass helped me get out of it.'

The man narrows his eyes. I wait for Myo to tell him about Jori. Instead, he tells the man, 'I need to talk to you.' He doesn't say *without Cass listening*, but I know from his tone that's what he means. 'And one of the horses we brought with us is injured. It fell on the hill. Can you take a look at it?'

I realize this must be Ben. 'Horses?' he says.

'They were Danny's.'

'Were?'

Myo gazes levelly at him. 'Like I said, I need to talk to you.'

Ben rubs a hand across his face. 'OK, OK. Let's go and look at this horse. You can tell me what's going on while we're there.'

And without even so much as a glance in my direction, the two of them walk out of the hall, leaving me alone with a large group of glaring strangers.

# Chapter 25

## MYO

As Ben and I head back to the bunker entrance, I tell him everything: how I managed to track Mara and the other Fearless she was with all the way to Hope – God knows how she managed to hook up with him, or where – and how I got trapped when the building collapsed and was arrested by those guards; how Mara and the Fearless man took Cass's brother, and how I struck a bargain with Cass to get me off the island.

'So she knows about Mara?' Ben says sharply.

I know what he's thinking: *How much did you tell her? How much does she know about us?* I shake my head. 'Don't be daft. If I told her one of the Fearless that kidnapped her brother is my twin sister, she'd stick a knife in my guts.'

'I should never have let you go after Mara,' Ben says, shaking his head. 'I knew it would bring trouble.' His expression is as grim as I feel.

'You didn't let me,' I remind him.

He scowls. 'I didn't want you to go until the weather improved a little. But you went haring off anyway, and now you turn up again with this girl. We agreed years ago that no outsiders could come here. It's too risky! If this Carrie or whatever she's called finds out what we are—'

'Mara's the only family I've got!' I say. 'Waiting wasn't an option! And I tried to ditch Cass, OK? Anyway, if it wasn't for her, I'd be at the bottom of the sea, or back at the Torturehouse.'

As we go out to the stable, I tell him about the attack at Danny and April's, and how Cass helped me fight off the Fearless man and kill him. He listens in silence. 'If I turn round now and tell her I can't help her, what sort of person does that make me?' I finish.

'Your trouble is, Myo, that you want to save everybody,' Ben says as he goes into Apollo's stall to take a look at his leg.

'Aye, and you know what, if that means I'm not like them, then I'll keep on doing it.'

'And I keep *telling* you—' Ben gently runs his hands up and down Apollo's injured leg, 'You're not like them. You're not going to end up like them. It is not. Going. To. Happen.'

*That's easy for you to say!* I want to yell at him, and if it wasn't for the horses, I would. For some reason Ben's never seemed bothered about – well, I guess you could call it our inheritance. He's never struggled with it. He's never been worried about this thing inside us changing or growing. But me, I'm aware of it every single minute of every single day. Can you imagine, every time you lose your temper or you do something that makes you feel selfish or mean, worrying that it's starting to take over?

That's why I cut when I was younger. I wanted it *out*. But of course, you can't get rid of it. Once it's in you, it's there to stay – I've just had to learn to live with it.

'Her brother's only a bairn,' I say. 'And no one on that island could've cared less about trying to get him back.'

'*Shit*, Myo.' Ben clenches his teeth, carefully flexing Apollo's fetlock. 'Don't you even remember what happened to me after we got out of the Torturehouse?'

He's talking about after he found the bunker, and set it up as a community for people like us. Before he was caught, he was living with another community – him and his partner, Rajesh. He went back to try and find him, but by then Rajesh had been taken by the Fearless too, and when the people who were left found out what had happened to Ben, he was lucky to escape with his life.

'Aye, but she's not going to find out,' I say. 'And I'm not asking for anyone else to come with us.'

Ben snorts. 'What, so you two are going to go haring off to the Torturehouse by yourselves?'

I pretend not to hear the sarcasm in his voice. 'All we need is some decent weapons and a few more supplies. Surely you can spare us those?'

'Myo, how are you going to stop her finding out the Fearless responsible for taking her brother is your sister?' Ben says, turning to face me. 'How are you going to stop yourself getting *killed*? For Christ's *sake*!'

I take a deep breath. 'Once we get her brother back,

**207**

it doesn't matter, does it? She can take him back to that island of hers and get on with her life, and I can bring Mara back here and get on with mine. End of.'

Of course, I know it's not that simple. The memory of Cass saying I hate them, and *The Fearless, who do you think?* rises inside my head. I push it away.

'Sounds like you've got it all figured out.' Ben lets go of Apollo's foot. 'He's damaged the ligament, I think. I'm not sure how badly, and I'm not sure what I can do except bandage it and let him rest. I'll go and look in the medical supplies and see what we've got. You planning on riding the other horse to Sheffield, then?'

'It'll be quicker than walking.'

'She'll need to rest for a few days. Horses aren't machines, you know. And I know you won't listen to me about this, but you'd be better waiting for the weather to improve, too. Or at least wait until it's stopped snowing.'

'So you're not throwing Cass out?'

'No, but she'll have to sleep away from the others.'

'She can have Mara's room.'

'And she isn't to go wandering off anywhere by herself. You keep an eye on her at all times.'

I nod.

As we walk back to the bunker, Ben fixes me with a grave stare. 'Seriously, Myo. It's up to you to make sure she doesn't find out about us. Don't screw up.'

I resist the temptation to salute. Ben's not known for his sense of humour at the best of times, and right now, he'd probably deck me if he thought I was messing with him.

When we get back to the Comms Hall, Cass is standing near the door, arms wrapped around herself. I don't need to be a mind-reader to figure out the look she gives me: *Thanks for leaving me on my own, you bastard.* No one's talking to her. Only Lochie, who's been getting a fuss from Cy and Gina, is pleased to see us, trotting over and wagging his tail.

Ben strides into the middle of the room and claps his hands. 'Listen up!' Everyone stops speaking and turns to look at him.

'Cass here helped Myo out of a couple of very bad situations. In return, he's promised to help her get her brother back, who's been taken by a Fearless. I'm calling a community meeting immediately.'

Everyone starts muttering among themselves.

'Myo, why don't you show Cass to her room before we start?' Ben adds. 'You can fetch her back once we're done.'

'Come on,' I mutter to Cass. I'm already starting to feel apprehensive about this meeting. 'It's this way.'

We leave the Comms Hall with everyone's stares drilling into my back. Mara's room is several tunnels away – some nights she'd scream for hours, and if she'd been nearer the dormitories, no one would've got any sleep.

I go in first to check the room is OK. When Mara and I got here, it was stuffed with filing cabinets and junk, and Ben helped me clear it out and make it secure for her. A mattress is shoved against one wall, the covers heaped up in the middle, but we had to remove the rest of the furniture so Mara couldn't hurt herself. Even so, the walls are scuffed and scored from where she'd scratch at the paintwork until her fingers bled. I blink, seeing her sitting on the mattress with her knees drawn up and her arms locked around them, her hair falling over her face as the cravings for the serum sends tremors through her body.

I gather up the bedding and take it out into the tunnel. 'It's all yours,' I tell Cass. 'I'll be back soon, OK? And I'll bring you some more blankets.'

She stares at the heavy bolts on the outside of the door. 'What is this, a prison cell?'

*Yes*, I think. 'No, it's just a room. I'm not gonna lock you in. But you have to stay here until the meeting's finished. And do me a favour, OK? Don't go wandering off on your own. It's a big place – you could get lost.'

She nods, pressing her lips into a thin line. I have this crazy moment where I think about explaining, telling her who we are and why we're hiding here from the rest of the world. And her miraculously understanding and telling me it doesn't matter.

Luckily, I realize just how crazy that would be before I open my mouth.

'I'll see you in a while,' I say. Then I head back to the Comms Hall.

Ben and the others are waiting.

'So you believe Mara is on her way to the Torturehouse,' he says.

'Aye.' I tell everyone else what I told Ben when we

were going to see to Apollo. They listen in shocked silence.

'I'm not asking any of you to come with us,' I say. 'I'm just asking for some weapons and supplies. And I won't bring Cass back here afterwards, so you don't need to worry about that.'

'Wait, you want to get Mara back from the Torturehouse on your own?' Cy says.

'I'll not *be* on my own,' I say.

'OK, you and that girl are going to go off to the Torturehouse by yourselves, to face God knows how many Fearless.' Cy shakes his head. 'That's *insane.*'

'What other option is there?' I ask, trying to keep the irritation out of my voice. 'I have to get Mara out of there. And Cass's brother. I *promised* her.'

Cy glances at Ben, then at Gina. 'A few of us could come with you. I mean, if you're sure that's where Mara is—'

Some people shake their heads, looking doubtful, as I expected they would. But Gina rubs her hands through her dark curls, and says, 'I'm in. We were going to try to get her back anyway, right?'

I feel a sudden, overwhelming rush of gratitude towards her and Cy. If this was anywhere else – Cass's island, for example – I know this conversation would have gone very differently. *Who are you kidding?* I think. *If we were anywhere else, no one would have even agreed to bring Mara here in the first place, never mind rescue her for a second time.*

'Well, I guess I'm in too, then,' Cy says.

Ben sighs. 'I guess that means I am too, seeing as I said I'd help you find her once the weather improved. Tana, can you keep an eye on things here while we're gone?'

Tana nods, twisting one of her plaits around her fingers. Her face is grim. She and Cy only got together a year ago, but they're pretty serious about each other. I know she's not happy about Cy coming with us.

But whenever we need something from outside, Gina, Cy and Ben are the ones who can get it. They're the strongest, fittest and fastest here. The best with guns and knives. And they're the ones I'd pick to come with me and Cass to the Torturehouse, every time.

'Thanks, guys,' I say, and despite everything that's happened over the last few days, I smile.

# Chapter 26

*Three days later*

## SOL

'No.' My father thumps the desk. 'No. You're not going with them, Solomon. I forbid it.'

I gaze at him, my arms folded, my face impassive. *Have you quite finished?* I want to ask him. But the only way to get what you want from a man like my father is to bide your time, strike at exactly the right moment.

So I wait.

As he carries on ranting, I think back over the last three days. Ever since David Brett arrived with the woman, whose name is Sofia, and his half-dead Fearless, Hope's been in a state of uproar. They've stayed for a few days because they needed to rest, they said, but really, I think Brett's playing some sort of sick game with my father, trying to mess with his head.

'We've found a way to cure them,' Brett told us in the office after he said to my father, *You helped create them, Simon. Now's your chance to help us make things right.* 'A simple operation. It's a bit hit and miss – an unfortunate consequence of having to work in the field, I'm afraid – but as you can see, when it *does* work, it's completely successful.'

He indicated the Fearless, who was just standing there, his expression vacant, his mouth gaping open. The stench coming off him was worse than ever. I glanced at the window. My father saw me looking and nodded. I went to open it.

'And then what?' my father said.

'They become biddable again. All their aggressive tendencies disappear.'

'Who are you people?' I demanded.

Brett turned that sneering smile on me. 'Haven't you heard of the Magpies, son?'

I shook my head.

He shook his head too. 'My, they really do shelter you on this island of yours, don't they?'

He handed the chain to the woman and sat down on a corner of the desk. 'Once upon a time, son, your father and I were colleagues. We both worked for a company called PharmaDexon—'

'David,' my father said in a warning tone.

'—where we created a drug we hoped would stop people in the armed forces suffering from post-traumatic stress disorder. But it did more than that. It stopped them feeling fear altogether. And then—'

'David, he knows all this,' my father said.

'I do,' I told Brett. 'We had a . . . a talk about it.'

I wasn't about to tell him what had really happened.

A year ago, my father had got drunk on some moonshine brought to the island by the barterers. I'd found him in our apartment, weeping over a picture of my mother, and without any warning at all, he'd spilled the whole sorry story of how he and his team at PharmaDexon had been the scientists responsible for creating the drug that would eventually turn people into Fearless. Then, because he was up to his neck in debt, my father and David Brett decided to sell the formula to a group of scientists working for the enemy for a crazy amount of money and split the proceeds. It was shortly afterwards that it emerged the drug wasn't just stopping soldiers from feeling fear, but turning them into super-strong, psychopathic lunatics. By then, the scientists my father and Brett sold the formula to had strengthened it so the side effects started immediately.

The rest, as they say, is history. And although my father and Brett had never intended the drug to be used for evil, it was too late. All they could do, my father said, was watch as the world started to fall to pieces around them.

I'd listened in surprise, then fear, then anger. The Invasion had happened *because of my father*, and instead of trying to stop it or owning up to what he'd done, he'd fled to Hope – which he'd got ready as soon as he realized things were going wrong – like a rabbit disappearing into its burrow.

Was that when I started to hate him?

I'm not sure, but I think it might have been.

'I see,' Brett said. 'And what about the rest of the Islanders? Do they know?'

'No,' my father said in a low voice. 'And I'll thank you not to tell them, either.'

'Seems to me we're in an ideal position to strike a bargain, then.' Brett smiled, and the Fearless shifted restlessly from one foot to the other. The woman gave a hard yank on its chain, making it moan. I saw how the metal cuff was cutting into its flesh, despite the bandage, and felt a secret thrill. Neutralized or not, it was still a freak. Why wasn't Brett going round shooting them all? Surely that would be easier? Not to mention a whole lot more fun.

'A bargain?' My father's voice was guarded.

Brett nodded. 'The Magpies are growing steadily in number, but we can always use more pairs of hands.'

'Why? What are the *Magpies* doing, exactly? Except for parading round with *those*—' My father jerked a thumb at the Fearless, who was drooling slightly, 'and threatening to blow up innocent communities?'

I glance at him in surprise. What does he mean, *communities*? There aren't any other communities, are there? Or does he know something we don't?

'We're taking back the country, Simon. We've already had major success overseas—'

'Is that where you went?' my father said, as I considered what Brett had just said, and more pieces of a puzzle that minutes ago I had no idea existed slotted into place. *Major success overseas* . . . Was it possible the world beyond Hope's shores wasn't quite as dead and dangerous as my father had always led us to believe?

'Never mind where I went,' Brett said, and for the first time I wondered why, if he and my father were working together so closely before the Invasion, Brett never came to Hope. Did they fall out over the stolen formula? Was my father scared Brett would tell people what they'd done? 'The point is, there's a huge, untapped resource out there – thousands of Fearless we can cure and use as labourers to rebuild towns, cities, the country's infrastructure – leaving ordinary people free to do the more difficult tasks, like forming a government and so on.

'Our mission right now is to round up as many Fearless as possible. I have people from all over Europe and Asia working under me, a large number of them ex-military. But the work is difficult and hazardous. We're launching a mission to Sheffield in a week or so's time, where there's rumoured to be a large Fearless lair. We expect casualties to be high.'

'So you're here because . . .' my father said.

'The population on Hope is young and strong,' Brett said. 'Surely you can spare a few of them to join us?'

My father's face went pale, then flushed red. 'Absolutely not. That's preposterous!'

'As preposterous as you keeping people here, continuing to pretend the world has ended so you can cling onto a little bit of power?'

'You are not taking anyone from Hope to join the Magpies!'

I imagined going after the Fearless, helping to round

them up, and wondered how many it might be considered acceptable to kill in self-defence. My skin was prickling all over with excitement.

'I wonder what they would say, then, if they were to find out they've been in exile for the last seven years because of you – that you're the reason they lost their homes, their families . . .'

'You wouldn't dare!' my father choked.

'Try me.' Brett's smile had become cold and humourless.

'You're just as culpable as I am!'

'Yes, but *I'm* taking steps to put what I did right. What are *you* doing? And anyway, Simon, selling the formula was your idea. I still have the documents to prove it.'

My father went pale again. 'Solomon, go and ring the Meeting Hall bell,' he told me. 'I want every Islander over the age of sixteen here in five minutes' time.'

'Excellent,' Brett said, and his smile returned to full wattage.

Shortly afterwards, everyone was packed into the Meeting Hall's main room. David Brett had covered the Fearless in a blanket again, and when he whipped it off, people gasped. He went through his spiel about rebuilding the country, and all the great work the Magpies had done so far. Then he asked people to consider joining them.

'You don't have to decide immediately,' he said. 'Think about it and let me know. We'll be here for a few days.' He smiled at my father, who shifted uneasily in his chair.

And inside, I was smiling too, because I'd already made my decision.

'I'm going, Dad,' I say once my father has finished ranting at me. 'You can't stop me. I've already handed in my armband to Captain Denning.'

My father stares at me, open-mouthed.

'But Sol . . .' His angry tone becomes almost pleading. 'There's a great future for you here – you could become Mayor of Hope yourself, in time—'

'I don't *want* to become Mayor of this shithole,' I bark at him. 'Brett was right. All you've done is hide yourself away here and refuse to take responsibility for what you did. This is my chance to make a difference. I'm no coward, even if you are.'

'*No!*' My father grabs his cane and struggles to his feet.

'Oh, shut up.' I turn and walk out of the office while he's still trying to get out from behind the desk. My pack is just outside the door, leaning up against the wall. I swing it onto my shoulder and jog down the Meeting Hall steps.

Colonel Brett and Sofia are already at the jetty, the Fearless bundled in the back of the boat. Marissa and Andrej are on board too. No one else was willing to leave their families.

'*SOLOMON!*' I hear my father yell from the other side of the sea wall as I step down into the boat. Brett sighs. 'Is everyone here?'

'Yes, sir!' we say.

He nods at Sofia, who starts the boat's engine. With six people on board, it sits low in the water, but we soon pick up speed. My last sight of the island is my father, waving his stick at us from the top of the sea wall. I turn away from him and watch the docks approaching on the other side of the channel.

I feel a grin spreading across my face.

Future, here I come.

# JOURNEY

# THE BUNKER

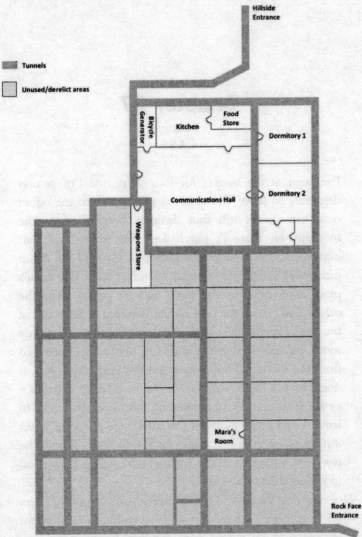

Tunnels

Unused/derelict areas

Hillside Entrance

Bicycle Generator

Kitchen

Food Store

Dormitory 1

Dormitory 2

Communications Hall

Weapons Store

Mara's Room

Rock Face Entrance

# Chapter 27

## CASS

I've been at the bunker for four days, and I'm getting desperate to leave. Myo's being pretty civil to me again now, but there's still that distance between us – the moment on Danny's porch feels like something that happened in a dream. And although Cy and the Asian girl, who's called Gina, seem friendlier now, Ben is just plain rude most of the time, and it's pretty clear the others don't want me here either. Wanting to keep out of the way, I spend most of my time in that depressing little room, ploughing through a pile of books I've borrowed from the Comms Hall to stop me thinking about Jori. It doesn't work. We're waiting for the weather to improve – or for it to at least stop snowing long enough for us to leave – and every moment I'm stuck here is agony. What if it takes less than two weeks for Jori to Alter? What if he never even made it to the Torturehouse and is lying dead in a snowdrift somewhere?

I decide to go and ask Myo if there's anything I can do to help prepare for our journey to Sheffield. It seems so *wrong* to be sitting here, reading books, when my brother is in so much danger. And even though Ben is being so rude, I'm grateful that he and Gina and Cy are coming with Myo and me to Sheffield. I feel as if I should be making myself useful. I grab the little wind-up torch Myo's given me and crank the handle to power it up. The lights – powered by a generator made out of a bicycle, which someone has to pedal like mad on every few hours to top up the current – don't work this deep inside the bunker. I head up to the Comms Hall, but it's empty. I can hear someone in the kitchen, but when I peek around the door, it's not Myo. I retreat before they see me, thinking about going deeper into the bunker to look for him, but then I remember his warning about not wandering off in case I get lost.

I give a frustrated sigh. Where is everyone? Elsewhere in the bunker, I guess – sleeping or cleaning or mending stuff or doing whatever else it is they do here. The routine at the bunker isn't as strict as on Hope; stuff gets done, but everyone's much more casual about it. It feels odd to me. But then this place *is* odd. There are so many things that puzzle me, like how there aren't any kids, or how Ben is the oldest person here. I asked Myo about that, but he just shrugged and said, 'Dunno. That's how it's always been.'

Looks like I'll have to wait here. Needing a distraction, I wander over to the bookshelves.

There are hundreds of books, crammed onto the shelves two deep – everything from kids' books to battered paperbacks, Stephen Kings, dictionaries and fat volumes of Shakespeare and Dickens. Some of the books

I've already borrowed have names in them, or library labels with dates stamped on them; it gives me a pang to see them because I'm reminded that before the Invasion, these books were in people's homes, on bookshop shelves and in libraries – things that simply don't exist any more.

There's magazines, too, yellowed and crinkled – page after page of celebrities and recipes and interviews and fashion. Back in my room, I've got an issue of Vogue with an article titled *Post ApocalypChic*: glossy photos of models posing inside derelict buildings, snarling into the camera. They're wearing combat gear, backcombed hair and make-up that's supposed to make them look like zombies. The date on the magazine's cover was six months before the Invasion. *If only you knew*, I thought as I stared at the pictures, a shudder going up my spine.

I pull books out at random, glancing at the covers before putting them back. Then, at the back of one of the shelves, I find a large scrapbook with *Afterwards* scrawled across the cover in thick black ink. It's full of newspaper articles and pieces of paper. Curious, I take it over to the couch and sit down to look through it properly. To start with, the articles are dated from before the Invasion, and are the sort of thing I saw in that newspaper I found in the kitchen the day before that terrible night – stories about the first encounters with the Fearless, and about other countries being overrun.

Then I see a headline that says *CITIES ALMOST EMPTY AFTER FEARLESS INVASION*. I assume it's about the invasions in Europe too until I read on.

Familiar place names leap out at me: Manchester, London, Birmingham, Glasgow.

I look at the date. Five days after the Invasion.

I flick through the rest of the scrapbook, my mouth dry. *Everything* after those first few articles is dated after the Invasion. The headlines jump out at me: *CALL FOR CIVILIANS TO SIGN UP TO PROTECT NEIGH-BOURHOODS; FIRES IN POWER STATIONS LEAD TO BLACKOUTS; ROYAL FAMILY AMBUSHED DURING EVACUATION; GAS, ELECTRICITY AND WATER RESTRICTIONS TO BE BROUGHT INTO FORCE TOMORROW; FEARLESS NUMBERS ON THE INCREASE.*

And there's leaflets, too – *leaflets from the government* – about food and water rationing, and shelters for people who've been made homeless by the Invasion, and where to go for medical care in an emergency. There's even a leaflet about a drug called Neurophyxil, which I realize is the original drug that was given to the military before people found out what it was doing to them. It and many of the articles are stained and burned, and the Neurophyxil leaflet has what looks like a bloody hand-print across it. I turn the page quickly.

The newspaper articles seem to stop about six months after the Invasion. After that the scrapbook is filled with hand-printed leaflets asking people to sign up to fight the Fearless; posters about meetings, with dates and times on them; and lists of names, most of which have been crossed out with large 'A's or 'D's scrawled beside them. I realize, with a lump in my throat, that this is someone's record of people who have been Altered or are dead.

And then those end too. The rest of the scrapbook is empty.

Suddenly, it's snatched out of my hands. 'What are you doing with that?' someone snaps.

I look up, startled, to see the woman with her hair in little plaits standing over me. Her name's Tana; she's Cy's girlfriend, I think.

'I—' I begin, getting to my feet.

'It's not yours! It's none of your business! Who do you think you—'

'Tana, leave her alone!'

Myo is striding across the Comms Hall.

'She was looking through Ben's scrapbook,' Tana says.

'It was right there on the shelves,' I say.

'Aye.' Myo narrows his eyes at Tana. 'That stuff's no secret. What's the problem?'

Tana scowls at me for a moment. 'The sooner you're out of here, the better,' she snarls at me, before thrusting the scrapbook under her arm and storming out of the hall.

Myo looks at me. 'Are you OK?'

I nod, although I feel embarrassed and shaken.

'Don't let her get to you,' he says. 'She's pissed off because Cy's coming with us to Sheffield.'

'I'm fine.' I push a loose strand of hair out of my face, my heart beating faster again. 'Myo, what *was* that stuff?'

'What d'you mean?'

'Those articles and posters and things – they were dated *after* the Invasion. I thought everything stopped when the Fearless came here.'

Myo's frown changes to a puzzled look. 'Who told you that?'

'We – everyone on Hope – thought that's what happened.'

'Why?'

'Because – because that's what we were *told* happened. The Invasion came, the government fled, society ended.'

'In *one night*?'

'There was that announcement on the TV—'

Myo shakes his head. 'Aye, someone panicking, I reckon. The TV and internet came back on – for a little while, anyway.'

I stare at him. 'But Mr Brightman said—'

*Mr Brightman.*

Realization hits me with a thud, and I sit back down on the couch.

'He – he told us there was nothing left,' I say. 'He said everyone got killed or Altered straight away and that the government abandoned us. But it wasn't like that, was it? Why did he say it was?'

Myo sits down too. 'I don't know. Maybe he thought it was like that, if he never left the island. I mean, yeah, things were bad. And the government *did* disappear eventually. But people didn't just give up. Ben and Cy and the older ones here – they were part of groups that tried to fight the Fearless and take the country back.'

'But they didn't succeed.'

Myo shakes his head. 'There were too many of them, and not enough of us.'

'Did you fight too?'

He laughs humourlessly. 'No. I was only a kid. But I managed to survive. Me and my sister—'

'You have a sister?'

He swallows. 'I – I did.'

*So you've lost someone too*, I think. What about the rest of his family? What happened to his parents?

'I'm sorry,' I say.

'Thanks.' He gives me a small, sad smile. We look at each other for a second too long, and I feel a jolt like the one I got on Danny's porch. Myo must sense it too because his face closes up. 'I'd better get on with . . . stuff,' he says, that stiff politeness returning to his voice.

'OK.' I turn back to the bookshelves so he won't see the way my face has heated up. It's only after he's gone that I remember I was going to ask him when we were going to leave.

As it turns out, I don't need to. That evening, Ben tells me, Myo, Cy and Gina that we'll be on our way the next morning. We spend hours getting ready – preparing weapons and packing food and supplies. My eyes widen when I see the guns Ben's fetched from the bunker's weapons store. I don't know what sort they are, but they're sleek and high-tech with night-vision sights, making the Patrol's Brownings and Lee Enfields look like kids' toys.

'I don't suppose you know how to shoot?' Ben asks when he sees me staring at them.

I nod. 'I was part of the Patrol on Hope. They were the island's guards. I trained for five years.'

His expression is sceptical, but he hands me one of the guns and an ammo belt.

Once everything is ready, we return to the Comms Hall, where Ben spreads out some maps on one of the tables, tracing out our route with the stub of an old pencil. 'We've got to go north-east across the Peak District up to the city, and through part of Sheffield itself to the station,' he says. 'Then we'll follow the railway line up to the Torturehouse. It goes all the way there – it used to have its own station before the Invasion, when it was still a shopping centre.'

'Is that a good idea?' Gina says.

'It's the most straightforward route. Otherwise we have to do a big loop round, which will take another day, maybe more.'

Gina nods, although she looks as pensive as I feel. Even after what Danny told me about most of the Fearless staying at their hideouts these days, the idea of going into the middle of a city makes me go cold all over.

But this is my only chance to get Jori back. I have no choice.

I don't get a lot of sleep that night.

# Chapter 28

## MYO

Crossing the moors is hellish. We have to plunge through waist-high snowdrifts, trying to follow what's left of the roads, and by the time we make it to our first stopping point, an old factory, it's dark. All of us are wet and pissed off and chilled to the bone. I wish we could have taken the horses, but Apollo needs time to heal, and even though Flicka's healthy, one horse between five of us isn't much use. Anyway what would we do with her once we got to the Torturehouse? Abandon her?

The next day, we make it as far as a farmhouse that reminds me of the one Cass and I stayed in on our way back to the bunker. As I lie there, wide awake, I wonder what might've happened if Cass hadn't said she hated the Fearless.

*How else do you expect her to feel, you idiot?* I tell myself fiercely. But now I'm thinking about the other day in the bunker, when she looked at me, then turned away, and I had to walk off so she wouldn't see the disappointment on my face, even though there wasn't actually anything I needed to do.

*Stop.*

At last, I doze off, managing a few hours of crappy, broken sleep before Cy shakes me awake for my turn on watch.

The third day is the longest: fifteen miles to cover before we reach the village marked on Ben's map, where we shelter in an old hotel that looks like a castle. We can't go upstairs 'cos the roof has given way in several places, so we bunk down in the bar on some mouldy leather sofas. No one sleeps well. Mice and rats keep us awake with their squeaking and scuffling. I wish Lochie was here. He'd see 'em off. I don't know why Ben insisted we leave him behind.

The next morning, Cass looks done in, dragging her feet. On the journey to the bunker, we could go at her pace, but now we're moving at Ben, Gina's, Cy's and mine, and I think she's finding it hard.

Then, as we come round a bend, Ben says, 'There it is.' I tear my gaze away from Cass and see houses and bungalows instead of snow-covered fields. The city. The houses are big and fancy looking, even though their windows are broken and their doors are caved in. It must have been a posh area once.

The road, which has been empty for days, is choked up with abandoned vehicles. We pass a double-decker bus, leaning to one side on deflated tyres. The headlights and most of the windows are smashed, and there's a skeleton slumped over the steering wheel, wearing the shredded remains of a bus driver's uniform. Snow has drifted in through the broken windscreen, burying it up to its waist. 'You'll be waiting a long time for that bus,' Cy says, and he, Gina and I share a wry smile.

Ben shakes his head, and Cass keeps plodding along, still staring at the ground. I think about asking her if she's OK, but I don't want Ben to realize she's struggling. 'Guys, I need to rest. I don't feel so good,' I say.

'We've only been walking an hour,' Ben says, sounding irritated.

'Are you OK?' Gina asks.

'Aye.' I try to make my voice sound weary. 'Just tired. I just need to sit down for a bit.'

Ben sighs sharply, but lets us stop at a burned-out Texaco garage for half an hour while we check our weapons. The relief on Cass's face as she sits down on her pack is plain.

'Keep as close to the buildings as you can,' Ben says when we're getting ready to leave again. 'No one, but no one is to walk out into the middle of the road unless I say so.'

We all nod. I glance at Cass and see her biting her lip. We make our way through the city, constantly on the alert for Magpies or Fearless. The houses have given way to large commercial buildings and skyscrapers with broken windows, drifts of rubbish piled up in the entrances. 'What was that?' Gina says, stopping in front of me so suddenly I almost collide with her.

Ben and Cy, who are in front, look round. 'What was what?' Ben says.

'I heard something,' Gina says.

We stand there, listening. Once, the air would've been filled with the roar of traffic and the sound of people. If it was like that today, it would deafen us – well, me, Gina, Ben and Cy, anyhow. Now, all I hear is the creak of Ben's boots in the snow as he shifts his position slightly, the sound of our breathing, and the faint caw of a crow, calling from two, maybe three miles away.

Ben shakes his head. 'I don't hear anything,' he says.

Cy and I glance at each other and shrug.

We carry on walking. Half of me is hoping Mara will appear right in front of us, holding onto Cass's wee brother, and it'll be bam, job done – as long as I can keep Cass from shooting Mara.

But it's just like the barterers have always said: the city is frozen, silent, dead. We stop to eat and rest again in the entranceway of an apartment block that looks as if it was only half-finished when the Invasion hit – it's covered with rusting scaffolding, a crane sticking up from the roof.

Then I hear it, faint but unmistakable.

Laughter.

Ben drops his pouch of beef stew, grabs his rifle and jumps to his feet.

'What? What is it?' Cass says, looking alarmed, and I realize it's still too far away for her to hear it.

'That's what I heard earlier,' Gina hisses.

'Stay here,' Ben orders. He walks to the edge of the steps and peers out at the street.

I hear the laughter again. It's shrill and bubbling. Is it Cass's brother?

It stops.

'Let's get going,' Ben says, his expression grim.

As we walk, we listen for the laughter, but we don't hear it again. The road opens up into a dual carriageway, and we dart between abandoned cars, buses and lorries, our fingers curled round the triggers of our guns. When the buildings close in around us again, I should feel relieved, but all I can think is, *We're getting closer to the Torturehouse.* I start to get flashes of memory – pain and cages and screaming and smoke – that make me go cold all over.

Ben stops and holds up a hand. 'What?' Gina whispers.

'We're here,' he says. He points across the street, and I see a long stone building with arches along its front. The railway station.

'We need to get across there,' Ben says. 'We'll go one by one, and the rest of us can cover. Agreed?'

'I'll go first,' Gina says.

'OK.'

Gina checks her gun, then runs across the road. When she reaches the station, she presses herself into one of the archways and gives us a thumbs-up.

Cy goes next, and then it's my turn. Now it's just Cass and Ben.

I see her swallow. Then she's running too, sprinting across to Gina and me. As she reaches us she stumbles and instinctively, I reach out and grab her arm. For a second, our faces are so close I can feel her breath against my face. Ben runs across the road. I let go of Cass and she leans against the wall beside me, gasping.

'Right,' Ben says. 'This is—'

'Ben,' Gina says.

He looks round at her. 'What?'

She points.

Footprints.

My heart leaps.

'They're not ours, are they?' Gina says.

Ben shakes his head. I glance round at the churned snow where we ran across to the station. Whoever made these was walking, and they're frozen solid, as if they were made hours or even days ago. They snake past the front of the station and disappear through one of the archways further along. They're too big to be Mara's, but they're *somebody's*. Another Fearless's, maybe. Someone could have met her here.

Ben lets out a slow breath. 'We have to go this way. There isn't a quicker route.'

'Come on, then,' Cy says. 'The sooner we get this over with, the better.'

We follow the footsteps through the archway and into the station. When I see the shops with metal shutters half-pulled down across the fronts, the blank departure screens and the steps, I get a rush of déjà vu. Even with the gaps in my memory, I remember this place. I remember screaming, because the pain in my head was so bad.

'Up there.' Ben points at the steps. I glance at the shuttered shops. I know there's no one there, 'cos I'd be able to hear them breathing if they were, but I still feel on edge. In less than an hour, we'll be there.

Then we hear the laughter again.

# Chapter 29

## CASS

It's coming from somewhere on the station – not close, but not too far away either. We all shrink back, guns aimed in the direction of the laughter.

'Shit,' Ben says, closing his eyes.

'What do we do?' Gina says.

'Carry on. What choice do we have?' He shifts his gun into a more comfortable position. 'When I say go – go.'

We wait, listening for the laughter.

Silence.

'*Go!*' Ben says.

We pelt up the steps, our feet thudding against the crumbling concrete. The others are much faster than me, and once again, I have to fight to keep up, my heart pounding, my chest burning. I thought I was fit after all my Patrol training, but compared to them, I'm useless.

At the top of the steps is an enclosed bridge. 'Keep going!' Ben snaps, jabbing a finger to his left as I pause, trying to catch my breath. I sprint along the bridge after Myo, and as we pass places where the glass has been broken I get glimpses of the platforms and the railway lines underneath us, buried in the snow.

At the other end, Ben tells us to wait, and uses the sights on his gun to peer through one of the gaps in the glass. Then he crosses to the opposite side and does the same.

'Are you OK?' Myo asks me in a low voice, at the same time as Gina asks Ben if he can see anything.

I nod.

Ben shakes his head. 'We'd better wait a minute. We made a lot of noise just now. Whoever's here is going to know they're not alone.'

We cluster near the top of the steps. Myo's right next to me, and every muscle in my body is tensed with the effort of trying not to brush against him.

When five minutes have passed and we haven't heard the laughter again, we creep down the steps.

'We need to go that way,' Ben says, pointing. 'Trains to Meadowhall used to leave from up there.'

'We know,' Myo says, and I glance round at him. He sounds almost angry.

Ben looks apologetic. 'Sorry. I wasn't sure if you remembered.'

To my surprise, Gina reaches out and gives Myo's arm a comforting squeeze. I'm even more surprised – and yes, a tiny bit jealous – when he puts his hand over hers for a moment and gives her a quick smile. What was all that about? Has he been here before? *When?*

'OK. Follow me,' Ben says. 'And stick together.'

We make our way to the end of the platform, where

a train sits against the buffers, its sloping nose buried in a snowdrift. I'm relieved the doors are closed and the windows are too grimy to see through. Who knows what could be in there?

'Which way?' Gina whispers. Ben points to a tunnel just up the tracks.

'More footprints, look,' Myo says. He's right; they're going into the tunnel, and this time, they're fresh.

'Then we must be going in the right direction,' Ben says. 'Assuming they're made by a Fearless, of course.'

We run to the tunnel in single file, listening out for that laughter again. The hairs on the back of my neck are standing up, the skin on my arms prickling.

On the other side of the tunnel is a cutting. The trees at the top are so overgrown that their branches form a thick, mat-like roof across it, keeping out the snow so we can no longer see if we're following the footprints.

Then, directly ahead, we hear the laughter.

'Oh, *shit*,' Gina says. 'It's *here*.'

'Keep your guns ready, OK?' Ben whispers back.

We edge along the tracks, the laughter bouncing towards us as we pass through another series of tunnels. I can hear scraping noises, and a muttering voice. Sometimes it sounds like one, sometimes two.

The last tunnel we enter is much longer and curved; I can't see through to the end. A faint, shuddering light plays across its walls, and something's burning, filling the air with a thick, greasy smell that instantly takes me back to my apartment on Hope: oil lamps.

Whoever's there gives another burst of laughter.

Holding up a hand, Ben walks forward, flat-footed and almost silent.

Gina and Cy exchange glances, then go after him. Myo and I follow. Ben looks round and motions frantically for us to get down. We all drop into a crouch.

The tunnel is choked with rubbish: paper, rusty cans, old plastic bottles, bags and boxes, even bits of furniture, and sitting cross-legged in the middle of it all is a Fearless, his wrists bound with rope and a metal collar around his neck with a chain. The other end of the chain is fixed to a heavy metal post, which has been driven into the tunnel floor.

I gasp.

'Shut up!' Ben mutters through clenched teeth as the Fearless scrambles to his feet and jerks his head round, trying to find the source of the sound. I clap a hand across my mouth so the word I want to scream can't escape.

*Dad.*

# Chapter 30

## CASS

I don't know how. I don't know why. But it's him.

It's *him*.

His mouth has been sewn shut with thin wire, dried blood crusted around the holes in his lips where it's gone in. He's so thin his cheekbones stick out like blades, his hair hanging over his face in filthy strings.

My vision goes grey at the edges. I put a hand against the wall to steady myself.

'Cass?' Myo whispers.

I shake my head fiercely. One of Dad's hands is bandaged, and I remember, with a stab of nausea, Danny telling us how the new drug the Fearless made to replace the serum rots them from the inside out. I wonder if I'm actually in the middle of a nightmare, and if in a moment, I'll wake up back at the hotel we slept in last night, or the farmhouse, or the factory; or if, perhaps, this whole journey has all been a nightmare and I'm actually still at the bunker.

Then, in the middle of one of the piles of rubbish, something stirs. At first, I think I'm hallucinating; that the exhaustion from days of walking and the shock at seeing Dad have finally caught up with me, and my brain's trying to trick me into thinking the rubbish has come to life. It's not until the shape rises up that I see it's a man, so grimy and grey he's almost indistinguishable from the junk he was hiding in. I shoot a glance at his eyes, my heart beating faster than ever, but they're brown, not silver. He gets to his feet and brushes himself down.

'What is it, what is it?' he asks Dad in a voice that sounds squeaky and thin, as if he doesn't use it very much. 'Is someone coming, are they coming, are they?'

Dad looks in our direction again and makes a thin *gnnnnh* sound behind the wire.

'Who's there?' the ragged man says in his rusty voice. 'Who's there, who's there?' He turns from side to side, craning his skinny neck. 'Show yourself or I'll let him off his chain, I'll let him off, oh yes!'

Ben steps forward, then Cy, then Gina, aiming their guns at the man's head. 'I wouldn't if I were you,' Ben says. Myo and I follow them, even though I'm shaking so hard I can barely walk.

The ragged man throws back his head and lets out the cackling laugh we heard earlier. He's almost as thin as Dad. His gaze dances over us, his eyes shining, and I think, *He's crazy. Completely crazy.* Who is he? A barterer? Or just someone like us, who's somehow managed to survive?

Dad strains on his chain, and the ragged man gives another laugh. 'I thought you were one of them,' he says, looking over his shoulder at Dad. 'But you're not, you're not, that's good, now why don't you put those guns down, eh, and we can all have a chat, oh yes.' He grins, showing teeth that are various shades of orange and black. Dad struggles harder against his chains, and the ragged man takes a step away from him.

'What's with the wire?' Gina asks in a low, tense voice.

'He's a biter,' the man babbles. 'A biter, a biter, oh yes, had to stop him biting, didn't I?'

'But what – what are you *doing* with him?' I say. I'm trembling harder than ever. My voice sounds high and faint.

'He guards my things, guards my things, oh yes.' The ragged man sweeps out a hand to indicate the piles of rubbish – his hoard. 'I found him at the Torturehouse, he was gonna get me so I got him instead. He won't last long, can't feed him, I can't, but I can always get myself another, oh yes.'

The man starts babbling in a singsong voice. 'The Torturehouse, the Torturehouse, lots like him there, oh yes. People in cages, wanted me in a cage too, but I outsmarted them, oh yes.'

Ben clenches the fingers of his free hand into a fist, uncurls them again. 'We're looking for a Fearless,' he says, slowly, patiently, as if he's speaking to a very young child. 'A girl in a blue dress. Have you seen her?'

'The Torturehouse, the Torturehouse, they're not taking me to the Torturehouse, oh no,' the ragged man says. 'No, no, n—'

'Hey!' Myo snaps his fingers. The man blinks, his gaze focusing again briefly. 'Have you seen a Fearless girl about my age? With long black hair? And a wee lad with red hair?'

The ragged man gazes at him for a moment, then turns and begins sifting through the rubbish, muttering to himself.

Ben lowers his gun and, never taking his gaze off the ragged man or Dad, removes his pack and pulls out a meal pack.

'Want something to eat, buddy?' Ben's voice is friend-lier than it was a few moments ago. He opens the meal pack and takes out a pouch of chilli con carne. The ragged man's eyes widen. So do Dad's. From behind his wire-stitched lips, he moans, and I feel another sob try to rip its way out of me. *Dad, it's me, Cass!* I want to yell at him, to see if there's a spark of recognition in those dead, silvery eyes.

But I can't. Because I know it won't work, and that will hurt even more than seeing him as a Fearless.

'Food, food, oh yes, food.' The ragged man wades through the rubbish towards us, smacking his lips, a thread of drool hanging from one corner of his mouth. The smell coming off him is awful: a rank combination of urine and rotten breath and dirt and oily hair and fermenting armpits. I take shallow breaths through my mouth, trying not to gag. He makes a grab for the pouch.

'Not until you tell us if you've seen the girl,' Ben says, pressing the muzzle of his gun against the side of the

**246**

ragged man's head. The ragged man's eyes widen, showing veiny, yellowish whites.

'The Torturehouse, the Torturehouse!' His voice rises to
a reedy shriek. 'Please don't kill me, please, please don't!'

'Tell me if you've seen the girl.' Ben's gripping the gun
so tightly his knuckles have turned white.

'Ben,' Gina whispers. He gives no indication he's
heard.

'*DID YOU SEE HER?*' he roars at the ragged man, so
loudly the rest of us – except for Dad – jump.

'She was here! She was here!' The ragged man's
gleeful air has gone, and I think how much like a child
he seems, despite the deep creases in his face and his
grizzled hair and beard. 'The blue dress, the blue dress,
pleasepleaseplease don't shoot me *please*!'

Ben scowls. 'I know what she was wearing, you crazy
old bastard. When was she here?'

The ragged man gives him a blank look.

'One day ago?' Ben says, holding up a finger.

The ragged man shakes his head.

'Two days?'

Another head-shake.

'Three?'

The ragged man nods.

'Are you sure about that?'

'Y-y-yes,' the ragged man squeaks. 'She was walking
up the tracks, up the tracks, oh yes.'

'And did she have a boy with her?'

I hold my breath while I wait for him to answer.

The ragged man nods. 'She was carrying him on her back, she was. And a baby. She had a baby, oh yes.'

Slowly, Ben lowers his gun. A tear escapes the corner of one of the ragged man's eyes, cutting a track through the dust and grime on his face. Ben snorts. 'Right,' he says, glancing up the tracks. 'Let's get going.'

The ragged man reaches a trembling hand out towards the chilli. Just as his fingers brush against it, Ben lifts his gun again and aims it at his head.

'No!' Gina grabs his wrist as he fires. The shot goes wide, the bullet smacking into the tunnel wall. The sound leaves my ears ringing.

'What the hell, Ben?' Cy says as the ragged man shrieks and runs away down the tunnel, while Dad pulls frantically at his chain.

'He deserves everything he gets,' Ben snarls. 'Keeping a Fearless as a guard dog – it's disgusting.'

He raises the gun again, and this time it's Cy who steps forward, snatching it out of his hand.

'God*dammit*, Cy,' Ben says.

'Come on,' Cy says. 'Let's go.'

Ben lets out his breath in a frustrated hiss.

We edge past Dad, pushing through the rubbish, and hurry to the end of the tunnel. Once we're outside, my knees give way, and I collapse in the snow.

'Cass? Cass!' It's Myo, somewhere above me. 'Are you OK?'

'That was my dad,' I jerk out, my teeth rattling

**248**

together, shudders wracking through me. 'That Fearless was my dad.'

There's a moment of shocked silence. Then Myo says, 'Jesus . . .'

'*Seriously?*' Cy says. 'Shit. What are the chances, eh?'

Suddenly, Gina's beside me too. She and Myo help me to my feet and we head up the tracks until we're a safe distance away from the tunnel. I sit down on my pack, hugging my arms around my knees as fresh shudders wrench through me.

Myo crouches down beside me. 'I'm so sorry,' he says. He touches my hand, but there's no buzz as his fingertips connect this time; no tingle of electricity or spark of heat. I'm too devastated, too raw. I bury my head in my arms and let the tears flow, year upon year of them spilling out of me until I feel exhausted and empty.

No one speaks for a long time. Then Ben says, his voice gentler than usual, 'We'd better get moving.' And he startles me by adding, 'Cass, can you manage?'

I nod, and get shakily to my feet.

As we walk on, we huddle together, keeping close to the tangle of trees and scrub at the edges of the tracks. Everyone looks sombre and sad. A couple of times, I see Myo looking at me, but when I try to catch his eye, he quickly glances away again. I can't get the image of the ragged man or Dad out of my head. Part of me wants to run back there and rescue him, but I know that's crazy. You can't save a Fearless, not even if they're your family.

They're *Fearless*. It's too dangerous. The man I knew as my father is gone.

But, oh, I don't know if I'll ever be able to accept it.

*Please be OK, Jori,* I plead inside my head as I trudge through the snow after the others, my pack heavy on my back, my heart heavy in my chest. *You're all I have left. I can't lose you too.*

# Chapter 31

## CASS

Warehouses loom either side of the tracks. Already, the light is failing, shadows gathering around us, the temperature dropping. 'Bloody hell, I'm cold,' Cy mutters. 'I'd give anything to light a fire right now.'

'No fires,' Ben says sharply. 'We're nearly there. We mustn't give ourselves away.'

Not long after that, we reach another station – two narrow platforms overgrown with dead weeds and leafless shrubs, a bridge arching overhead. Even in the near-dark, the signs along the platforms are still readable: *Meadowhall Interchange.*

Ben stops.

'We need to go up there.' He points at the bridge. 'It's best we do it now, while it's dark, so we're less likely to be seen. Then we can figure what we're up against.'

When we get up there, I see a vast sprawl of buildings along the horizon less than a quarter of a mile away, silhouetted against the darkening sky. At first glance, the buildings look derelict, but when I look again I notice pinpoints of flickering light here and there – lanterns, or fires. A high-pitched whoop drifts through the still, cold air towards us. It sounds like a war cry.

'It hasn't changed,' Gina murmurs. I wonder what she means. Then I remember the exchange between Myo and Ben at the station. Ben hasn't looked at a map all day. They must have been here before. But when? When it was still a shopping centre? Or did they get caught during the Invasion, and manage to escape, somehow?

'How are we gonna get in there?' Cy says.

'We need to get closer,' Ben says. 'Find out if there's anyone guarding the place, or if they're all inside.'

At the end of the bridge, a footpath leads down to another glassed-in walkway, like the one at Sheffield Station. We run across, our feet skidding on the filthy, snow-wet tiles, and into a building with a deep stairwell in the middle. The signs here read *Meadowhall Interchange* too. We hide our packs behind a fall of rubble that's come down from the roof. 'No point in taking them over there,' Ben says. 'If we have to run, they'll get in the way. Everyone check your weapons and make sure you've got plenty of ammo.'

We do as he asks.

'OK,' he says. 'All we're going to do tonight is work out where the Fearless are, and where they're keeping the people they've taken. They mustn't know we're here. And I don't want anyone launching any crazy rescue missions tonight.' Although it's so dark now I can't really make out his face, I know he's looking at me.

I think of Jori — how I'll feel if I see him — and swallow hard. 'I won't,' I say.

'That's the walkway that leads directly inside,' Ben continues. 'I think it's better if we find a way round to one of the old car parks.'

I wonder how any of us will be able to see where we're going. Outside, even at night, it's never completely dark. But here, the darkness will soon be absolute, and it will be the same in the Torturehouse. We can't light a lantern, not if we don't want to give ourselves away.

As we get to our feet again, I realize I've never wanted to see the inside of my apartment on Hope again as badly as I do right now.

The others are already walking off. 'Wait!' I call. 'I can't see where I'm going!'

'For God's sake,' I hear Ben mutter.

'Hold out your hand,' Myo says somewhere to my left.

I stretch out my hand, and he takes hold of it. My heart starts thumping. I tell myself it's just nerves at the thought of negotiating the stairs when I can't see properly — nothing to do with his fingers wound tightly through mine.

'The first step's just here,' he says as I wonder again how on earth he can see anything. A tiny, nagging suspicion starts up in the back of my mind, but I'm too busy trying not to fall and break my neck to pay it any attention. 'Shuffle your feet forward and you'll find it.'

'Keep your voice down, can you?' Ben hisses below us.

'Sorry,' Myo mutters.

He guides me carefully down the stairs, so close I can feel his hair tickling my cheek as he whispers, 'Next step. Be careful, it's slippery. We're halfway down now.'

Then Ben says 'Stop,' his voice quiet but sharp.

'What was that?' Gina whispers.

'I don't know.'

We wait, listening. I squeeze Myo's hand, and am ridiculously grateful when he squeezes it back.

'It must have been one of us,' Ben mutters. 'Come on.'

'You stay right where you are,' a voice says in the darkness above us. I hear the scratch and hiss of matches being struck, and suddenly, the stairwell is filled with light.

They're everywhere: up at the top of the stairs, standing around the railing, and down at the bottom.

A ring of Fearless men and women, staring at us with their strange silver eyes.

# Chapter 32

## MYO

Some have lanterns, others have guns. We don't have time to go for our own weapons – we're outnumbered three to one.

'Hands where we can see them,' barks the Fearless who spoke before – a gigantic woman with short hair and one eye, her arms marked with scars and tattoos, a filthy dressing taped across her elbow.

Ben lets his hands drop to his sides. I remember, just in time, that I flipped my eyepatch up so I could see where I was going, and pull it back down before Cass sees.

'Get up here,' the woman says.

We trudge back to the top of the stairs.

Every muscle in my body is screaming at me to run, and Cass is clutching my hand so hard it feels like she's gonna break my fingers. But I'm not scared. I'm *furious*. I can't believe we let ourselves get caught like this.

Ben looks angry too. 'You—' he says.

'Shut up,' the Fearless woman says. She smacks him across the face with the butt of her gun, rocking his head back. The other Fearless laugh, which makes several of them start coughing – a nasty, wet sound.

'Give me your weapons,' the Fearless woman says. We put our guns on the ground in front of us.

'And that.' The woman points at the pistol on Ben's waist. Scowling, blood leaking out of one nostril and a bruise already rising on his left cheekbone, he takes it out of its holster and puts it with the rest of our guns.

Then I remember my knife – it's hidden under my jumper. And I think Cass still has hers in her boot.

'That way,' the Fearless woman says as a man beside her picks up the guns. She points at a doorway to our left. Most of the Fearless move ahead of us, leaving the woman and four others to escort us. They're all limping, but they still move fast.

The doorway leads onto another bridge like the one we came over before. The stench is overpowering; everywhere I look I see skeletons and bundles of rags. One body still has mottled, purple flesh on it, and angry-looking marks at the base of its neck – a child.

*I hope that's not Cass's brother*, I think as the Fearless hustle us past it. Cass is trembling. I know she's thinking the same thing. I squeeze her hand again. *Be strong.*

The Fearless march us to the top of some escalators. I know exactly where we are now. To our left are the double doors that lead outside – that's where Ben got us out, running across the car park with me in his arms, and Cy right behind him with Mara in his. To our right is the entrance to a huge store, the doors gaping open. They still have a white M and a yellow & above them. I remember there being an S, too, but it must have fallen off.

Ben, Cy and Gina stop suddenly. Two of the Fearless in front have got into an argument, swearing at each other. One of the lanterns goes flying. The Fearless woman barges past us to break it up.

I give Cass's hand a quick double squeeze. She looks round, and I glance at Marks and Spencer.

She gives her head a tiny shake.

I raise an eyebrow, looking at the doors to the car park. Between them and us are three Fearless. Between us and the store, there's no one.

On the escalator, the woman is shouting at the two Fearless who were arguing. She'll come up here again soon.

Cass squeezes my hand back.

I shuffle forward and bump my foot against Gina's, making it look accidental. She glances round and I look at the store again.

She pokes Cy in the side, takes his hand, then reaches for Ben's.

One of the Fearless notices. 'Aww, sweet,' he sneers, his voice muffled-sounding because one side of his face is swollen with an abscess, the skin purple and shiny-looking. Anyone else would be in agony with it, but it seems to hardly bother him.

The arguing has stopped.

'*Now!*' I say.

Behind us, I hear gunshots, and Cy cries out, but there's no time to stop or look back. I've forgotten about the eyepatch; as the darkness inside the store swallows us up, I collide with something, sending it crashing to the floor. Gasping, I flip the patch up. The enhanced vision in my right eye isn't enough to make out any details, but the remains of the store loom in grainy black and white around us, like those infra-red images you used to see on cop shows on TV: upturned racks and shelving, piles of boxes and discarded goods, and bodies. So many bodies. Most of them are nothing but skeletons; they must have been here a while. Are they Fearless victims who didn't make it, or Fearless who've died from the effects of the serum?

'I can't see,' Cass gasps. She's kicking bones out of the way without even realizing. 'It's OK, just hold on,' I tell her. I wish I knew where we were going, but my memories of the Torturehouse are scattered and jagged. When I try to remember more, my mind locks down. I told Ben about it once, and he said he was the same, and he thought it was some sort of unconscious coping mechanism, our minds' way of trying to protect themselves. Frustration wells up inside me. The Fearless know this place inside out. Wherever we hide, they'll find us. We should have tried to get outside. I've screwed up. Big time.

Then, up ahead, I see bundles of wire hanging down from the ceiling. I pull Cass towards them. 'There's a hole in the ceiling above us,' I whisper, hearing the shouts of the Fearless coming ever closer. 'We need to get up there. I'm gonna lift you, OK?'

'How can you even see?' she whispers.

I let go of her, then wrap my arms around her waist and lift her up. 'Put your hands out. Feel for the edge.'

She does as I say, gripping the tiles. 'Go!' I say, and she hauls herself up and into the hole. Moments later she reappears, reaching down.

'Where are you?' she whispers. I grab her hands and she pulls me up.

We collapse side by side, breathing hard.

A few seconds later, someone runs right underneath where we're hiding. Even though my heart is racing and it feels as if my lungs are going to burst, I hold my breath. Cass does the same.

More running feet. Shouts from somewhere deeper inside the store. Gunfire.

Silence.

There's no sign of Gina, Cy or Ben.

Cass is pressed right up against me. I reach for her hand again. She winds her fingers tightly through mine and presses her face against my shoulder.

I close my eyes, breathing in the scent of her hair. Everywhere her body presses against mine feels electric. I close my eyes, half-despairing, half-elated. How am I supposed to fight this? And why do I even want to? If I can feel like this, it means I'm human, I'm *whole*. They didn't get me. It didn't work.

I feel Cass lift her head. When I open my eyes, she's gazing at me, even though I know it's too dark for her to see me. The electric feeling in my body rises to a roar, all the dials turned up to max.

'You saved my life,' she whispers. 'Thank you.'

I manage a small laugh. 'I guess we're even now, eh?'

One corner of her mouth twitches up in a smile. 'I guess so.'

She hasn't let go of my hand yet. My heart is thudding so loud I'm surprised she can't hear it.

I open my mouth to say something. I don't know what. All I end up doing is taking a gulp of air and closing it again.

*Don't do this*, the small part of my mind that's still functioning logically tells me. *She'll find out what you are.* But the rest of my mind isn't listening.

I close my eyes. Take another deep breath.

And then, before I can lose my nerve, I kiss her.

# Chapter 33

## CASS

When Myo's lips touch mine, I feel a jolt, and then a slow, spreading joy which chases away the dark and horror and stink all around us. For a few moments, I forget that we're stuck here with no water, no food, no guns and no way out. There's only us, this moment, now.

When we come up for air, I close my eyes and lean my forehead against his. He kisses me again, a quick brush of his mouth against mine. I want to stay like this for ever, but the awareness of where we are, of the danger we're in, comes crashing back.

'Have they gone?' I whisper.

'I'm not sure,' he says. 'I'll go and look.'

He disentangles himself and I hear him shuffle towards the hole in the ceiling. I sit up and lean against an air-conditioning pipe, hugging my arms around my knees.

A few moments later, he's back. 'I can't see anyone, but we need to get further inside and hide for a while. They'll still be looking for us.'

We don't have room to stand up, so we crawl on our

hands and knees through a tangle of pipes and wires. Myo guides me around the holes in the ceiling. The smell of rot and death is stronger than ever.

Eventually, we reach a wall, and can go no further. We draw our knees up and sit back against it, hip to hip, shoulder to shoulder.

I shiver. 'It's so cold.'

'Here.' Myo puts his arms around me, pulling me closer still. I lean against him, grateful for the warmth. I want him to kiss me again, to prove that what just happened wasn't a dream or a hallucination, but he doesn't.

I feel him move, and realize he's adjusting his eye-patch. I reach out and touch it. 'What happened to your eye?'

'It was a Fearless,' he says. 'I was attacked.'

'Is that how you got those scars on your arm, too?' I say.

I feel him stiffen. 'No. That was me.'

A silence yawns between us while I try to comprehend what would make him feel so bad that he'd do something like that to himself. 'Why?' I say. We're both talking quietly, careful not to let our voices get picked up by the Fearless's heightened hearing. I can still hear far-off shouts and crashes.

'It was when I was a lot younger. Stuff had happened and I couldn't deal with it. I thought it would help. But Ben made me stop. And he was right to – I mean, what if I'd got an infection or something? There were no hospitals or doctors about any more. It was pretty stupid, really . . .'

'I'm sorry,' I say. I wonder if by *stuff*, he means the Invasion. What happened to his family? I realize that apart from his sister, he's never mentioned them.

We're quiet for a moment. Then he says, 'Was that really your dad back in the tunnel?'

A sudden, savage ache starts up in my throat. 'Yeah. He was attacked by the Fearless the night of the Invasion. My mum made it to Hope with me, but she killed herself a couple of years later.' I take a shaky breath. 'She walked into the sea and drowned herself. Captain Denning – that's the guy with the moustache – was furious. But she'd lost my dad and had a baby and I think it was just too much for her.'

'Jesus,' Myo says. 'That's awful. I had no idea.'

'What about your parents?' I say.

He snorts. 'They were junkies. We didn't even live with them when it happened. We were . . .'

He trails off. Inside my head, something goes click. 'You were caught, weren't you?' I say.

He doesn't answer me.

'Myo?'

'Aye,' he says softly. 'Not straight away, though. It was about a year afterwards.'

'Oh, God,' I say. 'But you got away. You must have, because you're still . . .' I trail off. *Normal* doesn't even begin to describe what it means to escape being Altered.

'It was Ben. He rescued us and took us to the bunker.'

'And is that why you—' I nod at his arm, even though it's pitch-black in here.

'Yeah.'

'I'm sorry. It must be terrible for you to have to come back.'

'It's fine.' His voice is gruff. 'I don't plan on being here any longer than I have to, y'know? We'll wait until things have calmed down, and then we'll try and find Ben and the others.'

'OK.'

We lean back against the wall. 'Anyway, it's me who should be saying sorry,' Myo whispers.

'What for?' I whisper back.

'For trying to leave you at the docks. And being so weird at the farmhouse and the bunker.' He pauses, takes a deep breath. 'If we make it out of here alive, I'll explain everything, I promise.'

'You'd better,' I say, grabbing his collar and pulling him towards me. Our kisses are fiercer now, hungry, both of us trying to push away our dark memories, even if it's only for a moment.

Myo sits up abruptly.

'What is it?' I say.

'Someone's here,' he hisses.

'What, in the ceiling?'

'No. In the store.'

He falls silent. We listen. At first I don't hear anything. Then I do: footsteps, passing slowly underneath us.

'Stay quiet,' Myo murmurs in my ear.

We listen as the footsteps fade, then circle back again. My heart is thudding. So is Myo's; I can feel it through his jacket.

'Myo! Cass! Are you here?' someone whispers.

'That's Gina!' Myo says.

'Are you sure?' I say.

'Only one way to find out.' I feel him move.

'Where are you going?'

'To see if it's her.'

'But what if it isn't? What if it's a Fearless, trying to trick you?'

'Stay here.' He kisses me one last time, and then he's gone, the kiss tingling on my lips.

I pull up my trouser leg and take my knife out of my boot.

After a while, I hear someone moving through the roof space towards me. I grip the knife, my muscles tensed.

'Cass, it's me,' Myo says, his voice drifting towards me through the dark. 'It *is* Gina. Ben's with her, and he's hurt. We're going to try and get him up here.'

'Can I do anything?' I say.

'No, just stay put.'

I wait again, the darkness pulsating around me like something living. 'Can you make it?' I hear Gina ask Ben. He gives a soft groan. Then Myo's beside me again. Moments later, so are the others.

'Where's Cy?' I ask.

'They got him,' Gina says.

Horror washes over me. 'Oh, no.'

'Oh, no is right,' Ben says. There's no mistaking the sarcasm – or the pain – in his voice.

'What happened?'

'I got clipped by a bullet,' he says shortly.

*Crap.* I think of our packs, back in the building at the other end of the bridge. We left all the medical supplies inside them. Myo must have read my thoughts, because he says, 'I can go back, get bandages and stuff—'

'No chance,' Ben says. 'They've got Fearless on guard at the top of the escalators. They know we're still in here somewhere.'

'How many?'

'Four. You won't stand a chance without your gun.'

'How bad is it?'

'It didn't go in. Hurts like hell, though.'

We sit there for hours, rats scampering and chittering around us. Ben and Gina talk in whispers; Myo and I sit without speaking, our fingertips just touching. We don't move any closer to each other, but the memory of our kisses warms me as we wait for morning. Every time I think about them, my heart skips a beat.

Eventually, I must fall into a doze, because next thing I know, greyish light is stealing through the holes in the roof above us. Looking over at Ben, I see the blood darkening the shredded fabric of his trousers near his left ankle.

'Let me look,' Gina says as he tries to draw his leg back and grimaces. Gently, she pulls his trouser leg up.

Across Ben's shin is a furrow where the bullet has grazed across it. It isn't bleeding, but it looks sore.

'Are you sure it didn't go in?' Myo says.

'You think I'd still be here if it had?' Ben snaps.

'OK, OK, I was only asking.' Myo holds up his hands.

'We need to clean the wound,' Gina says briskly. 'There's bits of fabric in it – it'll get infected.'

'We can't go anywhere until those Fearless are gone,' Ben says through gritted teeth. 'And even if we do get out, how will we get back in for Cy and – and her brother? Getting in was hard enough. We'll not do it a second time.'

He's right – now we're in, we have to stay. My stomach cramps with fear and hunger.

'One of us is going to have to see if they can find some water, then,' Gina says. 'Though God knows where.'

'I'll go,' Myo says. 'I can crawl through the roof spaces. Some snow might have come in somewhere.'

'I'll come with you,' I say, and Ben's eyes narrow, suspicion flickering across his face as he looks from Myo to me and back again.

I square my shoulders, looking straight at him, daring him to say anything.

'Come on,' Myo says. 'We'll go that way.'

He points to where the daylight breaking through the gaps in the roof is strongest. We crawl side by side, trying to make as little noise as possible. I pray that if the Fearless hear anything, they'll think it's rats.

The roof spaces are connected; when I look down

through another hole in the ceiling, we're over a completely different store. Paper and books are scattered everywhere, fat with damp and mould. And under the piles of rotting books . . .

'Oh, God,' I say, my hand flying to my mouth. 'Are those bodies?'

'They're everywhere,' Myo whispers. 'Maybe people locked themselves in the shops when the Invasion happened because they thought it would be safer. Or else they're Fearless who've died from the effects of the serum.'

'Ugh.' I shake my head, trying to chase away the image of what I just saw.

'Are you sure you want to do this? You can go back to the others if you want. I don't mind.'

I shake my head. 'I'm fine.'

He gives me a quick kiss, and we carry on, avoiding the gaps in the ceiling when we can hear voices directly underneath us, or see the flickering glow of lamplight.

At last, we come to a place where the roof has caved in, letting in a broad shaft of daylight. A layer of snow coats the rubble. 'How are we going to get it to Ben?' I ask.

'I'll fill my gloves,' Myo says. 'It won't melt before we get it back – it's too cold.' Straightening up into a crouch, he strips them off and begins packing snow into them. I'm still wearing mine, so I do the same.

'We should get back,' Myo says when I've finished. I rub my fingers to get the circulation going again, thinking about Jori. He's somewhere underneath us. So is Cy.

When I look at Myo, I know he's thinking the same thing.

He sets the gloves down on the heap of snow-covered rubble. 'You want to find your brother?'

I nod.

'OK. I know where he'll be, if he's here.'

I take my knife out of my boot again, and crawl after him through the roof space.

# Chapter 34

## MYO

I should tell her that us kissing was a mistake, a heat of the moment thing. But how can I? She's bewitched me. And worst of all, I'm glad of it.

We steal through the roof space, freezing whenever we hear voices underneath us. I wish we had our guns. Our knives aren't gonna be worth shit if those bastards realize we're here and send a gang up after us.

Suddenly, the roof space opens out. I hear more voices – not Fearless, but ordinary people, moaning and crying. I remember my body cramped and folded, my face pressed against cold metal bars.

I stop, squeezing my eyes shut.

'Are you OK?' Cass whispers.

I hold a finger to my lips. We mustn't make a sound. We're in more danger than she can possibly imagine.

She nods, and I wish fiercely that our lives were not like this, and the Invasion had never happened; that I'd met her at school or college or something.

That I was as normal as she thinks I am.

But instead, we're stuck here in the roof space of

the Torturehouse, surrounded by Fearless. And I'm . . .

*Enough. Don't think about that now.*

We crawl over to another hole in the ceiling. The cage room is the place I remember the least about, but as we peer down at it, those memories start to return too. The smoky half-light from the lamps; the stink of blood and piss and vomit and shit, so strong it makes my eyes water; the rubble-strewn floor and rows of cages, crammed with bodies – cages thrown together out of whatever scraps of wood and metal the Fearless could find. It looks exactly the same.

In a cage directly below us, a bairn who can't be older than eight or nine throws himself against the bars of his cage, making guttural noises deep in his throat. Then he looks up. Cass and I both draw back, but not before I've seen the cuts on the kid's forehead where he's smashed them against the bars. Blood streams down his face.

I look round at Cass. Her eyes are completely round. *Is that your brother?* I mouth.

She shakes her head. Relieved, I crawl back to the hole.

That's when I see her.

She's moving between the cages, carrying a heavy wooden stick. As she passes the cage with the bairn in it, she swings it against the bars. He screams and she smashes the stick against the cage again, her hair swinging across her face. The Fearless woman with one eye hobbles up to her and pulls her away. She cuffs Mara's face and Mara tries to hit her with the stick. The woman

**271**

snatches it and cracks her across the head, sending her to her knees. Then she stalks away, leaving Mara kneeling on the ground.

I want to call out her name. I want to jump down there and see if she's OK. But I can't.

Suddenly, Cass is beside me again. 'What's going on down there?' she whispers in my ear.

'What does your brother look like?' I whisper back.

'Curly hair like mine, but it's red.'

I don't see anyone fitting that description. I can't see Cy, either. 'Let's try over there,' I murmur. 'Keep an eye out for Tessie and Cy, too.'

We belly-crawl to another hole in the ceiling. Suddenly, Cass punches me on the arm. *Cy*, she mouths.

*Where?* I mouth back.

She points. He's in a cage almost directly underneath us. His eyes are closed, his face bruised, his wrists and legs bound with strips of plastic.

I glance at Cass. *Do you see your brother?* I mouth when she looks round at me again.

She shakes her head.

I back away from the hole and pull her close.

'He's not here, is he?' she says in a tiny whisper. 'He's dead.'

'You don't know that,' I whisper back. 'There are loads of people here.' I rest my chin on the top of her head. I feel so helpless.

'Let's go back,' she mutters. 'I've seen enough.'

We crawl away from the cage room and head back to

the snow pile to collect our gloves. My head's aching, a hundred thoughts crowding into my mind all at once. *What if Cass's brother is dead? What's going to happen to Ben and Cy? Where's Tessie? How am I going to get Mara out of here? And what am I going to do about Cass?*

I have no idea.

# Chapter 35

## CASS

When we get back, Ben seems to be asleep, leaning against the wall, but as we approach, he opens his eyes. 'Where the *hell* have you been?' he snaps at Myo. 'We thought you'd got caught.'

In reply, Myo tosses him one of the snow-filled gloves. 'Here,' he says.

'Did you run into any Fearless?' Gina asks as, grimacing, Ben pulls up his trouser leg and begins applying the snow to the wound.

'We went to find out where they were keeping Cy,' Myo says.

'And?'

'Same place as before. In the old restaurant complex.'

'And . . . ?' She gives Myo a meaningful look.

He nods.

'We need to figure out how to get down there,' Gina says, as I wonder what that look meant.

'We need food and water first,' Ben cuts in. 'None of us are going to be able to do a damn thing if we're dehydrated and starving.'

'We have to go back for the packs,' Myo says.

'But those Fearless are guarding the entrance,' Gina says.

'I'm gonna see if they're still there.' Before any of us can stop him, he crawls away through the roof space.

As the minutes stretch out and he doesn't return, my stomach churns with dread. When he finally reappears, I'm so relieved I could kiss him, and never mind what Ben thinks.

'They've gone,' he says. 'They must think we escaped somehow.'

Ben and Gina look at each other. 'Right then,' Ben says, bending his knees and trying to get to his feet. 'We need to—'

The rest of his words are lost as his injured leg buckles underneath him and he collapses back against the wall, biting back a cry of pain.

'Oh, for—' he hisses, leaning back and closing his eyes again, beads of sweat standing out on his forehead.

'You two stay here,' Myo says. 'Me and Cass will go.'

He looks at me and raises his eyebrows – *OK?* – and I nod. 'We only need one of the packs, anyhow,' I say.

'Be careful,' Ben says. He's looking at Myo and me with his eyes narrowed. I'm sure he's guessed something's happened between us, but right now, what Ben thinks is the least of my worries.

When we reach the hole in the ceiling, Myo drops through first, landing catlike on the floor below. Then he reaches up, making a step with his hands so I can lower myself down too. We take out our knives and zigzag through the store in a series of almost-silent dashes, stopping every few moments to listen for Fearless.

The atrium at the top of the escalators is empty, bathed in spooky, whitish light. We sprint along the walkway, swerving round the bodies. Outside are huge car parks, piled with the snow-covered wrecks of cars. The horror of what must have happened here when the Invasion hit is almost too big to comprehend.

Then, as we run into the hallway, we see a Fearless man bent over our packs, which he's dragged into the middle of the floor. Despite the cold, he's only wearing a short-sleeved shirt, ragged and filthy. His left arm, hanging uselessly by his side, is puffy and greenish, two of his fingers no more than bones sticking out of dead-looking stubs of flesh. The new Fearless serum has literally rotted them away. He whirls, reaching for the gun by his feet. We don't have time to escape. We launch ourselves at him, and before he can shoot, Myo jams his knife into the man's stomach and I plunge mine into his solar plexus, yanking the blade upward towards his throat. The Fearless drops the gun and staggers back, blood fountaining from the top of the wound. I must have hit an artery.

But even with the blood draining from his body, he stays on his feet, trying to get the gun. Myo grabs it and smashes the butt into his face, while I kick out, both of us driving him backwards to the top of the stairs. He staggers, loses his footing and falls, howling with rage until he hits the floor at the bottom with a sickening crump.

Myo and I dive behind the rubble pile where we hid our packs and huddle, side by side, waiting.

At the bottom of the stairs, the Fearless starts making choking sounds. He still isn't dead. I close my eyes, sure that more Fearless will come running, drawn by the noise he made as he fell.

Eventually, the choking stops.

Myo straightens up. 'We have to get rid of him. If any more of them turn up—'

Wiping my knife blade on my trousers, I follow him down the stairs. The Fearless is lying on his back at the bottom, his silver eyes glaring at nothing. We struggle back up the stairs with him and take him onto the bridge that leads back to the station. Underneath it is a river. Heaving the body through one of the empty panes, we watch as it hits the surface with a splash and sinks, bubbles spiralling up in its wake. Then we run back, reorganize the contents of the packs, transferring as many supplies into the biggest one as we can, and make our way back to Marks & Spencer. I feel as if I'm in some sort of simulation, a test set up by the Patrol.

'You go first,' Myo whispers when we reach the hole in the ceiling. 'I'll pass the pack up to you.'

I give him the gun and my knife, and he removes the pack and makes a step for me with his hands again. Clambering into the roof space, I lie on my belly to reach down for the pack and the weapons.

But he doesn't pass them up to me. He's staring at me.

'What are you waiting for?' I hiss, at the same time as he starts to say, 'Cass, look ou—'

A hand grabs the back of my jacket, yanking me upright. Twisting round, I find myself staring straight into the face of the one-eyed Fearless woman. 'Well,' she says, her tone as matter-of-fact as if she was just discussing the weather. 'Looks like I caught myself a rat.'

'*Hey!*' Myo hauls up through the hole with my knife gripped between his teeth and leaps at the woman. 'Get off her!'

The woman swings me round in front of her so I'm directly in the path of the knife, and when Myo falters, she lashes out, her meaty fist smashing into his jaw. Myo drops the knife and goes flying backwards, cracking his head against a metal pipe.

'*Myo!*' I yell, as he collapses in a heap.

'Let's have a look at you,' the woman says, clamping her arm tighter around my neck. She lunges forward and rips off his eyepatch. Myo groans, his eyelids fluttering open for a moment.

I stare.

Not only does he have a right eye, but it's silver.

*Fearless* silver.

He closes his eyes again. My last sight of him, before the woman pushes herself through the hole in the ceiling with me hanging from her choking grip, is his slumped form lying beneath the pipe.

As she drags me through the store, I scream and kick,

struggling to get free. 'Shut up,' she growls, smacking me round the head so hard it leaves my ears ringing. I sag against her, all the fight leaving me in a rush. We're not going towards the exit, but deeper into the store. The Fearless loosens her grip. 'Walk,' she says, twisting her fingers into my hair so viciously that tears of pain spring into my eyes. 'And don't even think about trying to get away. I'll rip your scalp off.'

She marches me along a parade of derelict shops, until we reach a huge archway. 'In!' she barks.

On the other side, it's dark, and the foul smell that lingers everywhere, as thick as soup, gets stronger. I stumble, putting my hands out blindly in front of me, and the woman gives my hair another eye-watering tug.

Then I see the flicker of lanterns, and the cages. They're arranged in rows across what was once the floor of a restaurant. The room is circular, with a high ceiling, the wreckage of tables and chairs piled up round the edges.

The woman drags me towards the cages. From somewhere I find the energy to fight her again. 'You want me to snap your neck?' she spits at me, grabbing both my wrists in a meaty fist and twisting my arms up towards my face. She takes me to the cage right next to Cy. I scream his name, but he doesn't even open his eyes.

'You!' the woman barks, turning her head. A girl shuffles out of the shadows. The girl with the black hair who took Jori and was at Danny and April's. She has a heavy-looking bunch of keys round her neck on a frayed, stained piece of ribbon. 'Get that cage open,' the woman says. The girl starts fiddling with the padlock, and through my terror, I realize she reminds me of someone. Who?

But now the door is undone and the Fearless woman is shoving me towards the cage, and I forget about anything except trying to get away from her again.

'I warned you.' The woman punches me in the side of the head. The pain is red-black, explosive. I see sparks, and hear a roaring sound, growing louder and louder.

Then everything goes dark.

# Chapter 36

## SOL

I've been at the Magpies' camp for four days now. Four days of mud and rain and cold and barely enough sleep to function. The training is brutal: all-weather cross-country runs, flanked by armed Magpies on horseback as we stumble through woods and fields and icy rivers; hours on the camp's gigantic assault course, scaling wooden walls, swinging from ropes and wriggling through sticky, freezing mud; rifle drills; fieldcraft. We also have to join the Magpies on patrol around the camp's perimeter, which is protected by a huge electric fence powered by diesel generators. They get to ride horses – the jeeps are only for long-distance travel – but the rest of us have to walk.

And it's not just the training that's tough. Everything here is about pushing you to your absolute limits. We're in the middle of goddamn nowhere – a valley with a river running through the middle and steep hills either side, covered in trees, which are permanently cloaked in fog. The camp itself consists of row upon row of large, rectangular canvas tents with stoves inside them, which do nothing to keep us warm or the damp or the cold out. The food is terrible, and I'm beginning to think coming here was a huge mistake. I'm already fit; I already know how to shoot, and defend myself, and climb and run. I want action. It's a total waste of time. And meanwhile, a huge group of Magpies is getting ready to leave for the Fearless lair near Sheffield. Everywhere you look, people are loading up trucks, hurrying between tents with maps and supplies and weapons.

I wish I was going with them.

That evening, I'm lying on my bunk, thinking about Cass, when a Magpie marches into my tent. 'Colonel Brett has asked to see you,' she says in a heavily accented voice. I think she's Spanish – a lot of the Magpies are from other countries. Irritated at having my daydream about miraculously being reunited with Cass interrupted, I suppress a sigh and sit up. 'Yes, ma'am,' I say. The girl is only a few years older than me, and only a private, but right now, even she ranks above me. Which pisses me off no end.

I step into my boots, adjust my uniform – a black jacket, shirt and combats – and slosh along the muddy paths between the tents to Colonel Brett's office, a Portakabin near the fence. I'm still stunned at how organized the Magpies are. They have horses, vehicles, seemingly endless supplies of weapons and clothes and food. God knows where they get it all.

I knock smartly on the Portakabin door, and wait for Brett to call, 'Enter!'

'Ah, Brightman, take a seat,' he says from behind his desk when I go in. The office is dimly lit by a single bulb, run off the same generators that power the fence. A little wood stove burns in one corner. Brett has papers spread out in front of him. As I sit down, he pushes them to one side. 'You're probably wondering why I've asked you to come here.'

'Yes, sir,' I say.

'I've been keeping an eye on you, Brightman. And I'm impressed. You're fast and you're strong. Just the sort of person we need in the Magpies.'

I smile. 'Thank you, sir.'

Brett's expression remains serious. 'However, I get the feeling, sometimes, that you're not taking things here quite as seriously as you should.'

'I – I don't understand, sir.'

He leans his elbows on his desk, steepling his fingers. 'I've had reports from my field commanders that you often appear bored, or try to cut corners. I know, Brightman, that you feel your training on that island of yours was adequate preparation for you to become a fully fledged Magpie – no pun intended – but believe me, what we're trying to do here is in a whole different league from those *bodyguards* your father employed.'

I feel anger building up inside me, and clench my fists down by my sides where he can't see them.

'Yes, sir,' I say.

'It's imperative that everybody here sticks to the plan. We're not just trying to rebuild the country here – we're

**283**

trying to rebuild the whole *world*. If you could see some of the things I've seen, Brightman . . .'

'What *have* you seen, sir?' The question bursts out of me before I can stop it, and, deciding I'm probably screwed anyway, I go on, 'I mean, where did you come from? Where did the *Magpies* come from? How did they get all these supplies?'

I tense, waiting for him to yell at me for disrespect. Instead, he smiles. 'I suppose it's only fair I fill you in, seeing as your father and I worked together so closely at one time.' Then his smile vanishes. 'I'm only telling you this because you already know what we did, mind you. This is not common knowledge, understand?'

I nod.

He leans back in his chair, making it creak. 'Just before the Invasion hit, I fled the country and used my share of the money from what your father and I did to buy a military bunker in a remote corner of the French Alps. Other people paid me to let them have a place there too.

'But guilt ate away at me. In the end, I decided I had to stop sitting around and do something. So I started gathering people together. Getting organized. We met up with other groups who had managed to survive and, slowly, we started building armies of people to go after the Fearless and take them down. We killed them at first, but then we realized we were letting a huge resource go to waste, so we came up with the procedure we use now, which allows us to put them to use again.'

*The procedure*. I've heard rumours about it, but I've never actually seen it. I'd love to, though.

'We were more successful than we could ever have hoped,' Brett goes on. 'All over Europe, and even further afield, societies are being rebuilt. That's why I decided it was time for me to return here and see what I could do. There are still many unAltered people left who, with help, could return this part of the world to the way it used to be, but better.'

Brett leans forward. Suddenly, his expression, which has been almost friendly, is grave again. 'I must say, Brightman, I was very disappointed in your father. We both acted like cowards in the beginning, but when I came to Hope and explained what we were doing, I hoped he would see the error of his ways.'

*I've been disappointed in him for years*, I think, although what I say is, 'Did my father know about you?'

Brett shakes his head. 'Our trip to the island was the first time I'd spoken to him since everything went wrong.' He fixes me with a steely glare. '*You're* not going to let me down, are you?'

'Absolutely not, sir!' I say.

'Your father owes society a big debt. Eventually, he won't have any choice but to come on board, but in the meantime, it's up to you to prove that not all Brightmans are quitters or cowards.'

The enormity of what he's saying slowly sinks in. My father's debt is my debt, and because he won't pay it back, I have to. Brett owns me. My dreams of a glittering future in the Magpies crumble, and in that moment, I despise my father more than I've ever done in my entire life.

'Yes, sir,' I say. My throat is so tight with rage that my voice sounds stiff.

'You are dismissed,' Brett says.

I return to my tent and flop down on my bunk again, my thoughts returning instantly to Cass. If only she was here, I could bear this, somehow. Where is she? Is she even alive?

*Please, please, please let her be OK*, I think, closing my eyes.

Because the only thing that's keeping me going now is the hope that I might see her again.

# Chapter 37

## MYO

'Myo. Myo. Wake up!'

It's Gina. I wish she'd go away. My head hurts. I want to go back to sleep. It can't be time to get up yet.

'Myo, wake up, or I'll slap you, I swear to God.'

She shakes my shoulder, making pain bolt through my skull. I prise my eyelids open. 'Screw you,' I say. My voice sounds weird – blurry and thick.

'Oh, thank God,' she says, and I remember I'm not in my bed. I'm not at the bunker at all. I'm in the roof space of the Torturehouse.

'Cass!' I gasp, sitting up. 'Where is she? Did the Fearless woman get her?'

'She must have done,' Gina says. 'She's not here.'

'We have to get her back!' I touch the back of my head, steeling myself for the sticky, wet feel of blood, but to my relief, my fingers come away dry. Then I realize, with a stab of panic, that I'm not wearing my eyepatch. What happened to it? I've never been able to wear lenses like the others do – I'm allergic to them –

so it's the only way to hide my eye. What if Cass—

'No,' Gina says.

'What do you mean?' I say. 'Cy's down there, and Mara – we saw them! Cass's brother could be there too!'

'We have to get out of here. It's too dangerous. That woman or some other Fearless will come back for us soon. We need to find somewhere where Ben can rest so his leg can heal.'

'So we're just gonna *leave* them?'

'I'm sorry. We don't have any choice. We haven't got our weapons, and Ben's leg's too badly hurt for him to fight.'

'No.' It comes out as a guttural moan. '*No.*'

'Stop being so bloody stupid,' Ben says behind us. He's sitting beside my pack. I remember dropping it when I saw the Fearless woman behind Cass; he must have fetched it. 'If we stay here, we'll all get caught.'

'But we can't leave her!' I cry, not caring if the Fearless hear me.

'Who?' The sarcasm in Ben's voice is bruising. 'Mara? Or Cass?'

I don't answer.

'Maybe we need to accept that this is where Mara should be,' Ben says. 'Among her own people.' Gina looks round at him with a shocked expression and starts to say something, but he cuts her off with a shake of his head. 'And as for Cass, seriously, Myo, what were you thinking?'

'She saved my *life*,' I say.

'You're in love with her, aren't you.' It's not a question. His tone is blunt and accusing.

And I want to tell him no, of course I'm not.

But I can't.

'*Jesus Christ*,' Ben snarls. 'You're even more of an idiot than I thought. We're half-Fearless, Myo. People like her and people like us don't mix.'

I move towards him, but Gina steps in front of him and grabs my wrists.

'Myo, get a grip,' she says through clenched teeth. 'It's over.'

'You're leaving Cy, too,' I hiss at her. 'You think Tana will be OK with that? And what about Tessie? We don't even know if she's here.'

She drops my wrists and turns to Ben. 'I'll take the pack. Me and Myo'll go either side of you and help you walk.'

And I know, then, that there's nothing I can do. I can't fight this many Fearless on my own, even if half of them are incapacitated by the effects of the serum. I've failed Cass. I've failed her brother. I've failed Mara.

Gina's right.

It's over.

# Chapter 38

## CASS

I drift back into consciousness through a haze of un-familiar sounds. I'm freezing, and my whole face hurts, giving me a pounding headache. My mouth is dry, my lips stuck to my teeth. I'm lying on my side on something hard and rough and I can't feel my right arm. Where am I? What's happened?

I open my eyes. I still can't feel my arm. I start to panic, then realize it's gone numb because I'm lying on it.

Wincing, I roll over. I'm in a cage, which is just tall enough for me to sit up in if I hunch over and tuck my chin into my chest. The bottom is made from a sheet of plywood, spongy around the edges with damp, and the bars look like they're made from table legs and bits of fencing, roughly welded together and powdery with rust.

My palm and fingers buzz with pins and needles as the circulation returns to my right arm. Carefully, I touch my nose. *Broken*, I think, licking blood off my top lip. I've been caught by the Fearless. How? The last clear memory I have is of helping Myo get rid of the Fearless man's body. After that, my mind is blank.

'Cass?' someone whispers.

I look round, and my heart skips a beat.

'Jori!' I cry. My brother is in a cage directly opposite, no more than ten feet away. His green T-shirt is stained and ripped and filthy, his face pinched with exhaustion and fear. I scan his face anxiously, trying to see what colour his eyes are. To my relief, they're still green.

'Cass?' he whispers again, as if he can't quite believe it's me.

I press myself against the front of the cage, wrapping my hands around the bars. 'Are you OK?' I say, my voice shaking.

Tears well from the corners of his eyes. 'They keep giving me medicine. It makes me feel good at first, but then it makes me poorly.' He turns his head sideways, lifting his hair up at the back, and I see, at the top of his spine, a two-centimetre-wide circle of bruised, scabby puncture-wounds. My heart skips a beat. How much serum has he had? Frantically, I feel the back of my own neck, but there's nothing there.

*Yet.*

More tears spill down Jori's cheeks. 'My head hurts.'

I want to tell him that it's going to be OK, that I'm going to get him out of here. But this isn't like the times I comforted him after he'd had a nightmare or convinced himself there was a monster lurking in the stairwell outside our apartment. This is *real*, and there's absolutely nothing I can do to make it better.

Someone moans. I look round. Cy's scrunched up in

the cage right next to me, one side of his face black and blue where someone's hit him.

'Cy,' I say. '*Cy.*'

He looks at me with a dazed expression. At first, I'm not sure he even knows who I am, but then he says, 'We really messed up, didn't we? Where are the others?'

I scan the other cages, trying to see who's in them. 'I don't think they're here. Maybe they got away,' I say, and feel a brief surge of hope, thinking they could be out there still, looking for a way to rescue us. Then I remember that Ben's hurt.

And suddenly, with that one memory, everything else comes back to me.

I remember returning to the store with Myo.

I remember the Fearless woman grabbing hold of me as I climbed up into the ceiling.

I remember her punching Myo.

I remember her tearing off his eyepatch.

I remember his silver right eye.

Then I hear footsteps. Four Fearless walk into the middle of the circle of cages: the woman with one eye, two men, and the girl in the blue dress, who's carrying a metal bucket. Again, I'm struck by how familiar she looks. She sets the bucket down. It contains little plastic syringes filled with a murky-looking liquid.

The other Fearless grab handfuls of the syringes, and the girl starts unlocking the padlocked cages, using the keys on the piece of ribbon around her neck. I watch in horror as one of the Fearless men reaches inside a cage and injects a girl in the back of the neck. The girl struggles briefly, then goes limp. The Fearless slings her against the back of her cage and moves on, leaving the girl to lock her up again.

'No!' Jori shouts when the one-eyed Fearless woman gets to him. '*No! Cass, help!*'

'*Leave him alone!*' I scream. All four Fearless ignore me. As soon as the woman injects Jori, he loses consciousness, the only indication he's still breathing the faint, rapid up-down movement of his chest.

'Jori . . .' I whimper.

The girl in the blue dress stops in front of my and Cy's cages. Her eyes are so pale they're almost white. They seem to look right through me.

'Mara, don't do this, mate,' Cy says as she steps towards his cage. 'You know me, right? It's Cy.'

Shock slams through me. Cy knows her? *How?*

Then I remember the tattoo on Myo's hip.

*Mara.*

As she unlocks my cage, I realize what's been nagging at me. Her resemblance to Myo is unmistakable. She could be his twin.

*You were caught, weren't you?* I hear myself asking him, and his muttered reply: *Aye.*

That's why he was able to see where he was going, even when it was pitch-dark.

And what about his strength, and his speed?

What about his eye?

*Of course he was here before, you idiot,* I tell myself. *He was Altered. He's FEARLESS.*

And this girl, Mara — the girl who kidnapped Jori — is the sister he told me about back at the bunker. *That's* why he was on Hope.

He was with her and the man all along.

# Chapter 39

## CASS

*I kissed him*, I think, going cold all over with revulsion. *I kissed him*.

The Fearless who injected Cy reaches into my cage, grabs my hair and pulls my head forward. I don't even have time to scream before he jabs the syringe into the base of my neck.

For a fraction of a second, I feel nothing at all. Then warmth spreads up into my skull, and a heavy, woozy, pleasant feeling overcomes me. My vision starts to recede, closing in at the edges. I gasp, trying to fight it, but it's as if every cell in my body is shutting down.

As the door clangs shut, I slump against the cage bars, and pass out.

When I wake up again, my headache is a hundred – a thousand – times worse than the one I had before, the light from the lanterns stabbing into the backs of my eyes. When I try to move, my stomach clenches, and I double over, retching into a corner of the cage, even though I have nothing to bring up except bile and strings of saliva.

'The first time's a killer,' someone says as I spit, trying to clear the rancid taste out of my mouth – an older girl in a cage nearby. Her face sags downwards on one side, her mouth drooping. I wonder if it's some sort of nerve damage caused by the serum.

'Close your eyes and take deep breaths,' the girl says as another band of pain squeezes around my skull. 'It'll pass in a bit.'

I try to do as she says. All I can think is, *I need more serum.* Anything to take this headache away.

When the nausea has eased a little, I open my eyes again and heave myself upright, avoiding the stinking puddle in the corner of the cage. I look across at Jori. He's sitting up too, his face wet with tears. 'Jor,' I croak, reaching out through the cage bars towards him. My brother stretches out his hand too. In the next cage, Cy is lying on his side, his knees drawn up, his eyes flickering underneath his closed eyelids. I can't tell if he's asleep or unconscious.

A while later, Mara returns, bringing cups of water and some sort of greyish bread which she shoves through the cage bars. I don't want it, but the girl with the drooping face says softly, 'If you don't eat, you'll Alter much faster.' Even though I'm not remotely hungry, I cram the bread into my mouth and wash it down with the brackish-tasting water, encouraging Jori to do the same.

The smell of cooking meat drifts into the cage room from somewhere close by. The Fearless must be preparing a meal. My nausea returns with a vengeance as I imagine what that meat might be. They all look fairly well fed, even the ones who are badly affected by the serum, and - well, where *do* they get their food if it's not . . .

No. *No.* I don't want to think about it. To distract myself, I watch Mara shuffling from cage to cage. She's still wearing the keys. I wish I could get hold of them.

Cy coughs. He's awake, sitting up with his arms, which are still tied at the wrists, hugged around his knees.

'Did you know?' I ask him. 'About Myo, I mean?'

He jerks his head round. His gaze is blank and staring, the spider-web tattoo across the top of his skull standing out in stark relief against his pale skin. He mumbles something, then launches himself at me, crashing into the side of his cage so hard it rocks against mine. I scramble back as he shoves his fingers through the bars, trying to reach for me even though his wrists are bound. He begins to laugh, a screeching cackle that fills my veins with ice. What's happening? Has he Altered already? No – he can't have – his eyes are still blue. And he's only had a few doses of the serum.

The one-eyed woman strides into the room with a Fearless man who's as fat as she is. They drag Cy out of his cage, and the man holds him while the one-eyed woman does something to his face – I can't see what, because they're facing away from me. Cy howls and bucks in the man's arms.

'A clever trick,' the woman says, flicking something

away. 'Put him back. Another twenty-four hours, he'll be ready.'

The man bundles Cy back into his cage.

*Another twenty-four hours, he'll be ready.*

I huddle against the side of my cage, trying to put as much distance between myself and Cy as possible. When he turns to look at me, I already know what I'm going to see.

One eye is silver, and the other is a muddy grey.

He's almost Altered. *Already.*

'He was wearing lenses,' the woman with the drooping face says. 'I saw them take them out.'

*So he must have already been Fearless,* I think.

Just like Myo, who wore that eyepatch to hide his silver eye.

What else did Myo lie about? And how did he manage to act so *normal*? It was totally believable. I fell for it hook, line and sinker. I bet they couldn't believe how gullible I was.

I lie down on my side, curling into a tight ball. What will it feel like when I Alter? Will I be aware of it? How long have I got left? How long has Jori got?

*So you're just going to give up?* a little voice in my head says. *You came all this way just to GIVE UP?*

I try to ignore it, but it keeps on nagging at me. With an angry sigh, I sit up again. What the hell can I do? The one-eyed Fearless woman took my knife. And the cage bars might be rusty, but they're strong.

I gaze at the chunks of stone and concrete strewn

across the floor, wondering if I could use a piece to smash the lock. No, it would make too much noise. But nearby – near enough for me to reach – is a metal chair leg with a jagged end. I prod the damp-softened wood at the edges of the cage floor. Could I use the sharp end of the chair leg to gouge it out and get the bottom of the cage loose?

*They'll see you*, the little voice in my head says.

*No they won't*, I tell it. *Not if I'm careful. I can lie on top of what I'm doing to hide it.*

Cy's rocking back and forth, muttering. So are some of the others – they must be nearly Altered too. I reach through the bars for the chair leg, and see Jori watching me. I raise a finger to my lips. Jori's eyes widen.

The chair leg is further away than it looks, and at first I think I'm not going to be able to get it after all. With a grunt of frustration, I shove my shoulder right up against the bars, and finally manage to snag it with my fingertips.

The cage floor is even more rotten than I thought; it takes me less than an hour to dig a narrow trench almost six inches long. My hands get blistered and sore, but I carry on digging, forgetting the pain in my head as the trench, which I disguise by stuffing the pieces I dig out back into it, slowly lengthens. Jori watches, his face solemn.

'They're coming,' the woman with the drooping face says. I look round and see, with a jolt of horror, that one of her eyes has started to go cloudy. Even though I can't hear anything, another memory pops into my head: the way Gina heard the ragged man's laughter from across the city. Enhanced hearing; enhanced night vision – why did it take me so long to realize what they were?

I push the chair leg up my sleeve and lie on my side so the curve of my body hides the gouge in the plywood. A few moments later, Mara, the one-eyed woman and the two men enter the cage room.

With every ounce of self-control I possess, I force myself to lie still as Mara unlocks my cage and steps back to let one of the men inject me again. There's that instant of bliss, and I just have time to think *please don't let them find out what I'm doing* before I lose consciousness.

When I wake up again, my head feels like it's on fire, but I'm still in my cage, and the chair leg is still up my sleeve. I wait until the Fearless have brought round the food – more bread and water – then start digging again. I have to get out of here before Jori Alters.

And then I have to get us both as far away from the Torturehouse, Myo, Mara, and the rest of the Fearless as I can.

# Chapter 40

*Two days later*

## MYO

'For God's sake, Myo. You're making me nervous,' Ben growls from the bed in the corner as I pace across to the window.

I ignore him. The window has no glass, and the damp, chilly air blasts against my face. For the last two days, Ben, Gina and I have been holed up on the tenth floor of an old apartment block. Half a mile away, the Torturehouse is just visible through the rain, which started last night, washing away the snow.

'How's your leg?' Gina asks Ben, going over to the bed.

'Sore, but it's healing OK.' He glances at me. 'I guess being part-Fearless has *some* advantages.'

'Let me see.' Gina's been applying antiseptic cream and changing his bandages twice a day. 'You're right. It looks fine. No infection. Another day or two and you should be able to walk on it without opening it up again.'

'Good,' Ben says. 'I can't wait to get out of here.'

I carry on staring out of the window. Even though I

already know that we're not going back there, Ben's words are like a punch in the gut. Every night since Cass was captured, I've dreamed of her, and when I wake up and she's not there, it's like I've lost her all over again.

I think about the first time I ended up at the Torturehouse. The Invasion happened when Mara and I were ten. We were back in the children's home in Glasgow after our latest set of foster parents decided they didn't want us any more, and I hated it. So did Mara. But there was nowhere else for us to go.

The night of the Invasion, we were woken up by the fire alarms. I staggered out of my room and found Mara as we were being herded down the stairs. Most of the kids were in their pyjamas. I thought it was a drill, but when we got out into the car park, there was a bus waiting. Everyone was loaded onto it and told that something bad had happened and we were being taken somewhere safe. Most of the kids started crying. So did some of the staff. I huddled next to Mara, wondering what was going on.

We got caught in traffic as everyone tried to leave the city, and on the outskirts of Glasgow the bus was surrounded by men and women with guns and silver eyes. They boarded, and shot the driver. Mara and I managed to escape through an emergency exit window at the back. After a few days holed up in an abandoned office block, we were found by Ben, a student who'd been doing veterinary medicine at Glasgow University. He took us under his wing, and with a small group of other survivors that included Gina and Cy, we fled to England.

For almost a year, Ben and the other adults fought the Fearless, but one night, the warehouse we were living in was ambushed. There were so many Fearless that we were overwhelmed, and everyone who didn't die or manage to escape was taken to Sheffield, to the Torturehouse.

That's when my memories get weird and broken. I remember Ben being at the Torturehouse with us, but not how he got us out of the cages. I remember him carrying me through the station, but not the journey to Staffordshire. The first thing I recall clearly is waking up at the bunker, weeks after we were rescued. After that, I had to come to terms with what had happened – that I was half-Fearless, and my sister was full Fearless, and that she'd be like that for ever, even if we did manage to keep her off the serum. I was terrified that Ben would throw her out, but he agreed to let her stay.

A sound jerks me back to reality. Engines. I lean forward, my elbows on the window-sill as I scan the horizon, trying to work out where it's coming from. Between us and the Torturehouse there's a road bridge littered with old cars and the burned-out shell of a helicopter, the word POLICE still visible along the tail.

'What's wrong?' Gina says behind me.

Then I see them: two black specks – no, three – no, *seven* – coming over the bridge.

Jeeps, and a covered lorry.

'Magpies!' I say.

'What?' Gina says, and comes over to look. 'Are you sure?' Then she sees them. 'Oh, *shit*.'

I glance at Ben. He's looking at me through narrowed eyes. 'Don't even think about it,' he says.

'Screw you.' I walk over to the corner where the guns are leaning against the wall.

'I mean it, Myo.' Ben sits up and swings his legs round off the bed.

'So do I.' Picking up a rifle, I grab a box of ammo and tip the contents into my pocket.

Ben tries to stand up and gives a hiss of pain. 'Gina, stop him!' he cries. Gina makes a grab for me, but I'm too quick. I flee through the apartment. Ten flights of stairs later I burst out onto the street, and with the gun strapped across my chest and the shells clinking against my leg, I sprint up the road towards the bridge.

# Chapter **41**

## CASS

With no other way of knowing how long I've been here, I measure time in injections of the Fearless serum. It takes two more for me to dig the cage floor out all the way around the edge.

Cy and the woman with the drooping face have been taken away. Jori's still hanging in there, but he seems weak and dispirited. I don't feel so good either. My head aches permanently, and I'm shaky and irritable. I tell myself it's from the stress and bad food and lack of sleep, but deep down, I know it's because my body's starting to need – to crave – the serum, and because the serum is starting to sink its claws into my brain.

I make the last cut through the wood not long after coming round from the third injection. Glancing around to check for Fearless, I take a few deep breaths, and put my palms flat against the top of the cage and push upwards, straining against the weight of the metal. The bars lift neatly away from the floor. *Done it*. I feel an instant of dizzying elation, then a wave of fear.

Because this is only the beginning. It's pointless trying

to escape unless I have the keys. Mara's due to bring our food soon; I tuck the chair leg back up my sleeve to use as a weapon if I need to, my stomach churning. I have one chance at this. One chance to rescue my brother. One chance to get us both out of here. I think briefly about Dad, wondering if I should try to get back to Sheffield and find him. But what good would that do? He's not my dad any more – he's Fearless. He'd probably try to kill us both.

When Mara comes in with the water and bread, I wait until she's opposite me, her back turned. Willing her not to look round, I lift my cage up and wriggle out from underneath it, grabbing a lump of stone. As Mara turns, hearing me, I jump up and smash it down on the top of her head with a strength I wasn't even aware I possessed. She crumples to the floor. I yank the keys from around her neck, snapping the frayed ribbon, and drag her limp body backwards into the shadows.

She's still breathing, but her eyes are closed, and blood trickles down from her hairline. A boy in one of the cages nearby, who's almost Altered, shrieks at me. 'Shut up,' I hiss, dropping Mara beside a heap of rubble. I dart across to Jori's cage.

With a racing heart, I unlock it and help him out. He flings his arms around me, body heaving with silent sobs. I hug him back. 'Can you walk?' I whisper.

He tries, and his legs buckle. 'OK, OK,' I whisper, my gaze darting everywhere as I look for more Fearless. 'You'll have to get on my back.' I crouch down. He wraps his arms around my neck, and I shake the chair leg out of my sleeve. As we run for the exit, people call after us, begging me to save them too, but there isn't time. I have to get out of here before their shouts draw the other Fearless, or before the Fearless realize Mara's been gone too long.

I sprint along the parade of ruined shops the Fearless woman dragged me past who knows how many days ago, trying to remember the route we took. Everywhere looks the same. And soon, I'm too exhausted to run any more. I slow to a fast walk, looking behind me every few seconds. Jori is completely still. I'm scared he's passed out and that he'll lose his grip, but I can only hang onto him with one hand; I need the other free to hold the chair leg.

Then the parade branches, and at the end, I see the M&S sign. My heart leaps, and for the first time I allow myself a tiny spark of hope that Jori and I might actually make it out of here.

Then someone grabs my wrist from behind. I whirl and try to yank my arm free, aiming a savage kick at my attacker, my breath catching in my throat in a sob that's half fear, half rage. I haven't come this far to get caught again. I *haven't*.

'Cass! Don't! It's me!' hisses a voice.

I freeze.

'It's me.' Myo steps in front of me, still holding onto my wrist. He has a shotgun over his shoulder and he isn't wearing his eyepatch. His right eye is as silver as the sea. 'Oh my God. I can't believe it's you. I was coming to get you.' Then he sees Jori. 'You found him! Is he OK?'

I slam my palm into his chest, stopping him from coming any closer. 'Don't.'

'What? Cass, it's *me*. Myo.'

'I know who you *are*. Do you think I'm stupid? I'm guessing you do, as I fell for all your lies.'

'My . . . lies?'

'Yes. When were you going to tell me you and your sister are Fearless, exactly?'

The colour drains out of his face, and he lets go of my wrist.

'I'm guessing that would be never,' I say.

'Wait, let me explain,' he croaks as I try to push past him.

'Explain *what*?' I try to push past him again.

'Don't!' he says. 'The Magpies are outside. They've found out the Fearless are here – they've got the place surrounded!'

I let out a harsh laugh, so furious with him I'm past caring if anyone hears. '*Bull*shit. I can't believe I trusted you. I can't believe I *kissed* you. If you want your sister, she's back there.' I jerk my thumb savagely behind me and barge past him, walking to the M&S store without looking back.

It's not until I'm inside, weaving my way through the junk and bones, that the tears come, stinging my eyes and blurring my vision. I tuck the chairleg into my waistband and swipe angrily at my cheeks with the back of my hand. *Christ's sake, Cass, get a grip*, I tell myself. *You and Jori could have died or been Altered because of him.*

But it feels as if there's a huge, empty space inside my chest where my heart used to be. And it's Myo who's taken it from me. He had *no right*.

When I reach the escalators, the first thing I notice is that outside, it's raining and the snow is almost gone. On my back, Jori whimpers. I wonder where we'll find shelter and food; how we'll ever make it back to Hope.

*Don't think about that*, I tell myself. *Don't think about how far you have to go. Just think about getting out of here. And then getting out of Sheffield. You'll find a way.* Maybe the packs Myo and I left behind are still at the top of those stairs. Maybe we'll be able to—

'Woah woah woah, where d'you think you're going?'

I jump and look up to see a man in a black coat and a black cap pointing a gun at me – not a shotgun but a slim-barrelled rifle with a metal canister fixed underneath. Instinctively I pull the chair leg out from my waistband.

A memory surfaces inside my aching head. Jeeps. Hiding with Myo in a wood at the side of a road.

*Magpies.*

'I'm not Fearless!' I say.

'Put that down.' The man nods at the chair leg, which I'm still gripping like a club.

I drop it. It hits the ground with a clang. Keeping the gun trained on me, the man turns his head and shouts, 'Mikael!'

Another man with a gun, also in a black coat and cap, comes running up the walkway.

'She appeared outta nowhere,' the first man says. 'You got your light? She says she's not Fearless, but we need to check her.'

The second man, Mikael, reaches inside his jacket and brings out a narrow torch no longer than my finger. The first man shoves the end of his gun into the soft space under my jaw and grabs my hair, pulling my head back. Mikael snaps the torch on and shines it into my eyes. The beam is so bright, I wince.

'She's clean, boss,' he says. He has a slight accent, which I can't place – almost American, but not quite.

The first man lets go of my hair and lowers the gun. I scowl at him. 'Check the kid,' he says. With the gun pointed at me I can't do anything except set Jori down and help him stand while Mikael shines the light into his eyes too. He moans, trying to twist away.

'Not sure, boss. Some cloudiness at the back of the right eye, maybe.'

'What were you doing in there?' the first man asks me as Jori presses his face against my stomach and I stroke his filthy, matted hair, trying to comfort him.

'The Fearless caught us. We escaped,' I say.

The man gives a low whistle. 'Seriously?'

'Seriously. So why don't you let us go, and get on with rounding them up?'

'How much of the serum did you get?'

'Two – no, three injections,' I say, the ever-present throb in my head intensifying just at the thought of it.

'And what about the kid?' The man pushes Jori's hair

aside to look at the wounds on the back of his neck.

'I – I don't know.'

'Then you're coming with us. You need to be tested.'

'For what?'

'To see how close you are to Altering.'

A chill snakes through my veins.

'Put restraints on 'em and take 'em back to the jeep,' the first man tells Mikael.

'*Ja*, boss.' Mikael pulls what look like lengths of plastic strapping from another pocket in his oversize coat. 'Please hold out your wrists.'

I think about doing as he says. I have Jori. The other man has a gun. And I'm tired. So tired. I don't want to fight any more.

But I don't want Jori to be taken away by these people, either.

I hold out my wrists, and, just as Mikael's about to bind them, I grab Jori and make a dash for the stairs. If I can just get down them – get outside—

I hear a *crack*, and something thuds into my hip. Jori screams as I stagger and grab the rail at the top of the stairs, trying to stop both of us from tumbling headlong down them.

I look down. The metal canister from the first man's gun is sticking out of me. As I reach to pull it out, my vision swims and doubles, and I fumble and miss it.

'What have you done?' I ask the men as I slump against the railing, hooking an arm over it to keep myself upright. My words come out as *whaave yoo dun*.

Then I realize. It's a tranquillizer. He shot me with a tranquillizer.

'Get the boy,' the first man tells Mikael. 'We'll take them back to the truck while we round the rest up.'

Mikael pulls Jori away from me. The first man grips my arm. 'Can you walk?' he says. I try to pull away from him and next thing I know I'm sitting on the floor with no clear idea of how I came to be there. Shaking his head, the first man swings me over his shoulder as if I weigh almost nothing. He carries me through the smashed double doors opposite M&S, down some steps and across the car park to a group of jeeps and a tarpaulin-covered truck with huge wheels. The rain, fine as mist, soaks my clothes and hair.

'You'll have to stay with them,' the first man tells Mikael as he lays me on the floor of the truck. I can hear Jori crying, and I want to tell him it's OK, that I won't let anything bad happen to him, but I can't speak.

The first man leaves. I can see out of the back of the truck, and watch as a bird, the same washed-out grey as the sky, flaps towards the Torturehouse.

Then, from across the car park, I hear a muffled pop. Guns.

*Myo's still in there*, I think, before remembering I don't care what happens to him any more. I close my eyes, letting the chemicals surging through my blood stream shut the noises out, and drive any lingering thoughts about him out of my head.

# MAGPIES' CAMP

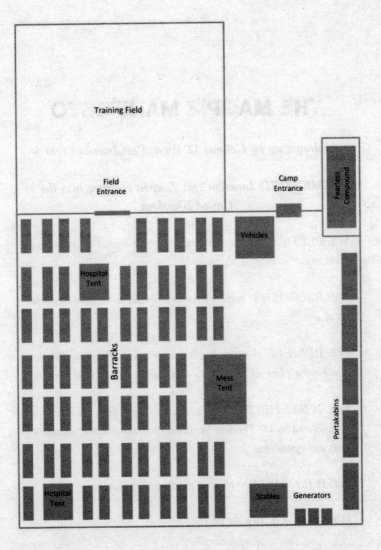

Training Field

Field Entrance

Camp Entrance

Fearless Compound

Vehicles

Hospital Tent

Barracks

Mess Tent

Portakabins

Hospital Tent

Stables

Generators

# THE MAGPIE MANIFESTO

*As drawn up by Colonel D. Brett, Post Invasion Year 5*

*AMENDED Invasion Year 7, upon re-entry into the
United Kingdom*

*WE PLEDGE to bring the Fearless under control by any means
necessary.*

*WE PROMISE to build a new society that is fair and equal for
all of you.*

*WE BELIEVE that the Fearless, once cured of their tendencies,
also have a place in this society and can be put to good use.*

*WE WILL HELP all of you who have been displaced or
dispossessed by the Fearless Invasion, in return for your assistance
with our operations.*

*WE WILL LISTEN to your needs and requirements.*

*WE WILL FIGHT FOR YOU.*

# Chapter 42

## CASS

When I open my eyes, it takes me a moment to remember where I am: in a bed in the hospital tent at the Magpies' camp. It must be daytime, because the tent's gloomy, but not dark. A little wood-stove, hooked up to a flue angled out of the side of the tent, burns brightly.

'How are you feeling?' the Magpie medic, Nadine, says as she crosses over to my bed. Like the rest of the Magpies, she wears a black military-style uniform, and around her neck, a fine silver chain shimmers against her dark skin. 'I've got some good news. All your test results have come back clean.' She smiles so broadly at me I can't help grinning back. But almost immediately, my smile fades. 'What about Jori?' I say.

Her smile fades a little too. 'We're still waiting. Don't worry about him, OK? We're looking after him.'

When she's gone, I sink back against my pillows. It's been six days since I arrived at the camp, which is deep in the countryside north of what used to be London. We drove through the night and into the morning to get here, long enough for the sedative I'd been shot with to start

317

wearing off. Ever since, I've been quarantined with the other adults they got out of the cage room; the children must be in another tent. The Magpies brought plenty of Fearless back too, piled into the jeeps, but I have no idea if Myo, Mara or Cy are here. Not long after my arrival, I came down with a fever, which left me weak and exhausted. It's gone now, but today is the first time I've felt anything close to normal.

I look round the tent. There are six of us in here: a girl and a boy about my age, three older women, and a man in his mid-twenties. The man is hooked up to a drip, and everyone looks pretty sick. I'm the only one who's awake.

I need to find out how Jori's doing.

I sit up again. It makes me dizzy, but the light-headedness soon passes. I open the little metal locker next to my bed and find the clothes I was wearing when I got here, washed and neatly folded. My boots are in the bottom of the locker, also clean. I'm already wearing a pair of thermal leggings and a long-sleeved T-shirt, so I pull the clothes on over the top, push my feet into the boots and pull the woollen cap down over my ears, tucking my hair up inside it.

Outside, it's chilly, mist brushing the tops of the tents. The ground is churned and muddy. I can hear the chug of machinery, a horse nickering and, far away, a voice shouting orders, but at this end of the camp, there doesn't seem to be anyone around. The tents are laid out in rows. I peek inside one, but it's empty save for more beds, laid out as neatly as the tents themselves, and a stove, dark and cold.

A hand lands on my shoulder.

I gasp, expecting it to be one of the men who brought me here, shoving his trank gun in my face. Instead, I see a girl in a Magpies' uniform with her hair tied back in a thick plait, escaped strands hanging in corkscrews around her face. 'What the hell do you think you're doing?' she says.

My mouth drops open. 'Marissa?'

For a moment, she looks at me blankly, and then recognition dawns in her eyes. '*Cass?*'

We hug, half-laughing, half-crying. 'Oh my God,' Marissa says when she lets go of me. 'I thought you were dead. How did you get here?'

'How did *you* get here?'

'A group of Magpies came to Hope, recruiting. Being in the Patrol was OK, but after everything that happened with that boy, and you and Jori going missing, everyone was so scared. When the Magpies told us there was a way to actually stop the Fearless – really make a difference – I just had to sign up. Mayor Brightman wasn't happy, but . . .' She shrugs.

'Do you know if Jori's OK?' I say. 'He was brought here with me – I was looking for him—'

'He was?' Marissa frowns. 'I'm not sure. We can ask someone, though. Hey, are you hungry? It's almost lunchtime.'

No sooner have the words left her mouth than the

smell of food drifts towards me through the fog, making my stomach rumble.

'Yeah,' I say.

'Come to the mess tent and eat with us, then, and we'll ask someone about Jori afterwards. I want to know where you've been and what you've been up to.' Concern passes over her face like a cloud on a sunny day. 'You look so *thin*, Cass.'

'I'm OK,' I say, although my legs are starting to feel shaky and I want to sit down.

As we walk, she tells me about her time with the Magpies so far. Apparently the guy in charge, Colonel Brett, has been taking back countries all over Europe, and now he's come here to do the same. Marissa is among a large group of new recruits being trained to round up the Fearless, who the Magpies are going to put to work to rebuild everything. I listen in amazement. I can hardly believe it's true.

Then, as we reach a clearing in the middle of the tents, she looks back over her shoulder at me. 'Oh, and did you know Sol's here?'

My heart skips a beat. 'What?'

'Yeah, and Andrej. Rob wanted to come as well, but he got in trouble for something with Captain Denning and he told the Magpies not to take him. He was *furious*, but I'm glad he's not here.'

'Me too,' I say, and I mean it.

'Oh, but Sol is going to be *so* glad to see you! He was really cut up when you disappeared – he wanted to go after you, but his dad forbade him. It was awful to think that that boy had kidnapped you and there was nothing any of us could do.'

'What? Myo didn't kidn—' I shut my mouth again with a snap. I don't want to talk about Myo. I don't even want to think about him. If that's what people assume happened, then fine. He deserves it. Luckily, Marissa's already talking again and doesn't seem to have heard me.

Although, if people do think he kidnapped me, what happened to my note?

Marissa takes me to a big, open-sided tent in the middle of the camp. It's packed, people sitting at long wooden benches that remind me of the refectory back on Hope. They all wear the Magpies' uniform, and conversations in many different languages and accents fills the air. I glance over at the long tables at the back of the tent where people are standing beside big metal pots of food, and my heart skips another beat. The people serving have silver eyes. They're *Fearless*.

I look for restraints, and don't see any. How can they be just standing there, calmly doling out the food? Then I notice their empty expressions, their slack faces, their slow, jerky movements, as if they're operating on some sort of autopilot. One of them, a woman, has bruised, swollen eyes, her eyelids the colour of raw liver.

Marissa sees me staring at them. 'Amazing, isn't it?' she says. 'You'd never think an operation that quick could cure them.'

'An operation?' I say.

'I won't tell you now. It might put you off your lunch.'
She makes a face and leads me across to a table at the
back of the tent.

I see Sol and Andrej at the same time as they turn
round and see me.

'*Cass?*' Sol sounds as incredulous as Marissa did when
she first saw me. He gets up and comes over.

'Hey,' I say.

'I thought you were dead,' he says.

I give him a small smile. 'Not yet.'

'For God's sake, Sol, let her sit down,' Marissa says.
'She looks like she's about to pass out.'

'Of course. Sorry.' Sol leads me to the table, and
Andrej, who's staring at me as if he's just seen a ghost,
scoots over so I can sit down.

'I'll get you some food,' Marissa says. The others
already have bowls of broth in front of them. As she
hurries off, Sol pours me a cup of water. The other
people sitting here are all about our age; I'm guessing
they're new recruits too. Most of them smile, but one boy,
dark haired with freckles, just looks at me through
narrowed eyes. His stare makes me uncomfortable, and
I'm relieved when Marissa returns with a bowl and a
spoon and I have something to do with my hands.

'OK, tell,' Marissa says as I eat my broth. 'What
*happened* to you?'

Realizing I don't have any choice but to tell them, I
give them a highly edited version of the truth, leaving
many things out – comforting Myo after Danny and

**322**

April and their baby were killed; that night in the farm-house; escaping from the Fearless and our kiss in the roof space of the Torturehouse. I have to forget that. Forget *him*. It meant nothing.

*Nothing.*

'So he didn't kidnap you?' Andrej says when I've finished.

I shake my head, feeling my face grow warm. Across the table, the dark-haired boy continues to watch me through narrowed eyes.

'I can't believe you helped him escape.' Andrej sounds disgusted.

I look him squarely in the eye. 'He said he could help me. I had to get Jori back. And I did. I'm not going to apologize for anything.'

Marissa shoots Andrej a filthy look. 'It's OK. We understand. I would have done the same thing.'

'Cass!'

I look round. Nadine's striding towards us. 'What are you doing here?' she says. 'You should be resting.'

I explain. She doesn't look impressed, but I insist I'm OK. If I have to spend another minute lying in bed, I'm going to go crazy.

'I guess if you're feeling up to it, we should sort you out with a uniform, then.' She turns to Marissa. 'Will you take her? You can bring her back to me afterwards.'

Marissa nods, and when the meal's finished, she takes me to a long row of Portakabins at the edge of the camp, right up against the fence, which she says is electrified. I

**323**

remember the chugging sound I heard earlier; there must be a generator somewhere. One of the cabins, much larger than the others, is set apart, surrounded by another fence. The windows are boarded, and on our side of the compound stands a young Magpie with a gun – not a trank gun but a shotgun.

'Is that where they're keeping the——' I begin.

'Yup.' Marissa points at metal box with a lever sticking out of it. 'See that? If you hear a siren and it doesn't stop after ten seconds or so, run to the training field and don't look back.'

'What is it?' I ask, as something thuds hard against the Fearless Portakabin from inside.

'Alarm. For if any get loose.'

'Have they?'

She shakes her head.

'But why are they even here? What do they do with them?'

Marissa makes a face. 'It's pretty gross. Apparently they do something to their brains.'

I stare at her. 'Eh?'

'I know, it sounds brutal, doesn't it? But it obviously works. It could mean no more Fearless – can you imagine?'

I feel a stab of panic as I think of Jori, lying in one of those tents somewhere. What if he's Altered enough to need the operation? *I have to find him.*

Marissa climbs the steps of one of the other

Portakabins and knocks. A muscular woman with short blonde hair sticks her head out. 'Yeah?'

Marissa gently shoves me forwards. 'Cass needs a uniform.'

'Righto. You'd better come in, then.'

The Portakabin has an electric light. Inside, stacks of clothes are neatly folded on metal shelves. Where did the Magpies get all this stuff? The woman measures me and fits me out with new boots, combats, a T-shirt, lightweight zip-up jacket and a heavier, waterproof jacket to wear over the top. I have a scarf and a cap too. She drops my old clothes – the bunker clothes – into a metal bin marked *recycling*. I'm glad to see them go.

'Perfect!' Marissa says when I'm dressed. 'Now you look like one of us.'

And that's when I realize, like it or not, I've just been recruited into the Magpies.

# Chapter 43

## SOL

After Cass and Marissa leave the mess tent, I sit there, staring into my bowl. I've dreamed about seeing her again for so long, and now she's here.

She's *alive*.

I throw down my spoon with a clatter and run through the camp to the clothes store.

Marissa and Cass are coming down the steps. Cass is wearing a uniform now. With the weight she's lost and the shadows under her eyes, the black makes her look pale, washed out.

But she's still beautiful.

*So* beautiful.

God, I've missed her.

'Can I speak to Cass for a second?' I ask Marissa.

Marissa shrugs. 'I'll wait here,' she tells Cass. Cass nods, then follows me around the side of one of the tents, where it's more private.

'Are you really OK?' I ask her.

She nods again.

I swallow. 'I mean, that boy – he didn't . . . *do* anything to you, did he?'

A strange look flickers across her face. 'No. No way.'

'Because if he did, I'll find him. And I promise you I'll make him pay.'

She smiles at me. 'I'm all right. Don't worry about me.'

Silence. This doesn't feel like the big reunion I imagined. I thought she'd be happy to see me, but she seems sad about something. *Angry*, almost.

'I found your note,' I say.

Her eyes widen. 'You did?'

'Yes. I – I got rid of it. No one else who's still on Hope knows you went with that boy voluntarily. I thought, if you made it back . . .'

'Oh. Thank you. That was . . . good of you.'

I take a deep breath. 'Why *did* you go with him?'

'I told you. He said he could help me get Jori back. I had to trust him – no one on the island was even prepared to try.'

*Not even you*, her accusing gaze says, and I remember, with a wave of shame, how all I did that night was tell her to go back to her apartment.

'I'm sorry.' I look down at the ground. 'I was just—'

'Following the rules, I know.' Her tone is as hard as her eyes were a moment ago. Anger flares inside me, but when I glance up, she's looking apologetic.

'Sorry. That was uncalled for. Your dad's Hope's mayor. Of course you had to follow the rules.'

I close my eyes, open them again. 'I want to tell you something,' I say.

She frowns at me.

'My dad,' I rush on. 'The Fearless are his fault. I mean, it was him – his company – that created them.'

Her eyes widen. '*What?*'

'You know he worked for a medical research company?'

She shakes her head. 'I know he did something scientific, but I never really knew what.'

'His company, PharmaDexon, created the drug that turned people into Fearless. And then Dad sold the formula to the enemy, who made it stronger.'

'I knew it. *I knew it.*'

Now it's my turn to frown. 'You – what do you mean?'

'That's why Hope was so well set up, isn't it? He'd already decided who he wanted to save from the Fearless, because that was easier than stopping them. And that's why he pretended that after the Invasion, everything just stopped, and the mainland was still overrun with Fearless. I found these articles while I was away, Sol. The government didn't just disappear. People tried to fight the Fearless, and they almost succeeded. He must have known that.'

'I'm so ashamed of him,' I say, my voice hoarse. 'But I'm not like him, Cass. You have to believe me. That's why I'm here. I—'

'Cass?' Marissa calls.

Cass glances round. Is that relief on her face? 'I'd, um, better get back. I should go and find Nadine,' she says.

A siren sounds, marking the start of the afternoon's training. By the time it stops, Cass is gone, and every-thing else I wanted to say to her still hangs, unspoken, in the air around me.

# Chapter 44

## MYO

Standing with the others in the bottom of the hollow near the bunker, I watch Ben limp forward to light the lost candle. 'Goodbye, Cy,' he says, his voice cracking as he straightens up again. 'We won't forget you, buddy.'

Tana gives a gasping wail. She's clinging to Gina, her body heaving with sobs. 'This is your fault,' she hisses at me. Her eyes – one blue and one silver, because without Cass here, there's no need for any of us to wear lenses, or for me to wear my eyepatch – are bright with tears. 'If you hadn't gone off on that crazy mission for that sister of yours, he'd still be here.'

She storms out of the circle of candles, making the flames flicker. Gina goes after her.

In ones and twos, the rest of us return to the bunker as well, no one speaking. This was meant to be a memorial service for Cy – for all we know, he's still alive, even if he is Fearless – but it feels more like a funeral. The weather matches the sombre mood; it's only one in the afternoon, but the sky's full of cloud and it feels like it's getting dark already. Patches of snow still cling to the hills, and the

329

ground is as hard as iron. The cold bites through my clothes. I haven't been able to get warm since we came back.

Inside, Lochie trots over and pushes his nose into my hand. He's picked up on the tense atmosphere: his tail hangs down and his ears lie flat against his head. I rub them, then go to check on Mara, who's huddled on her bed with her hands over her face, shivering. They gave her more serum at the Torturehouse, and now her cravings are worse than ever. Someone hit her on the head, too – she has a nasty wound on her scalp, although as expected, it's healing fast.

She didn't want to leave. Not even when I'd already shot five Fearless just to get to her, and the Magpies were closing in on us. I still have scratches and bite marks where she attacked me. If Gina hadn't come after me and helped me restrain her, I would have never managed it. We'd have been caught – or Mara would have killed me. But between us we found a way out through the network of corridors that ran behind the shops. I wanted to find Cy, too, but there wasn't time. And there wasn't time to find Tessie either. I have no idea if she even survived the journey to the Torturehouse, and now I'll never know.

'How is she?' Gina says as I shut the door again. I jump and turn round. I was so deep in thought, I didn't hear her coming.

'Same,' I say.

'We'll give her some more codeine later.' Gina puts a hand on my arm. 'Come on.'

We return to the Comms Hall. When we walk in, Ben walks out. He won't speak to me, only Gina.

I slump into one of the armchairs. Lochie lies down at my feet with a grunt.

'Are you still thinking about Cass?' Gina says softly. 'Myo, you have to forget her.'

'I'm trying, OK?' I say through gritted teeth.

'And Ben will come round eventually—'

'He says I've put everyone here in danger by getting so close to her. And y'know what? He's right. All she has to do is tell the Magpies about us and we're screwed. Finished.'

'You don't even know she got caught by them.'

'You didn't see her face when she realized what I was. I bet she walked right up to them and begged them to let her join them.'

Gina sighs. 'I'm going to check if Ben's OK. I'll be back in a minute.'

I close my eyes. She's right. I shouldn't be feeling like this. OK, Cy's gone, and I miss the guy so much it *hurts*, but I got my sister back – as much as it's possible to get her back – and we made it here in one piece. Things will settle down eventually. Ben will speak to me again. I have my dog. I'm *home*.

So why do I still feel like I've lost everything?

# Chapter 45

## CASS

After I get my uniform, Marissa takes me back to the hospital tent, where Nadine is waiting for me. 'We don't want you getting ill again, Cass,' she says when I protest at being told to go back to bed. 'It's important you save your strength.'

'We'll meet you in the mess tent for the evening meal,' Marissa says.

I sigh. 'Try to make the most of it,' Nadine says as, reluctantly, I ease off my boots and lie down again. 'You'll be desperate for a rest by the time you've done your first day's training.'

When she's gone, I make myself wait ten minutes. Then I sit up again and put my boots back on. Before I leave the tent, I shove my blankets into a mound, stuffing my pillow underneath them so that it looks like there's someone in my bed.

Outside, I'm grateful for my uniform; at least I blend in now. I hurry along the rows of tents, switching direction whenever I hear voices. But I can't find my brother anywhere. Anxiety begins to gnaw inside me.

What if something's already happened to him? Or he got so sick he—

Eventually, I find myself at one end of the row of Portakabins, almost stepping into view of the guard outside the Fearless compound before realizing where I am.

I draw back, pressing myself against the side of the tent nearest to me. I can hear a commotion going on inside the cabin in the compound – shouting, thumps, a cry. The door flies back and two Magpies appear, dragging the limp body of a Fearless with a trank dart sticking out of his neck.

I stare. It's Cy, the spider-web tattoo across his scalp clearly visible. They carry him out of the compound and over to the tent I'm hiding beside, his feet, which are bare, leaving score marks in the mud. I notice a small tear in the side of the tent, about two feet from the ground, and crouch down to peer through it.

Inside is a rough wooden table a bit like the benches in the mess tent, with leather straps that the Magpies are using to bind Cy's wrists and ankles. Nearby is another bench loaded with plastic trays and little glass bottles; a third Magpie, wearing a medic's badge like Nadine's and a surgical mask over his face, is standing beside it, pulling on a pair of thin rubber gloves. He opens one of the bottles, tips something onto a gauze pad and swabs Cy's face, paying particular attention to his eyes. Then he picks something up from one of the trays. It isn't until he crosses back over to Cy that I see what it is: a thin metal spike with a bulbous wooden handle at one end. He's also carrying a small hammer.

'Hold his head,' he tells one of the Magpies who brought Cy in.

I watch, frozen with horror, as the medic buries the spike in the tear duct in the corner of Cy's left eye, aiming it upwards. Despite the trank dart in his neck, Cy screams, straining against the leather straps. The medic holds the hammer against the top of the spike's handle. 'Got him steady?' he asks the Magpie holding Cy's head. The Magpie nods.

With the brisk *tap-tap* of the hammer ringing in my ears, I straighten up and stumble back through the rows of tents, no longer caring if anyone sees me. I must find my brother. I need to know if he's OK.

I find him in another hospital tent that's almost identical to mine. 'Jori!' I call softly, and run across to him, wrapping him in my arms.

'Are you OK?' I say, trying, in the half-light from the stove, to see his eyes. They look normal, but didn't that Magpie, Mikael, say something about cloudiness? What if he . . .

'What's wrong?' Jori says. His face is pinched and there are faint shadows under his eyes, but he looks a whole lot better than he did at the Torturehouse.

'Nothing. I'm just glad to see you, is all.' I hug him again. 'Do you feel OK? Are they looking after you?'

A boy in the bed nearby, not much older than Jori, starts coughing, doubling over. I look round for water, but there isn't any. *Crap.* 'I'd better go and get someone,' I tell Jori as the boy's hacking reverberates around the tent.

'No, don't go!' he cries.

'I'll be back in a minute. I'm only going to get Nadine.'

'You mean that doctor lady? She's nice.'

'She is.' *Although I'm not sure how nice she'll be when she realizes I'm out of my tent again,* I think. I've wandered quite a way through the camp, and it's a while before I find her, checking over medical supplies near the mess tent, a Magpie girl about my age ticking off items on a sheet of paper.

'Cass, I thought I told you to rest!' she says, sounding exasperated.

'There's a boy in Jori's tent – he won't stop coughing.'

'OK, I'm on my way.' She grabs a bottle from a table behind her, and I follow her back through the maze of tents. 'But how do you know that?'

I blush. 'I had to find him.'

Nadine turns. 'Look, between you and me, I think your brother's going to be just fine. You've both been here nearly a week, and in my opinion, if he was going to Alter, he would have done so by now. He's not showing any cravings or aggression. He was lucky – they obviously didn't give him enough to make him change. So will you *please* go back to your tent and rest? I've got enough patients on my hands without you relapsing on me.'

A grin spreads across my face. '*Go*,' Nadine says, waving me away. When I get back to the hospital tent, I lie down again and close my eyes, trying to cling on to the good feeling that Nadine's words have given me.

And try to push away the thoughts of Cy – and Myo – that threaten to intrude.

# Chapter 46

## CASS

That evening, Marissa, Sol and Andrej are waiting for me outside the mess tent like they said they would be. They look exhausted, their clothes smeared with mud, and Andrej has a bruise on his forehead.

'What have you been doing?' I ask as we head into the tent. Now it's dark, the camp is lit by flickering electric lights like the one in the Portakabin where I got my uniform.

'What *haven't* we been doing?' Marissa rolls her shoulders. 'I am so sore. These guys make the Patrol look like they're playing toy soldiers.'

'You'll be coming with us soon, I bet,' Andrej says as we join the queue for food. I feel a burst of nerves. But I can hardly go up to whoever's in charge here and say, *Look, I know you saved my life and all, but actually, my brother and I would quite like to go home now*, can I?

Anyway, I'm not sure I want to go back to Hope. Not now I know about Mr Brightman, and how he's kept the truth about the Fearless and what happened after the Invasion from us all these years.

Behind us, someone laughs raucously. I look round and see the boy with dark hair, the one who was staring during my first meal in the mess tent, sneering at me.

Sol turns round too. 'What did you say?'

Even though Sol is a whole head taller than him, the boy stares at him insolently. 'None of your business.'

'Oh, I think it is, actually,' Sol says. 'Especially if it's about Cass.'

My stomach gives an unpleasant little lurch, and I tug on Sol's sleeve. 'It's fine, leave it.'

'No, I won't *leave it*.' Anger burns dully in his eyes. My unease deepens. I've seen him look like this before – when he asked me to go out with him and I said no.

Sol grabs the boy by the collar. 'Tell me what you said,' he spits through clenched teeth.

'You really wanna know?' A flush steals up the boy's neck and into his cheeks. 'I was just wondering what it must have been like for your girlfriend, getting it on with a Fearless. D'you think they'll send her in as bait and try to trap them?'

Sol lets go of his collar and punches the boy on the jaw so hard he actually lifts into the air, people dodging out of the way as he sprawls onto the muddy ground.

'*Sol!*' Marissa shrieks, her hands flying to her mouth.

'Speak about Cass like that again, and I will kill you,' Sol tells the boy. The icy calm in his voice scares me even more than the look on his face. 'I won't have anyone saying stuff like that about her.'

'What is going on?' a voice barks. Shock prickles

through me. It's the guy I saw when Myo and I were hiding in that wood, the one with the scar on his face who was driving the second jeep. Up close, he's even more imposing. His neck and arms, which are bare despite the cold, bulge with ropes of muscle, and the jagged mark down his cheek looks like it came from a bite.

'He hit me, sir!' the boy says, pointing at Sol, as some- one helps him up.

The man regards Sol through narrowed eyes. 'Is that correct?'

'Sir! Yes, sir!' Sol says.

'Both of you get to my office now.'

The dark-haired boy scowls, holding his jaw, but Sol's expression is triumphant. Shame pours hotly through me. What would he do if he knew that what the boy had said was very nearly the truth? He must have drawn those conclusions when he was listening to me talk to Marissa, Sol and Andrej.

That night, I'm moved out of the hospital tent and into one of the new recruits' tents. Marissa's there too, and convinces the girl beside her to swap bunks with me so we're next to each other. This part of the camp is much busier, and there are more of the Fearless – the cured Fearless – about, doing menial tasks. I keep an eye out for Myo, just in case he is here, but I never see him, so I assume he made it back to the bunker. Half of me is relieved, and half of me is . . . well, I don't know what it is.

A few days later, Cy is helping to serve breakfast. I

know it's him because of the spider-web tattoo. His eyes are so swollen and bruised, I have no idea how he can see out of them, and more than once, as he's serving the porridge, he fumbles with the ladle and drops it, making the Magpie standing nearby snap at him. Cy doesn't react, just picks the spoon up again and carries on serving. As I hold out my bowl, the image of the medic pushing the spike into his eye flashes into my head, and I hear the tap of the hammer as he knocks the spike through Cy's skull. My stomach clenches. When I sit down with Marissa, Andrej and Sol, I leave my porridge and sip my coffee instead.

'Why were you staring at that Fearless guy serving the food?' Marissa asks in a low voice. 'Was he one of the ones who tried to Alter you?'

I shake my head, staring into my mug. 'He was one of the guys from the bunker.'

When I look up again, Marissa's mouth is an 'O'.

'You need to tell them about that place,' Sol says. It's the first time I've seen him since last night. The boy he punched is sitting at a different table, glowering at us. I ignore him.

'Yeah, what if they're all Fearless?' Andrej says. 'They need rounding up too.'

'Can you remember where it is?' Sol asks.

In my head, I try to retrace my and Myo's journey from Hope Island. 'It was on a moor up north. There were a lot of high hills around it.'

'Was it an ex-military bunker?' Andrej asks.

I nod.

'They have maps here – it might be on one of them,' Sol says. 'I'll take you to Colonel Brett's office after breakfast.'

When I've finished my coffee, we head over there. The Colonel's office is in the largest of the Portakabins. Sol knocks, and we wait.

And wait.

'Shouldn't we go through one of his people?' I say nervously. 'I mean, he's in charge of this whole place.'

'I know what I'm doing, Cass,' Sol says. 'Don't you want those freaks rounded up?'

At last, the door opens, and I see the guy with the scar on his face again. So this is Colonel Brett.

'What do you want, Brightman?' he says.

Sol salutes. 'Cass has some important information she wishes to share, sir.'

'Um, yes, um, sir,' I stammer. 'It's – it's about a group of Fearless.'

Colonel Brett frowns. 'You'd better come in. Not you, Brightman,' he adds as Sol starts to follow me up the steps. 'Don't you have drill?'

A dull flush creeps up Sol's neck, but he salutes again. 'Sir! Yes, sir!'

'Well, get going, then.'

I follow Colonel Brett into the cabin.

'Sit down.' He indicates a chair in front of a little desk piled with papers. 'You're one of the group from Sheffield, aren't you?'

'Yes, sir,' I say.

'You had a lucky escape there.'

'Yes, sir.'

'Where are these Fearless you mentioned? My men tell me they caught everyone who was at that place in the city.'

'This is a different group, sir,' I say. Then his words sink in. *They caught all the Fearless.* Does that mean Myo's somewhere here too?

Haltingly, I tell him about Myo coming to Hope Island, about the Fearless kidnapping Jori, and the abridged version I gave Sol and the others of what happened after that.

'They don't sound like ordinary Fearless to me,' Colonel Brett says, pressing his fingers together. 'Otherwise the boy would have tried to kill you or taken you to that place in Sheffield straight away.'

'I don't think they are either, sir,' I say. 'I think they're some sort of . . . hybrids.'

'Hmm. Interesting.' The Colonel regards me coolly.

'How many Fearless do you have here, sir?' I ask.

'Here, over two hundred cured, plus thirty or so still waiting for the reversal procedure. There are others in holding camps elsewhere in the country. The Magpies' operations in the UK are really gathering speed now, especially since we've been able to start recruiting from various refugee communities, like that island of yours. I hear from the medics that you've made a good recovery

**342**

from your ordeal. Do you think you'll be fit enough to start training in a day or two?'

'I think so, sir.'

'Good.' He stands up, and I take that as my cue to do the same. 'Thank you for the information about the bunker. Most useful.' He shows me to the door.

I spend the rest of the day working with Nadine, helping her tend to the patients in the hospital tents, and taking stock of the camp's medical supplies. While we're rolling bandages, I ask her about the reversal procedure.

'How do you know about that?' she says, frowning.

'I, um, heard some of the other recruits talking about it.'

'Well, you know how the serum affects the emotional centres in the brain?'

I nod.

'The reversal procedure physically severs the connections between the frontal lobes in the brain and reverses the effect of the serum.'

'You mean they—'

'Yep, hammer the spike into their brain and give it a stir around. It's not very exact, but most of the time, it does the job. Unfortunately, cutting their skulls open to operate isn't an option in a place like this.'

A chill runs down my spine. 'Have you had to do it?'

'A few times, in the beginning. Not any more, though. I can't stomach it.'

I don't think I'd be able to either. I concentrate on rolling bandages, trying not to think about what I saw the Magpies doing to Cy. One corner of Nadine's mouth lifts in a smile. 'So, what's going on between you and Sol Brightman, then?'

I look round at her, frowning. 'Huh?'

'The first thing he did when he got here was go round asking everyone if they'd picked up a girl called Cass Hollencroft. He said you'd been kidnapped by a Fearless. He was really worried about you, you know.'

I shake my head, heat stealing into my cheeks. 'Sol and I are just mates. And I wasn't kidnapped. My brother was. This boy – Myo – said he'd help me get him back. And he did, kind of, but . . .' I think about telling Colonel Brett about the bunker. About Myo being brought back here to have those spikes driven through his eye sockets. 'He . . . lied to me,' I say. 'He wasn't who he said he was.'

I turn and begin arranging the rolled-up bandages on a tray so Nadine won't see the way I'm pressing my lips together as I try to get my emotions under control.

She doesn't ask me any more questions.

# Chapter 47

## SOL

Cass began her training two days after she had her talk with Brett. They put her with the newest recruits at first, but now she's been moved up to my group. 'How'd she get here so fast?' I hear the boy I punched say at dinner one night. I turn and stare at him until he looks away.

I wish I knew why Cass was so preoccupied. She'll hardly talk to us, and when I ask what's bothering her, she brushes me off, tells me she's fine. What's *wrong*? She should be happy. She got Jori back, didn't she?

*Maybe she misses that Fearless freak*, a little voice keeps whispering in my ear. I try to ignore it, but it won't shut up.

What *really* happened when she went with him? What did they do?

A few days later, when we get to the training field after breakfast, Colonel Brett is waiting for us. As usual, it's raining, and my boots, which I spent yesterday evening cleaning, are caked with mud again.

*Goddammit.*

'Congratulations, troops,' Brett says. 'Your basic training

is almost over. I'm going to divide you into units, and throughout today, you will come in those units to my office to be briefed about the missions you're being sent on.'

I want to whoop and punch the air. *Finally*. Brett waits for the muttering to stop, then starts calling out names. I'm with Andrej, Marissa and Cass, plus another recruit, Halim, who's French, I think.

Andrej frowns. 'Why is our unit so small?'

As I listen to the Colonel call out the other names, I realize he's right. The other units have fifteen or twenty people in them. We have five.

I shrug. 'I guess we'll find out later.'

Then Brett leaves and it's back to scaling the climbing walls and wriggling through the mud in the endless drizzle. God, I can't wait for this to be over.

Our unit is summoned to Brett's office that afternoon. He's studying some maps. Next to him is a guy with a beard I've seen him working with a few times, I don't know his name, though.

'At ease,' Brett says, still looking at the maps.

The others relax, letting their shoulders drop. I stay standing tall and straight.

Brett looks up. 'You're probably wondering why your unit is smaller than the others.'

'Yes, sir,' I say. 'We were.'

'I've been looking at the information Hollencroft gave us when she first came here, about a bunker inhabited by people she suspects are part-Fearless, and I think I have located it.'

Cass, standing beside me, gives a start.

Brett jams a finger down onto one of the maps. I see a sprawl of empty land, tight contour lines and rocky outcrops, with *STAFFORDSHIRE MOORLANDS* printed across them. In the middle of it is an X drawn in red ink.

'The bunker is known to a few of my troops. It was originally built by the military to house government officials if the Fearless invaded, but it was never used. You'll be under the command of Corporal Jonasson here, and will also be assigned a medic. Your mission will be to go to the bunker and round up these part-Fearless. We hope that by studying them, we'll be able to find out more about the effects of the Fearless serum on the brains of people who are close to Altering, but haven't quite undergone the change. After that, they'll be given the reversal procedure.'

I glance at Cass. She's gone pale. *Whisper, whisper* goes that voice inside my head. I try to concentrate on what Brett's saying.

'You will leave at O-five-hundred hours tomorrow morning. It is expected that the journey to the bunker will take you until nightfall. Once there, you'll set up camp, and carry out your mission the following day. The reason your unit is so small is because you'll need to get into the bunker and take these . . . *people* by surprise. Corporal Jonasson will spend the rest of the afternoon discussing tactics with you. Does anyone have any other questions?'

'Sir,' Cass says, looking at Brett again and swallowing. My heart squeezes painfully inside my chest. She's going to ask him about that boy. I just *know* it.

'What will happen to my brother while I'm gone?' she says, and I feel my shoulders sag with relief.

Brett gives her a small smile. 'Don't worry about him. He'll be well cared for,' he says. 'You're only going to be away for a few days. Anyone else? No? In that case, you're dismissed.'

Corporal Jonasson gathers up the maps. 'We'll use one of the offices,' he says as we go outside. 'We have a lot to go through before we leave.'

We spend the afternoon poring over the maps and a plan of the bunker, Cass showing us where the main entrance is – a door set into the hillside, she says – and the rooms the freaks inhabit. There's one more entrance, under a rock face at the other end of the bunker. 'We need to figure out a way to get in and take the occupants by surprise, *ja*?' Corporal Jonasson says.

'A lot of the bunker is derelict,' Cass says. 'I'm not sure what the tunnels are like near the other entrance. But that main door is pretty secure.' She's biting her lip.

'Can't we blast the locks somehow?' I ask.

'But then they will know we are there,' Halim says. 'There is no surprise. And Cass says they have guns, no?'

I shake my head in frustration. 'Think about it. If we blast the locks, they'll send some of them up to see what's going on. *Those* will be the ones with guns. So we lie in wait for them outside and capture them. After that, we go down into the bunker and get everyone else.'

I look round at the little group, eyebrows raised. How can anyone argue with that? It's the perfect strategy.

'We do have a small supply of plastic explosive,' Corporal Jonasson says eventually. 'It might work.'

I allow myself a small, triumphant smile.

The rest of the afternoon is spent planning our route to the bunker and working out an exit strategy in case things go wrong. At dinner, everyone is talking at once, as excited as I am to finally be getting out of the camp and away from the dreaded training field.

Everyone except Cass. She pushes her food around her plate, not joining in the conversation at all. Halfway through the meal, she excuses herself and leaves the tent.

After a few moments, I follow her.

It's still light outside – just – and for once, it's not raining. I find Cass in the training field, leaning against the climbing wall. 'Are you OK?' I ask her.

'Yeah,' she mutters.

'You don't look it.'

'I'm fine, honestly.' She gives me an unconvincing smile.

'You really don't need to worry about Jori, you know. Like Brett said, it's only a couple of days.'

'I know. I wasn't thinking about Jori.'

My stomach twists. 'So what are you doing out here by yourself?'

'I just wanted to be on my own for a bit. Is that a crime?'

I curl my toes inside my boots. 'You should be happy.'

'Why?'

'Because we're going to get that boy. He's going to get what he deserves.'

When she doesn't respond, I move a little closer to her, until our shoulders are almost touching. 'And we're going together. At least you're not on your own with people you don't know.'

*Say it!* I scream at her inside my head. *Say you're pleased to be going with me!*

'I know,' she says, but her smile is still thin and unhappy.

I narrow my eyes. 'Is it that boy?'

Her head whips round and she stares at me. 'What d'you mean?'

*Aha.*

'You're worried about him, aren't you?'

'No!' She says it a little too quickly. 'Of course not!'

'So what's wrong?'

I don't want to say it. I want *her* to say it. To deny my suspicions, or confirm them.

*Anything's* better than not knowing.

But she doesn't answer me. *Goddammit, she's so beautiful*, I think. I should have watched her, followed her, stopped her from ever going near that boy. I wish I could make her realize how good we'd be together. What if something happens while we're up in Staffordshire? This could be my only chance.

My heart thudding, I take a deep breath. 'Cass?'

She looks round at me. '*What?*'

'I – I love you,' I tell her, almost overwhelmed by the emotions that rush through me as I finally say the words out loud. I lean towards her to kiss her.

'No!' She pushes me away before our lips can meet. 'Sol, *don't!*'

Humiliation burns through me. 'Why not?'

'I don't like you like that.'

I stare at her. 'I thought, maybe, after everything—'

'I'm sorry.'

'But I *love* you, Cass.' This time the words sound weak, a mocking echo. 'You must know that by now. We're perfect for each other!'

'No, we're not! You're my friend, Sol, but that's all.'

I feel sick. Stupid. Small. 'Are you *sure* there wasn't anything going on between you and that Fearless boy?'

'Of course not! I went with him to get Jori back. That's all.'

'Really,' I say flatly. For a second – just a *second* – I think about slamming a fist into her face.

Instead, I punch the climbing wall near her head, making her jump and gasp. Then, my knuckles throbbing, I turn and walk away.

'Sol, wait!' she calls after me, but I ignore her. When I find that boy, I'm going to kill him.

There has to be some way to make it look like an accident.

There *has* to be.

# Chapter 48

## CASS

When five a.m. rolls around, I don't need the alarm call that sounds across the camp to wake me up. I haven't slept at all. I've just stared up at the ceiling of the tent, reliving the moment Sol tried to kiss me.

The way he slammed his fist into the climbing wall inches from my head.

I'm so tired I feel as if I'm encased in thick glass. I eat my breakfast without tasting it, not even realizing people are talking to me until after they've finished speaking. Sol's face is stony, his shoulders squared. I want to say something that will make it OK between us again, but I don't have the words.

*Damn you, get out of my head*, I think, as memories of Myo threaten to surface yet again. I wish I could wipe him from my mind for ever. The reason I've thrown myself into the training so hard – that I'm forever in the medics' tent, having scratches and bruises and muscle strains tended to – is so, when I go to bed at night, I'm too exhausted to dream. Otherwise, I dream about Myo, and when I wake up, there are a few moments when I forget that he lied to me, and then I remember, and it crushes me.

After breakfast, everyone who's going out on a mission fetches their packs and then our unit – minus Sol, who Andrej says is still in his tent, looking for something – heads to the training field, where a truck is waiting.

Corporal Jonasson's standing beside it with Nadine. 'You're coming with us?' I ask her, surprised.

She nods. 'Is that a problem?'

'No, of course not,' I say, although I can't help wondering if she made sure she was assigned as our medic because she wants to keep an eye on me. *I hope Jori's OK while I'm gone*, I think, with a sudden pang. Since recovering from his ordeal at the Torturehouse, my brother has been living in one of the Portakabins with the other young children at the camp, some of whom were rescued from Sheffield, some of whom belong to the Magpies. He's been attending the camp school, and I see plenty of him in the evenings, but the thought of having to leave him again gives me a pain in my stomach. What if something goes wrong while we're up there and I never see him again?

'Is everyone here?' Mikael asks, opening the truck's passenger door.

'We're still waiting for Sol,' Marissa says. Then we hear a shout. Sol jogs up to the truck, sliding his pack off his shoulders and placing it gingerly on the ground.

'You bringing your best china or something?' Andrej jokes. Sol gives him a thin, humourless smile and glances at me, only for a second, but long enough for me to get the message: he's still angry about last night, and he's going to stay angry for a long time.

Maybe for ever.

*Oh, screw him*, I think.

The truck is one of the big ones with a cover over it. In the back, between the seats, is a large cage. *Oh, God*, I think. If we catch Myo, I'm going to have to travel back with him right next to me the whole way.

I shove my pack under my seat. Our weapons – shotguns and trank guns – are strapped into some webbing above our heads, and we've all been given pairs of high-resolution night-vision goggles. The plan is to go to the bunker in the small hours of tomorrow morning, well before it gets light.

'Want a hand with that?' Andrej says. I look up and see Sol trying to get into the truck with his pack hugged against his chest.

'No!' he snaps. 'I mean, I'm fine. Thanks.'

He takes the seat furthest away from me, still hugging his pack. Marissa shoots us a puzzled look, but I ignore her. I don't have the energy to explain.

Mikael twists the key in the ignition, and the truck shudders into life. The vehicles here all run on a modified form of diesel, which the Magpies make themselves; I'm not sure how.

The trip is long, cold and uncomfortable. Every time the truck jolts over a pothole, Sol clenches his teeth. The others tease him about it, until he starts to get a spot of colour high on each cheekbone. He looked the same last night when he punched the climbing wall.

'Everything OK back there?' Nadine asks.

'Fine,' Sol says with a tight smile. But the spots of colour on his face remain, and I'm glad when the others get bored and leave him alone.

Even though we only stop for half an hour that day, to eat and relieve ourselves, it's almost dark by the time we reach the moors. It's much colder up here, patches of snow still clinging to the hills. Mikael leaves the truck under some trees at the side of the road, next to a dry-stone-walled paddock with a tiny hut at one end where we set up our camp. All around us, the hills loom up into the dusk. I get a jolt when I turn and see we're right beside the two-pronged ridge Myo and I rode the horses over all those weeks ago, when it was snowing and I thought he was just a normal boy.

Once we've put up our tents – one for the boys, one for the girls and a small one each for Mikael and Nadine – we light fires to cook the evening meal. Sol picks up his pack.

'Where are you going?' Halim asks him.

He points at the hut. 'I'm putting this in there. The tents are tiny.'

Halim frowns. 'Why do you not keep it in the truck?'

'The building's closer.'

'OK. Maybe I put mine there too.'

I notice a strange look flash across Sol's face, but he says nothing. In the end, all of us take our packs over to the hut. Then we eat, decide who's taking first watch, and retire to our tents. I'm so tired that I fall asleep almost immediately.

Some hours later, I'm woken by something brushing against the side of the tent. '*Shit*,' I hear Sol mutter. He must be going to do his turn at watch duty. As I lie there, I realize that despite my thick sleeping bag, I'm cold. I decide to fetch the spare jumper from my pack.

Being careful not to wake the others, I crawl out of the tent. I can't see Sol anywhere, but when I reach the hut, I see a flashlight beam moving around inside.

I frown. Is Sol in there? I creep to the door and peer round.

It *is* Sol, crouching over his pack with a torch wedged under his chin to keep his hands free. He has his back to me; it looks like he's fiddling with some wires.

'Sol?' I say. 'What are you doing?'

He jumps, dropping the torch. 'Jesus Christ, Cass, don't startle me like that!'

'What are you *doing*?' The wires spill from the top of his pack in a great, tangled mass, and when I go closer, I see some blocks of a yellowish substance that looks a bit like clay. 'What's that?'

Sol picks up the torch again. 'It's the explosives. Mikael told me to bring them.'

'In your *pack*?'

'Any other questions?' Sol says in a bored tone, going back to fiddling with the wires.

'Yes. Why have you got so much? I thought we were just blasting the main entrance door.'

Sol looks up again and grins at me. The torchlight makes his face look skull-like and ghastly. 'You really wanna know?' His grin widens. 'I'm going to give those freaks a surprise.'

I stare at him. 'How?'

'I'm going to destroy their food supplies, and rig up the entrances so that if they try to leave, they'll get blown sky high.'

'But – but we're supposed to take them back to the camp.'

He shrugs again. 'And?'

'*And?* Sol, you can't do this! What will Corporal Jonasson say? And Colonel Brett?'

'They'll think that the freaks found out we were com-ing and set a booby trap, which detonated early.' Sol stuffs the wires back in his pack, then looks at me with his grin fading from his lips. 'As long as you keep your mouth shut, that is.'

I stare at him, wondering what happened to the freckle-faced kid I used to climb trees and read comics with – who I used to chase through the Shudders – and it finally hits me that the Sol I used to know hasn't been around for a long time.

'No,' I say. 'No way. I won't let you do this.'

'Oh?' Sol sounds surprised. 'Why not?'

'Because it's not what we've been sent here to do. It's—'

'Cut the crap, Cass,' Sol sneers. 'Why don't you

**357**

just admit you're in love with that Fearless boy?'

Shock stabs through me. 'What? No! That's not it at all! I'm not—'

He gets to his feet. 'Bullshit. I can see it in your face every time you talk about him. Every time you *think* about him. What's he got that I haven't?'

I glance behind me at the door, but Sol sees and steps round me, blocking my way.

He folds his arms. 'I'm waiting.'

I lick my dry lips, cursing myself for not realizing that Sol was jealous of Myo. An image of Myo's face rises, unbidden, in my mind, and I feel something squeeze inside my chest. 'Nothing happened,' I say, but my voice is shaky, and it comes out sounding like the lie it is.

'I don't believe you.'

'Why *not*?'

'Because I saw the way you looked at him when he turned up on Hope. You begged us not to hurt him. And you helped him escape. For God's sake, Cass. D'you think I'm *stupid*?'

My throat is dry. I'm all too aware that, only inches away from me, is the pack loaded with explosives.

Sol grabs me around the throat, pushing me against the wall. 'What happened?' he says, his voice a growl.

'Get off me!' I try to twist free. His fingers dig into my windpipe, slowly cutting off my air supply. I think of the guns we brought with us, but they're all in the tents. And with Sol's hand around my neck, I can't even draw enough air into my lungs to scream.

'Did you kiss him?' he says, shoving me back against the rough, damp stone again. I try to bring my knee up into his groin, one of the self-defence moves we were taught in the Patrol, but he shoots out his foot, blocking me.

'*Did you kiss him?*'

Choking, I nod.

'Did you do anything else with him?'

I shake my head.

'You're lying,' he hisses. 'I bet you were all over him.'

'Please, Sol, let go of me,' I wheeze, spots of light starting to dance in front of my eyes. I claw at his hand. My lungs are burning.

Suddenly, he releases me. I slide to the ground, gasping, still feeling his fingers around my neck.

He crouches down in front of me. 'You're disgusting. I should take you up to the bunker and trap you in there too.'

I draw in a great, hitching gulp of air, and glance round at the door, thinking, *if I can just get past him – warn the others—*

'Don't even *think* about it.' Sol whips something out of his pocket and pushes it into my neck, just under my ear. I feel a sharp sting, and then a spreading coolness. A trank dart.

My muscles go slack, the scream that's still inside me fading to a whisper. Everything begins to spin, and I sag sideways. The last thing I remember before I lose consciousness is seeing Sol snatch up his pack and walk out of the hut.

# Chapter 49

## CASS

When I wake up, I feel a burst of panic, thinking I'm back in the Torturehouse in one of those cages. Then I feel the ache in my throat and a sharper pain near my ear, and everything comes back to me in a rush.

Dizzily, I try to sit up. The torch is on the ground nearby, but the beam is much fainter now. Next to it is the trank dart Sol stuck in my neck. How long have I been out?

I pick the dart up, my hand shaking with the cold and the lingering effects of the tranquilliser still in my bloodstream. The tip of the needle is broken; it must have snapped when I slumped over, preventing me from getting a full dose. Otherwise, I'd have been unconscious until the morning.

Clinging to the wall, I haul myself upright and stagger to the door, calling for Mikael, Nadine, Marissa, *anyone*. Torch beams bob through the darkness. Nadine's the first to get to me.

'Cass? What the hell's going on?' she says, shining her torch in my face. 'Why is there blood on your neck?'

'Sol's gone crazy!' I say. 'He's going to blow up the bunker!'

Mikael comes up behind her. '*What?*'

I tell them about the explosives, and Sol trying to throttle me, then knocking me out with a trank dart.

Mikael swears. 'What the hell does he think he's doing? Our mission was to bring the people up there back alive, not murder them. Hollencroft, you have the maps and the bunker plan, don't you?'

'In my pack.' I point, and Mikael goes to fetch it.

He swears.

'What wrong?' I say.

'He's been through it. The plans and maps are missing.'

'Shit . . .' I go over and see it's wide open, the contents strewn everywhere.

'How long ago do you think he left?'

'I don't know. I have no idea how long I was out for.'

Mikael swears again. 'I'll go after him. Maybe he won't have got too far. You take the watch,' he tells Halim, and runs out of the hut.

The others help me gather up my things. Then Nadine takes me back to her tent to look at my neck. 'Those are some bruises you've got there,' Nadine says as she pulls the broken end of the needle out with a pair of tweezers and puts a dressing over the wound. 'Are you sure you're OK?'

I nod, even though, inside, I feel like screaming. How will Mikael find Sol? These moors are huge. I'm the only one who knows where the bunker is without looking at a map. I have to get up there and warn Myo and the others they're in danger.

I stand up, trying to hide the fact that my legs are shaky from the after-effects of the tranquillizer. 'I'm cold,' I tell Nadine. 'I'm going to get an extra jumper from my pack.'

She gets up too. 'I'll go.'

'It's OK. I could do with some fresh air, to be honest. I feel a bit sick.'

She nods. 'All right. Come straight back. I want to keep an eye on you for a bit – those trank darts are strong, and I don't know how big a dose you had.'

Promising her I'll only be a couple of minutes, I duck out of the tent. The only other person outside is Halim, sitting cross-legged in front of the boys' tent.

When I get to the hut, I pull my jacket out of my pack and put it on. We've each been issued with a small torch and a stick of camouflage paint; I tuck the torch in my pocket and streak the paint across my face. Then I pull on my night vision goggles. When I switch them on, the interior of the hut swims into focus in lurid shades of green. I wish I had a gun, but I don't have time to get one. This is all my fault. If I hadn't told Colonel Brett where to find the bunker—

I push the thoughts away. No time for that now. Tiptoeing to the hut door, I peer out. I can see the tents across the field almost as clearly as if it was daylight. When Halim is looking the other way, I slip around the

**362**

back of the hut, climb over the wall and drop into the bracken, where I lie still for a few moments in case Halim heard me. Then I scramble forward on my hands and knees until I'm far enough away from the paddock to stand up.

The hill is even steeper than I remember, littered with rocks and twisted heather stems that catch at my boots. When I reach the top of the ridge I lie down again, scanning the moors around me. There's no sign of Sol. My scalp prickles as I wonder if he's nearby, watching me.

About a quarter of a mile away are the two slabs of rock that lead to the bunker entrance that's set into the hillside. I scramble down there. When I reach the stable under the overhang, Flicka and Apollo are snorting and nickering to one another inside; something's disturbed them.

Then I hear footsteps. Instinctively, I draw back, pressing myself into a niche between the stable wall and the rocks behind it. Moments later, Sol walks past, heading back towards the hill. He's wearing his pack and a gun.

I wait until he's gone, then hurry up the path to the bunker entrance. There's a pile of rocks at the bottom of the door. Sol must have hidden the explosives amongst them.

As I knock on the door – five long taps and seven short ones – my breath catches in my throat at the thought of seeing Myo again. But I have to warn them. Sol won't have reached the other entrance yet; there might still be time for them to get out. It feels like hours before the porthole in the top of the door opens. 'Who's there?' a girl's voice says. My stomach lurches. *Gina.*

I push my goggles up onto my forehead so she can see my face. 'It's Cass.'

She's silent for a moment. Then she says, 'What the hell are you doing here?'

'Please listen to me,' I say. 'I'm here with a group of Magpies. We were sent to—' I pause. 'We were sent to round you and the others up. But one of our group has gone crazy. He's planning to trap all of you inside the bunker and destroy your food supplies. He's already rigged this door up. You have to get everyone out through the other exit *now.*'

Gina doesn't answer me. Without the night vision goggles, I can hardly see; I wonder if she has a gun, and if she's pointing it at me.

'You have to believe me,' I say. 'He has maps with both the bunker entrances on them. He could be laying explosives in the tunnels right now.'

She begins to laugh. 'Oh my God. That is the craziest thing I've ever heard. Seriously. You break Myo's heart, you join the Magpies, and then you turn up here with some insane story, expecting me to bring everyone out of the bunker so — what? You can shoot us all?' She laughs again. 'Nice try, Cass. Whoever's trained you did a *brilliant* job.'

She slams the porthole closed.

I hammer frantically on the door. 'Gina!' I shout. '*Gina!*'

She doesn't come back.

I snap my goggles back down, and with her words ringing in my ears I run back along the path and scramble back up the hill, trying to remember where the entrance under the rock face was on the map. Then, several hundred yards along the ridge in front of me, I see a bright green shape. *Sol.*

He's standing still, looking at the map. He hasn't seen me. I lie down in the heather, and when he starts walking again, I belly-crawl after him, being careful to keep my distance. He heads down the other side of the ridge. I follow as close as I dare, keeping low.

He stops again on a slope covered in loose rock. Sticking out of it is a concrete plinth with a hatch in the top. I drop into a crouch again and watch as he opens it and climbs inside. When it's clanged shut after him, I run down there, my boots skidding on the scree.

I count to ten, then quietly, carefully, open the hatch. On the other side, a ladder plunges down into a darkness so intense, even my goggles can't penetrate it. I climb in after Sol, and as I reach the bottom, a familiar damp smell steals into my nostrils. The tunnel branches left and right. I think about the map again. *Which way?*

To my right, I hear a faint scraping. I creep towards it.

But there's nothing there. Did I imagine it?

'*You*,' Sol says.

I whirl. He's standing right behind me, still wearing his pack, and a pair of night-vision goggles like mine. 'Come to save your boyfriend, did you?'

'Don't do this, Sol,' I say.

He pushes the gun into the small of my back. 'Start walking.'

'*No!*'

'*No,*' he mimics in a sing-song voice. He jabs the gun into my back again, hard enough to make me stagger. 'Get moving, or I'll shoot you in the legs and drag you.'

Shaking, I start walking. This part of the bunker is in total disrepair; the walls are streaked with slime, and we have to dodge around piles of rubble and past dangling wires. We get further and further into the bunker until, up ahead, I see a faint glow. I pull my goggles up onto my forehead. The glow is the lights in the Comms Hall, spilling out round the edge of a door.

Sol pushes past me and, keeping the gun trained on me, kicks the door open.

Everyone except Mara is in there, holding guns, which they appear to be in the middle of loading. Like Myo, each one of them has one silver eye, and distantly, I think, *I was right, they* are *all half-Fearless*.

When Myo sees us, his mouth drops open. Lochie, standing beside him, whines, then starts wagging his tail.

Ben points his gun at me and Sol. 'Who the hell are you?' he asks Sol.

Sol smiles. 'I wouldn't do that if I were you. See this backpack? It's got explosives in it. If you shoot me, or even try to shoot me, I'll detonate them, and you'll all be dead.'

Ben lowers his gun, his face draining of colour.

I look at Myo again. He's still staring at me. He looks exactly the same, his hair falling in a thick black curtain across his right eye. I feel a tug of longing inside my chest, and I realize that the whole time I was telling myself I hated him – that I never wanted to see him again – I was missing him so badly it hurt.

And now it's too late to do anything about it. I've as good as sentenced him to death.

# Chapter 50

## MYO

When Cass stumbles into the Comms Hall, I think I'm dreaming. I have to look again to make sure it's really her.

'I've rigged up the entrances to the bunker so that if you try to leave, they'll blow up,' Blondie says after he tells us about the explosives in his pack. 'I'm also going to blow up your food supplies. Any questions?'

Behind me, I hear people gasp. I reckon they're all thinking the same as me. *Is this guy for real?*

But I don't want to be the one who shoots him and finds out he is.

'Cass?' I say. 'Is he serious?'

She nods.

Blondie drags her across to where I'm standing and pushes her towards me, hard. I grab her hand to stop her falling. 'That's right. That's where you belong. With *him*,' Blondie hisses.

Cass stares at him. 'Sol—'

'I mean it,' Sol says. 'If anyone tries to stop me, I'll trigger the explosives in my pack.'

'What, and kill yourself?' Ben says.

368

Sol shrugs. 'It'll be worth it.'

'Sol, please!' Cass says.

'Too late,' he snaps. 'You had your chance.'

I glance at Cass. What's he on about? She shakes her head. 'I tried to warn Gina. That's why I came.'

Gina shoots us an agonized glance. I remember how scornful she was after she came running in to tell us Cass had turned up, and we hastily collected our weapons and got ready to face the Magpies. *Christ*, I think. *Why didn't you listen to her?*

Sol begins to walk across to the kitchen. I remember what Gina said Cass had told her. *She reckons this guy is going to come in here and destroy our food supplies.*

'You're a lunatic,' Ben says, raising his gun.

'*NO!*' Cass screams as he pulls the trigger.

The bullet smacks into Sol as he's opening the door. His body twists and he cries out and falls to his knees.

Nothing else happens. He was lying. Thank God.

And then he reaches round and does something to the side of his pack, tugging on a strap or a wire. There's a flash of light so bright it blinds me, a roar big enough to fill the whole world, and something slams into me, throwing me to the ground. I hear screams and a rumbling sound that goes on and on. The stench of smoke and dust fills my nostrils. When I try to sit up, I realize I can't move my legs. There's something pinning them down. In panic, I try to yank them free, and pain bolts up them, white hot and enormous. Gasping, I close my eyes, and everything drifts away for a while.

# Chapter 51

## CASS

The force of the explosion knocks me off my feet. My ears ringing with screams and the rumble of falling masonry, I land hard on my left hand and feel something snap in my wrist, sending a sickening jolt of pain up my arm.

Too stunned even to cry out, I roll onto my side, clutching at my wrist, coughing as I draw in lungfuls of smoke and dust. It stings my eyes, making them stream with tears. For a moment, I think I've gone blind. Then I realize the lights have gone out.

With my good hand, I reach up and pull my night vision goggles back down. The dust and smoke make it impossible to see anything except swirling clouds of white and green.

'Myo!' I say, but my throat is so full of grit that I can barely even raise my voice above a whisper. 'Are you there?'

No response. The rumbling has stopped now. I can hear coughing and sobbing.

Then I hear a soft whine.

'Lochie!' I say. 'Lochie, come here, boy!' For a moment, nothing happens, and I start to imagine the dog trapped under a pile of rubble, his back broken, his legs crushed. Then he sticks his cold, wet nose in my ear and licks my face. I put my good hand up and rub his wiry fur. 'Good boy. *Good* boy.'

'Gina? Is that you?' a hoarse voice says somewhere in the darkness. Ben.

I cough again. 'It's Cass,' I say. I try to get up, and knock my injured wrist against my leg. The pain is sickening. I grind my teeth, breathing fast.

'Is Gina there with you?'

'I don't know. I can't see.'

'*Shit.* I didn't think he meant it. I didn't think he really had explosives in there.'

'Are you hurt?' I need to distract him. If he panics, I'm going to panic too, and then we'll never make it out of here.

'No. Where are you?'

'Over here.'

'Keep talking. I can't see anything either – there's too much dust.'

As Ben's feet crunch towards me through the rubble, I clamber awkwardly to my feet, trying to avoid putting any weight on my injured arm.

'Gina! Myo!' Ben calls when he reaches me. No answer. He shouts some other names. People answer him in weak-sounding voices. The dust is making my chest burn. I pull my T-shirt up over my mouth to use as a filter.

Then, a few feet away, someone moans. Lochie shoves past me. 'Myo?' I say. I shuffle after the dog, feeling in front of me with my right hand. 'Myo, where are you?'

That's when I remember the torch in my jacket pocket. Praying it isn't broken, I fumble it from my pocket and press the switch. A fuzzy beam of light cuts through the smoke and dust.

'Can you see him?' Ben says.

'I think he's down here somewhere,' I say, shining the torch around me. Then the beam hits Lochie. He's standing over Myo, who's lying on his back, his face and hair coated in whitish dust, his eyes closed. I drop to my knees beside him, saying his name.

The lights stutter back on.

I push my goggles up. The dust hangs over the Comms Hall like fog. I can just make out where Sol was standing when Ben shot him; there's a waterfall of bricks and rubble in front of the kitchen door. In the middle of the mess lie dark, still shapes. People.

I look at Myo again and my heart skips a beat. A huge chunk of concrete lies across his legs. 'Oh, God,' I say.

Ben turns. 'What is it?' One side of his face is streaked with blood. When he sees Myo, he swears. 'We need to get that thing off him.'

'I can't, I think my wrist's broken.' I hold it up; it's puffy and turning purple-black. Ben swears again. 'Can I get some help over here?' he yells. Tana and a man I don't recognize appear out of the dust from the far end of the hall. As they lift the concrete off Myo's legs, he screams, the sound punching right through me. But he still doesn't open his eyes.

While Ben goes to look for Gina, I sit beside Myo, trying to ignore the pain pulsing up my arm from my wrist. 'Ben, over here!' Tana calls.

They bring Gina over and lie her down on the floor beside Myo. She doesn't look injured, but she doesn't respond when Ben calls her name.

One by one, the other residents of the bunker are found. A few are walking wounded, like me and Ben, dazed and in shock. Two more are unconscious like Gina and Myo, although they're starting to come round. And the rest . . .

'I'm so sorry,' Ben keeps saying, his voice raw and filled with pain. 'I thought he was just some stupid kid playing soldiers. I had no idea—'

'Ben, stop,' Tana says. 'You can feel guilty later. Right now, we need to work out how we're going to get out of here.'

'Sol hadn't laid any explosives around the entrance he brought me in through,' I say. 'I think he was going to do it on his way out.'

'You mean the entrance under the rock face?' Tana says.

Gina groans.

Ben helps her to sit up. 'Can you walk?' he asks her. She nods, and winces. 'How about you?' he asks me. I nod too.

**373**

'OK. You and Gina go with Tana and the others.' He turns to the man who was with Tana. 'Neil, can you find Mara? I'll bring Myo.'

At the mention of Mara's name, my stomach twists. I still can't quite get my head round the fact that she's Myo's sister. As I follow Tana and Gina, the lights go out again. I pull my goggles down, wishing for a moment that I was half-Fearless too so I didn't need them. Everything feels nightmarish and surreal. I keep seeing Sol's face as he told Myo, Ben and the others about the bunker entrances being booby-trapped, and then his body twisting as the bullet from Ben's gun slammed into him. I can't believe he's gone. What went so wrong? I knew he liked me, and I knew he wanted us to be together, but it's as if he viewed me as . . . as his *property*, or something. I shudder.

Out on the hillside, I collapse onto the scree, gasping for breath. Tana goes back inside to help Neil and Ben.

'I'm sorry I didn't believe you,' Gina says, her voice shaky and thin.

'It's OK,' I say. I don't know what else *to* say. 'I don't blame you for thinking I was trying to trick you. I would have thought the same.'

'Myo's been lost without you,' she says, and my pulse quickens as I remember her words earlier: *you break Myo's heart . . .*

Then I hear shouts. '*Cass! Sol!*' and see lights in the distance, bright blobs amongst the green of my night-vision.

'Who's that?' Gina sounds wary.

'The rest of my group.'

'Crap. We have to get out of here.'

'No! One of them's a medic. We have all sorts of supplies down at the camp. She might be able to help us.'

'Are you *crazy*? They're Magpies. You said yourself that they were here to round us up.'

Ben appears out of the hatchway, his hands hooked under Myo's armpits. A couple of people go over to help him, and they lay him down beside me. Neil and Tana follow with Lochie, and then Neil climbs back inside, reappearing with Mara. Her wrists and ankles are bound with strips of cloth, a piece of fabric tied between her ankles to allow her to take small, hobbling steps. She looks a lot cleaner than she did last time I saw her – her hair is washed and tied back, her scrappy blue dress replaced by trousers, boots and a warm jacket – and she seems quite docile. I wonder if they've drugged her.

'Is that everyone?' a woman with dark hair asks Ben, her tone frantic. He nods, and the woman's face crumples.

I look at Myo again. His face is waxy, just like Danny's was after the Fearless shot him. *You are NOT going to die, dammit*, I tell Myo inside my head. But I know he's slipping away from me.

'Please,' I say fiercely to Gina. 'He needs help.'

Gina looks at Myo, then turns towards Ben. The shouts drift towards us again, nearer this time.

'Cass says her group had a medic with them,' she tells Ben.

'The Magpies?' he says.

'You have to let them help Myo,' I say.

Ben closes his eyes, opens them again. Then he nods. 'But let us get away first.'

'What about you?' I ask Gina. 'Will you be OK?'

She gets unsteadily to her feet, biting her lip. 'I think so.' She squeezes my arm. 'Take care of yourself, OK?'

'Where will you go?'

'Don't worry about us,' Ben says, and for the first time since I've known him his voice sounds almost kind. 'Just look after Myo, yeah?'

'We need to get the horses, Ben,' Gina says.

'We'll collect them on our way.'

I watch the group disappear round the hill. Everyone's moving slowly, as if they're in shock. A few are limping badly, and one man has to be held up by the people either side of him, but I don't blame them for wanting to get away. If Myo survives, the Magpies will stick spikes in his brain and he'll be a zombie for ever. But if I don't get Nadine to help him, he'll die.

'*Cass! Sol!*' It sounds like Mikael; the others must have come after me when they realized I'd gone, and found him.

'*Over here!*' I yell.

They reach us a few minutes later. 'Oh my God,' Marissa says. 'Are you OK? We heard an explosion—'

Then she sees Myo and Lochie. Under her night vision goggles, her eyebrows shoot up.

I explain what happened, being as vague about the

others as I can. Nadine bends over Myo. 'We have to get him back down to the camp,' she says. 'I need to try and get a drip in.'

Butterflies flip and twist in my stomach. 'Will he be OK?'

'I don't know.'

'Is Sol . . . dead?' Andrej says as we make our way back down the hill, Mikael carrying Myo in a fireman's lift across his shoulders and Lochie trotting alongside them.

I nod.

'Christ. Why would he do something like that?'

Marissa looks over at me, and I'm relieved we both have our goggles on so I can't read her expression.

Back at the camp, Nadine splints Myo's legs, injects him with painkillers and hooks him up to a saline drip. She gives me some painkillers too, enough to send me drifting away so that next thing I know, it's light, and I'm lying in one of the tents with my wrist encased in a bulky bandage. It hurts, but not as badly, probably because I still have the drugs Nadine gave me buzzing around my system. She reckons it's not broken, just badly sprained, but she can't be sure, so I have to keep it still.

Thick-headed and dry-mouthed, I push myself up onto my elbow. Myo is lying on the other side of the tent. I'm startled to see Lochie stretched out between us too. Did he sneak in here, or did someone bring him in? Myo looks exactly the same as he did last night. I will him to open his eyes. He doesn't move.

Nadine ducks into the tent.

'How is he?' I croak.

'His blood pressure's OK,' she says, 'and his pulse is stronger. He hasn't woken up yet, though, and I don't like the look of those legs. The right is broken in several places. Is this the boy you were telling me about when you first came to the camp?'

I nod.

Nadine checks Myo's drip. 'What happens now?' I ask.

'Mikael's just come back from checking the bunker.'

'Did he find any more survivors?'

She shakes her head.

'What — what about Sol?'

She shakes her head again. 'I'm sorry. Once we've packed up, we'll head back. Myo needs an operation on those legs, and I can only do that back at the main camp.'

An hour later, we're all in the truck, jolting along with Myo and Lochie lying in the cage. Andrej keeps looking at the empty seat beside him with a faintly disbelieving expression on his face. I can't take it in, either. This time yesterday, Sol was there. And now he's nothing but dust and vapour and the memory of a person I still can't quite match up to the boy I thought I knew.

We reach the Magpies' camp just before nightfall. Myo and I are whisked off to the hospital tent, where Lochie stations himself beside Myo's bed, refusing to move. Dosed up with more painkillers, I drift in and out of sleep until Myo's taken away to have his legs operated on. I don't sleep again until he comes back. His face is clean, the blood and dust washed away. To my intense relief, his eyes don't appear bruised or swollen, and there's no sign he's undergone the procedure. Yet.

I wonder when he'll wake up. *If* he'll wake up. And how long it will be before they put him through it.

The only thing I'm sure of is that this time, there's nothing I can do to save him.

# Chapter 52

## MYO

The first thing I see when I open my eyes is Lochie. I'm lying in a bed in a tent, with no idea where I am or how I got there, and he's standing beside me, wagging his tail.

'Good lad,' I say. My voice is scratchy and thin. I reach out to stroke his head, dismayed at how weak I am. My legs hurt like hell, and when I pull my blanket back, I get a shock. Both of them are covered with wooden splints and bandages.

What happened? I can't remember. The last thing I recall clearly is being at the bunker, in the Comms Hall. Gina was there – she was agitated about something, and . . .

'Myo?' someone says.

I look round. It's Cass, sitting in a bed opposite. Her face is bruised and her left wrist is in a bandage. A hundred different emotions go flooding through me – relief and happiness and longing and anger and confusion and everything in between. I tried to forget her, I really did. But I couldn't.

'Where am I?' I say.

'We're at the Magpies' camp,' she says. 'You've been unconscious for three days.'

Terror zigzags through me. I throw back the blanket and try to climb off the bed, but the pain in my legs stops me dead. I fall back, gasping.

'How did I get here?' I ask when I've got my breath back. 'What happened to me? Is Mara here too?'

As she tells me, I feel myself sinking into despair. That's it, then. I can't get away. I can't even stand up. I'm screwed.

Lochie whines again, and licks my fingers. I look over at Cass again. 'So what changed?'

'What do you mean?' she says.

'Last time I saw you, you hated my guts. But you got me out of the bunker – got your pals here to help me instead of leaving me up on the moors to die—'

'I'm sorry I said those things to you,' she says, her voice formal and stiff. 'I know you're not Fearless.'

'I was trying to find Mara,' I say. 'That's why I was on the island. I had no idea she and that guy would take your brother, I promise.'

'I know. And I'm grateful. Thank you for helping us.' Before I can say anything else, she turns over, leaving me to frown at the back of her head. She doesn't *sound* grateful at all.

A little while later, a guy walks into the tent carrying a bucket and some cloths. I sit up with a gasp. 'Cy!'

He doesn't answer me.

'Over here, please,' the woman who's come in with

**381**

him says. They're followed by a guy with two missing fingers. As Cy hands the bucket and cloths to them, I see both his eyes are silver. But he's not acting like a Fearless. He looks half asleep. Lochie presses himself against my bed, his tail between his legs.

I lie back down, my heart thudding. What have they done to him? I think about asking Cass, but she's still lying on her side, facing away from me.

The woman and the other Magpie come over to my bed.

'How are his legs?' the man asks the woman.

'Healing well,' she says. 'Faster than usual, but of course, with him being half-Fearless, that's to be expected.'

*Hey, I'm right here!* I want to shout at her, but both of them have guns on their belts, so I keep quiet.

The man pulls back my blanket and frowns at my splinted legs. Then he takes a torch out of his pocket and shines it into my eyes. The light's so bright it gives me a headache. I turn my head away, but he grabs my jaw and turns it back.

'How long before he's ready?' The woman still looks worried.

'Sometime in the next few days. It'll be easier if we do it before his legs have mended.'

The woman frowns. 'Really? Weren't we going to study—'

'Brett's changed his mind. We have more and more of them coming in, Nadine. We don't want to be in a situation where there are so many of them needing the procedure that we can't cope.'

'What procedure? What are you gonna do to me?' I ask them, but they both ignore me, and leave. I stare up at the canvas above me, my heart thumping, my mouth dry.

The next morning, Cass is moved out of the tent, and I don't see her again. Without her there, the hours crawl by. I can't get anyone to tell me what the *procedure* is. I need to figure out a way to get Lochie and me out of here. But how – by crawling? How will I defend myself? And where will I go? How will I get food?

*Face it, you're screwed*, I tell myself, and I start wishing that they'd do whatever they're gonna do to me right now, so it's over.

Later, the man with the missing fingers comes back. The woman's already here.

'Nadine, hold his head,' the man says tersely. He shines the torch into my eyes again.

'How are his legs today?' he asks as I try to blink the after-image away.

'A little better, but he still can't stand,' she says.

The man nods. 'I think it's time.'

'What, now?'

The man shakes his head. 'We've a few waiting to go in already today. We'll do it first thing tomorrow morning.'

There's a clatter, and I see Cass at the entrance to the tent, the contents of the tray she was carrying scattered all over the ground. She turns and runs. Lochie barks and tries to go after her, but I put a hand on his neck and stop him.

'What's that dog still doing in here?' the man says. 'Get rid of it. And restrain the boy. I don't want him even *trying* to escape.'

'I don't think he'll be able to—' Nadine begins.

'*Restrain him.*'

The man stuffs his torch back in his belt, and leaves.

# Chapter 53

## CASS

I run back to my tent, where I sit on the edge of my bunk and hug my arms around myself, guilt surging through me. I should have been back to see him. Instead, I've avoided him. I should have fought for him. Instead, I'm letting them do the procedure on him without so much as a whimper. What sort of person am I?

But what was the point in getting close to him again when I knew that, at any moment, he would be taken away from me? The thought of seeing him emptying the latrines or serving the food, blank-faced and slack-jawed, gives me a pain in my chest like someone's stuck me with a knife. So instead of facing up to it and trying to do something, I've tried not to think about it at all. Too much has happened since that night Jori was taken; I want it all to go away.

And anyway, what can I do against people like Colonel Brett? We're all just cogs in his machine. If I try to defend Myo, he'll probably lock me up for insubordination.

'Are you OK?'

I look up. Nadine's standing there with Lochie.

*Yes, I'm fine*, I want to say, but the words won't come. Instead, I say, 'I thought they were going to study him before they did the procedure.'

Nadine presses her lips together.

'*Why?*'

'He means a lot to you, doesn't he?'

I look away again, staring at the ground.

'You probably don't remember this, but when we got back to the tents on the moors and you were doped up, you kept asking if he was OK. You were frantic.'

I shake my head. I have no memory of it at all. 'Does he know what's going to happen?'

'No. And I won't tell him, either.'

'But why do they even want to do it in the first place? He's not Fearless. They don't *need* to operate on him.'

'I know. And I've tried to tell them that, but . . .'

'Maybe *I* could tell them – talk to Colonel Brett—'

She gives me a small, sad smile. 'I doubt he'll listen. He's decided to accelerate the reconstruction programme. All he wants is for the Fearless to be neutralized so he can put them to work. Myo included.'

I twist my blankets in the fingers of my good hand (the other is still strapped up, although it's healing well). 'I wish I'd never told Colonel Brett about the bunker!' I say.

'I'm sorry, Cass,' Nadine says. 'I've done everything I can. Maybe you should go and talk to him, make the most of the time you have left.'

*We don't have any time*, I think. *It's over.*

Nadine gets up and touches my arm lightly. 'I'll let you know before he has it done. I'll make sure you can say goodbye. Look after the dog, OK? Make sure he doesn't get in anyone's way.'

She leaves me with Lochie, who places his head in my lap. I stroke his ears, wondering if he can sense what's about to happen to his master.

'When are we going home?' Jori asks me that night after dinner. I spend as much time in the evenings with him as I can; the others still want to talk about Sol and what happened at the bunker, and all I want to do is forget it.

'I don't know, Jor,' I say, while Lochie rolls over to let my brother tickle his stomach. The first time Lochie met Jori, they clicked, even though the dog is almost as tall as he is. As soon as Jori saw the dog, he marched up to him, ignoring my warning to be careful, and Lochie immediately washed his face, his tail thumping from side to side.

'We must be going *soon*,' Jori says as Lochie, still lying on his back, bats at him with one gigantic paw in an attempt to get another belly-rub.

I just shrug. I haven't the heart to tell my brother that we're probably *never* going back to Hope. I need to get me, him, Myo and Lochie away from the camp. It's the only way I'll save Myo. But how? The gate is heavily guarded. And we'd need to steal horses, because Myo can't walk.

When it's time for Jori to go to bed, I walk him to his cabin, which is near to the Fearless compound. The boy with the dark hair who Sol punched is standing by the fence with a gun, his collar turned up and his shoulders hunched. I watch him for a moment, until he sees me and sneers, 'What you looking at?' Then I walk away. But not in the direction of my tent. Instead, I head towards the makeshift stable where the Magpies keep their horses, halfway between the cabins and the hospital tent. A Magpie is checking their straw and water before turning in for the night, but there's no one guarding them.

An idea begins to form inside my head.

*This is crazy*, I tell myself as I lie in my bunk an hour or so later, fully clothed beneath my blankets, waiting for the camp to quieten down. *What if it goes wrong? What if you get caught?*

Outside, the lights go out. At night, everything is powered down except for the fence.

I get out of bed, put my boots on and whisper, 'Come on,' to Lochie.

The boy with dark hair is still guarding the compound. I stride up to him, trying to appear confident, even though, inside, I'm shaking.

'Colonel Brett wants to see you,' I say as the Fearless thump the cabin walls.

He looks at me and Lochie as if we've both got three heads. 'What, *now*?'

I shrug. 'Just passing on the message. I've got to guard the cabin while you go. Can you leave me your gun, please?'

*He'll never fall for it*, I think, but he passes me his gun.

'Not that way!' I say as he starts to walk over to Colonel Brett's cabin. 'He's at the mess tent.'

The boy gives me another funny look, shakes his head and walks away.

I count to twenty.

Then I walk across to the alarm and yank the lever down.

The siren is earsplittingly loud. I pull the gun's strap over my head and run with Lochie to Jori's cabin. 'Help!' I yell, hammering on the door. 'A Fearless is loose!'

As the Magpie adult who stays with the children at night opens the door, lights start to come on all over the camp. She hustles the kids out of the cabin. While she's looking the other way, I grab Jori's arm. 'This way,' I say in his ear. 'I'll explain later. Can you run?'

He nods, his eyes huge, and before the Magpie can turn around and see us, we sprint in the direction of the stables, the scream of the siren following us. Shaking with nerves, I put bridles and saddles on two of the horses, who are spooked and snorting. I help Jori up one-handed, climbing on behind him and telling him to hang on no matter what. Then, clinging onto the second horse's reins with my good hand, gripping its sides with my knees, I canter through the camp to the hospital tent. 'Get to the training field! This isn't a drill!' I yell as I go. Any second, I'm expecting to be stopped and questioned, but people see the horses, and the gun strapped across my chest, and flee towards the field.

When I ride into the hospital tent, Nadine is bending

over Myo, unfastening the straps around his arms and legs. She's on her own; the other occupants have already been moved out. She whirls, looking startled. 'Cass? What the—'

'Help me get Myo onto this horse,' I say, jumping off as Myo blinks groggily at me. I know I have only minutes now before someone discovers the Fearless are still secure inside their compound. And I still have no idea how we're going to get out of the camp.

'But what are you going to do?'

'Get us out of here.'

'*How?*'

'I—' Suddenly, inspiration strikes. 'Give me your coat and your cap. *Please*, Nadine.'

She looks at me a moment longer. Then she takes them off and hands them to me. I thrust them at Myo. 'Put these on.' He looks puzzled, but does as I say. I pull the collar of the coat up to hide his face.

'This is crazy,' Nadine says as she helps me lift him onto the horse and Myo bites his lip, his face white, his eyes shining with pain. 'You have no food, no tents, *nothing*.'

'We'll be OK,' I say, grabbing a blanket to cover Myo's splinted legs and hopping back up onto my horse.

'Wait!' Nadine turns and grabs something off the top of the locker by Myo's bed. She thrusts a handful of blister packs at me. 'These are painkillers. Two every four hours, up to eight a day. No more.'

I nod, and turn my horse towards the exit.

'And Cass—'

I look back at her.

'Good luck. And take care.'

'You too,' I say. 'Thank you.' I look at Myo. 'We have to gallop to the gates. Can you manage it?'

'Aye,' he says, although under the brim of Nadine's cap, his face is still white. Outside, the siren is still wailing. How long until it stops?

I squeeze my knees into my horse's sides, and we take off through the rows of tents. People are still streaming towards the field; they scatter out of our way. In front of me, Jori has his hands buried in the horse's mane, clinging on for dear life.

'Let us through!' I yell to the two guards at the gate, waving the gun. 'Colonel Brett's orders!' As they catch sight of Jori and Lochie, who thankfully hasn't started barking yet, confusion passes over their faces and I think, *that's it, I've blown it, we're not going to get out of here.*

And for a second – just a second – I consider firing at them.

They open the gates.

The siren stops.

'*GO!*' I yell, and we plunge forward.

As we thunder away from the camp, Myo and Lochie right beside me, I hear shouts, but we don't slow down or look back. Only when the camp is far behind us do we stop, steering the horses under a stand of trees. Their sides are heaving. I lean over and press my forehead against Myo's. 'Are you OK?'

He nods, although I can feel him trembling. 'Aye.'

'What about your legs?'

'Give us some of those pills.' He swallows them dry.

'I'm sorry I never came to see you,' I say.

'It's OK. Nadine explained. I understand.'

My heart is still pounding, my mouth dry and metal-lic-tasting. I keep expecting to hear shouts or gunshots behind us, but the valley is silent and still. 'So. Where to?'

He adjusts his cap. 'We should head back up north, I guess. Find out where Ben, Gina and the others have gone.'

'Who are Ben and Gina?' Jori says.

'Friends of mine,' Myo tells him. 'I'm Myo, by the way.'

'Hi, Myo,' Jori says.

'And don't forget Mara,' I say.

Myo glances at me. Then one side of his mouth lifts in a small smile. 'Aye. Don't forget Mara.'

Lochie wags his tail.

'We'd better get going, then,' I say. 'We need to find water, and food, and somewhere to rest up for a bit.'

Myo makes a soft clicking sound to get his horse moving. I do the same, and we ride on up the valley, the darkness folding over us like a veil.

# Acknowledgments

Writing a book can be a lonely process, not to mention daunting, especially when it's your second novel and there's a little voice nagging away in the back of your head saying, *You do know it was all a fluke the first time round, right? Do you really think you're capable of doing this again?* If it wasn't for the following people, that little voice might have got the better of me many times.

So, heartfelt thanks go to:

My parents, sister and aunt, for always being there to cheer me on and share my excitement over the smallest of things.

Pat and Graham, for being the best in-laws I could ever wish for.

My wonderful agent, Carolyn, for her wisdom and guidance, and for making me a better writer.

My amazing editor, Nat, for her hard work, insight, enthusiasm and kindness.

Everyone else at Random House Children's Publishing who's helped turn *The Fearless* from a collection of typed pages to a real, live book, in particular Laura for her amazing design work and Larry Rostant for finding the perfect 'Cass', and everyone on the publicity team who's helped get the word out there about my books.

Kate Ormand, beta reader extraordinare, for being at the other end of an email at all hours of the day. I'm so excited that people will get to read *your* books soon, too!

Lydia Kang and Lexx Clarke for medical advice — any errors are definitely mine, not theirs.

James Law, for telling me how to ventilate an underground bunker.

Geoff Allen, for telling me which guns to give the Patrol, and how they'd use them.

All my friends and colleagues who've cheered me on and supported me on this crazy ride so far.

All my writer buddies in the Author Allsorts, Lucky 13s and YA Think — you keep me sane!

All the bloggers and readers who've supported my writing and made me feel like there's nothing else I'd rather be doing.

G-Dog, for repeatedly dropping tennis balls and soggy toys onto my laptop keyboard and reminding me that there's a real world out there, and shouldn't we be going for a walk now?

And last, but most definitely not least, Duncan: for all those brainstorming sessions; for reading the same pages over and over again; for helping restore my confidence in this novel and convincing me Cass and Myo's story was worth sharing with the world; for saying 'I told you so' in the nicest way possible, and for making that little voice whispering doubts in my ear shut the hell up. I love you, and I couldn't do any of this without you. Thank you.